epic!

TIME HEIST

Written by
Matthew Cody

Illustrated by
Chad Thomas

Colors by
Warren Wucinich

Cat Ninja created by Matthew Cody and Yehudi Mercado

Andrews McMeel Publishing
a division of Andrews McMeel Universal
1130 Walnut Street, Kansas City, Missouri 64106

www.andrewsmcmeel.com

Epic! Creations, Inc.
702 Marshall Street, Suite 280
Redwood City, California 94063

www.getepic.com

23 24 25 26 27 SDB 10 9 8 7 6 5 4 3

Paperback ISBN: 978-1-5248-6758-4
Hardback ISBN: 978-1-5248-6808-6

Library of Congress Control Number: 2021934839

Design by Dan Nordskog

Made by:
RR Donnelley (Guangdong) Printing Solutions Company Ltd.
Address and location of manufacturer:
No. 2 Minzhu Road, Daning, Humen Town
Dongguan City, Guangdong Province, China 523930
3rd Printing — 7/24/23

ATTENTION: SCHOOLS AND BUSINESSES
Andrews McMeel books are available at quantity discounts with
bulk purchase for educational, business, or sales promotional use.
For information, please e-mail the Andrews McMeel Publishing
Special Sales Department: sales@amuniversal.com.

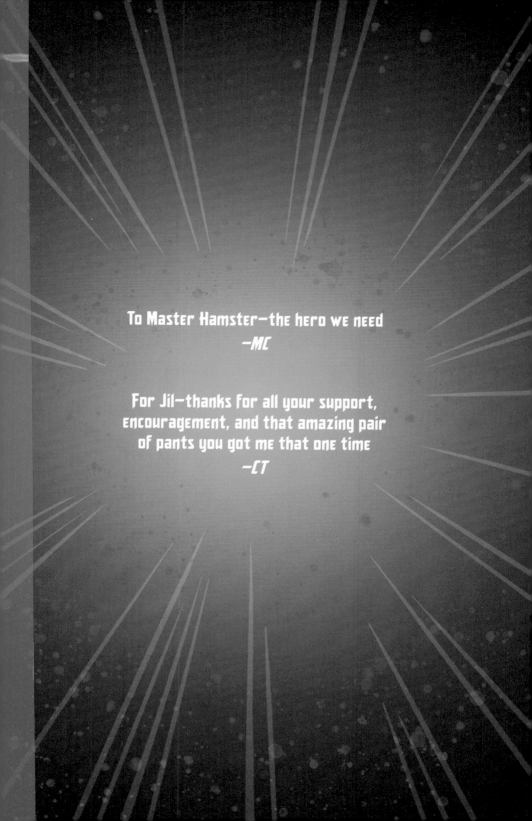

To Master Hamster—the hero we need
—MC

For Jil—thanks for all your support,
encouragement, and that amazing pair
of pants you got me that one time
—CT

Chapter 1: Fish of Legend

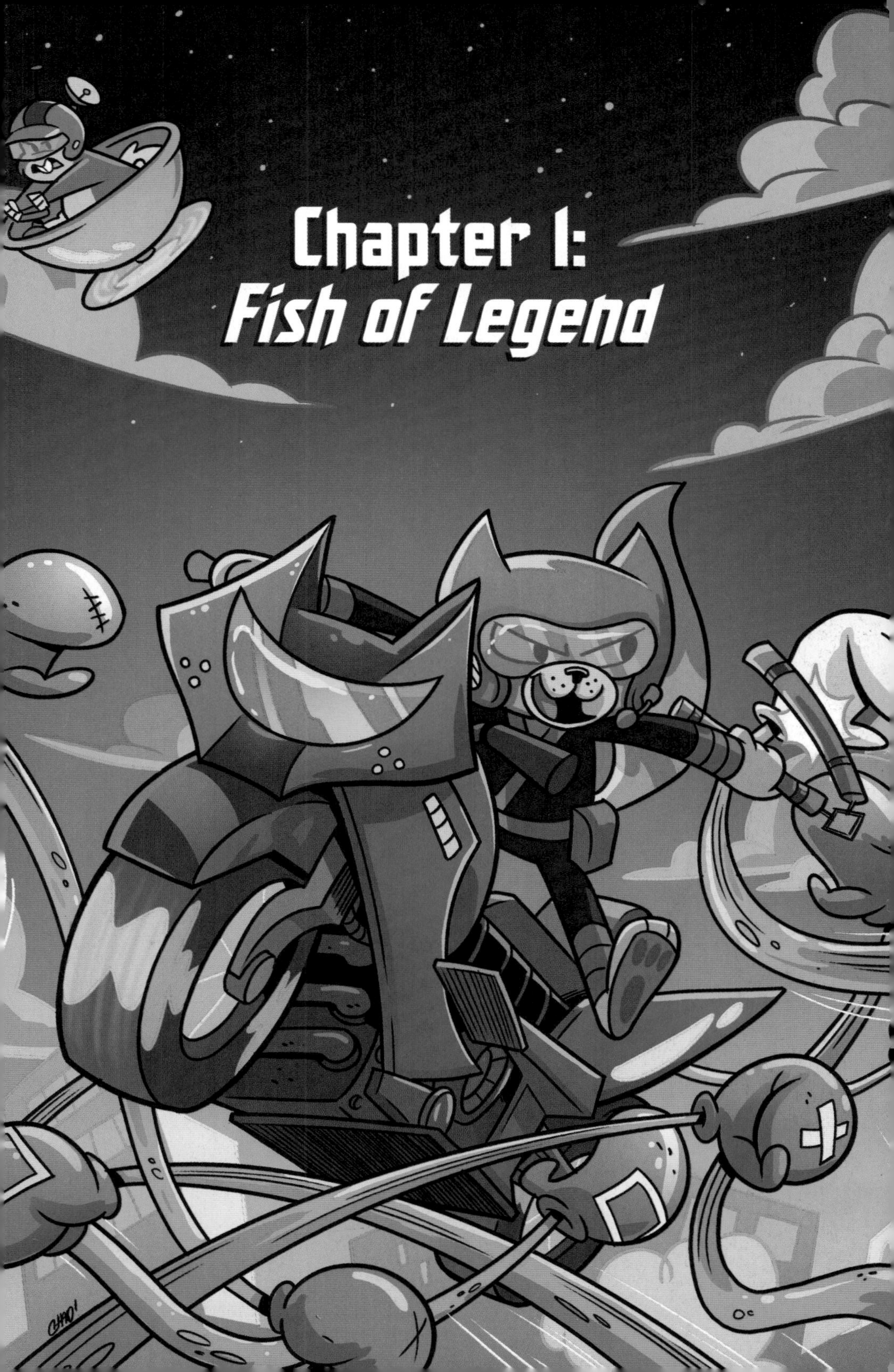

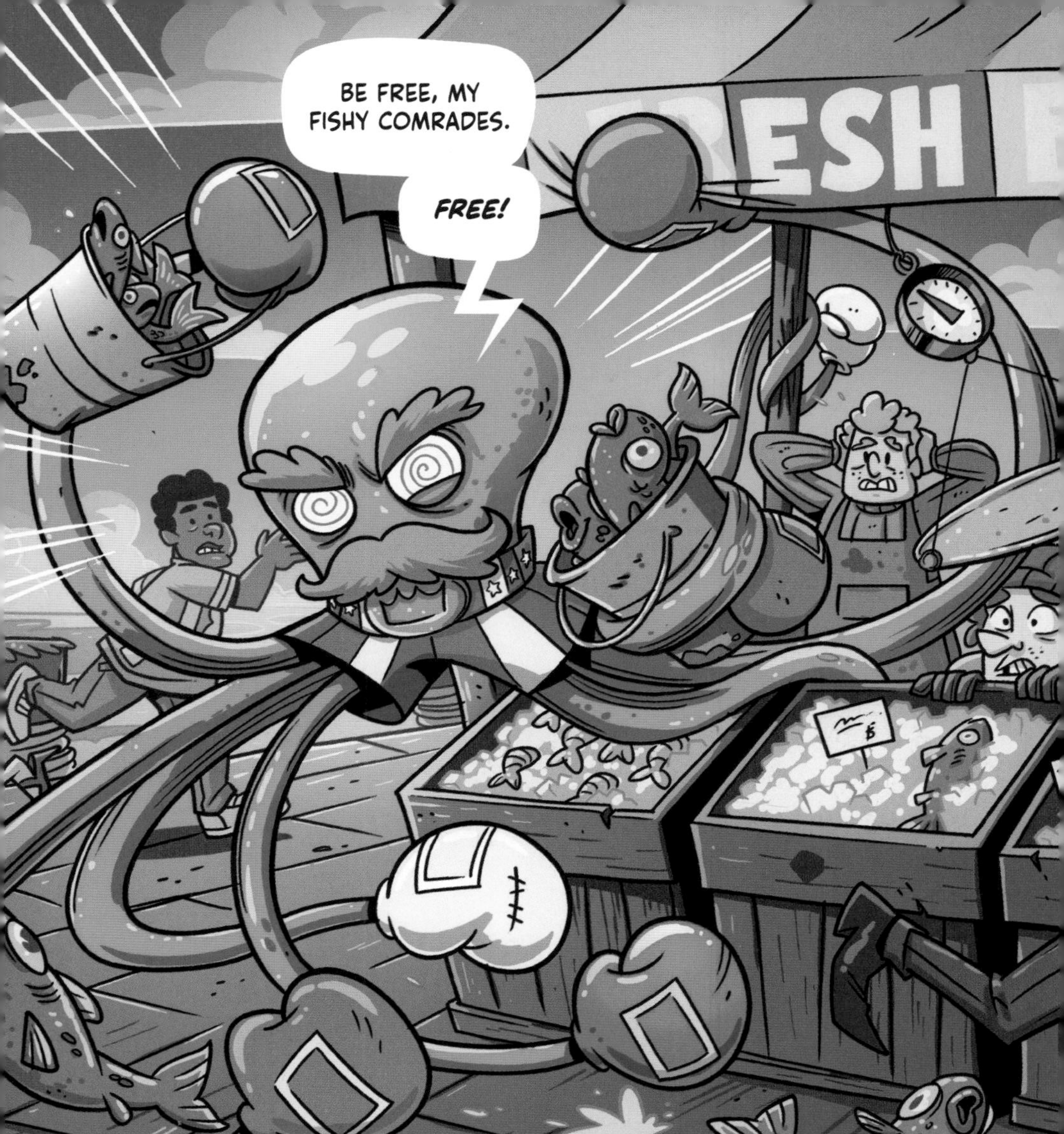
BE FREE, MY FISHY COMRADES.
FREE!
ESH
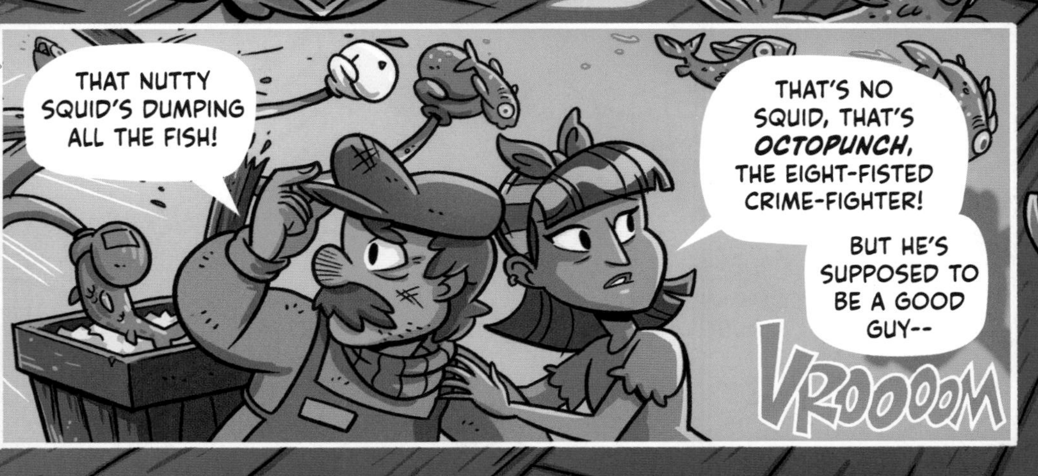
THAT NUTTY SQUID'S DUMPING ALL THE FISH!
THAT'S NO SQUID, THAT'S ***OCTOPUNCH,*** THE EIGHT-FISTED CRIME-FIGHTER!
BUT HE'S SUPPOSED TO BE A GOOD GUY--
VROOOOM

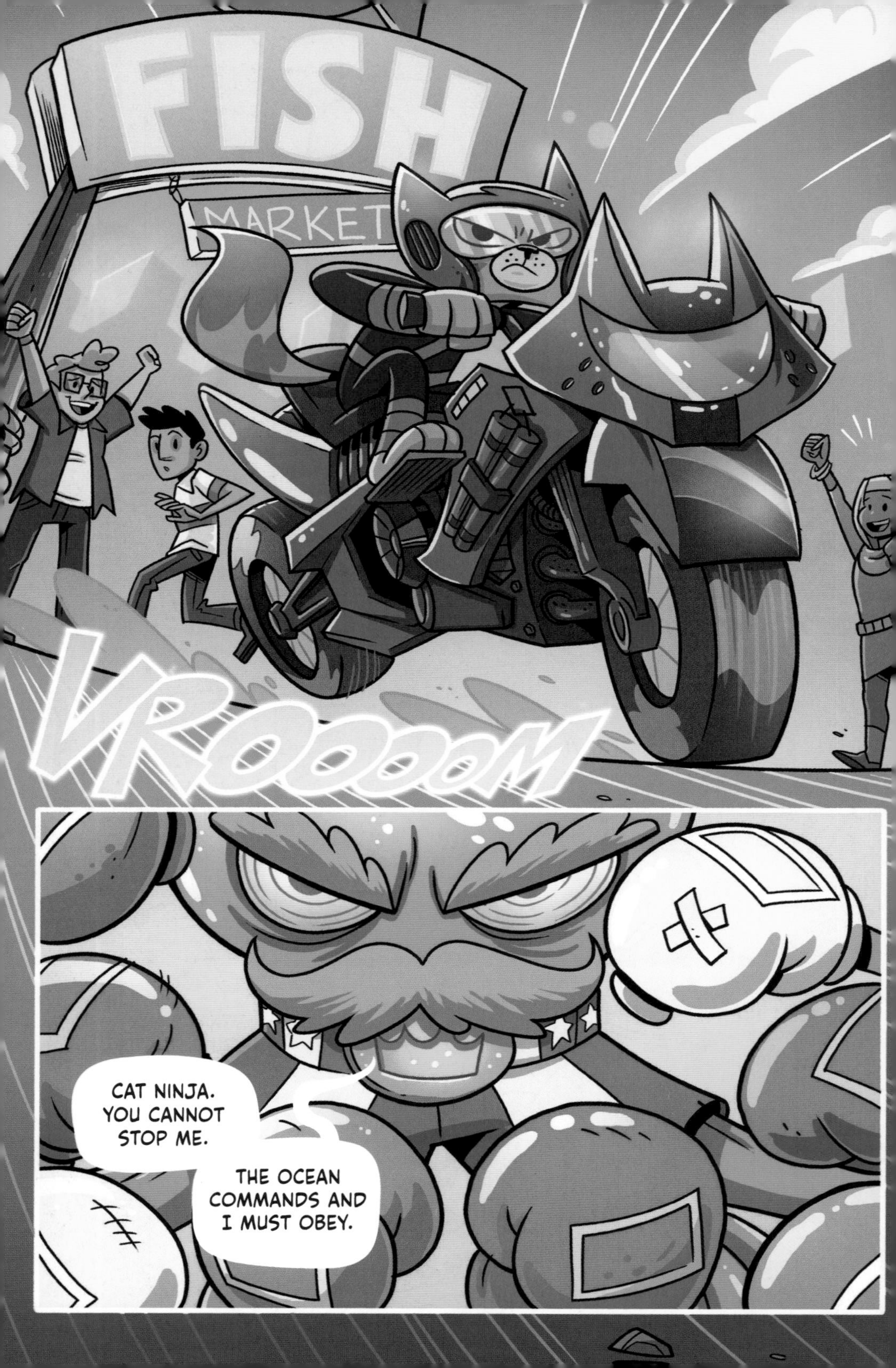
FISH
MARKET
VROOOOM
CAT NINJA. YOU CANNOT STOP ME.
THE OCEAN COMMANDS AND I MUST OBEY.

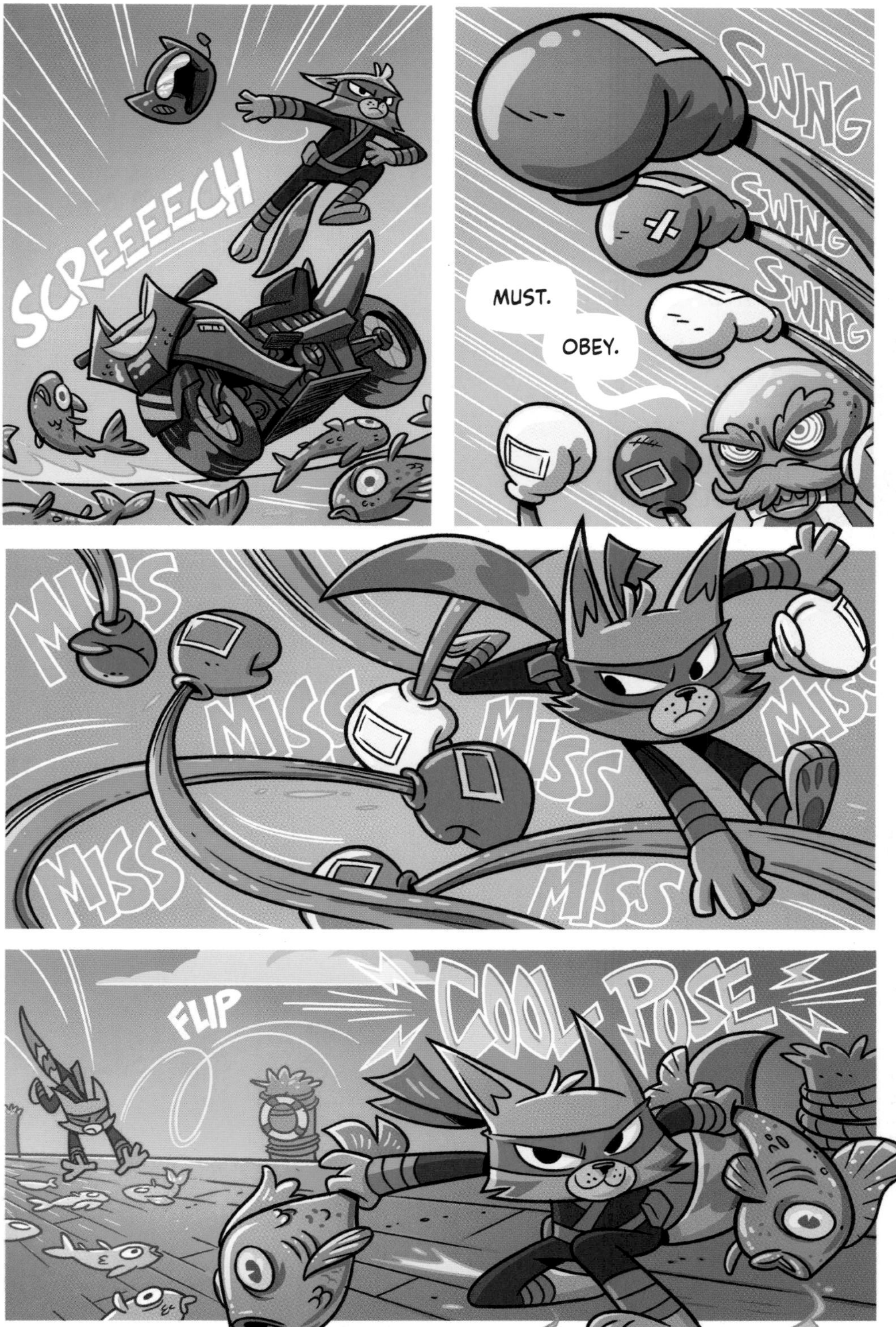
SCREEEEECH
SWING
SWING
SWING
MUST.
OBEY.
MISS
MISS
MISS
MISS
MISS
MISS
FLIP
COOL POSE

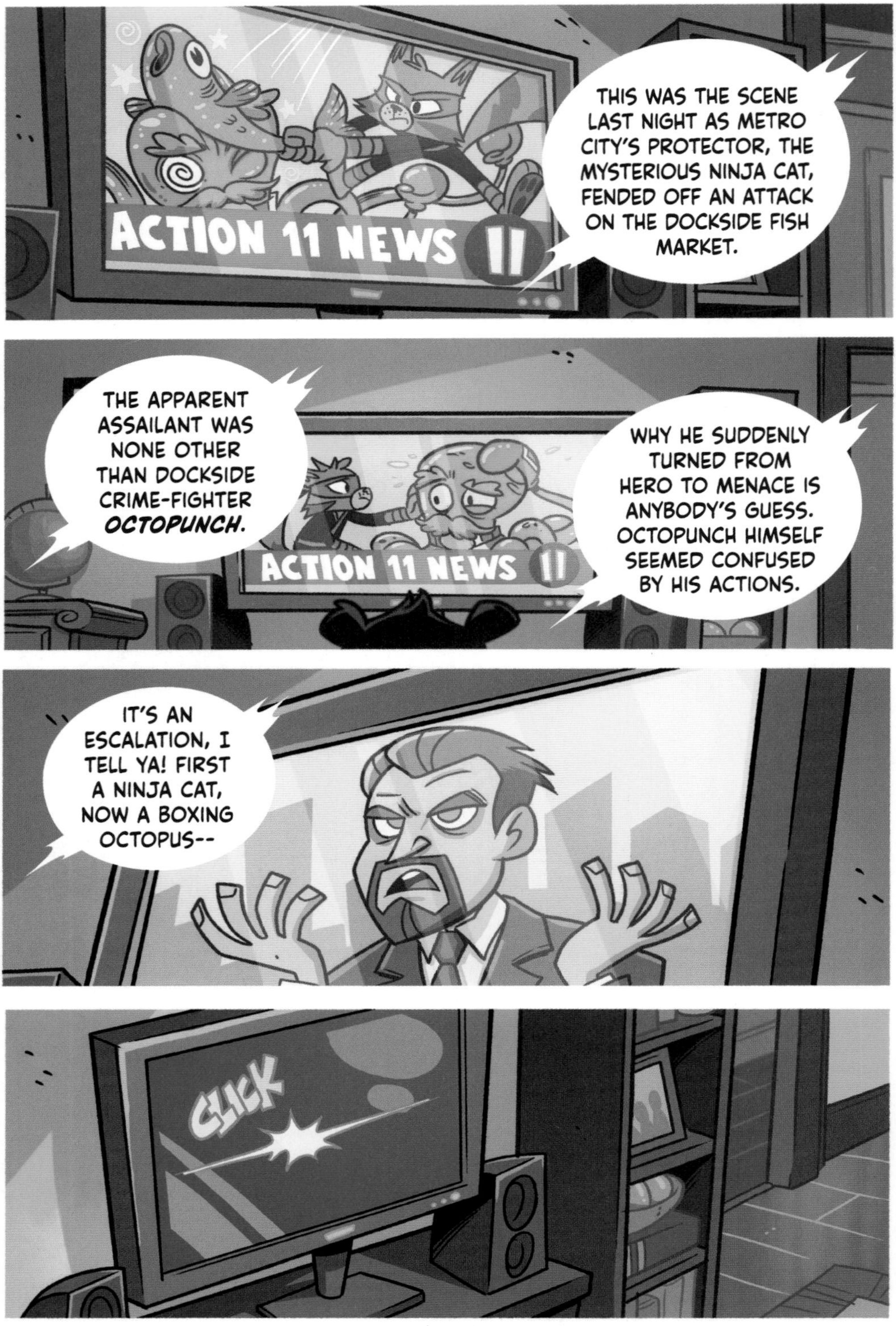
ACTION 11 NEWS
THIS WAS THE SCENE LAST NIGHT AS METRO CITY'S PROTECTOR, THE MYSTERIOUS NINJA CAT, FENDED OFF AN ATTACK ON THE DOCKSIDE FISH MARKET.
THE APPARENT ASSAILANT WAS NONE OTHER THAN DOCKSIDE CRIME-FIGHTER *OCTOPUNCH*.
ACTION 11 NEWS
WHY HE SUDDENLY TURNED FROM HERO TO MENACE IS ANYBODY'S GUESS. OCTOPUNCH HIMSELF SEEMED CONFUSED BY HIS ACTIONS.
IT'S AN ESCALATION, I TELL YA! FIRST A NINJA CAT, NOW A BOXING OCTOPUS--
CLICK

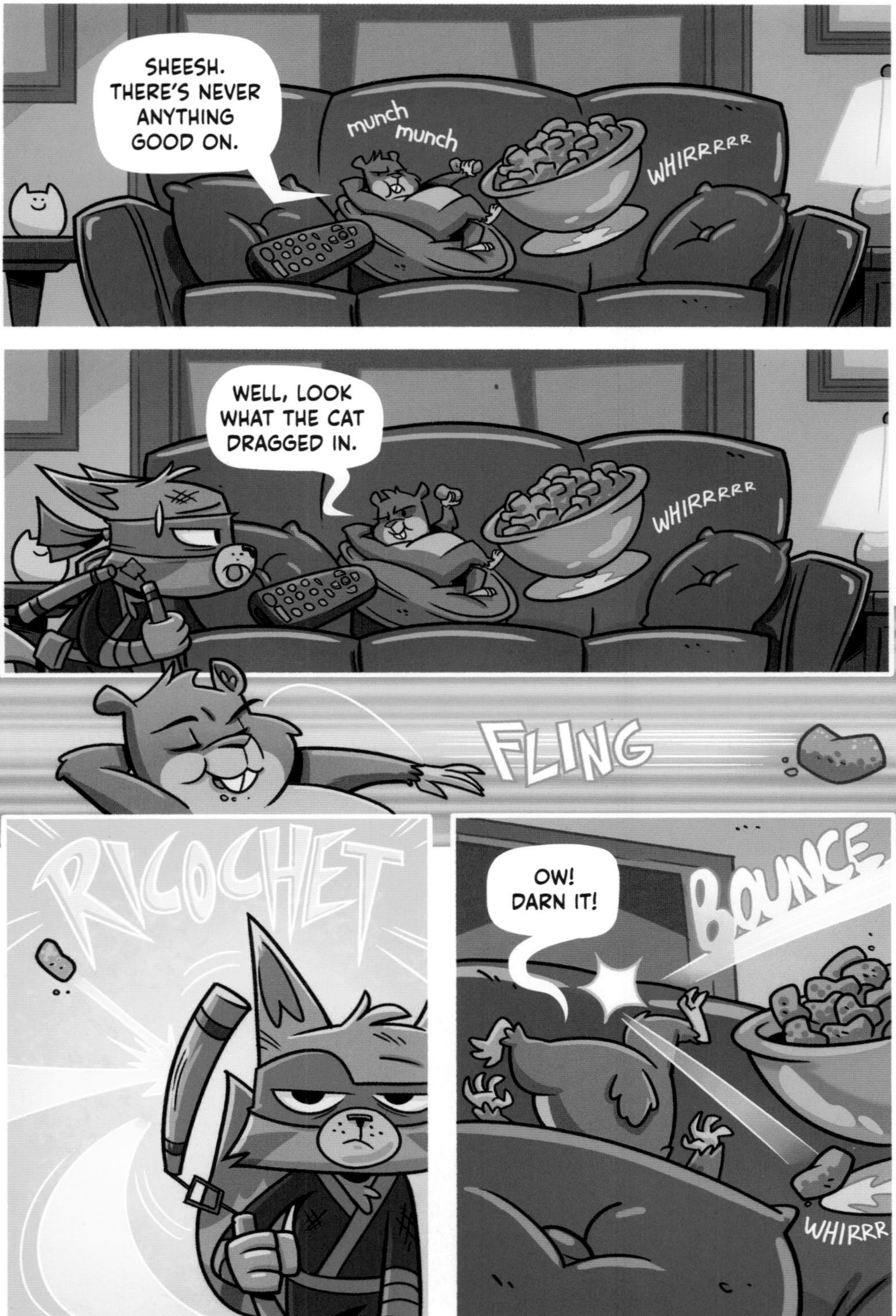
SHEESH. THERE'S NEVER ANYTHING GOOD ON.
munch munch
WHIRRRRR
WELL, LOOK WHAT THE CAT DRAGGED IN.
WHIRRRRR
FLING
RICOCHET
OW! DARN IT!
BOUNCE
WHIRRR

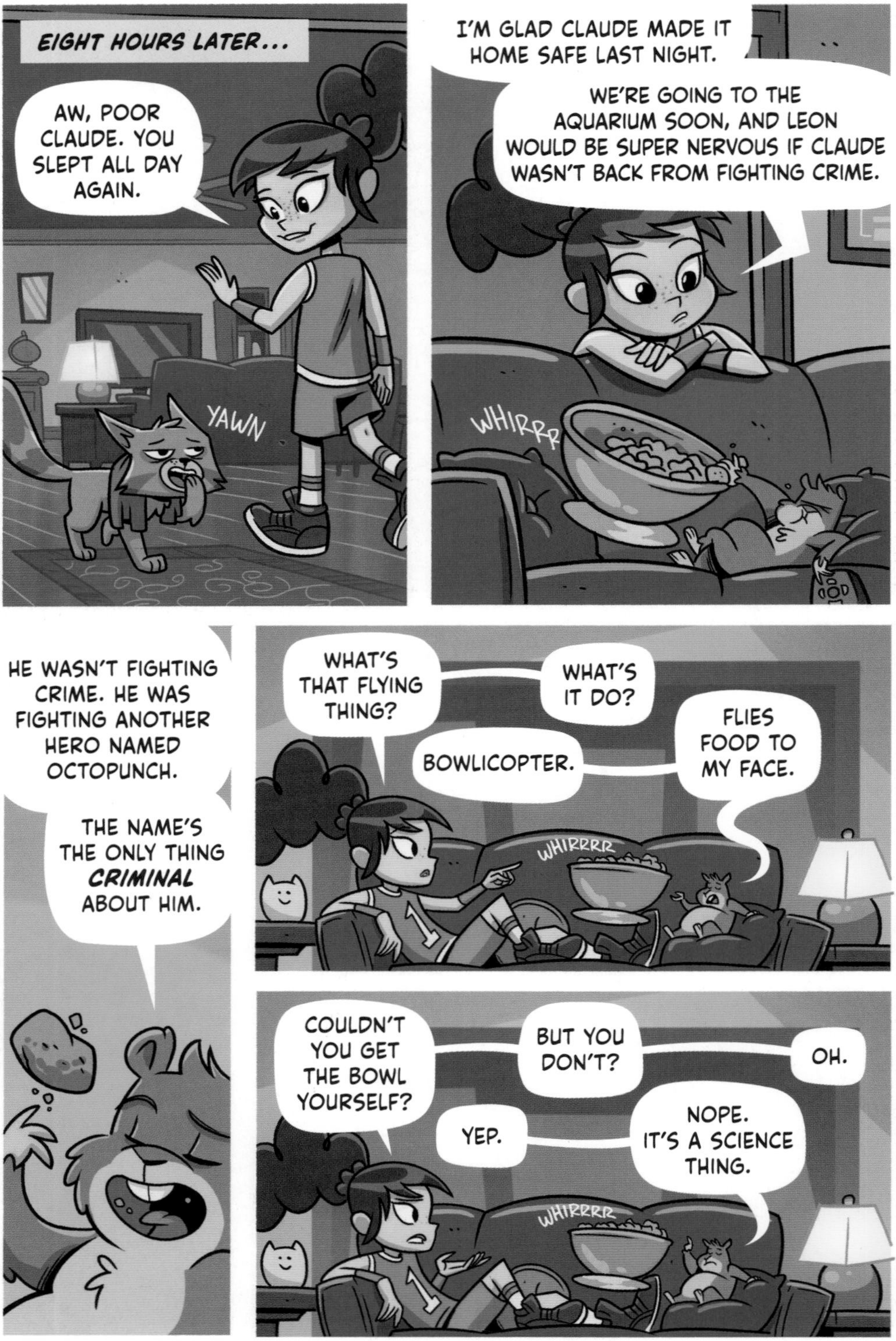
EIGHT HOURS LATER...
AW, POOR CLAUDE. YOU SLEPT ALL DAY AGAIN.
YAWN
I'M GLAD CLAUDE MADE IT HOME SAFE LAST NIGHT.
WE'RE GOING TO THE AQUARIUM SOON, AND LEON WOULD BE SUPER NERVOUS IF CLAUDE WASN'T BACK FROM FIGHTING CRIME.
WHIRRR
HE WASN'T FIGHTING CRIME. HE WAS FIGHTING ANOTHER HERO NAMED OCTOPUNCH.
THE NAME'S THE ONLY THING *CRIMINAL* ABOUT HIM.
WHAT'S THAT FLYING THING?
BOWLICOPTER.
WHAT'S IT DO?
FLIES FOOD TO MY FACE.
WHIRRRR
COULDN'T YOU GET THE BOWL YOURSELF?
YEP.
BUT YOU DON'T?
NOPE. IT'S A SCIENCE THING.
OH.
WHIRRRR

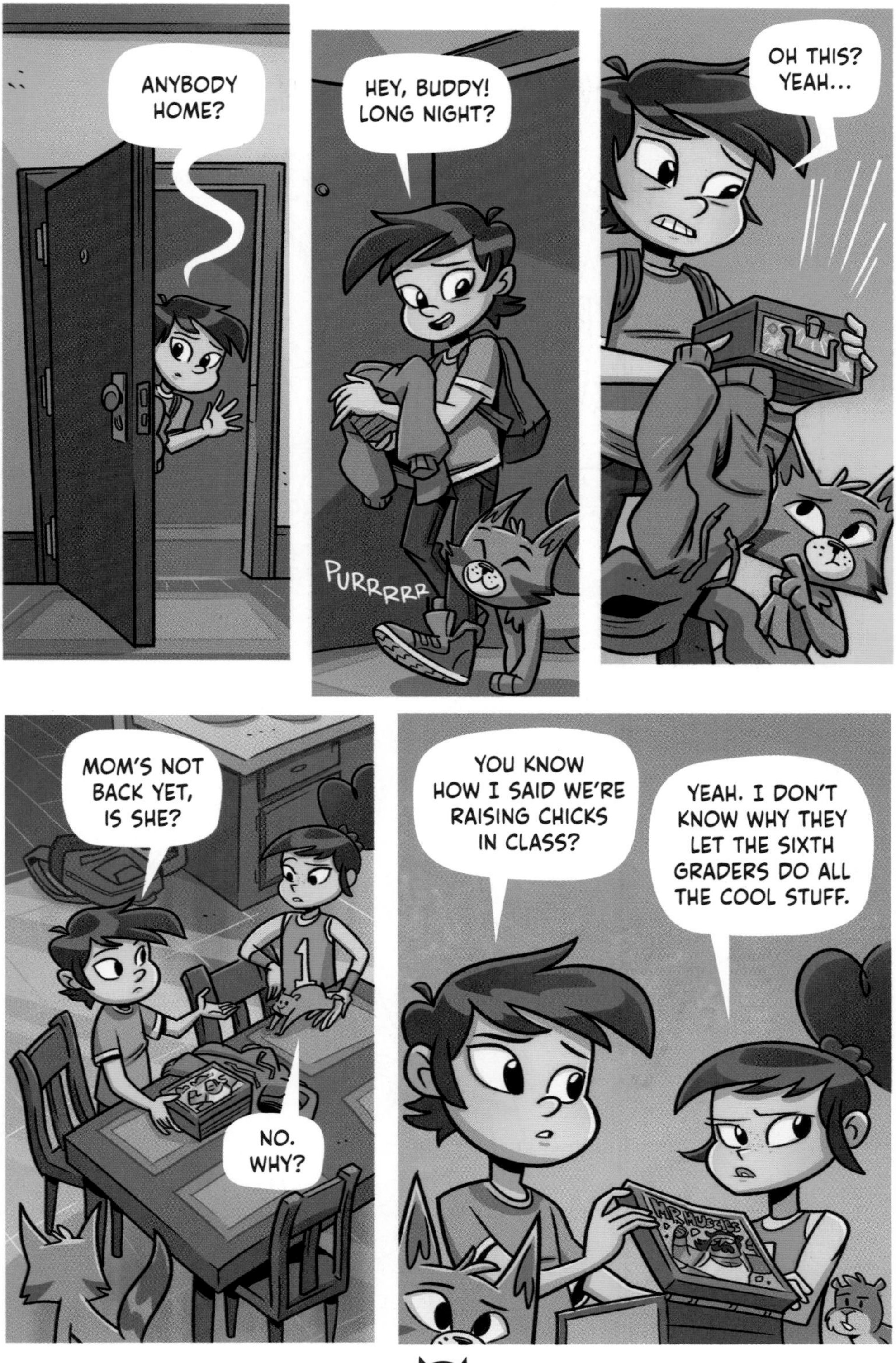
ANYBODY HOME?
HEY, BUDDY! LONG NIGHT?
PURRRRRR
OH THIS? YEAH...
MOM'S NOT BACK YET, IS SHE?
NO. WHY?
YOU KNOW HOW I SAID WE'RE RAISING CHICKS IN CLASS?
YEAH. I DON'T KNOW WHY THEY LET THE SIXTH GRADERS DO ALL THE COOL STUFF.

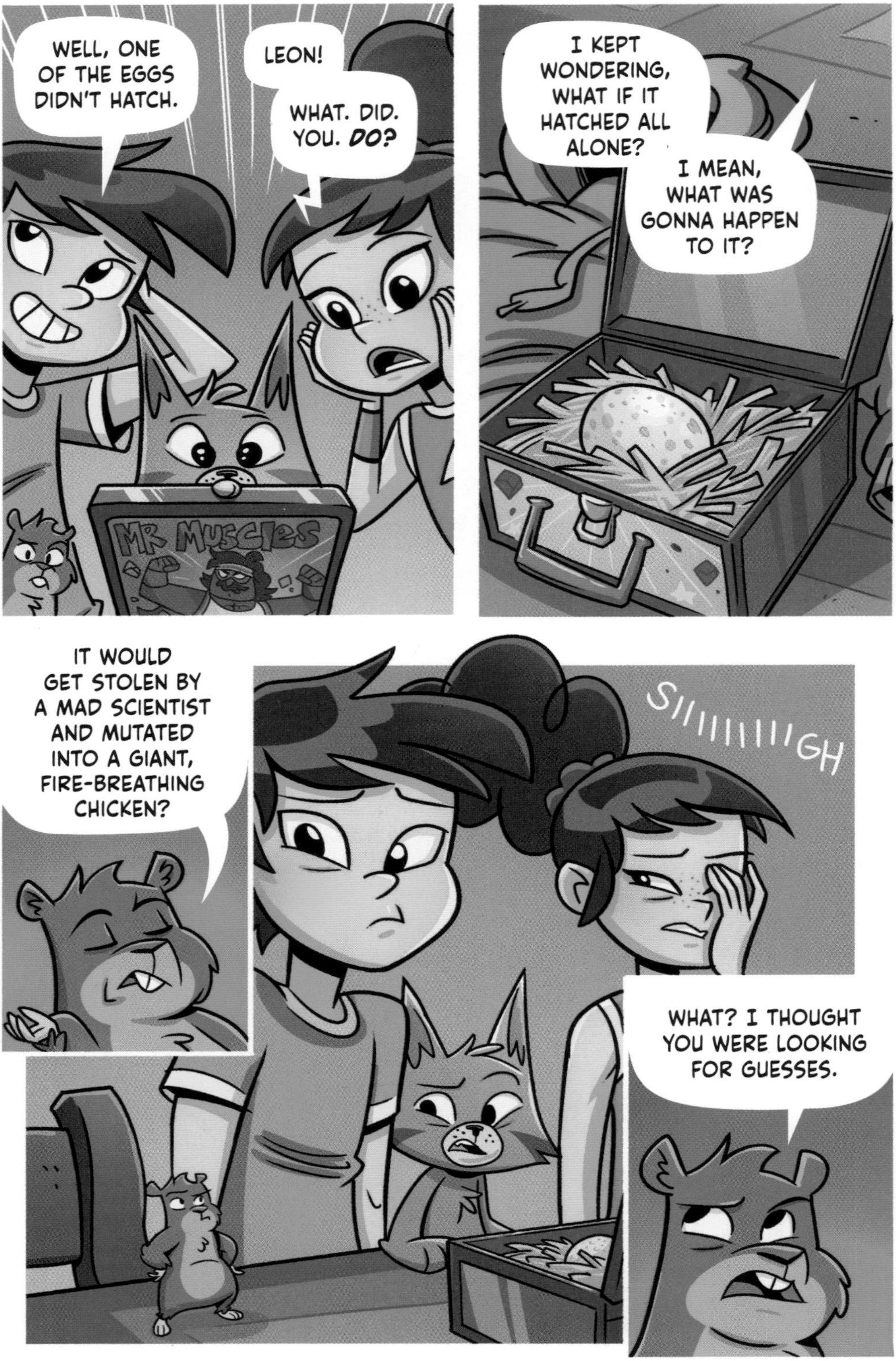
WELL, ONE OF THE EGGS DIDN'T HATCH.
LEON!
WHAT. DID. YOU. *DO?*
I KEPT WONDERING, WHAT IF IT HATCHED ALL ALONE?
I MEAN, WHAT WAS GONNA HAPPEN TO IT?
MR MUSCLES
IT WOULD GET STOLEN BY A MAD SCIENTIST AND MUTATED INTO A GIANT, FIRE-BREATHING CHICKEN?
SIIIIIIIIGH
WHAT? I THOUGHT YOU WERE LOOKING FOR GUESSES.

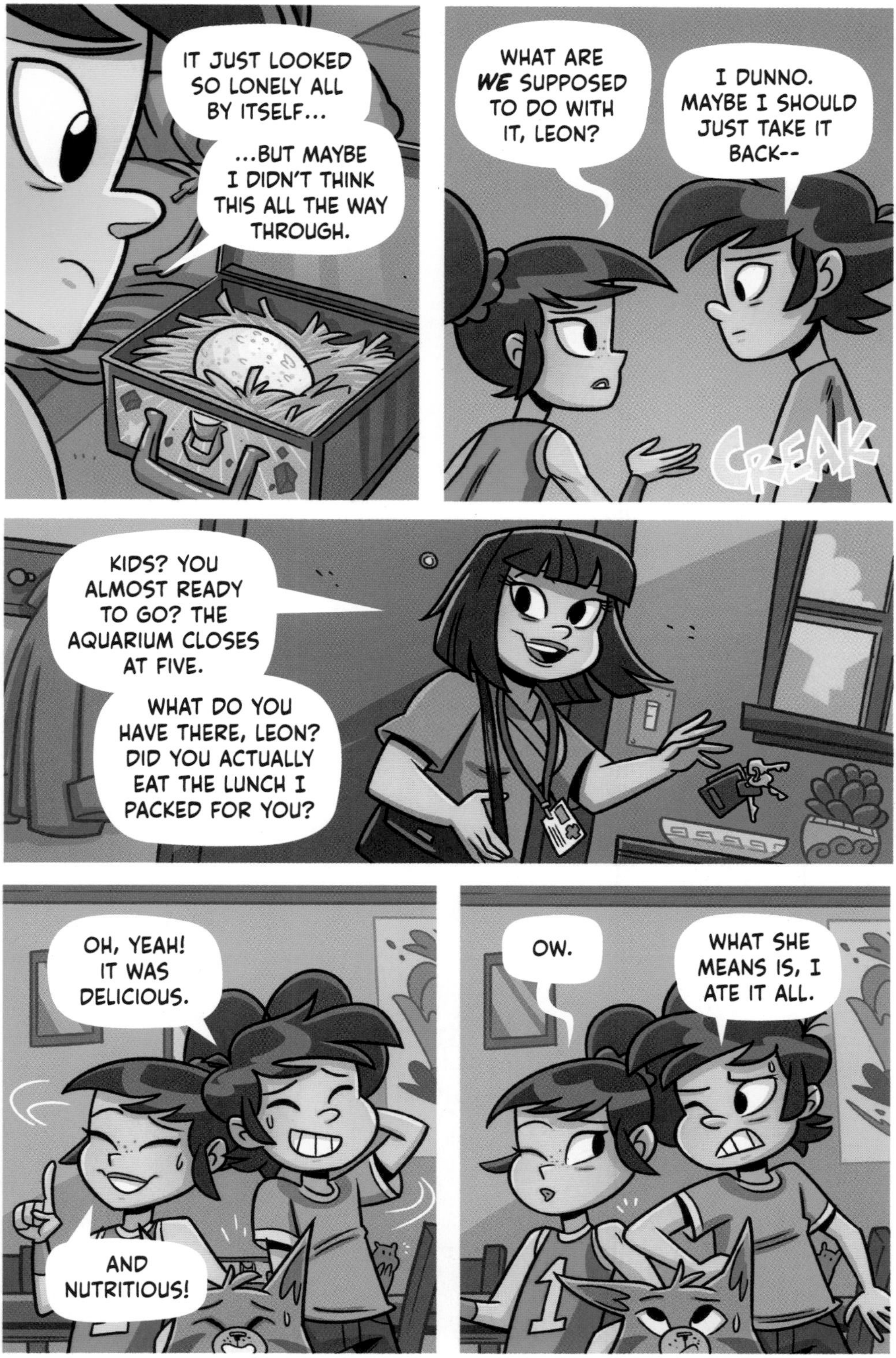
IT JUST LOOKED SO LONELY ALL BY ITSELF...
...BUT MAYBE I DIDN'T THINK THIS ALL THE WAY THROUGH.
WHAT ARE *WE* SUPPOSED TO DO WITH IT, LEON?
I DUNNO. MAYBE I SHOULD JUST TAKE IT BACK--
CREAK
KIDS? YOU ALMOST READY TO GO? THE AQUARIUM CLOSES AT FIVE.
WHAT DO YOU HAVE THERE, LEON? DID YOU ACTUALLY EAT THE LUNCH I PACKED FOR YOU?
OH, YEAH! IT WAS DELICIOUS.
AND NUTRITIOUS!
OW.
WHAT SHE MEANS IS, I ATE IT ALL.

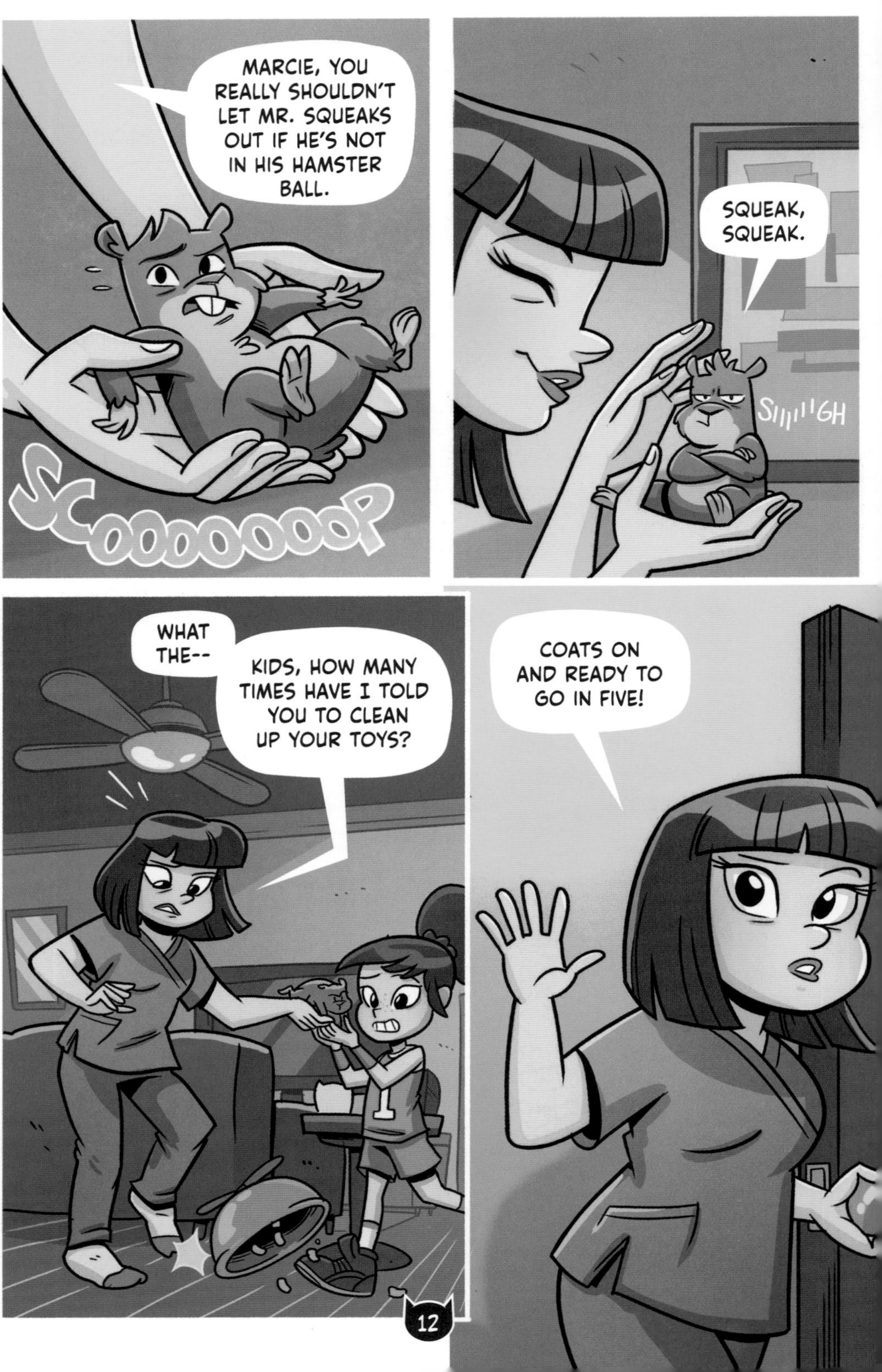
MARCIE, YOU REALLY SHOULDN'T LET MR. SQUEAKS OUT IF HE'S NOT IN HIS HAMSTER BALL.
SCOOOOOOOP
SQUEAK, SQUEAK.
SIIII'GH
WHAT THE--
KIDS, HOW MANY TIMES HAVE I TOLD YOU TO CLEAN UP YOUR TOYS?
COATS ON AND READY TO GO IN FIVE!

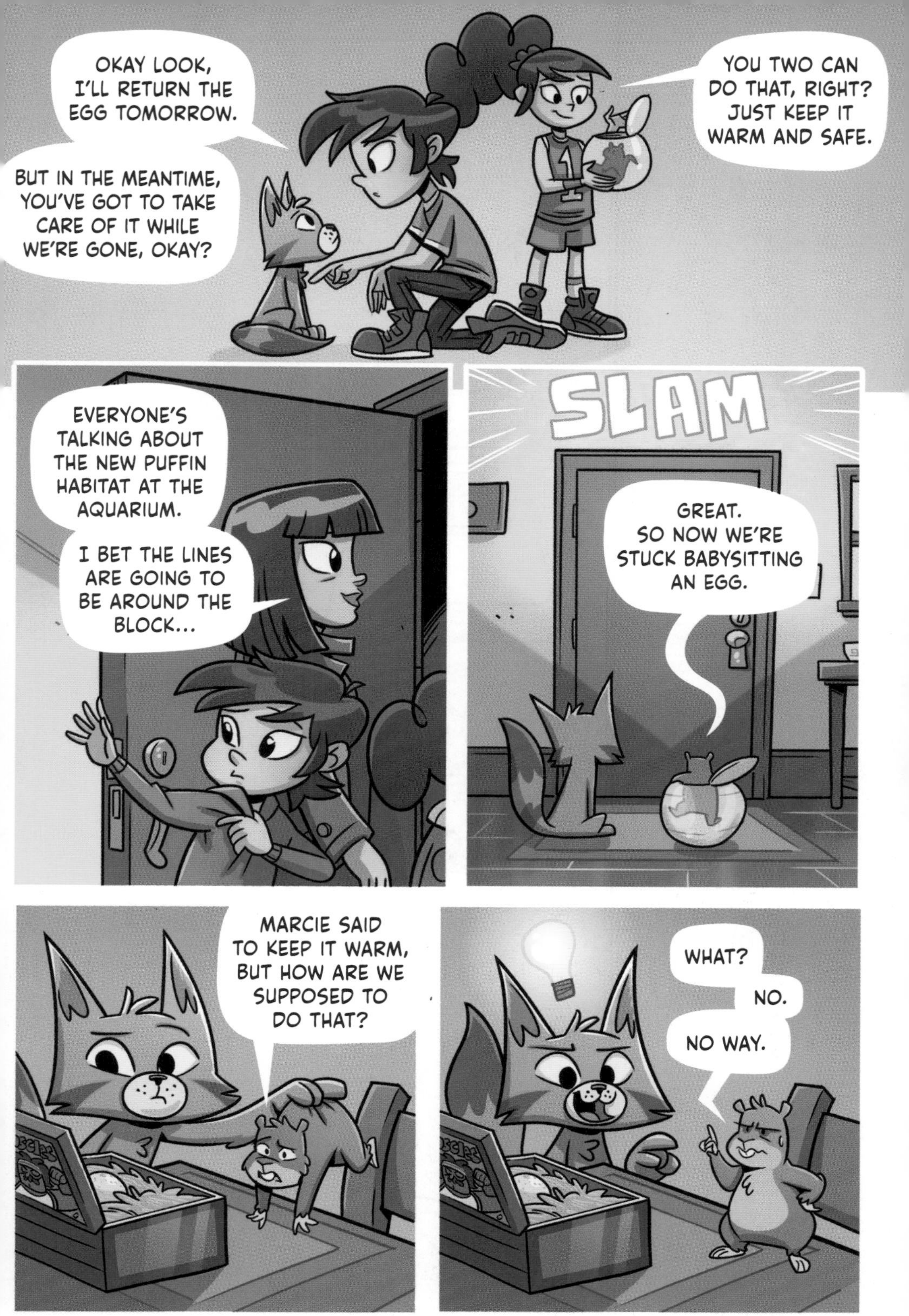
OKAY LOOK, I'LL RETURN THE EGG TOMORROW.
BUT IN THE MEANTIME, YOU'VE GOT TO TAKE CARE OF IT WHILE WE'RE GONE, OKAY?
YOU TWO CAN DO THAT, RIGHT? JUST KEEP IT WARM AND SAFE.
EVERYONE'S TALKING ABOUT THE NEW PUFFIN HABITAT AT THE AQUARIUM.
I BET THE LINES ARE GOING TO BE AROUND THE BLOCK...
SLAM
GREAT. SO NOW WE'RE STUCK BABYSITTING AN EGG.
MARCIE SAID TO KEEP IT WARM, BUT HOW ARE WE SUPPOSED TO DO THAT?
WHAT?
NO.
NO WAY.

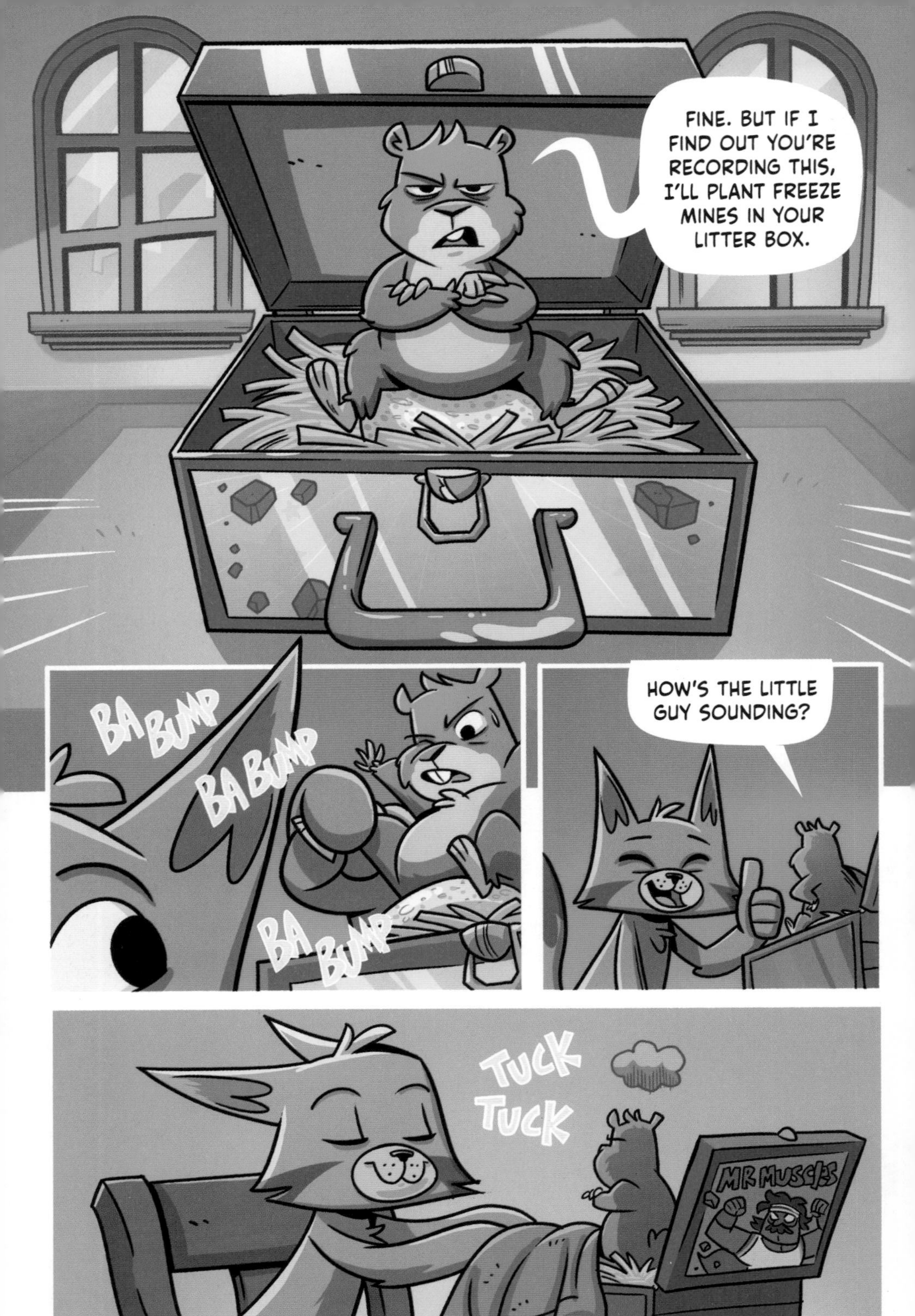
FINE. BUT IF I FIND OUT YOU'RE RECORDING THIS, I'LL PLANT FREEZE MINES IN YOUR LITTER BOX.
BA BUMP
BA BUMP
BA BUMP
HOW'S THE LITTLE GUY SOUNDING?
TUCK TUCK
MR MUSCLES

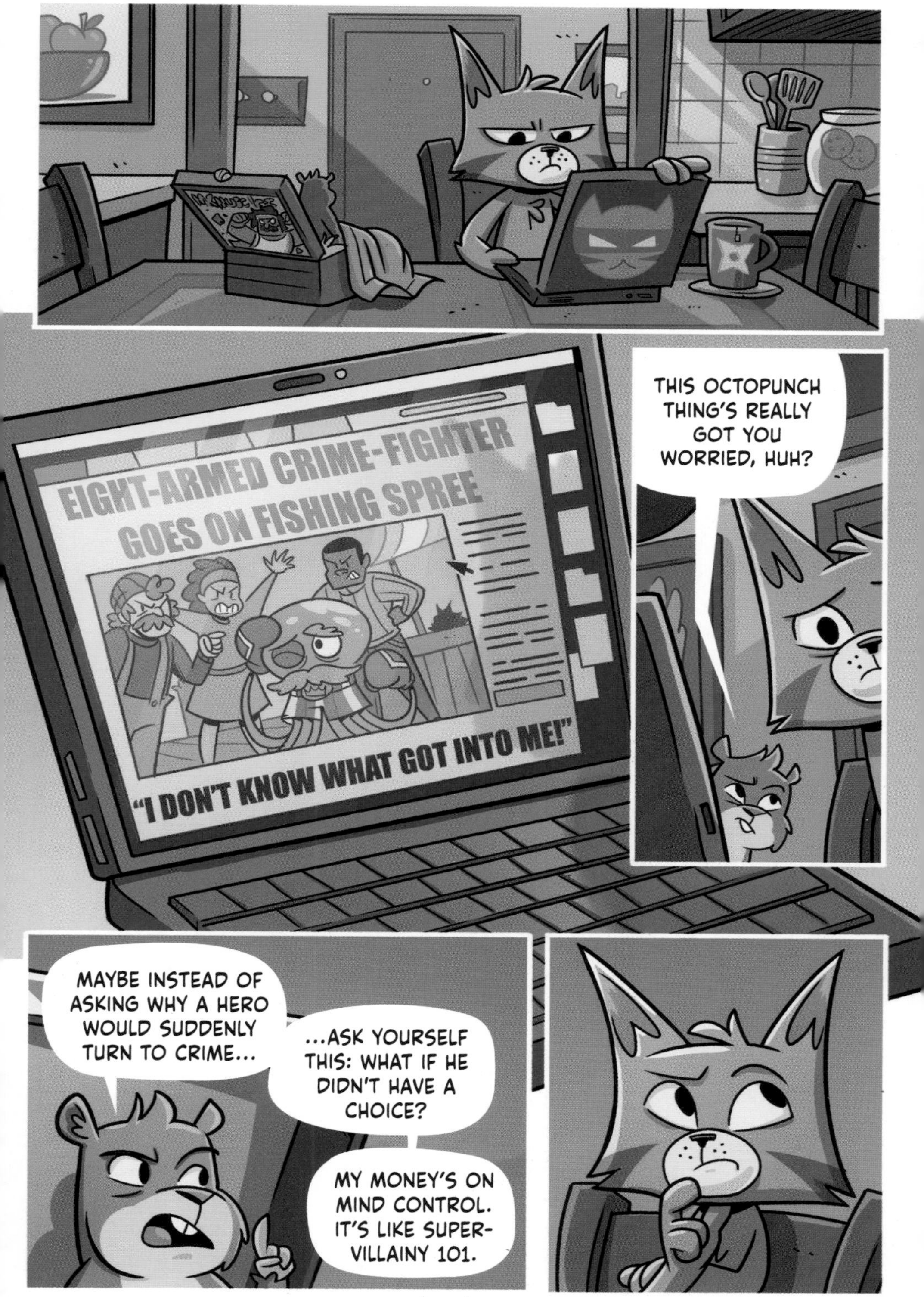
EIGHT-ARMED CRIME-FIGHTER GOES ON FISHING SPREE
"I DON'T KNOW WHAT GOT INTO ME!"
THIS OCTOPUNCH THING'S REALLY GOT YOU WORRIED, HUH?
MAYBE INSTEAD OF ASKING WHY A HERO WOULD SUDDENLY TURN TO CRIME...
...ASK YOURSELF THIS: WHAT IF HE DIDN'T HAVE A CHOICE?
MY MONEY'S ON MIND CONTROL. IT'S LIKE SUPER-VILLAINY 101.

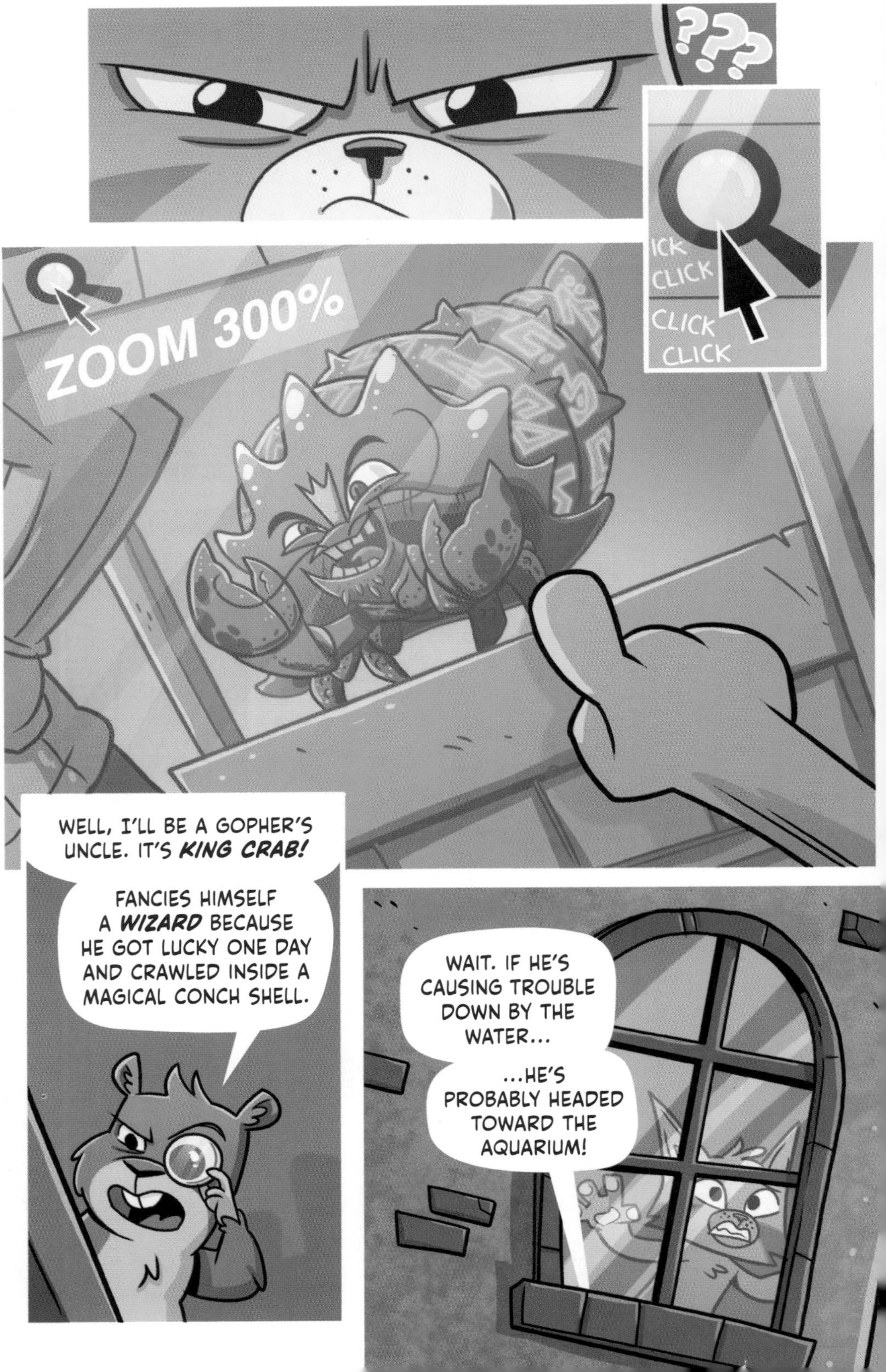
???
ICK
CLICK
CLICK
CLICK
ZOOM 300%
WELL, I'LL BE A GOPHER'S UNCLE. IT'S *KING CRAB!*
FANCIES HIMSELF A *WIZARD* BECAUSE HE GOT LUCKY ONE DAY AND CRAWLED INSIDE A MAGICAL CONCH SHELL.
WAIT. IF HE'S CAUSING TROUBLE DOWN BY THE WATER...
...HE'S PROBABLY HEADED TOWARD THE AQUARIUM!

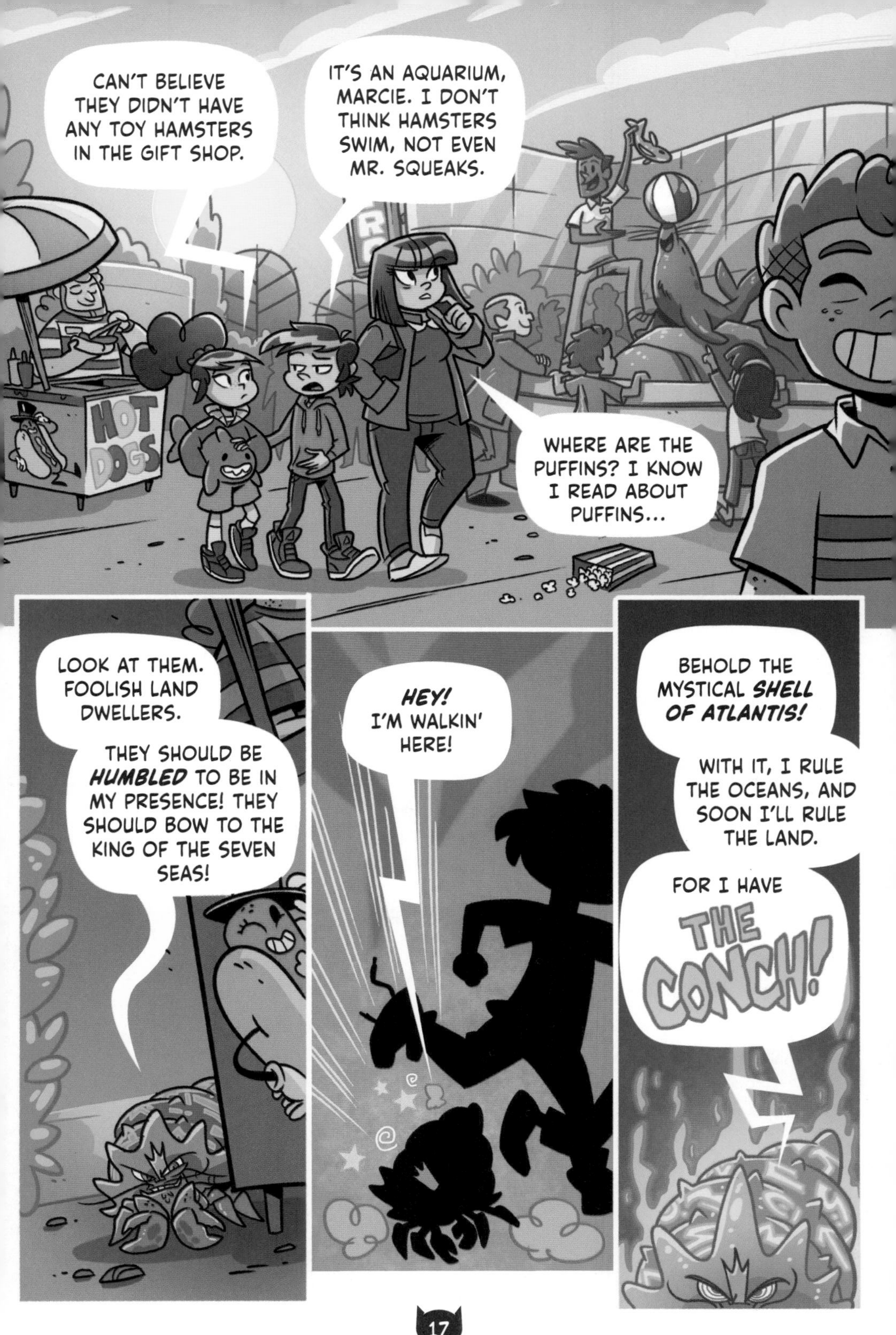

CAN'T BELIEVE THEY DIDN'T HAVE ANY TOY HAMSTERS IN THE GIFT SHOP.
IT'S AN AQUARIUM, MARCIE. I DON'T THINK HAMSTERS SWIM, NOT EVEN MR. SQUEAKS.
HOT DOGS
WHERE ARE THE PUFFINS? I KNOW I READ ABOUT PUFFINS...
LOOK AT THEM. FOOLISH LAND DWELLERS.
THEY SHOULD BE *HUMBLED* TO BE IN MY PRESENCE! THEY SHOULD BOW TO THE KING OF THE SEVEN SEAS!
HEY! I'M WALKIN' HERE!
BEHOLD THE MYSTICAL ***SHELL OF ATLANTIS!***
WITH IT, I RULE THE OCEANS, AND SOON I'LL RULE THE LAND.
FOR I HAVE
THE CONCH!

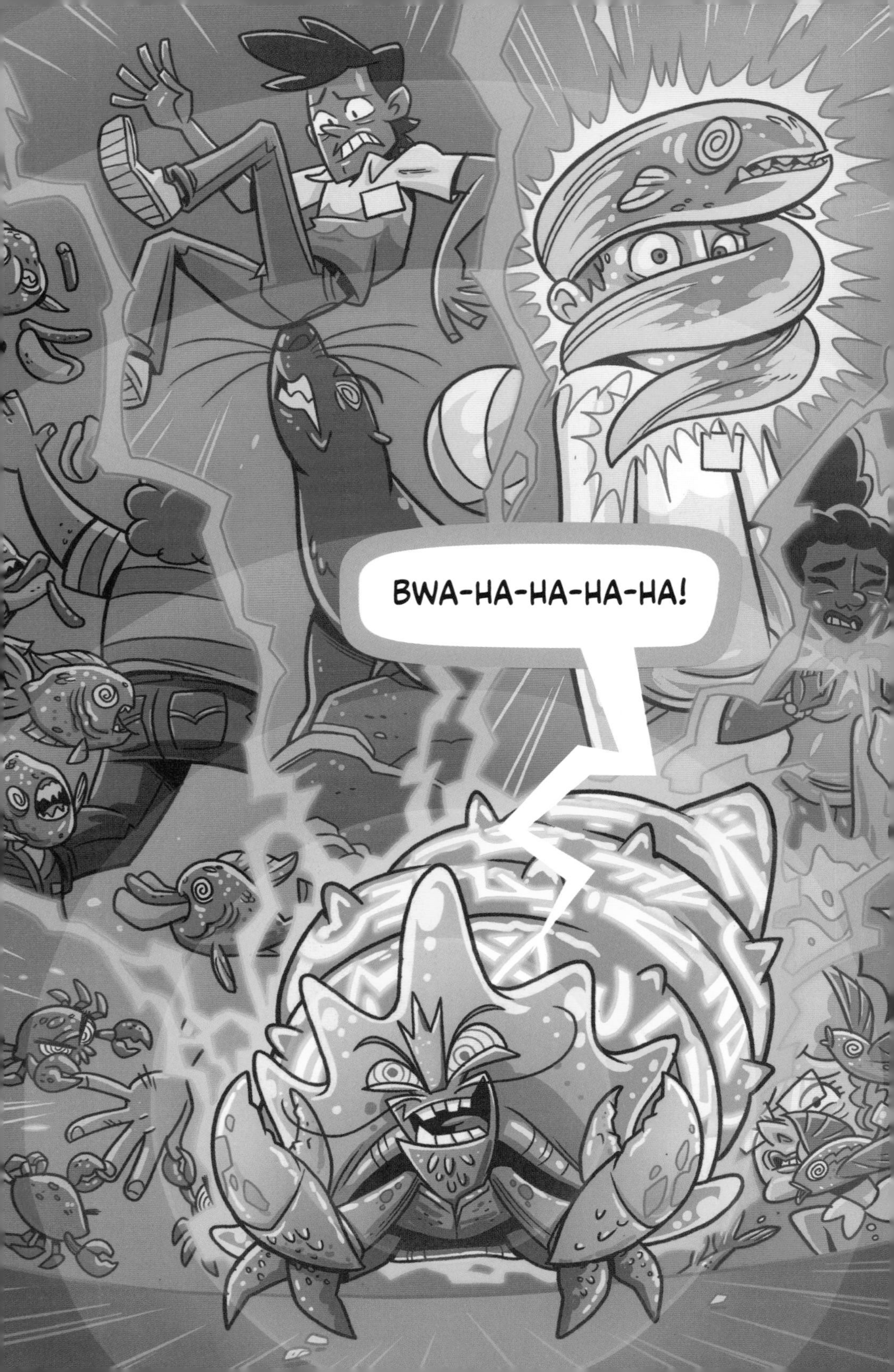
BWA-HA-HA-HA-HA!

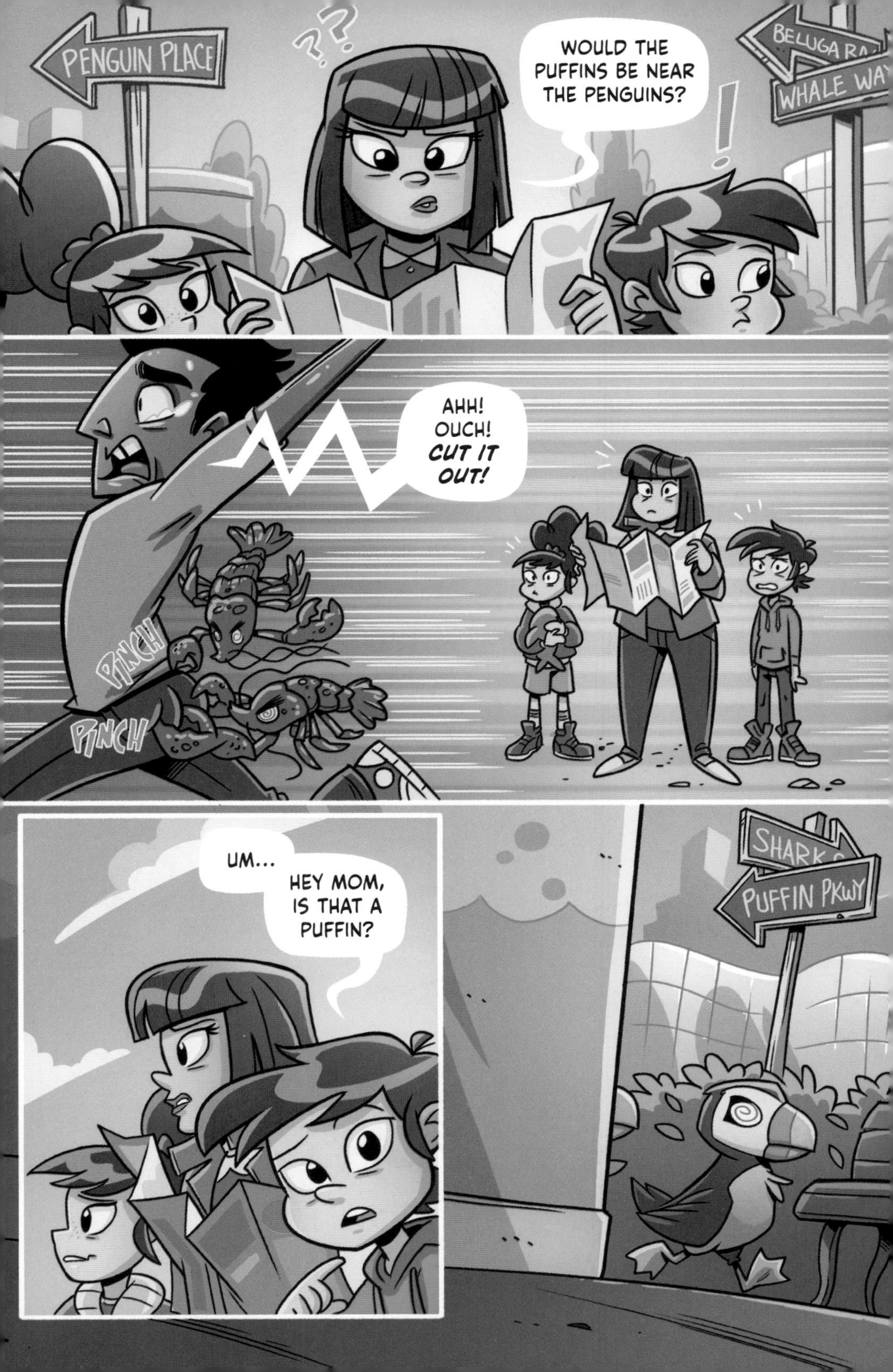
PENGUIN PLACE
BELUGA RA
WHALE WAY
WOULD THE PUFFINS BE NEAR THE PENGUINS?
AHH! OUCH! *CUT IT OUT!*
PINCH
PINCH
UM...
HEY MOM, IS THAT A PUFFIN?
SHARK
PUFFIN PKWY

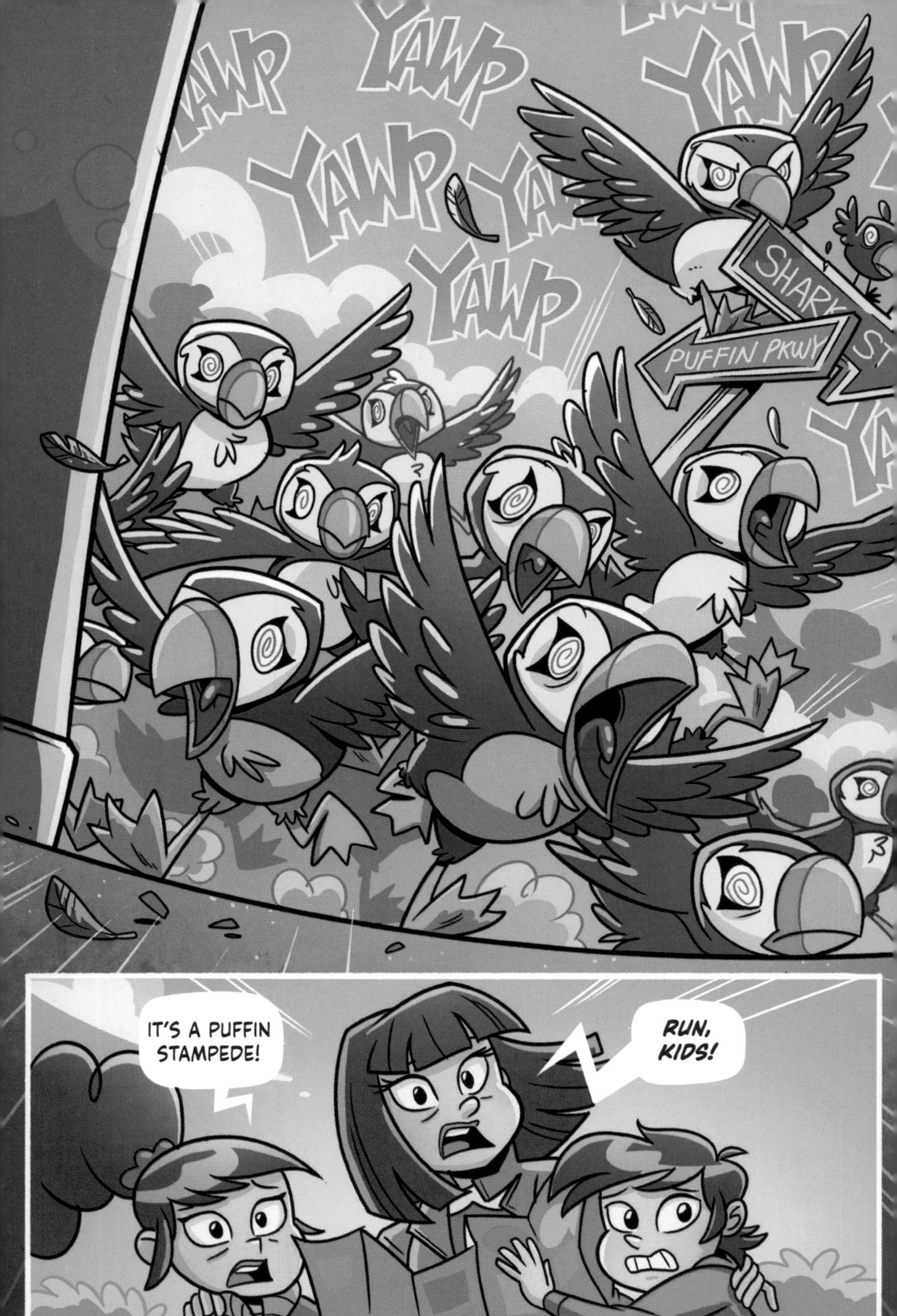
YAWP
YAWP
YAWP
YAWP
YAWP
YAWP
SHARK
PUFFIN PKWY
IT'S A PUFFIN STAMPEDE!
RUN, KIDS!

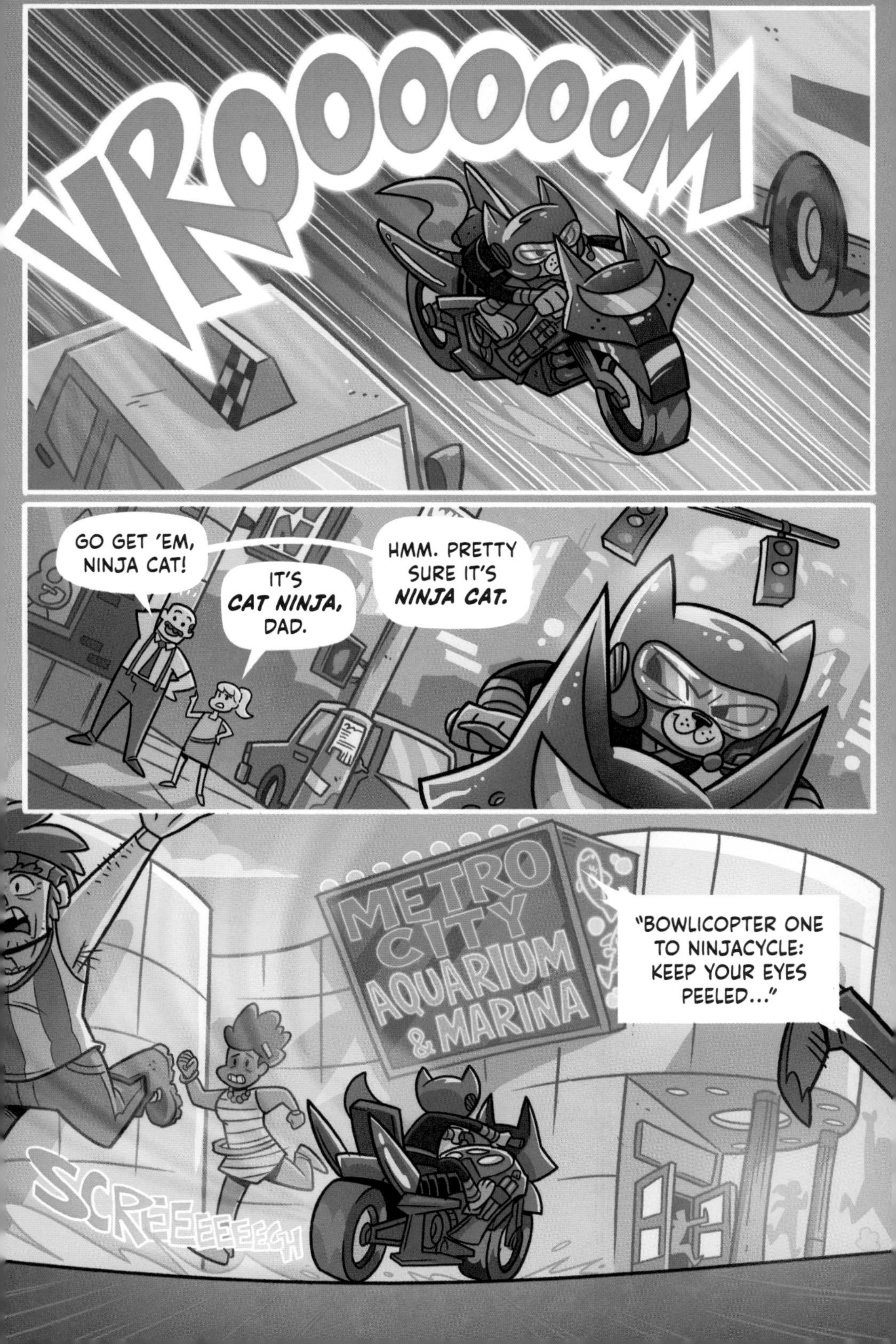
VROOOOOOM
GO GET 'EM, NINJA CAT!
IT'S CAT NINJA, DAD.
HMM. PRETTY SURE IT'S NINJA CAT.
METRO CITY AQUARIUM & MARINA
"BOWLICOPTER ONE TO NINJACYCLE: KEEP YOUR EYES PEELED..."
SCREEEEEEECH

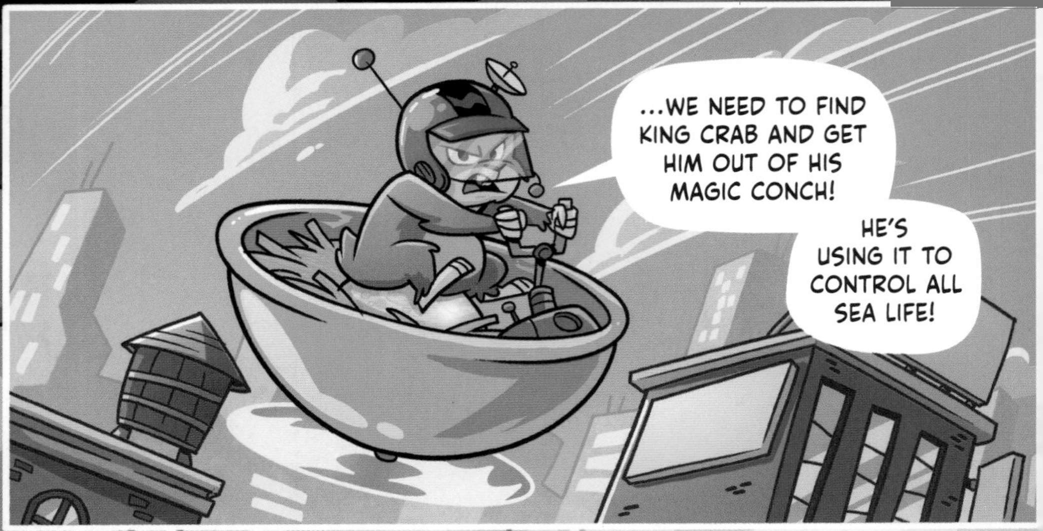
...WE NEED TO FIND KING CRAB AND GET HIM OUT OF HIS MAGIC CONCH!
HE'S USING IT TO CONTROL ALL SEA LIFE!

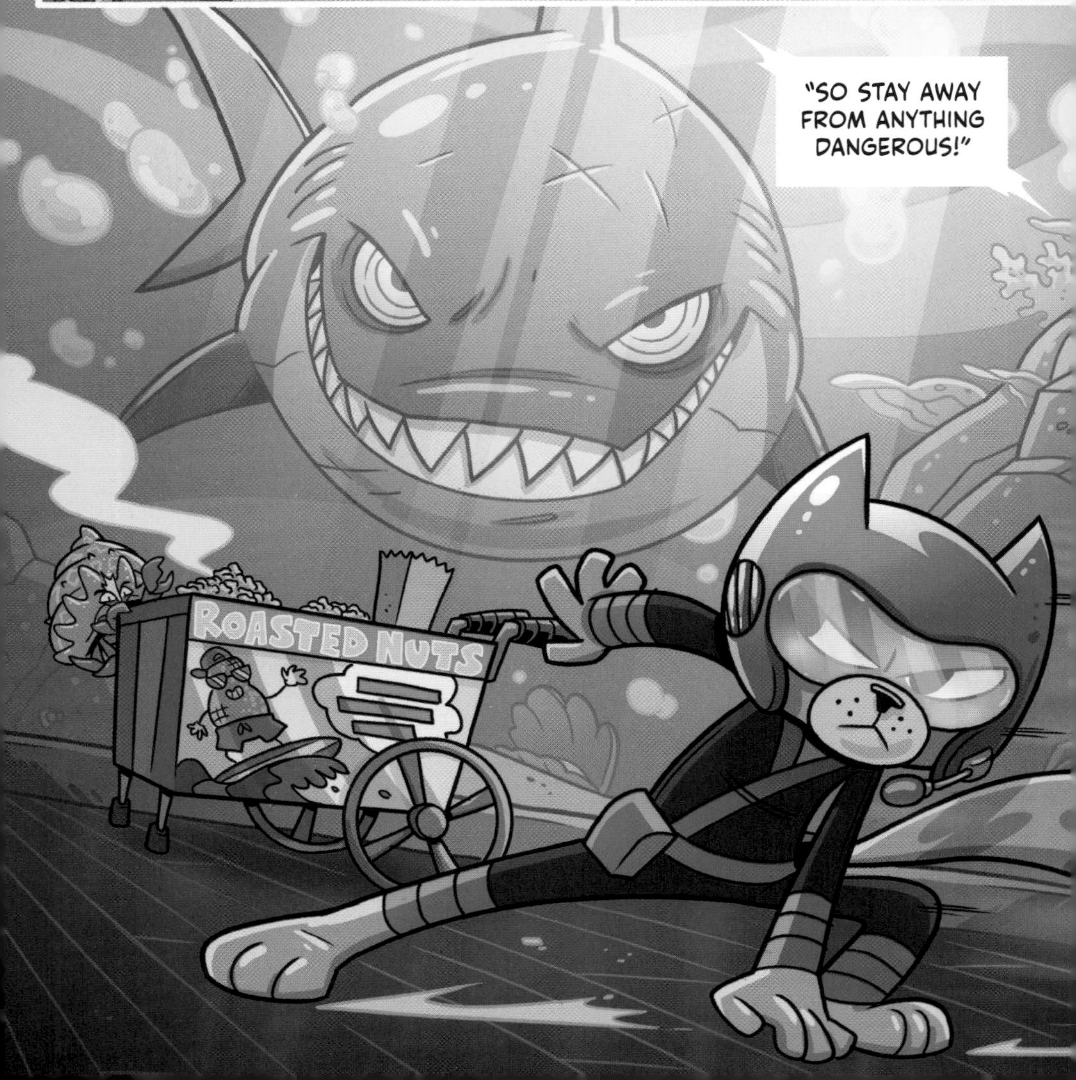
"SO STAY AWAY FROM ANYTHING DANGEROUS!"
ROASTED NUTS

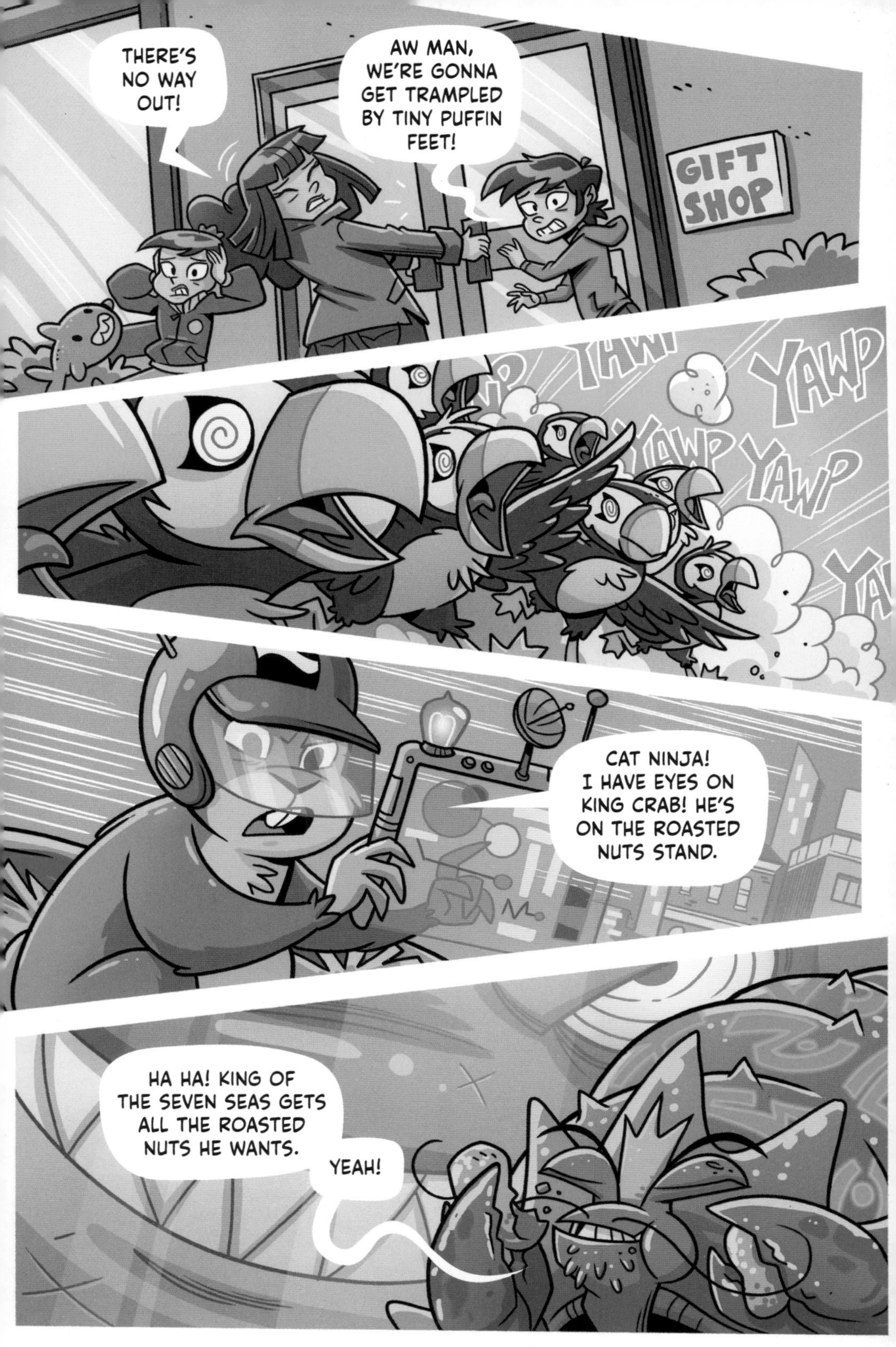
THERE'S NO WAY OUT!
AW MAN, WE'RE GONNA GET TRAMPLED BY TINY PUFFIN FEET!
GIFT SHOP
YAWP
YAWP
YAWP
YAWP
CAT NINJA! I HAVE EYES ON KING CRAB! HE'S ON THE ROASTED NUTS STAND.
HA HA! KING OF THE SEVEN SEAS GETS ALL THE ROASTED NUTS HE WANTS.
YEAH!

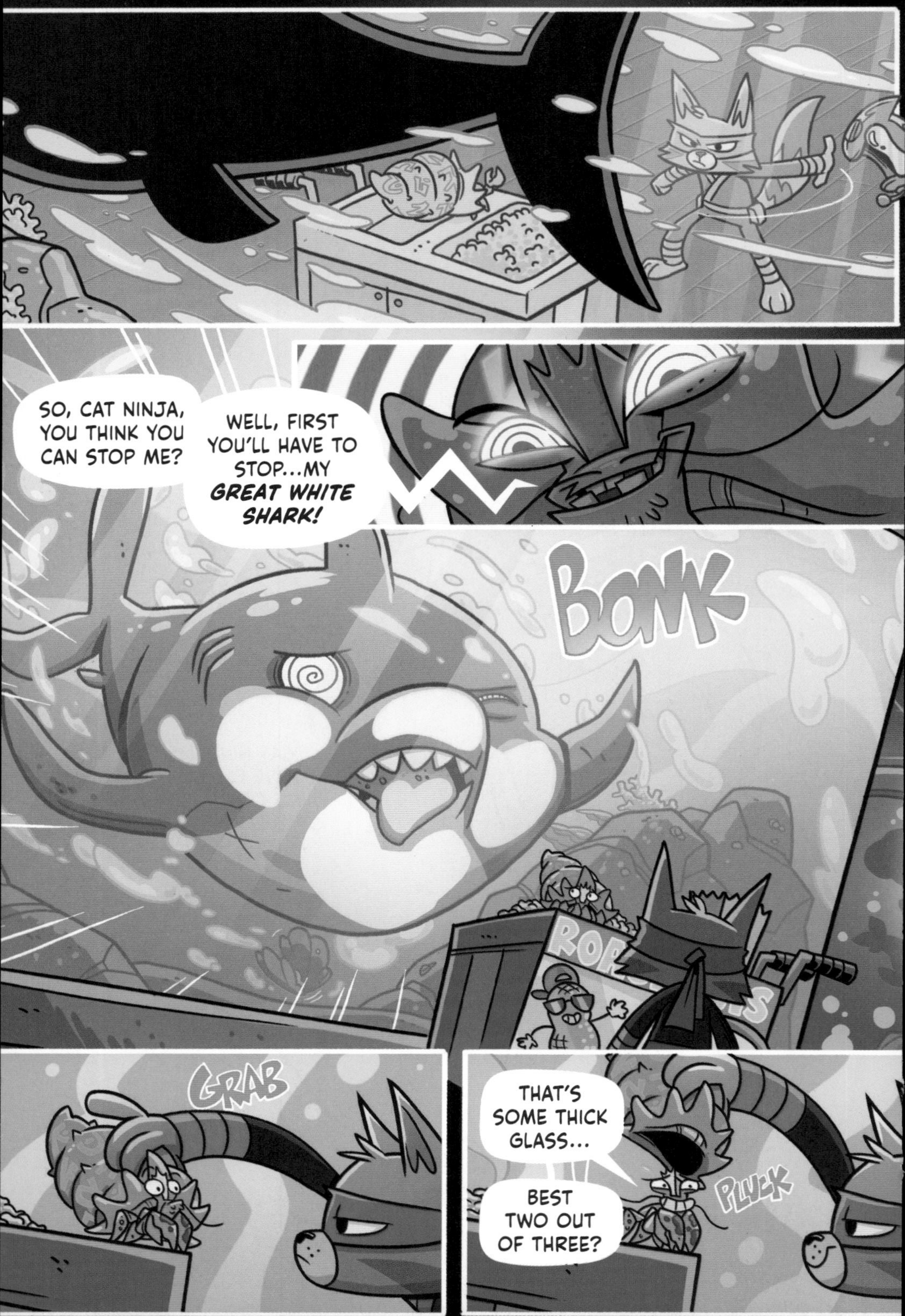
SO, CAT NINJA, YOU THINK YOU CAN STOP ME?
WELL, FIRST YOU'LL HAVE TO STOP...MY *GREAT WHITE SHARK!*
BONK
GRAB
THAT'S SOME THICK GLASS...
BEST TWO OUT OF THREE?
PLUCK

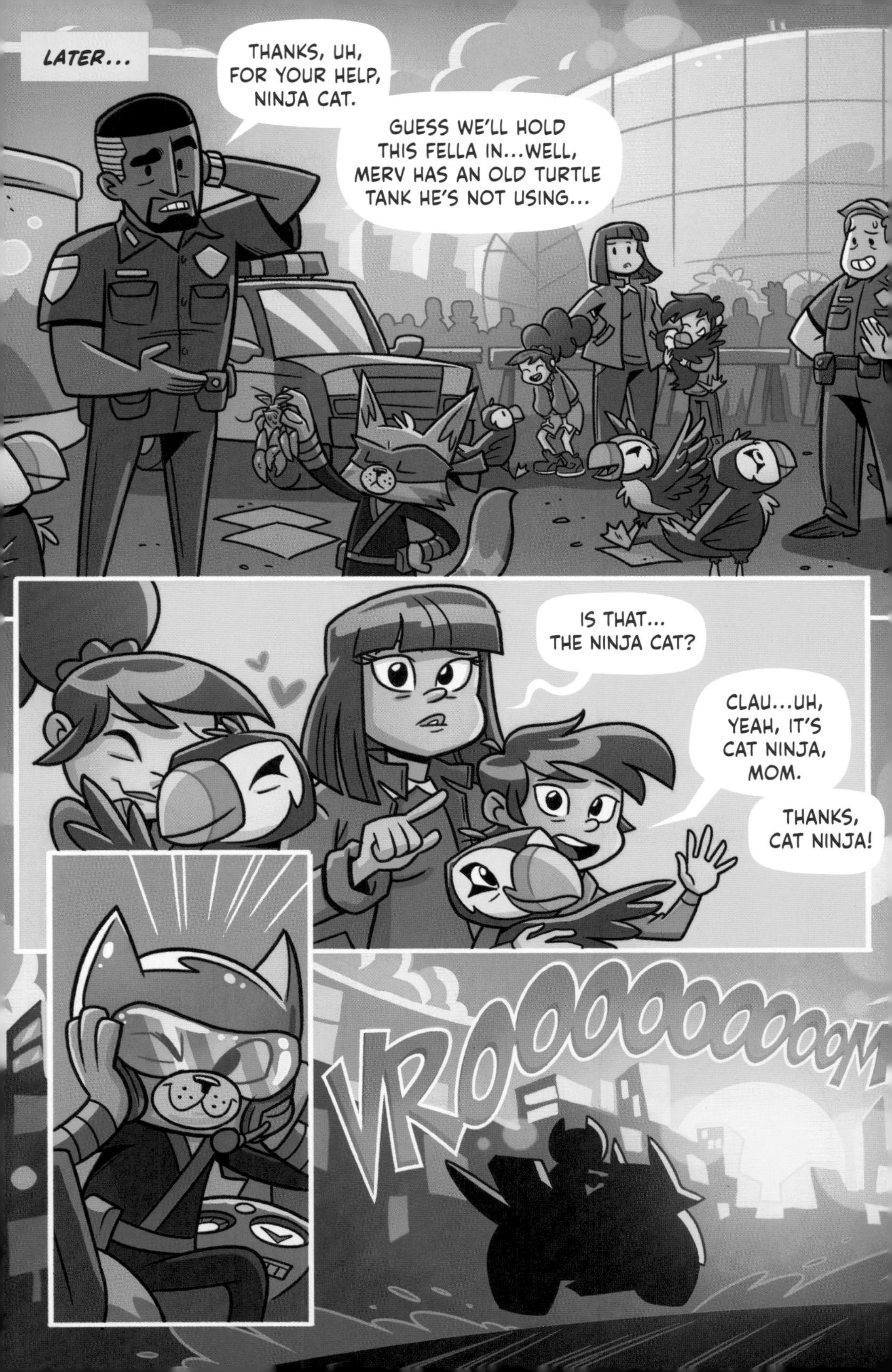
LATER...
THANKS, UH, FOR YOUR HELP, NINJA CAT.
GUESS WE'LL HOLD THIS FELLA IN...WELL, MERV HAS AN OLD TURTLE TANK HE'S NOT USING...
IS THAT... THE NINJA CAT?
CLAU...UH, YEAH, IT'S CAT NINJA, MOM.
THANKS, CAT NINJA!
VROOOOOOOOOOM

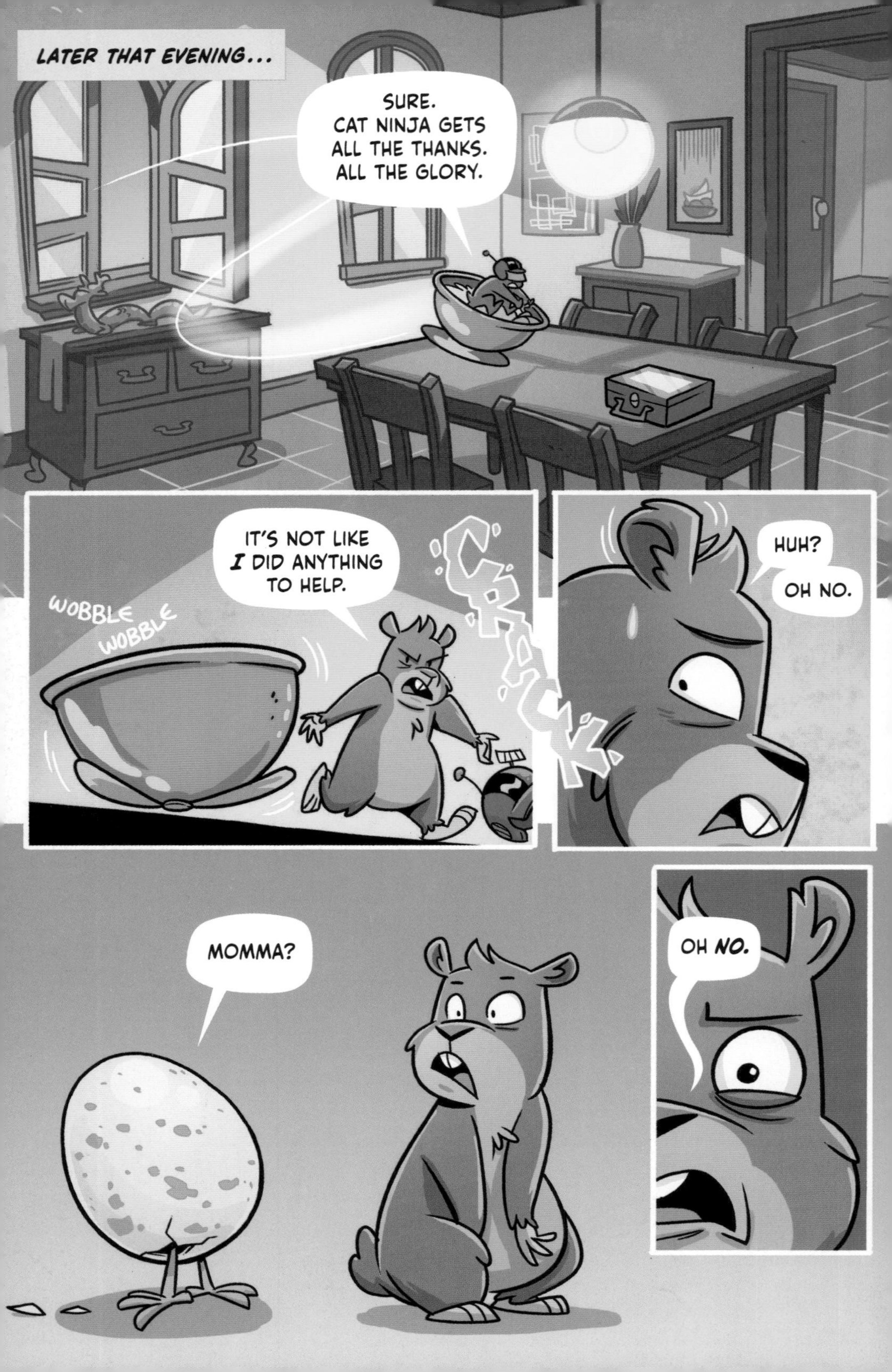
LATER THAT EVENING...
SURE. CAT NINJA GETS ALL THE THANKS. ALL THE GLORY.
IT'S NOT LIKE I DID ANYTHING TO HELP.
WOBBLE WOBBLE
CRACK
HUH?
OH NO.
MOMMA?
OH NO.

Chapter 2: *Baby's Day Out*

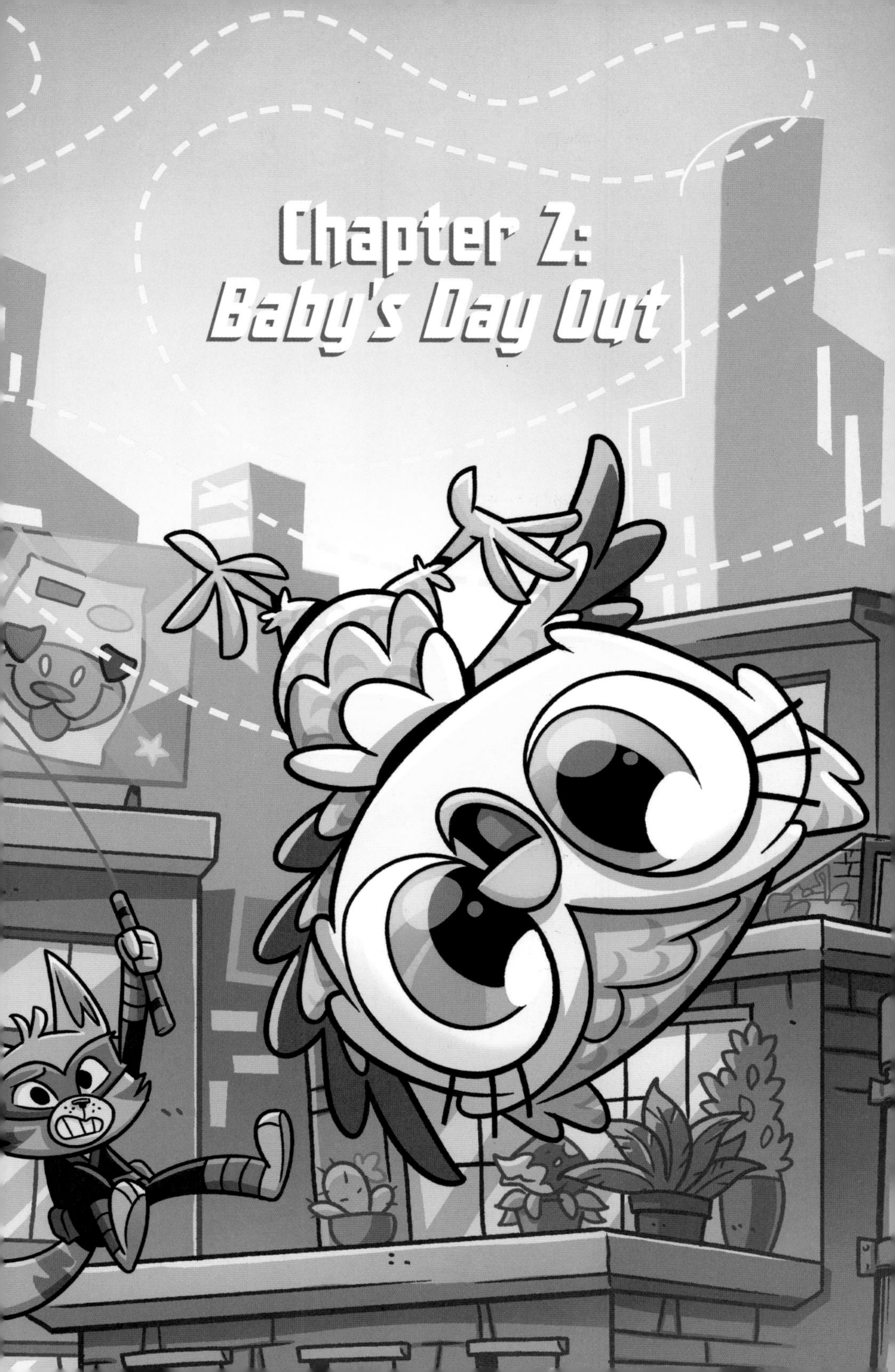

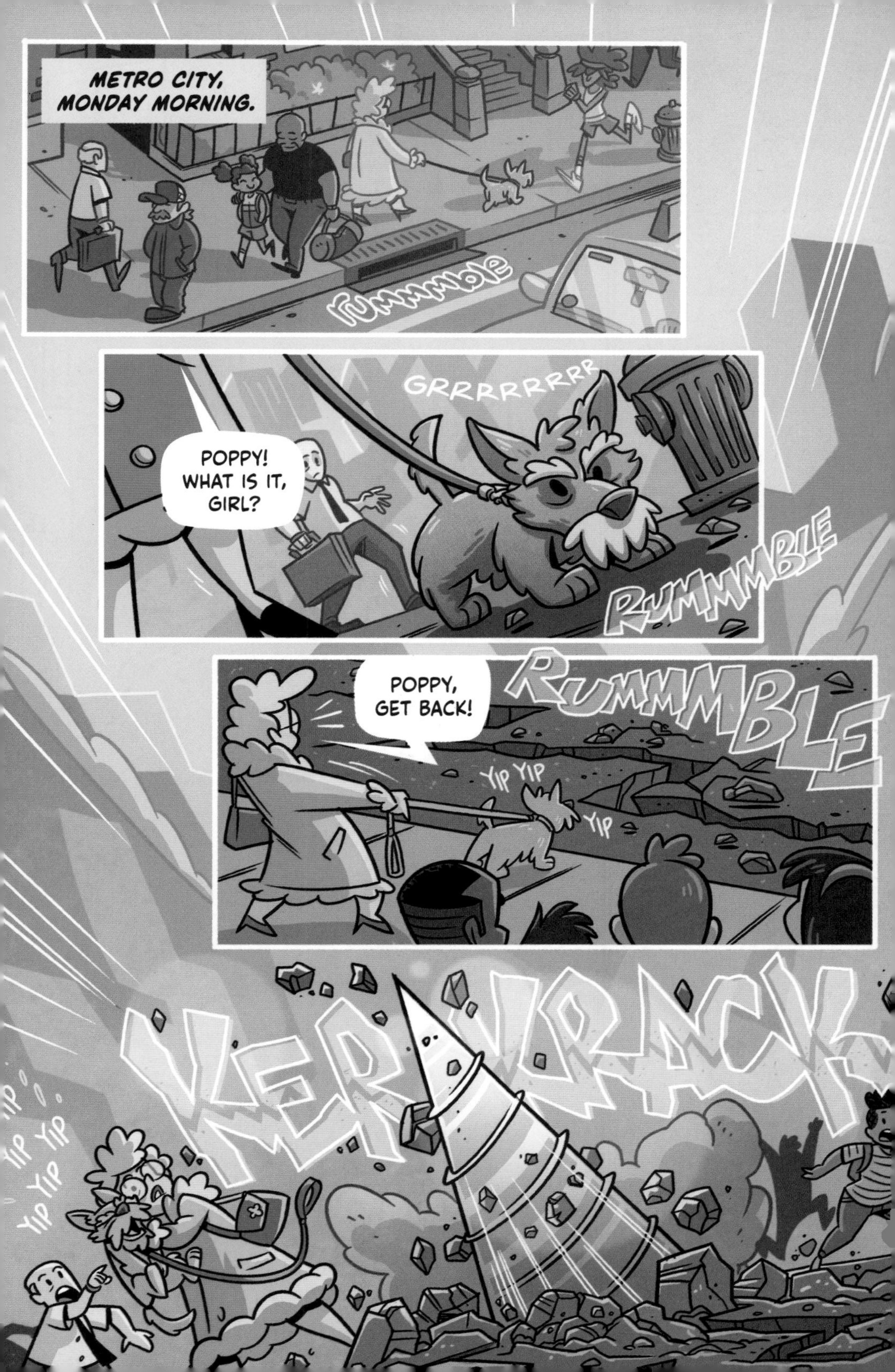
METRO CITY, MONDAY MORNING.
RUMMMBLE
GRRRRRRRR
POPPY! WHAT IS IT, GIRL?
RUMMMBLE
POPPY, GET BACK!
RUMMMBLE
YIP YIP
YIP
YIP YIP YIP YIP

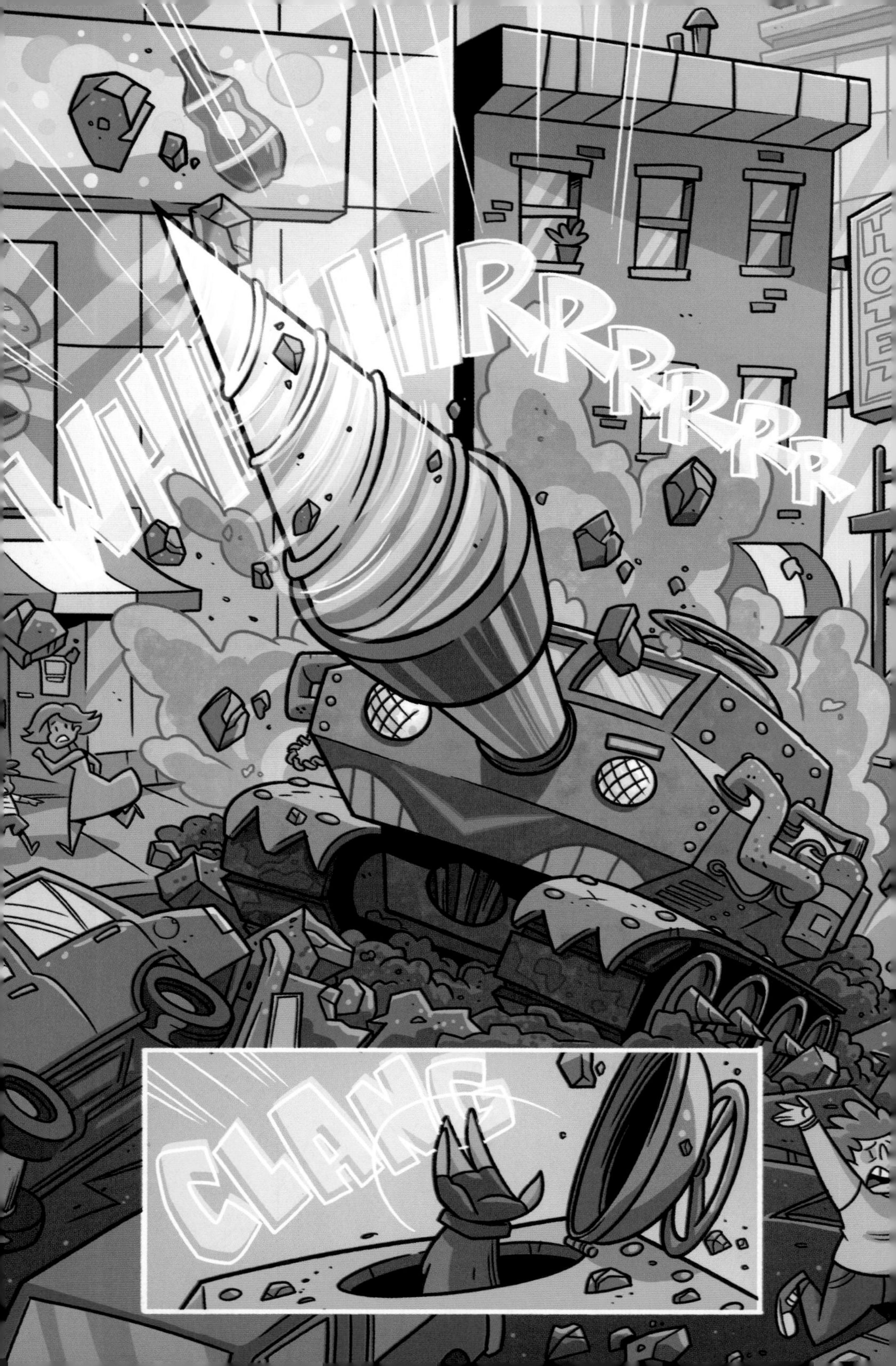

WHHIIIIRRRRRRRRR
CLANG
HOTEL

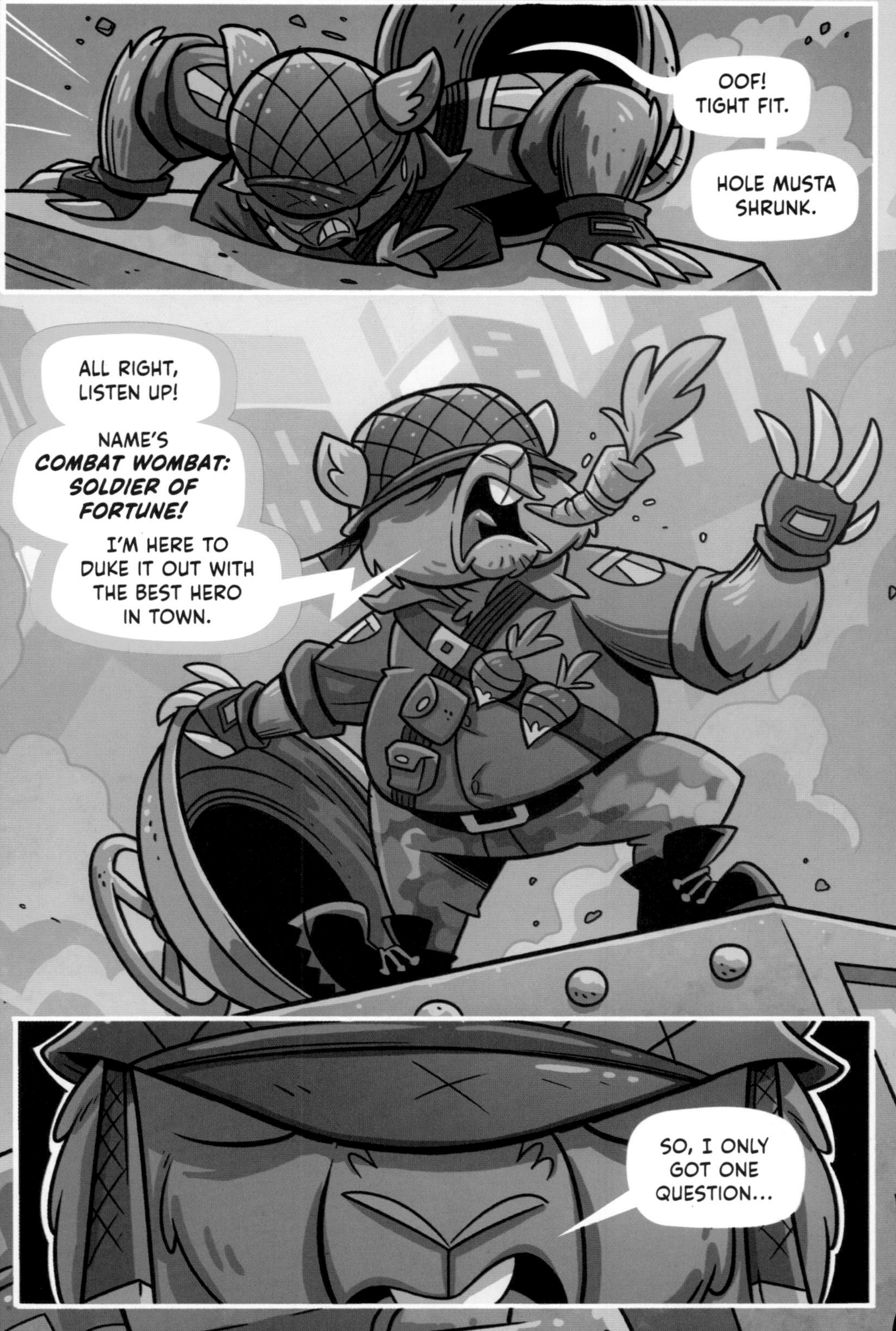
OOF! TIGHT FIT.
HOLE MUSTA SHRUNK.
ALL RIGHT, LISTEN UP!
NAME'S *COMBAT WOMBAT: SOLDIER OF FORTUNE!*
I'M HERE TO DUKE IT OUT WITH THE BEST HERO IN TOWN.
SO, I ONLY GOT ONE QUESTION...

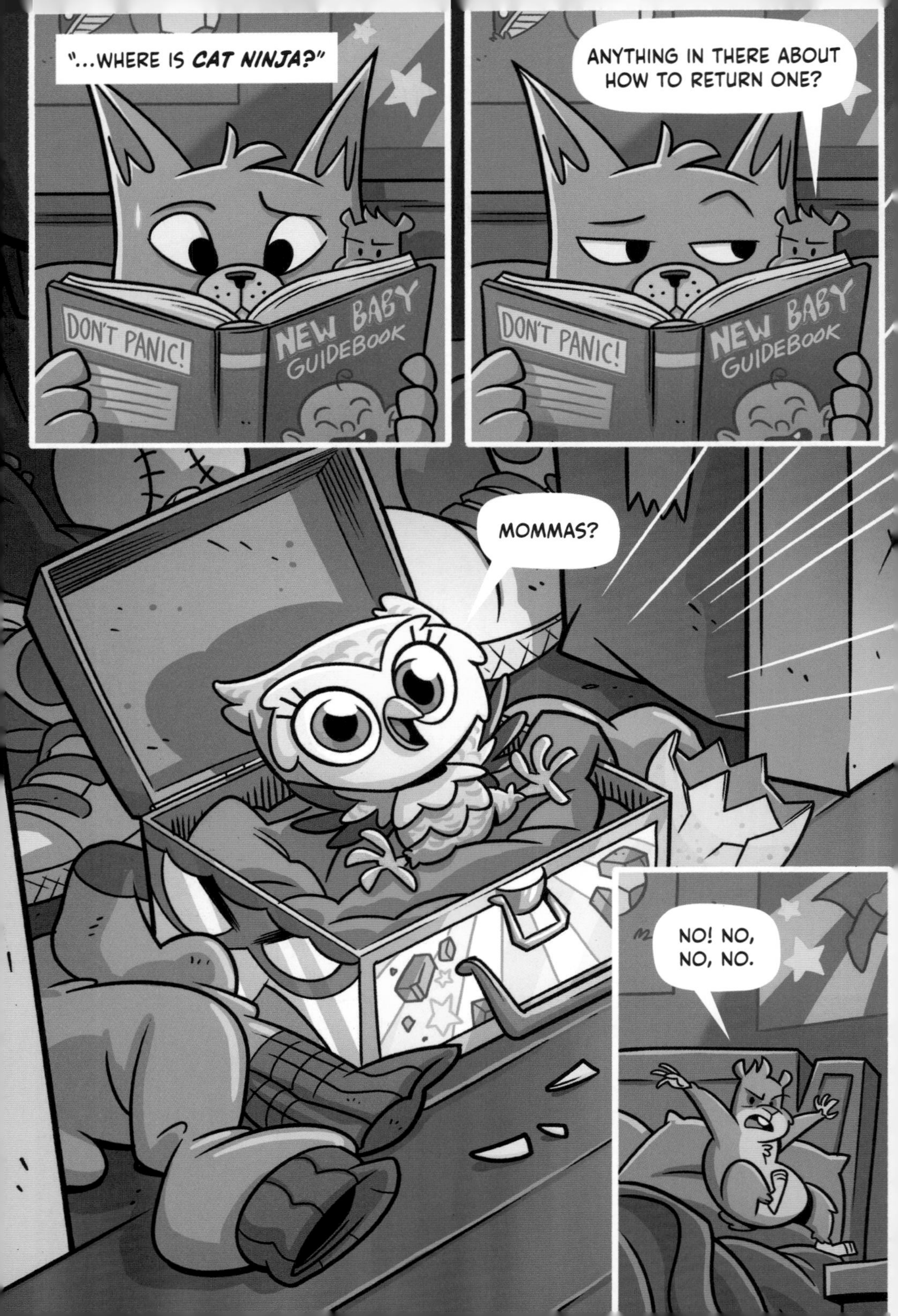
"...WHERE IS *CAT NINJA?*"
DON'T PANIC!
NEW BABY GUIDEBOOK
ANYTHING IN THERE ABOUT HOW TO RETURN ONE?
DON'T PANIC!
NEW BABY GUIDEBOOK
MOMMAS?
NO! NO, NO, NO.

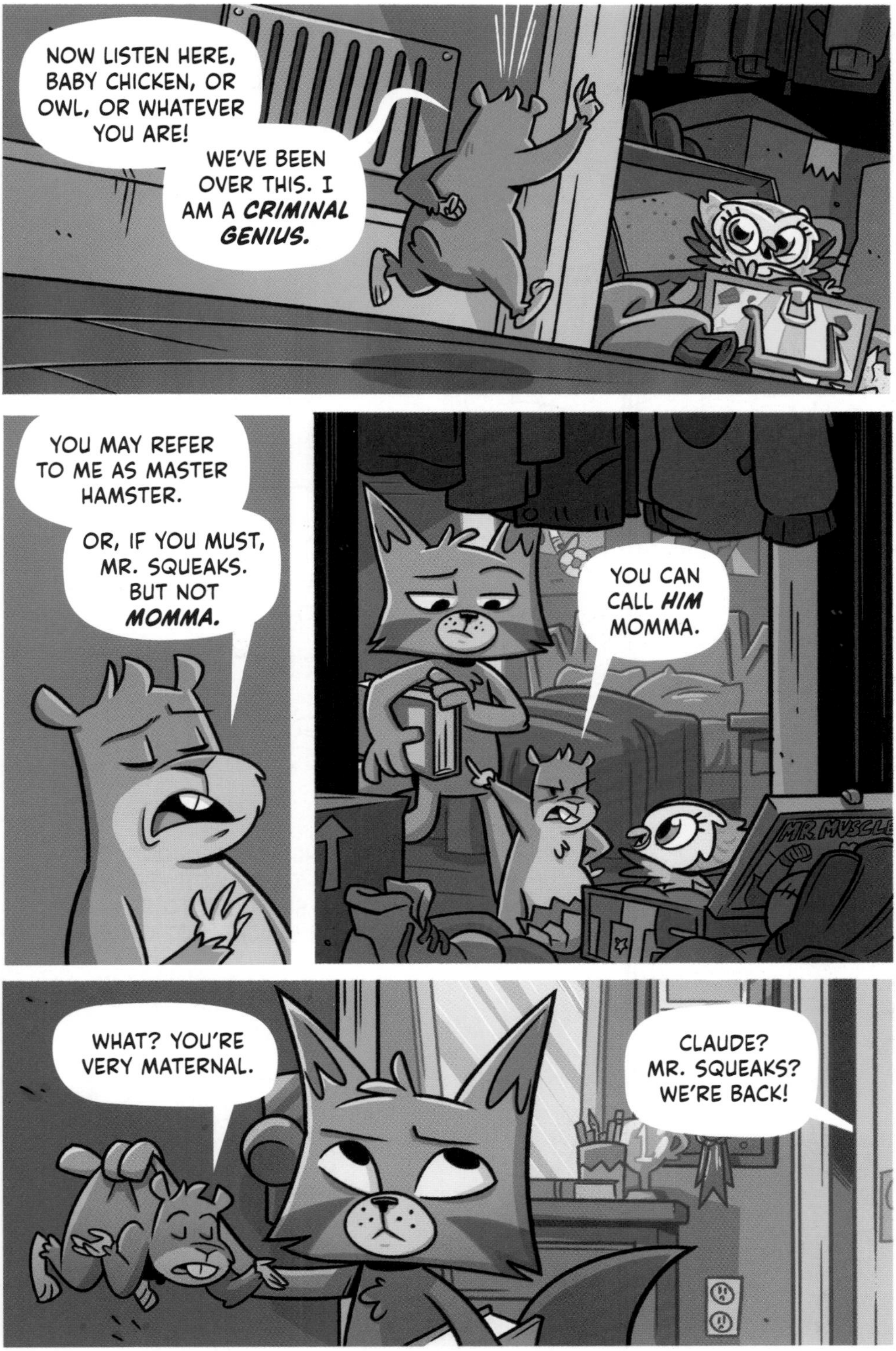

NOW LISTEN HERE, BABY CHICKEN, OR OWL, OR WHATEVER YOU ARE!
WE'VE BEEN OVER THIS. I AM A ***CRIMINAL GENIUS.***
YOU MAY REFER TO ME AS MASTER HAMSTER.
OR, IF YOU MUST, MR. SQUEAKS. BUT NOT ***MOMMA.***
YOU CAN CALL ***HIM*** MOMMA.
MR. MUSCLE
WHAT? YOU'RE VERY MATERNAL.
CLAUDE? MR. SQUEAKS? WE'RE BACK!

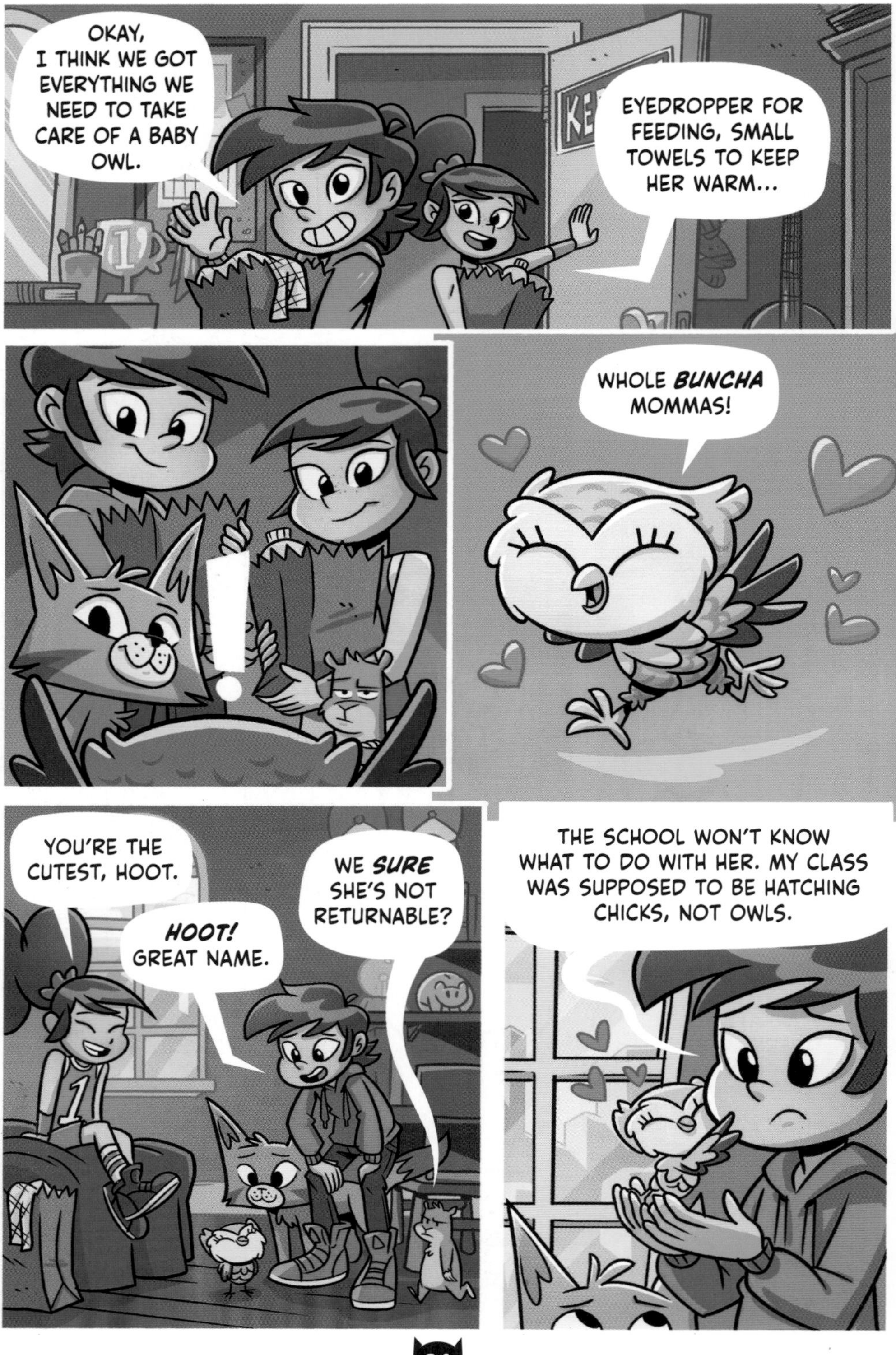
OKAY, I THINK WE GOT EVERYTHING WE NEED TO TAKE CARE OF A BABY OWL.
EYEDROPPER FOR FEEDING, SMALL TOWELS TO KEEP HER WARM...
WHOLE *BUNCHA* MOMMAS!
YOU'RE THE CUTEST, HOOT.
HOOT! GREAT NAME.
WE *SURE* SHE'S NOT RETURNABLE?
THE SCHOOL WON'T KNOW WHAT TO DO WITH HER. MY CLASS WAS SUPPOSED TO BE HATCHING CHICKS, NOT OWLS.

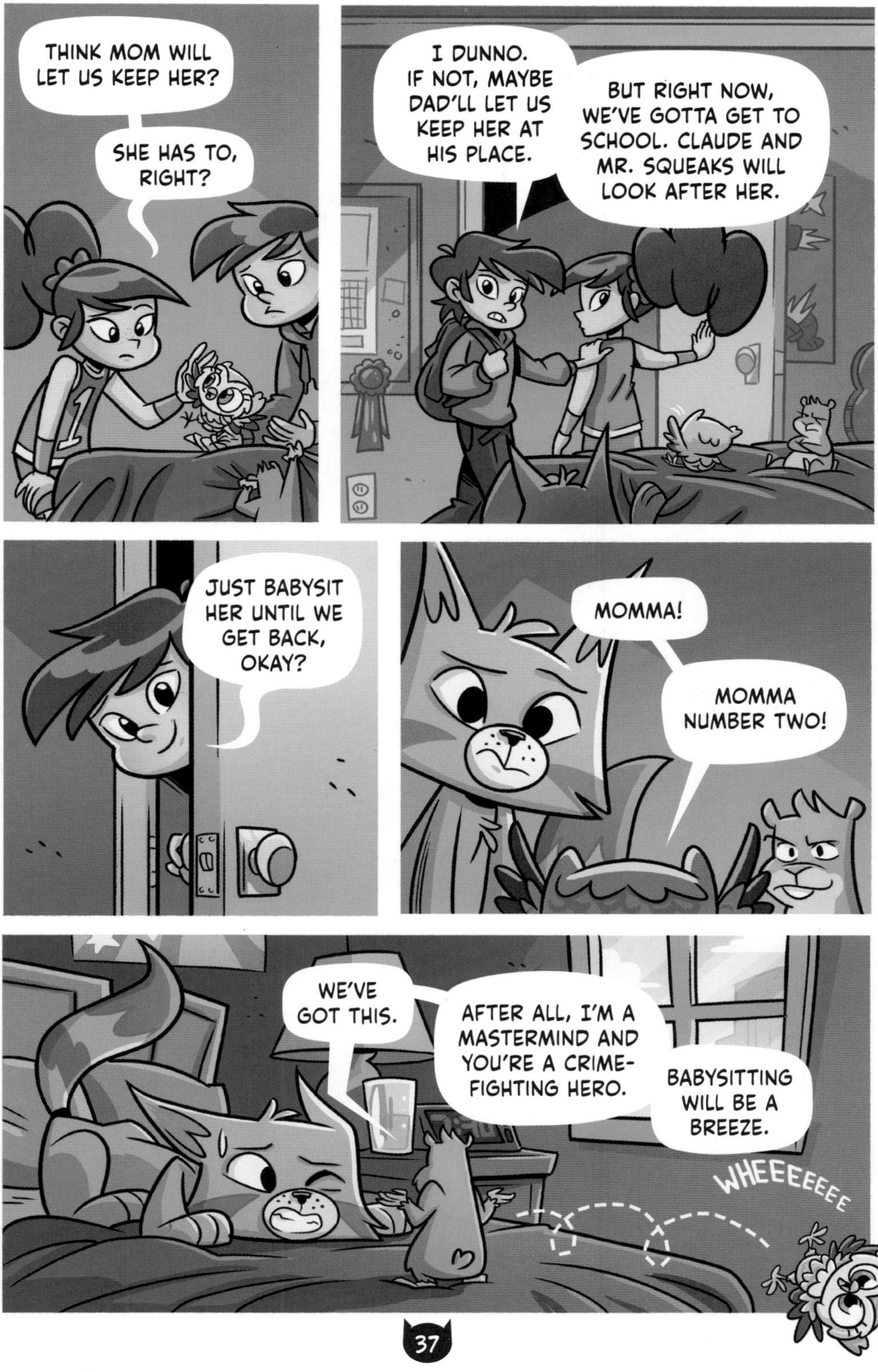
THINK MOM WILL LET US KEEP HER?
SHE HAS TO, RIGHT?
I DUNNO. IF NOT, MAYBE DAD'LL LET US KEEP HER AT HIS PLACE.
BUT RIGHT NOW, WE'VE GOTTA GET TO SCHOOL. CLAUDE AND MR. SQUEAKS WILL LOOK AFTER HER.
JUST BABYSIT HER UNTIL WE GET BACK, OKAY?
MOMMA!
MOMMA NUMBER TWO!
WE'VE GOT THIS.
AFTER ALL, I'M A MASTERMIND AND YOU'RE A CRIME-FIGHTING HERO.
BABYSITTING WILL BE A BREEZE.
WHEEEEEEE

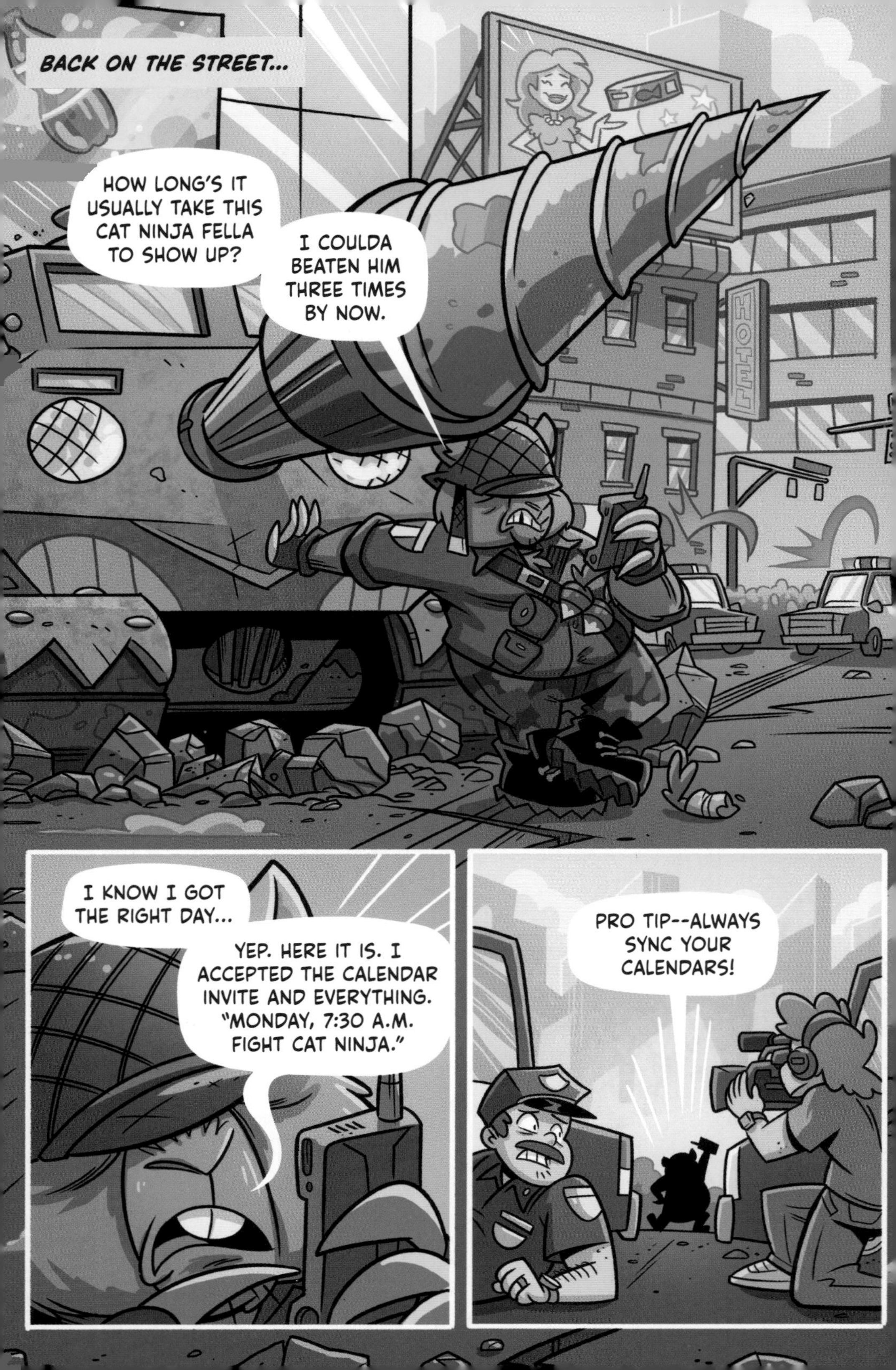
BACK ON THE STREET...
HOW LONG'S IT USUALLY TAKE THIS CAT NINJA FELLA TO SHOW UP?
I COULDA BEATEN HIM THREE TIMES BY NOW.
HOTEL
I KNOW I GOT THE RIGHT DAY...
YEP. HERE IT IS. I ACCEPTED THE CALENDAR INVITE AND EVERYTHING. "MONDAY, 7:30 A.M. FIGHT CAT NINJA."
PRO TIP--ALWAYS SYNC YOUR CALENDARS!

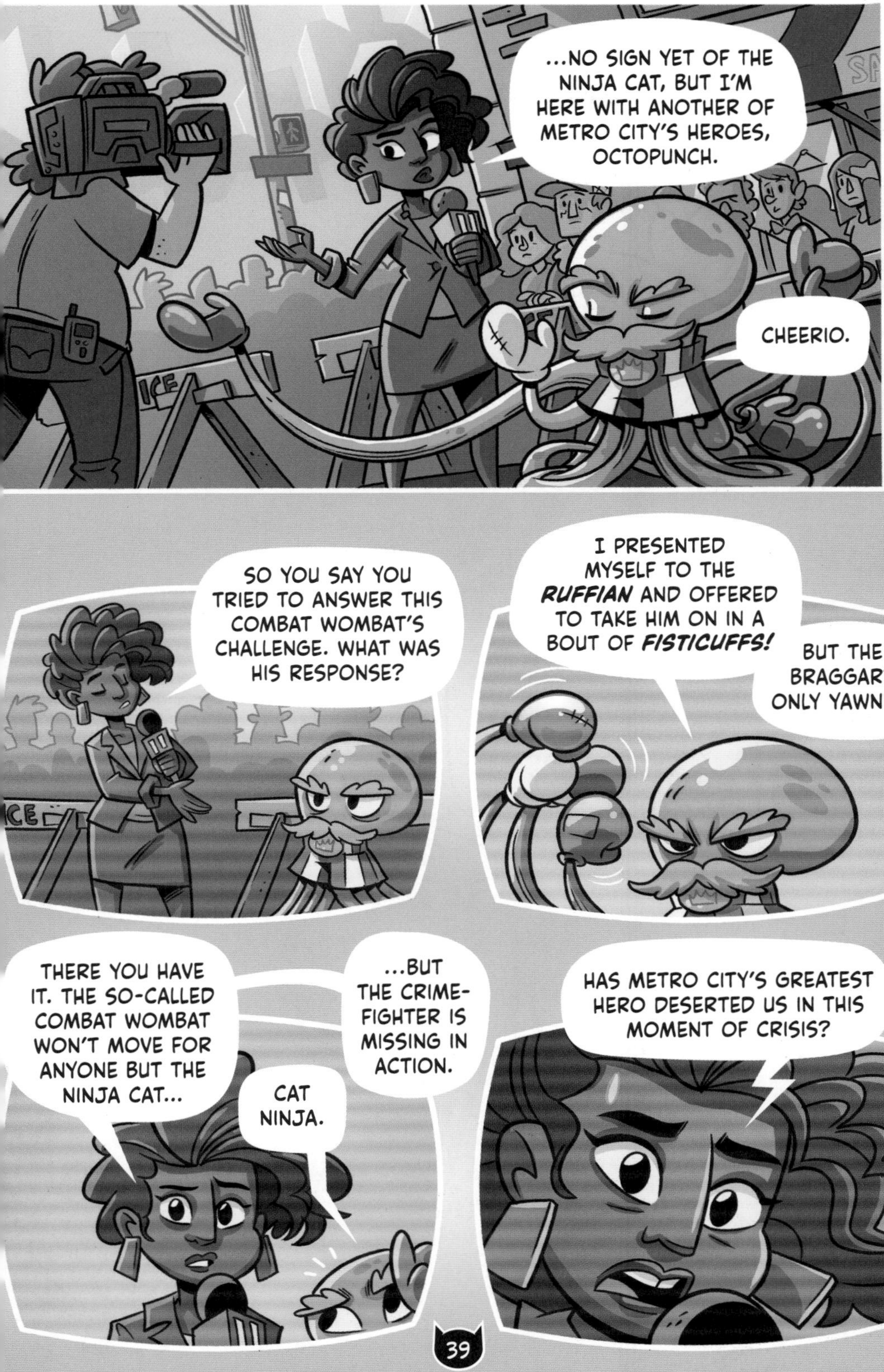
...NO SIGN YET OF THE NINJA CAT, BUT I'M HERE WITH ANOTHER OF METRO CITY'S HEROES, OCTOPUNCH.
CHEERIO.
SO YOU SAY YOU TRIED TO ANSWER THIS COMBAT WOMBAT'S CHALLENGE. WHAT WAS HIS RESPONSE?
I PRESENTED MYSELF TO THE *RUFFIAN* AND OFFERED TO TAKE HIM ON IN A BOUT OF *FISTICUFFS!*
BUT THE BRAGGART ONLY YAWNED.
THERE YOU HAVE IT. THE SO-CALLED COMBAT WOMBAT WON'T MOVE FOR ANYONE BUT THE NINJA CAT...
CAT NINJA.
...BUT THE CRIME-FIGHTER IS MISSING IN ACTION.
HAS METRO CITY'S GREATEST HERO DESERTED US IN THIS MOMENT OF CRISIS?

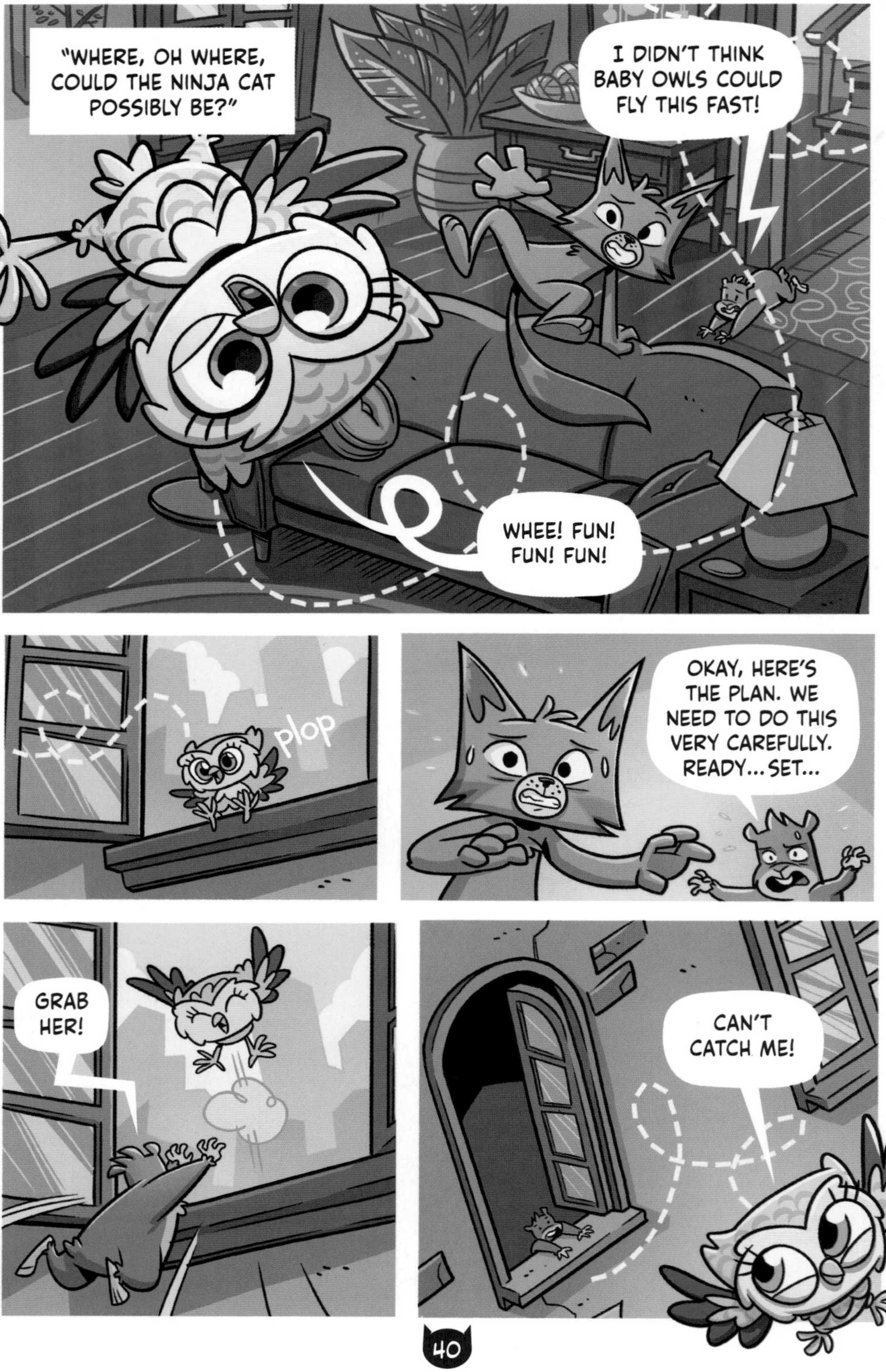
"WHERE, OH WHERE, COULD THE NINJA CAT POSSIBLY BE?"
I DIDN'T THINK BABY OWLS COULD FLY THIS FAST!
WHEE! FUN! FUN! FUN!
plop
OKAY, HERE'S THE PLAN. WE NEED TO DO THIS VERY CAREFULLY. READY... SET...
GRAB HER!
CAN'T CATCH ME!

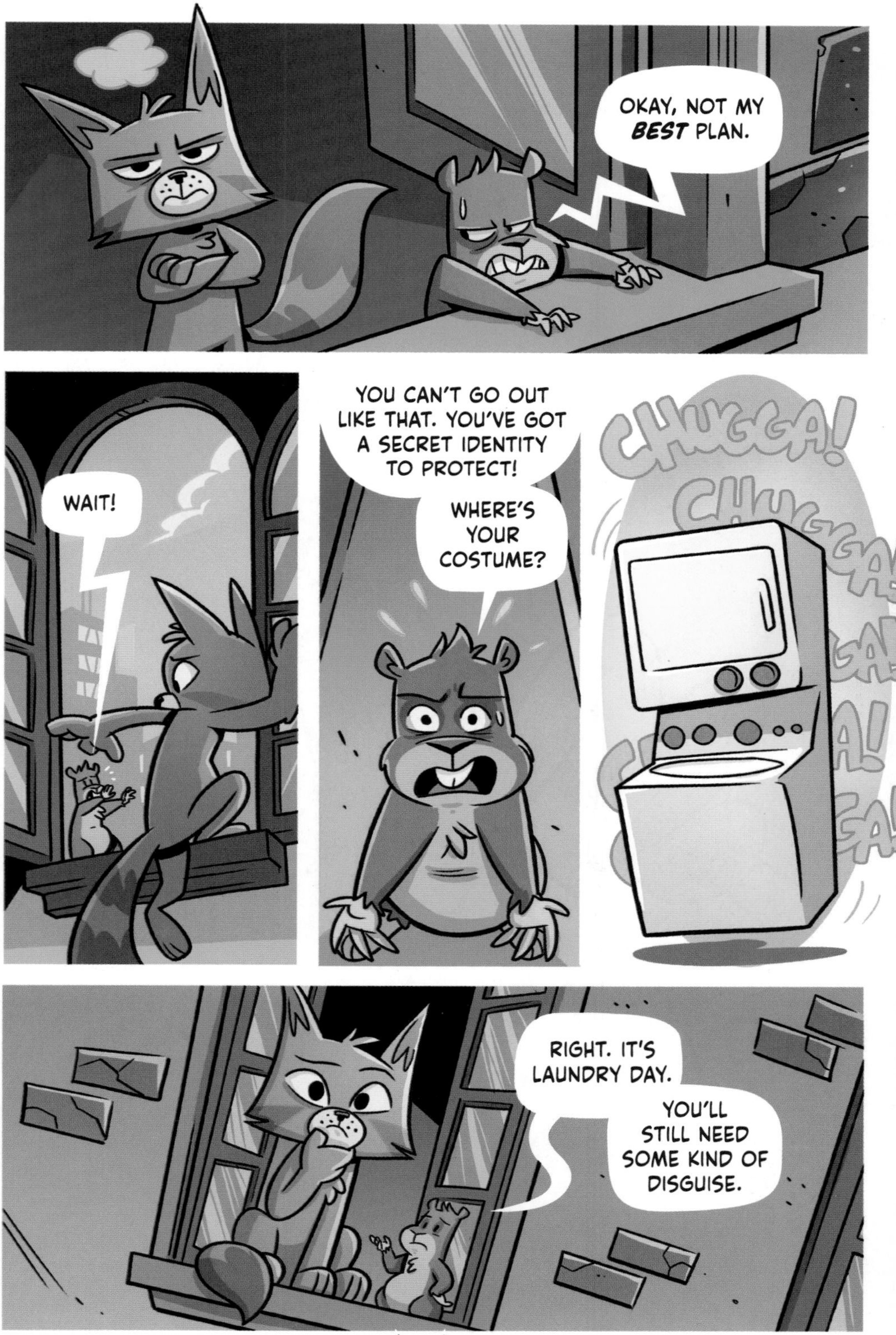
OKAY, NOT MY *BEST* PLAN.
WAIT!
YOU CAN'T GO OUT LIKE THAT. YOU'VE GOT A SECRET IDENTITY TO PROTECT!
WHERE'S YOUR COSTUME?
CHUGGA! CHUGGA!
RIGHT. IT'S LAUNDRY DAY.
YOU'LL STILL NEED SOME KIND OF DISGUISE.

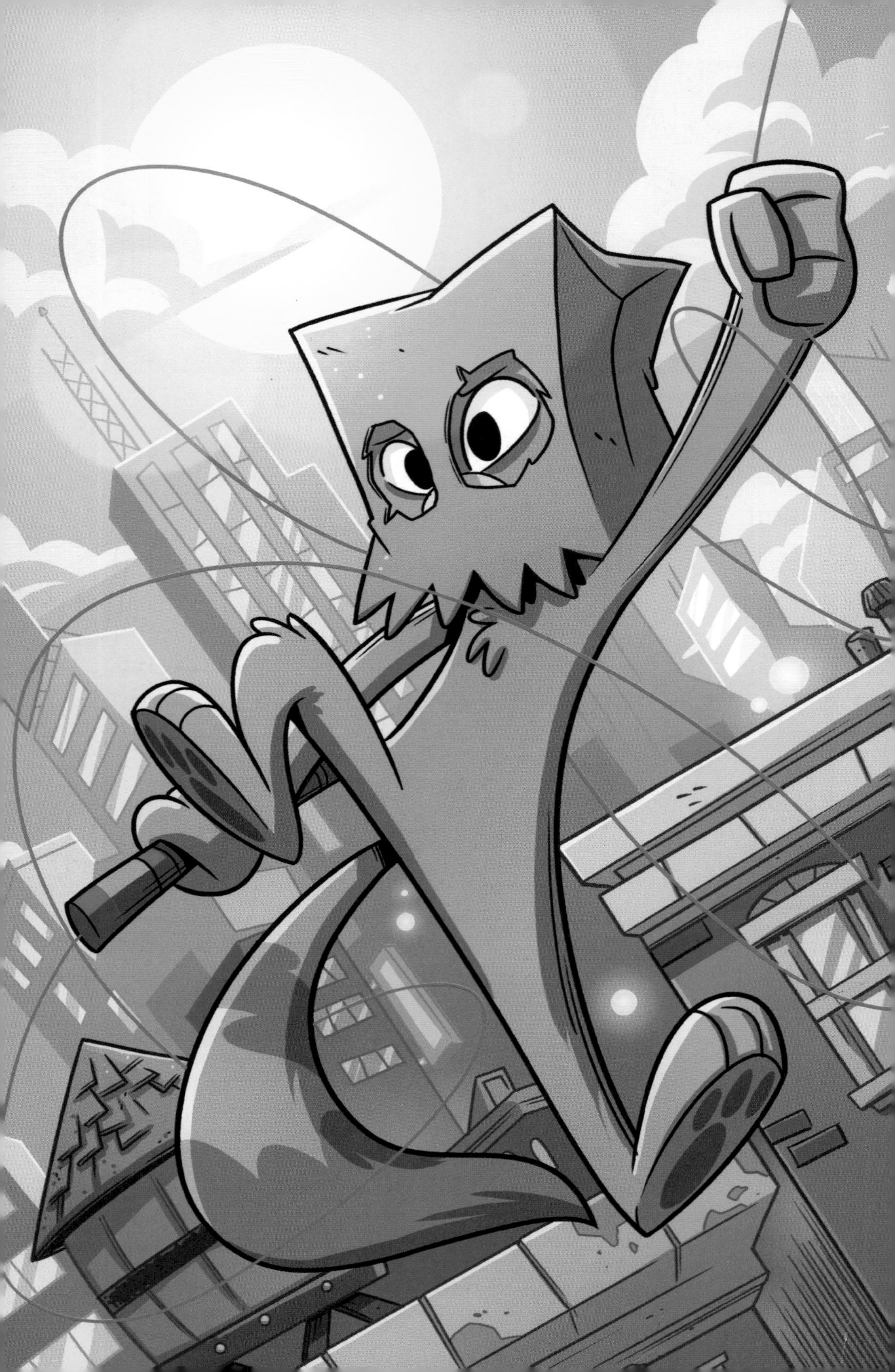

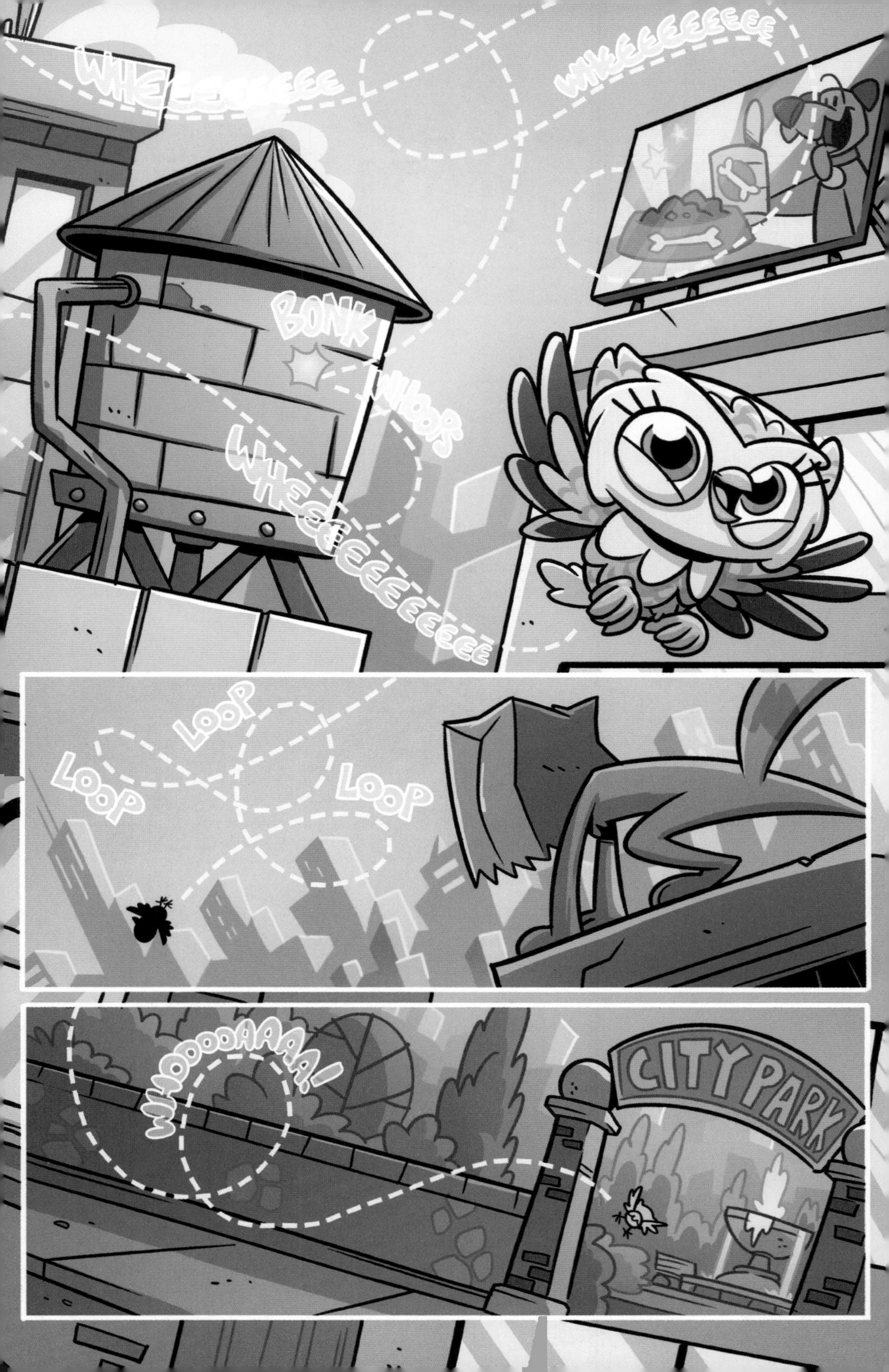

WHEEEEEEEE
WHEEEEEEEEE
BONK
WHOOPS
WHEEEEEEEEEEE
LOOP
LOOP
LOOP
WHOOOOAAAA!
CITY PARK

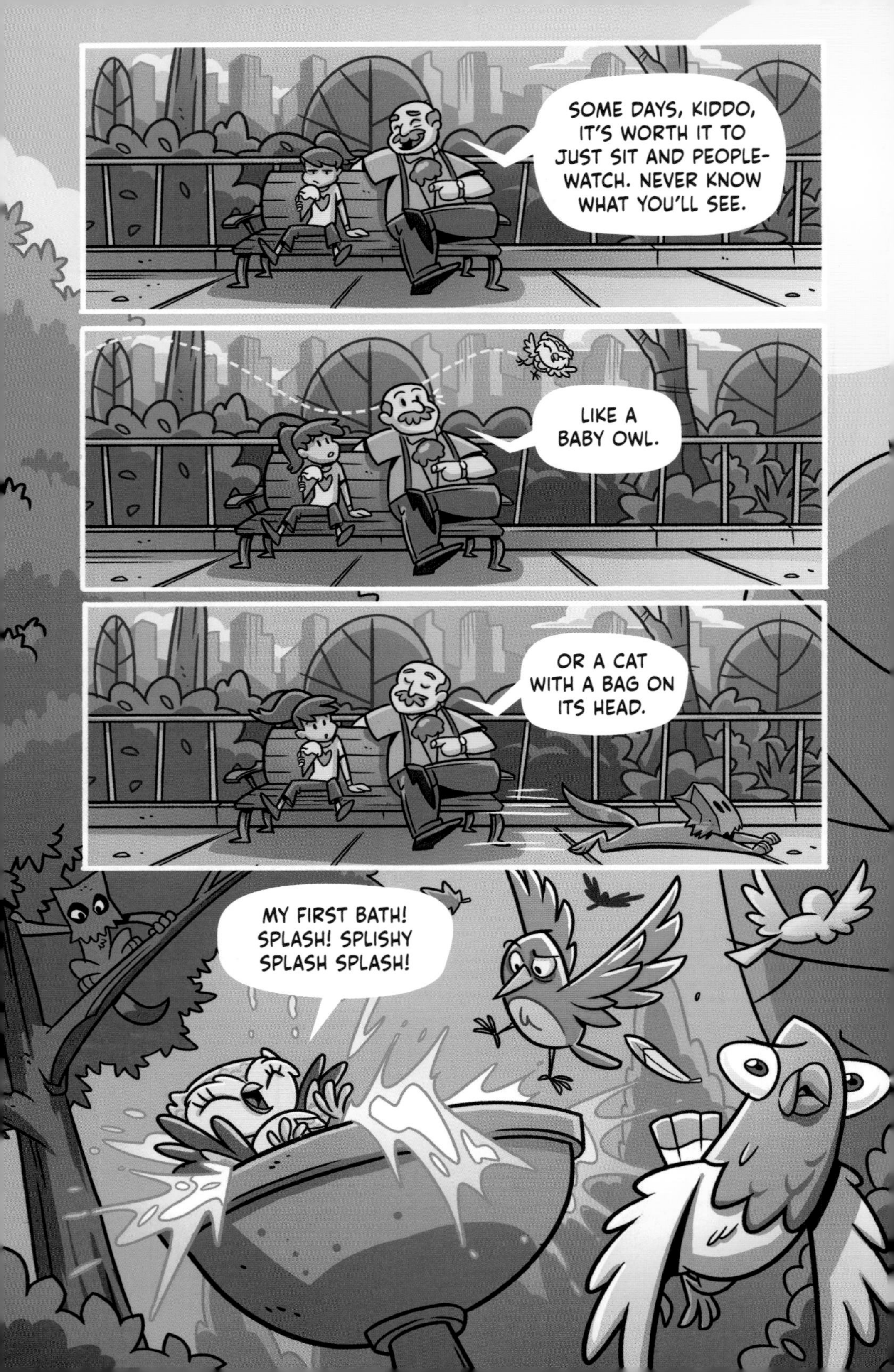
SOME DAYS, KIDDO, IT'S WORTH IT TO JUST SIT AND PEOPLE-WATCH. NEVER KNOW WHAT YOU'LL SEE.
LIKE A BABY OWL.
OR A CAT WITH A BAG ON ITS HEAD.
MY FIRST BATH! SPLASH! SPLISHY SPLASH SPLASH!

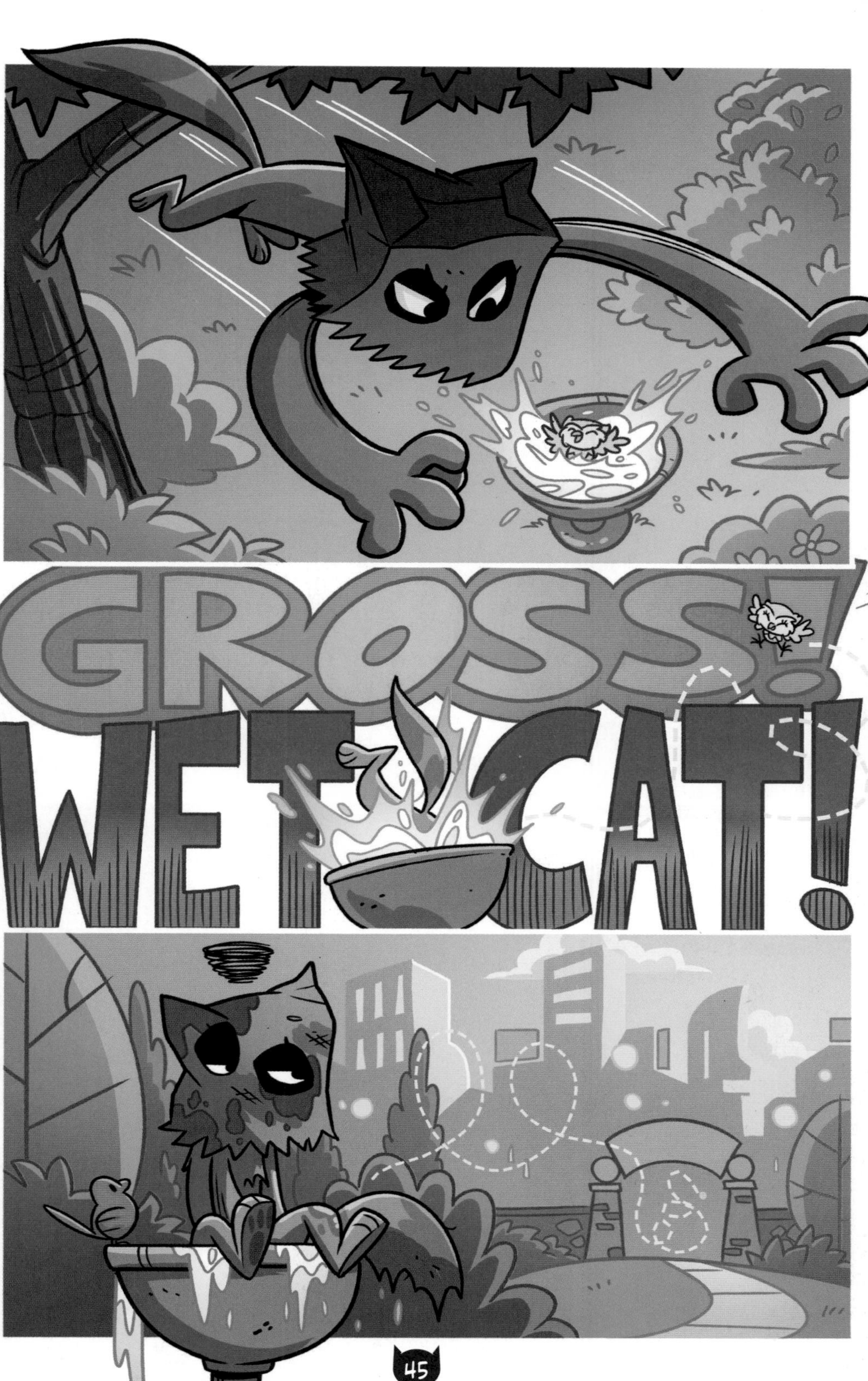
GROSS!
WET CAT!

HEY, I WONDER WHAT'S GOING ON?

DUNNO, BUT WE GOTTA GET TO SCHOOL.

I'LL JUST BE A SEC.

MARCIIIEEE!

LOOK, I'M MARKING THIS CAT NINJA DOWN AS A NO-SHOW AND MOVING ON TO THE NEXT GIG.

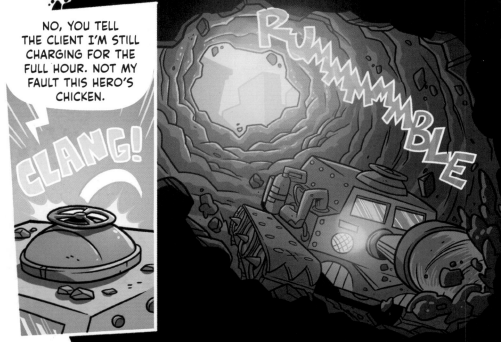

NO, YOU TELL THE CLIENT I'M STILL CHARGING FOR THE FULL HOUR. NOT MY FAULT THIS HERO'S CHICKEN.

CLANG!

RUMMMMMBLE

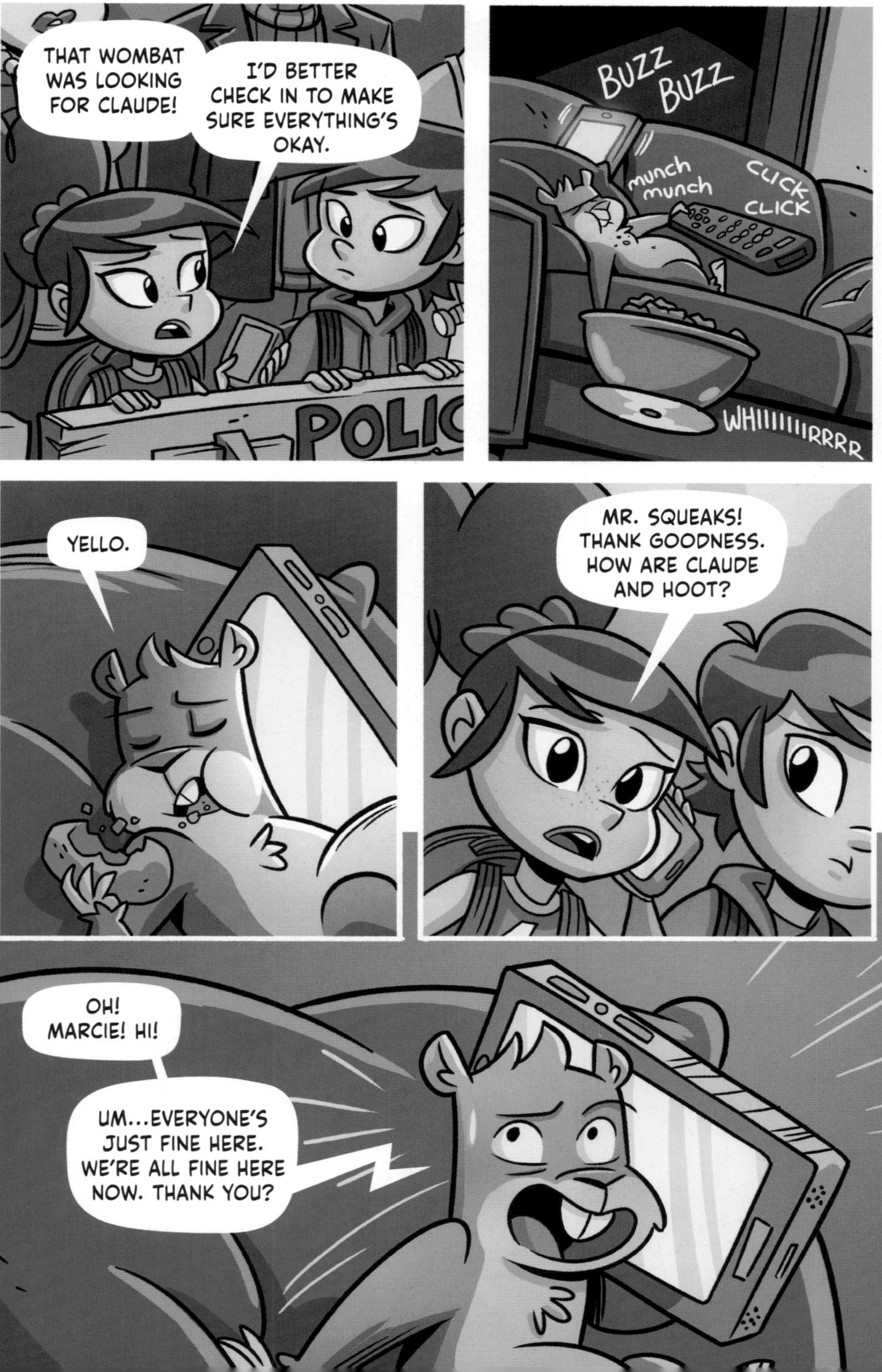
THAT WOMBAT WAS LOOKING FOR CLAUDE!
I'D BETTER CHECK IN TO MAKE SURE EVERYTHING'S OKAY.
POLIC
BUZZ BUZZ
munch munch
CLICK CLICK
WHIIIIIIRRRR
YELLO.
MR. SQUEAKS! THANK GOODNESS. HOW ARE CLAUDE AND HOOT?
OH! MARCIE! HI!
UM...EVERYONE'S JUST FINE HERE. WE'RE ALL FINE HERE NOW. THANK YOU?

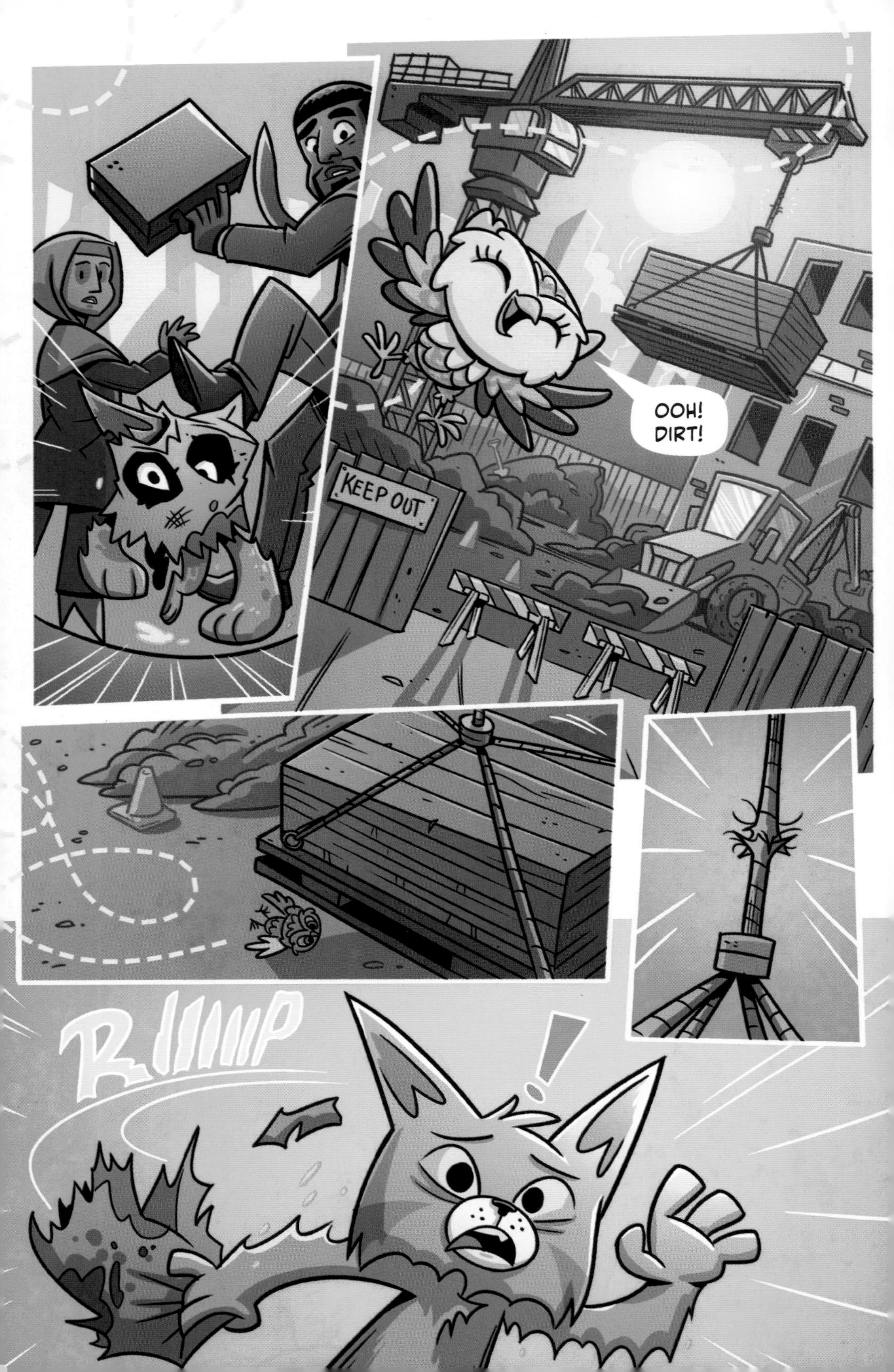
KEEP OUT
OOH! DIRT!
RIIIIP
!

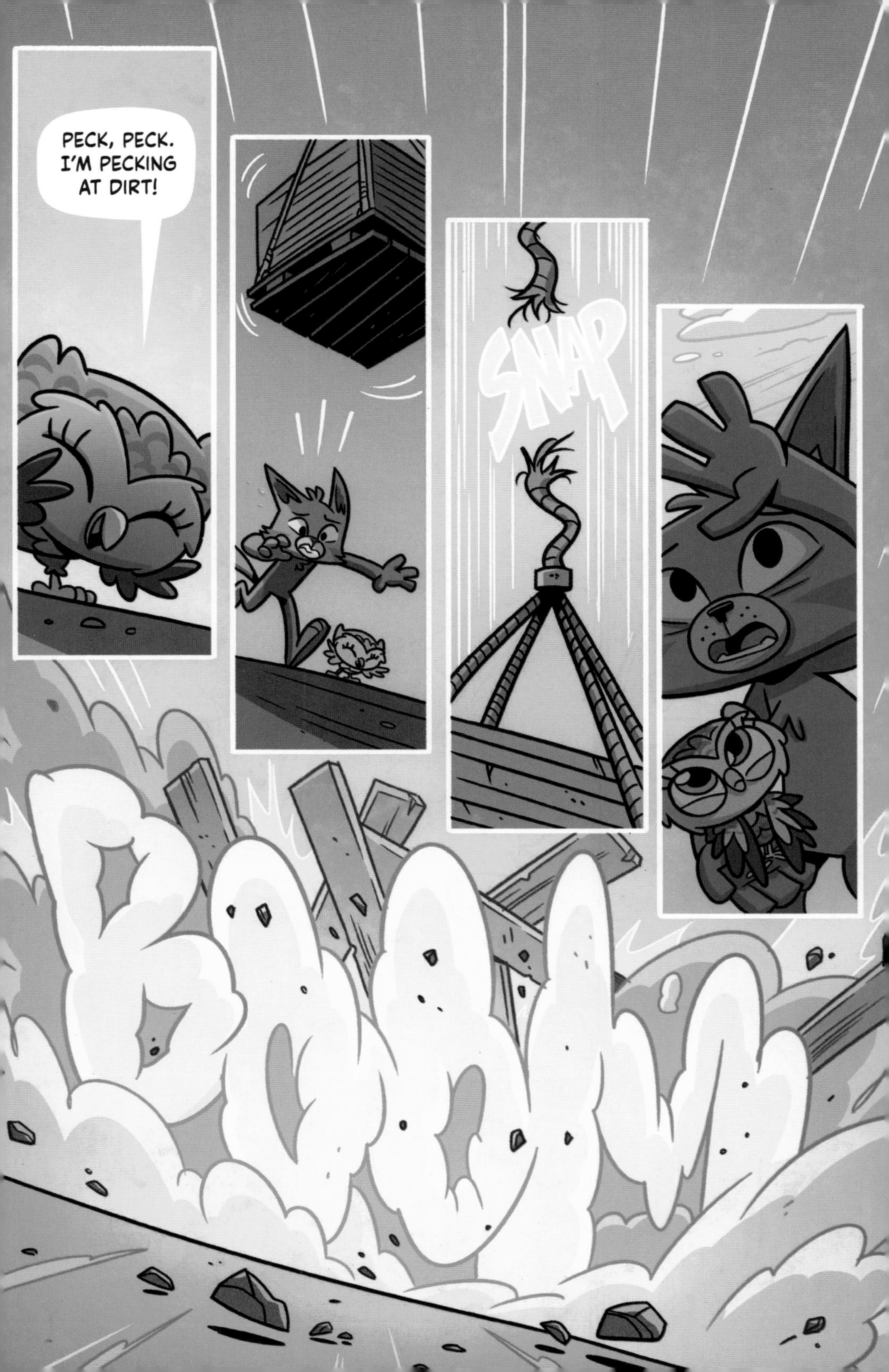
PECK, PECK. I'M PECKING AT DIRT!
SNAP
BOOOM

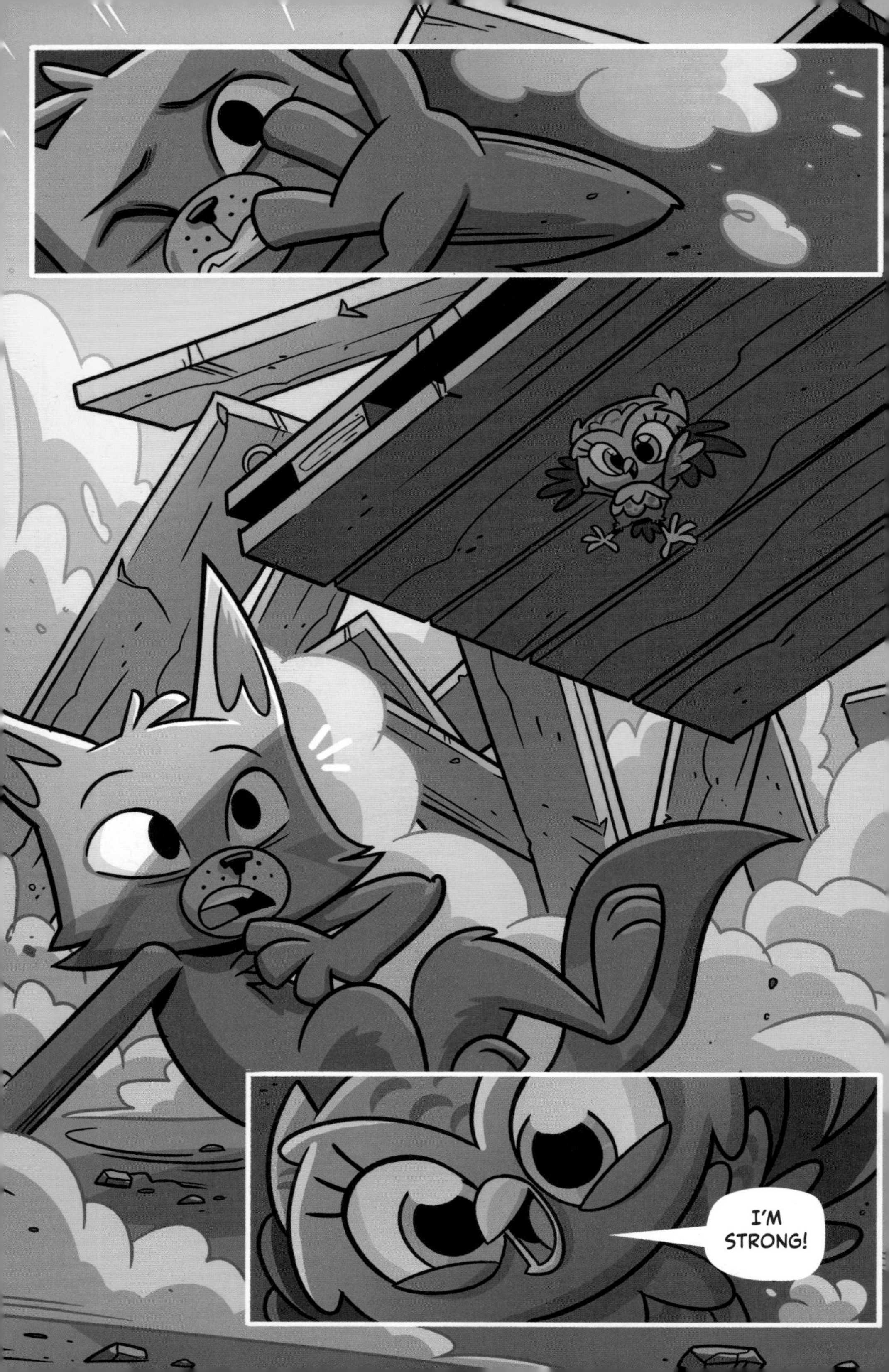
I'M STRONG!

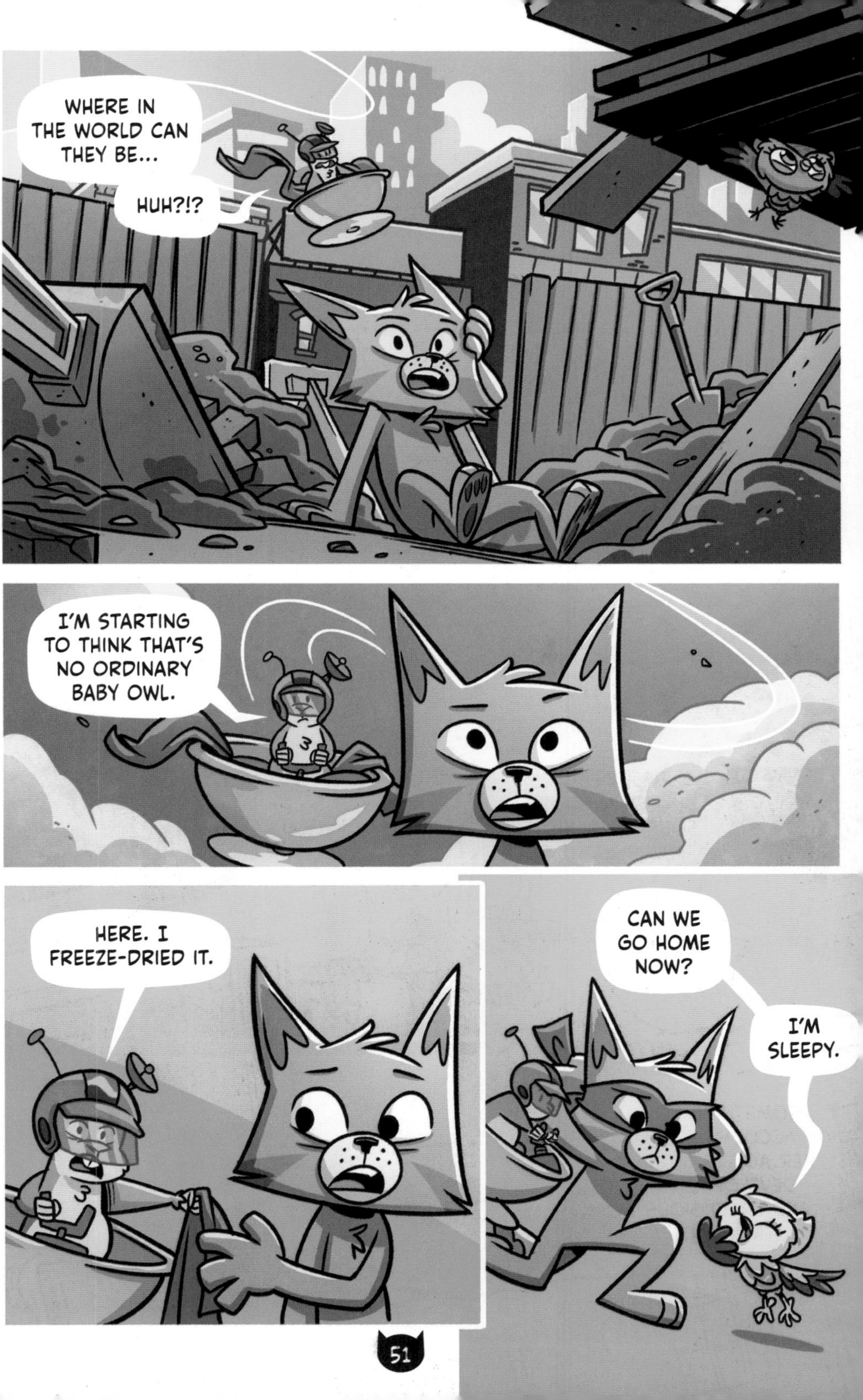
WHERE IN THE WORLD CAN THEY BE...
HUH?!?
I'M STARTING TO THINK THAT'S NO ORDINARY BABY OWL.
HERE. I FREEZE-DRIED IT.
CAN WE GO HOME NOW?
I'M SLEEPY.

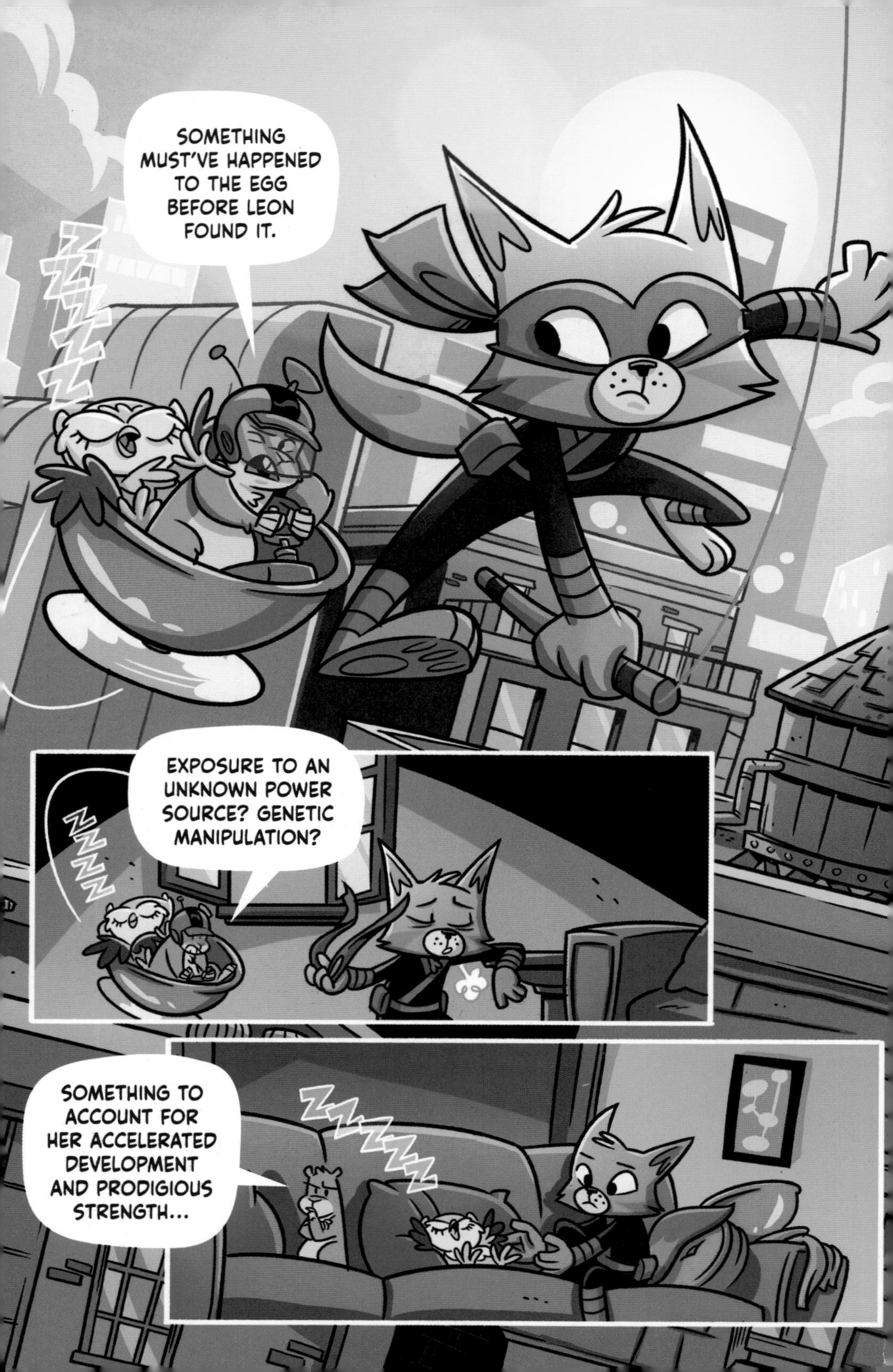
SOMETHING MUST'VE HAPPENED TO THE EGG BEFORE LEON FOUND IT.
EXPOSURE TO AN UNKNOWN POWER SOURCE? GENETIC MANIPULATION?
SOMETHING TO ACCOUNT FOR HER ACCELERATED DEVELOPMENT AND PRODIGIOUS STRENGTH...

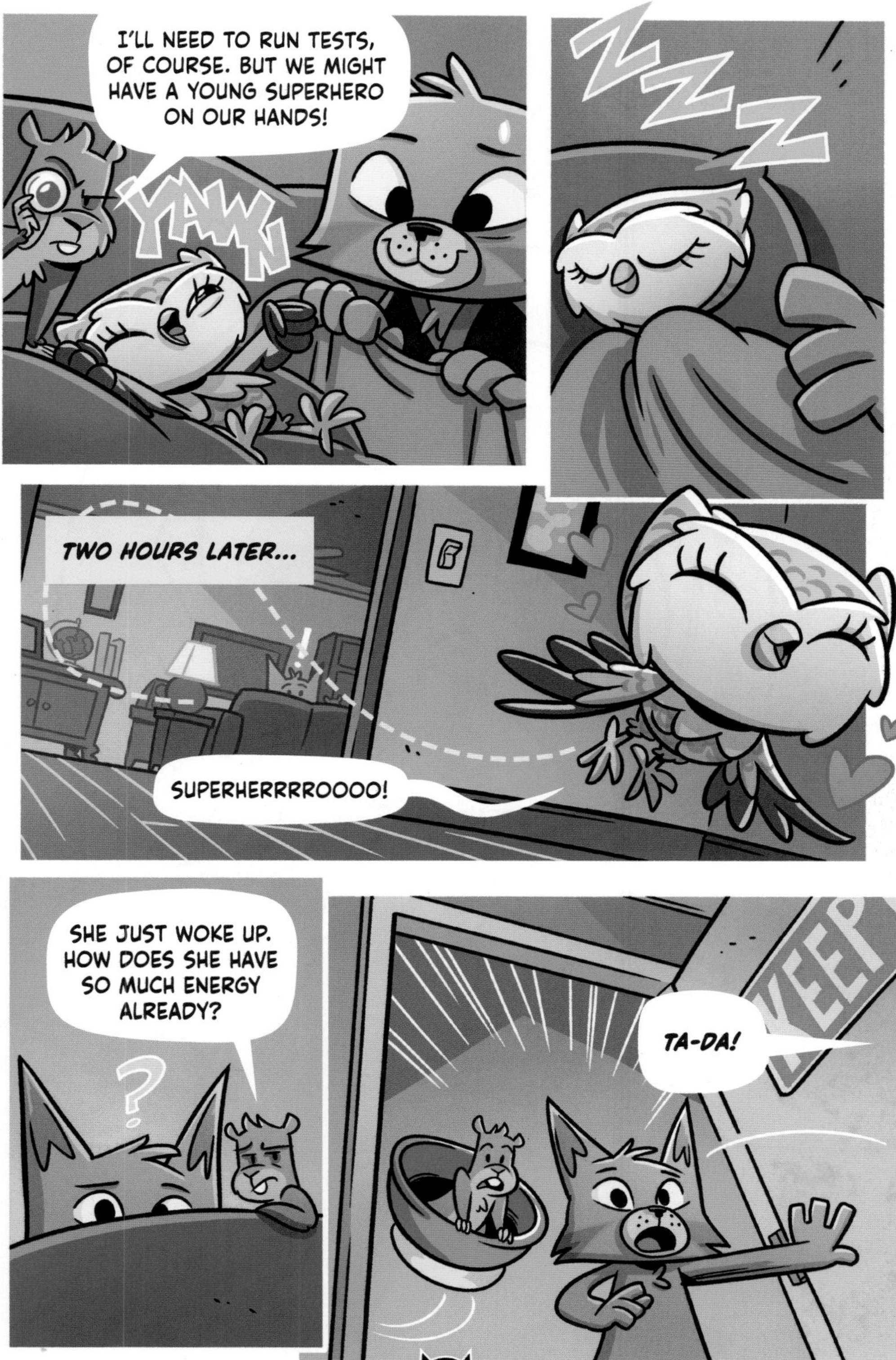
I'LL NEED TO RUN TESTS, OF COURSE. BUT WE MIGHT HAVE A YOUNG SUPERHERO ON OUR HANDS!
YAWN
ZZZ
TWO HOURS LATER...
SUPERHERRRROOOO!
SHE JUST WOKE UP. HOW DOES SHE HAVE SO MUCH ENERGY ALREADY?
?
TA-DA!
KEEP

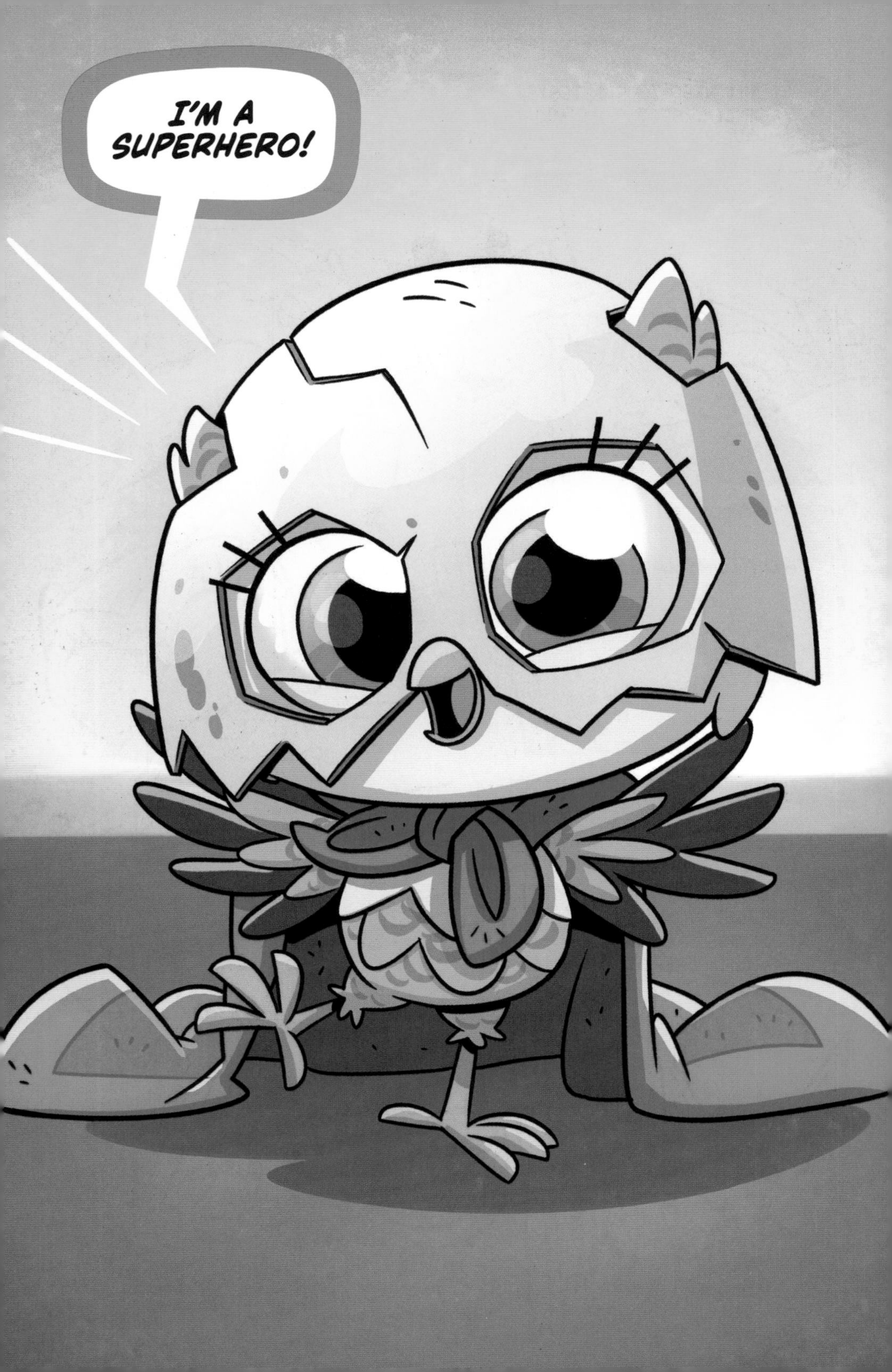
I'M A SUPERHERO!

Chapter 3: *Time Heist*

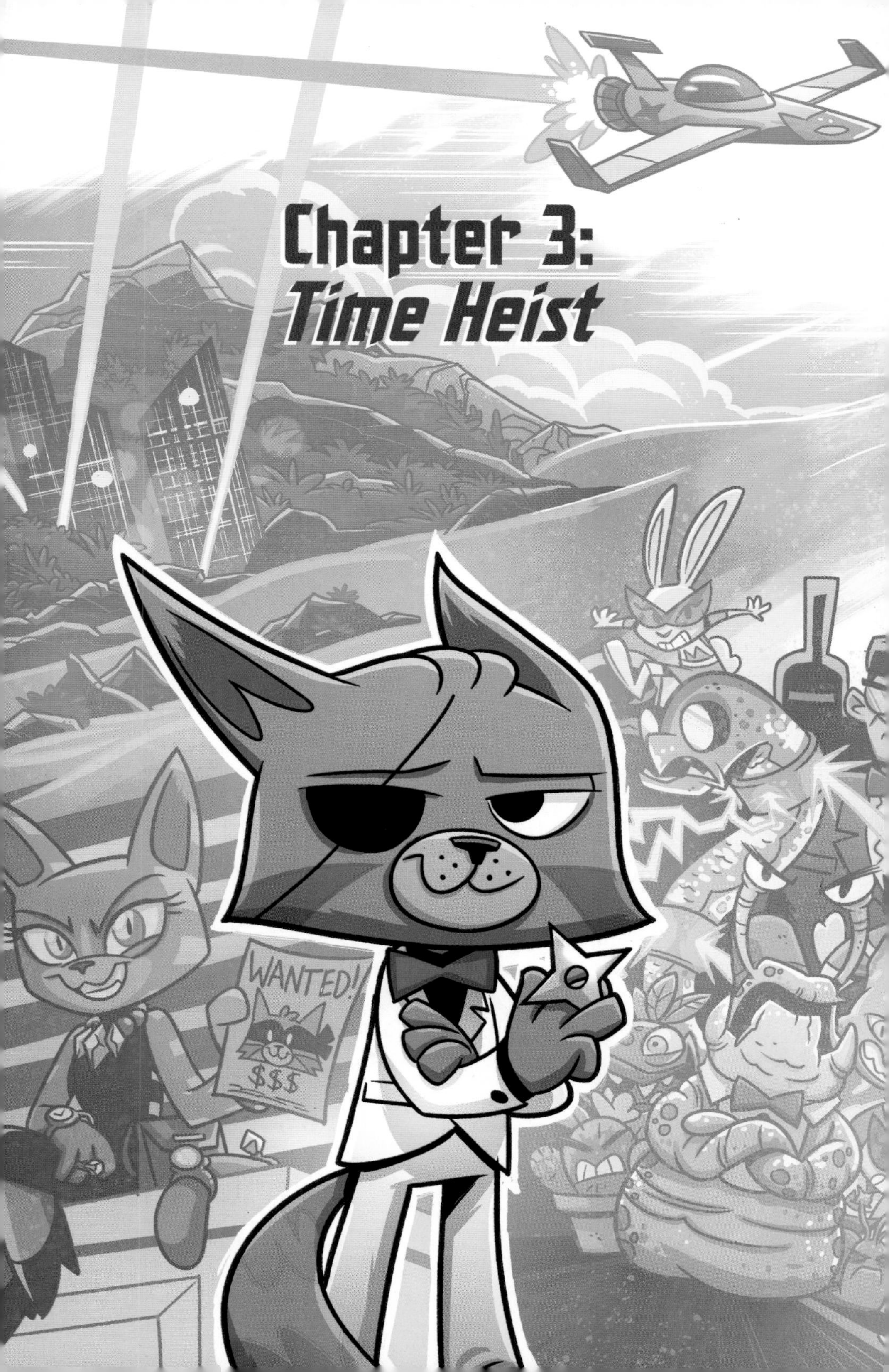
WANTED!
$$$

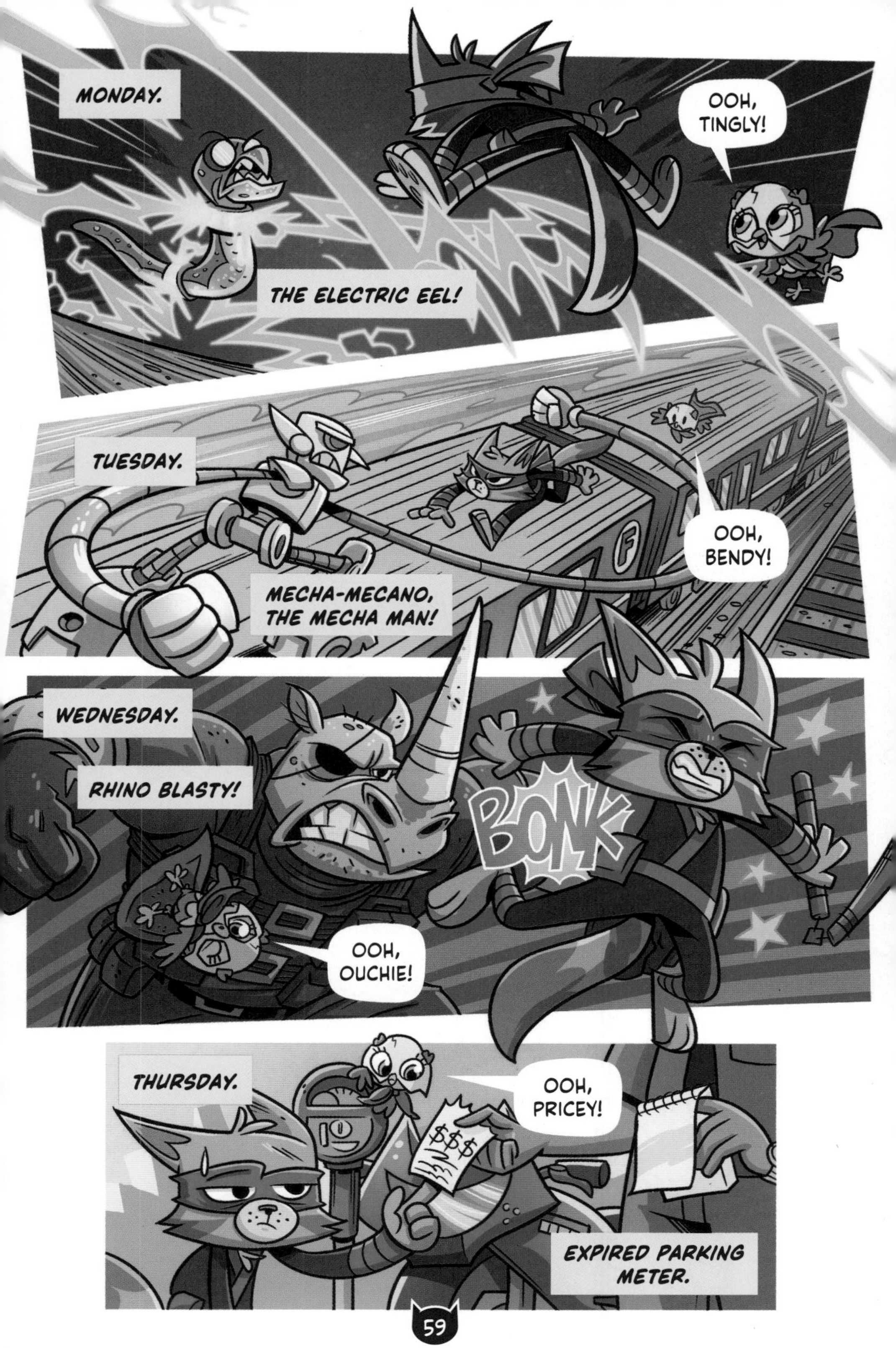
MONDAY.
OOH, TINGLY!
THE ELECTRIC EEL!
TUESDAY.
OOH, BENDY!
MECHA-MECANO, THE MECHA MAN!
WEDNESDAY.
RHINO BLASTY!
BONK
OOH, OUCHIE!
THURSDAY.
OOH, PRICEY!
$$$
EXPIRED PARKING METER.

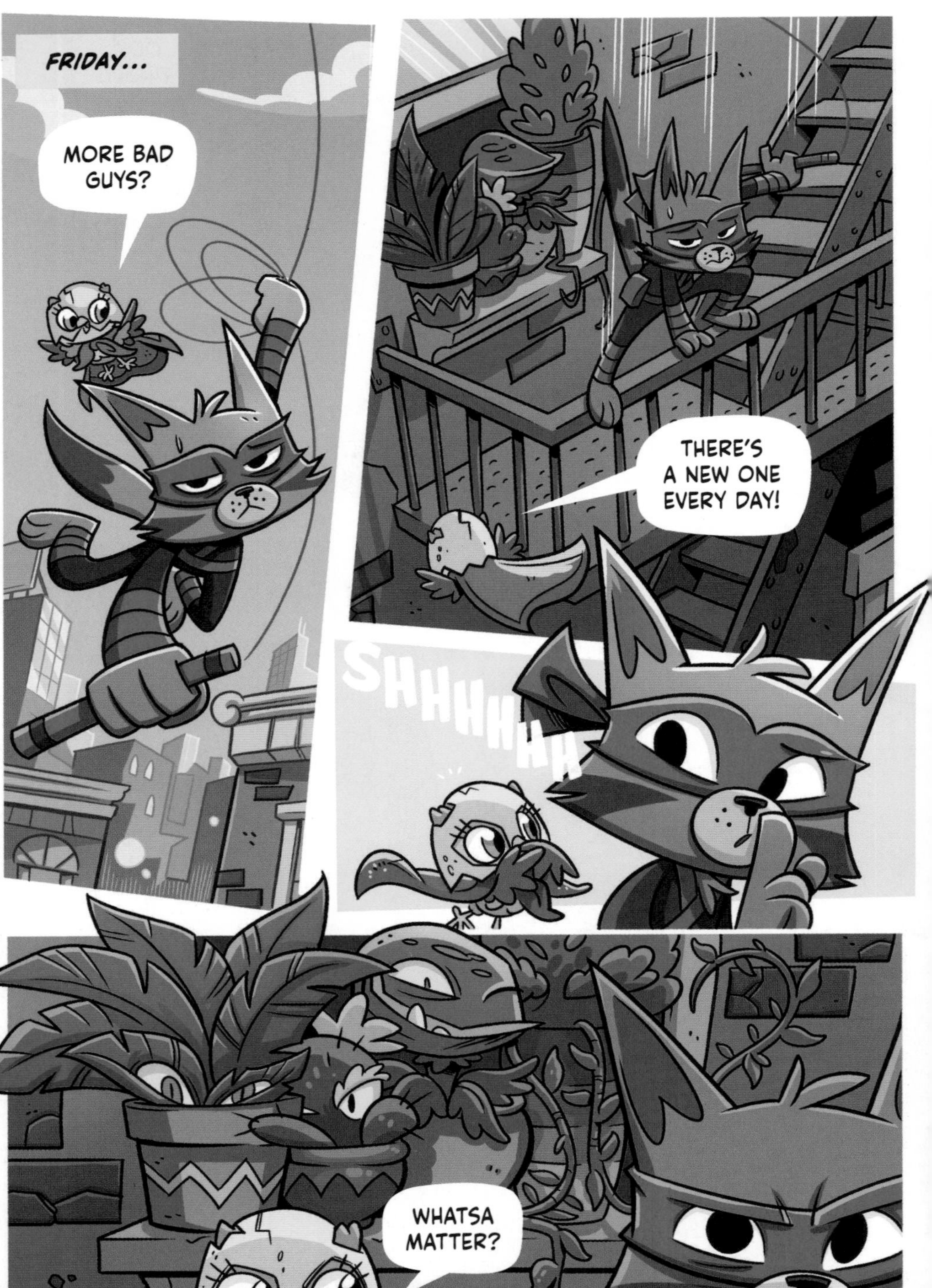
FRIDAY...
MORE BAD GUYS?
THERE'S A NEW ONE EVERY DAY!
SHHHHHHH
WHATSA MATTER?

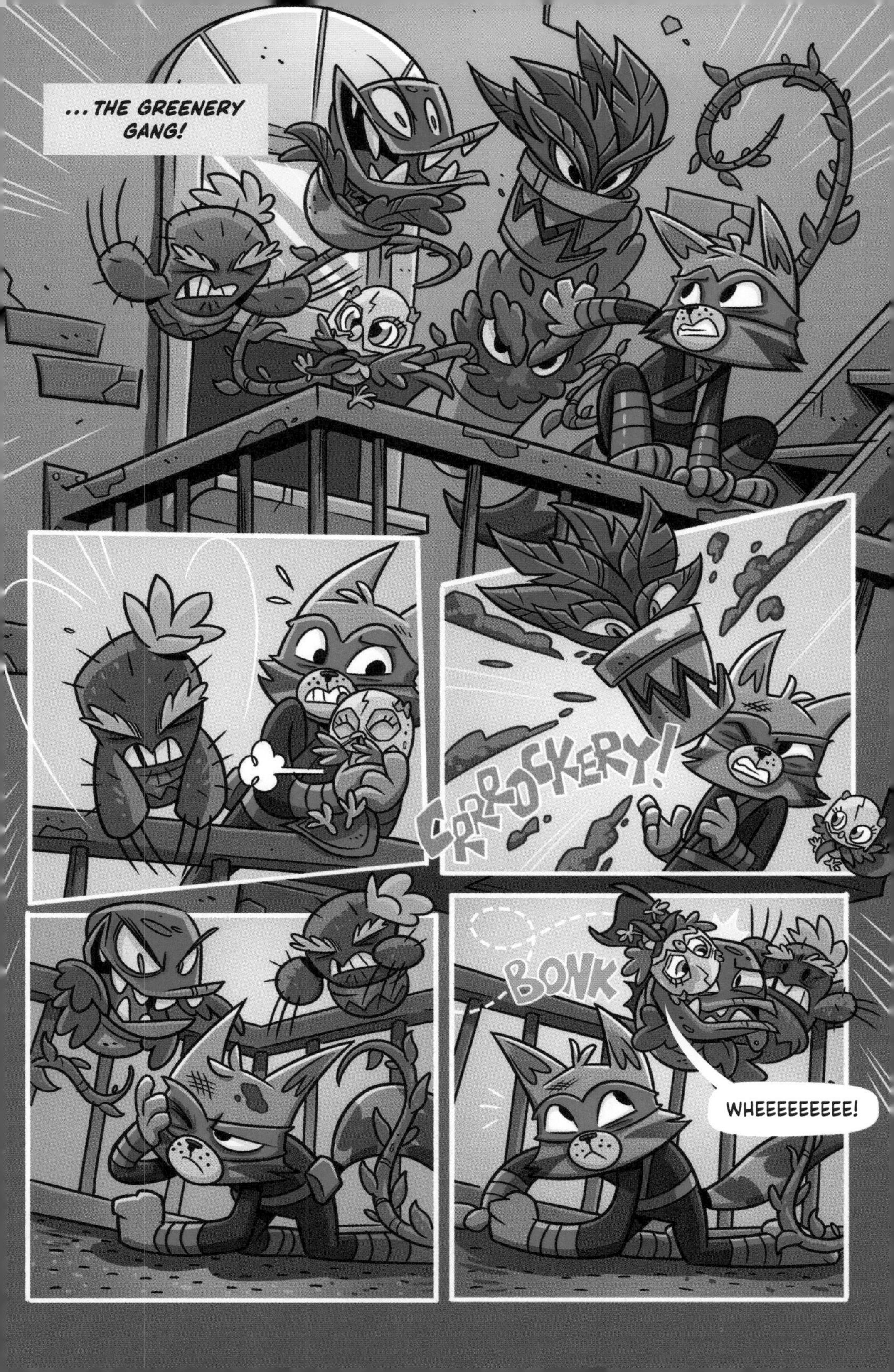
...THE GREENERY GANG!
CRRROCKERY!
BONK
WHEEEEEEEEE!

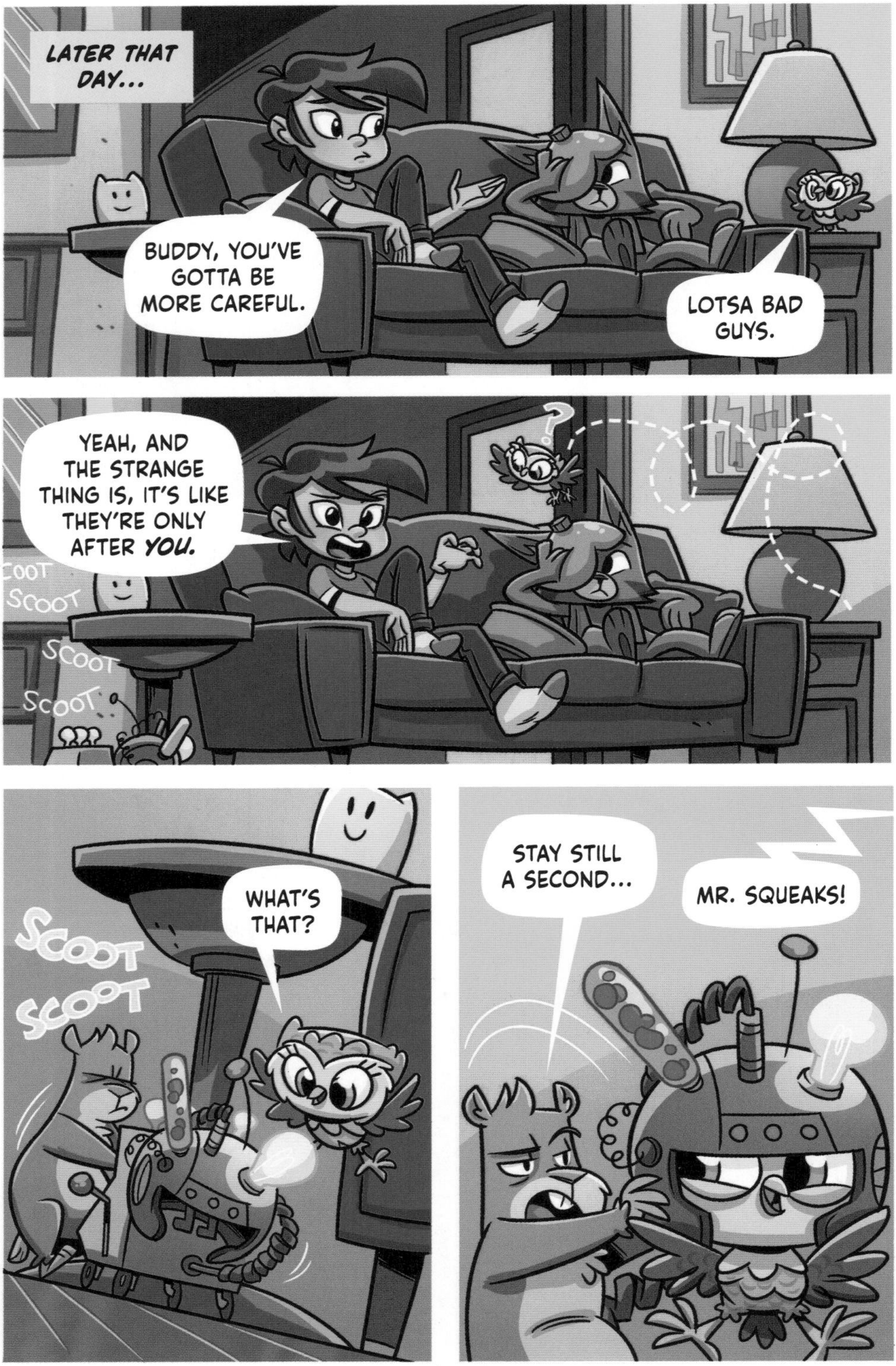
LATER THAT DAY...
BUDDY, YOU'VE GOTTA BE MORE CAREFUL.
LOTSA BAD GUYS.
YEAH, AND THE STRANGE THING IS, IT'S LIKE THEY'RE ONLY AFTER *YOU.*
SCOOT
SCOOT
SCOOT
WHAT'S THAT?
SCOOT
SCOOT
STAY STILL A SECOND...
MR. SQUEAKS!

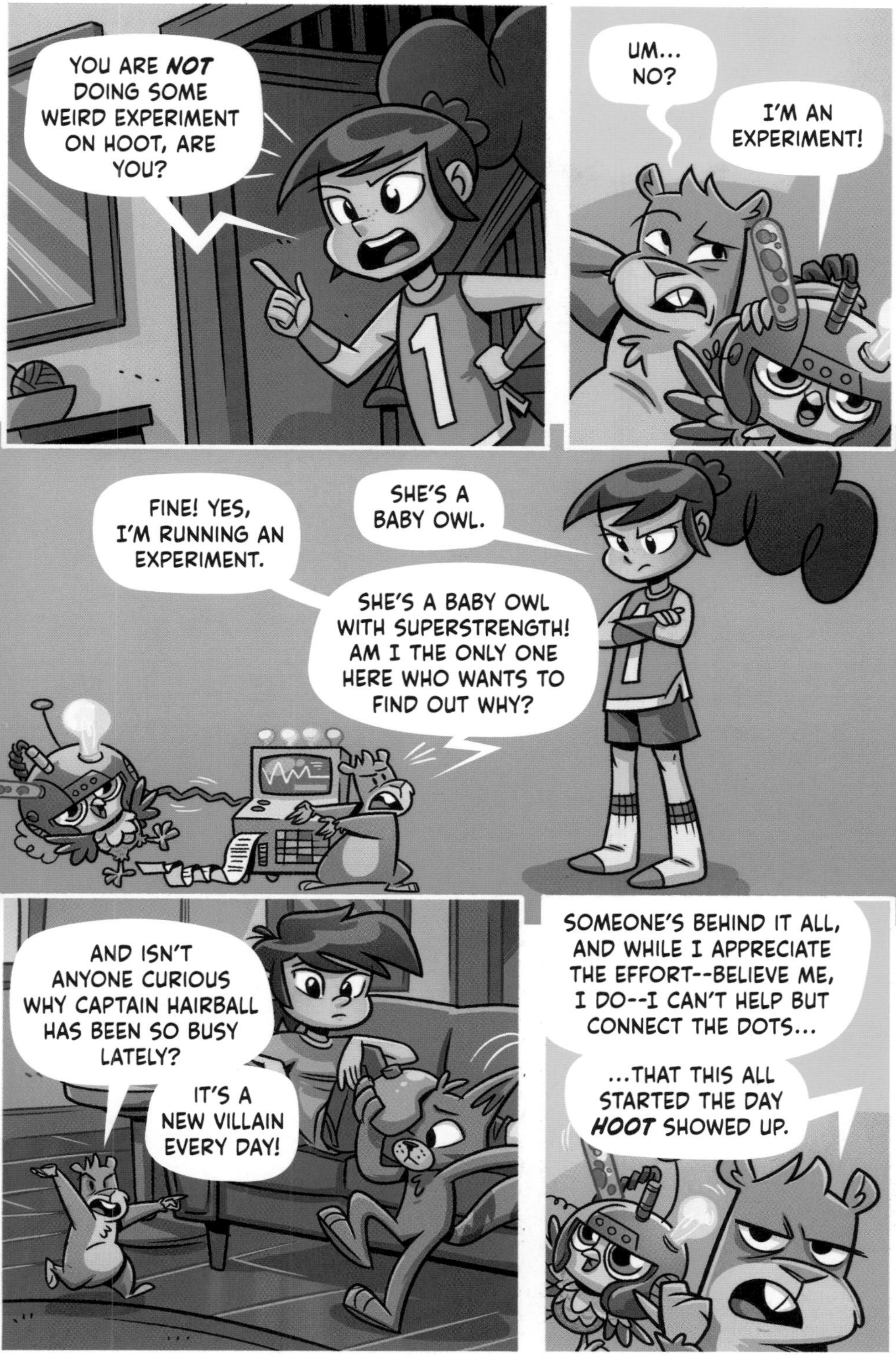
YOU ARE NOT DOING SOME WEIRD EXPERIMENT ON HOOT, ARE YOU?
UM... NO?
I'M AN EXPERIMENT!
FINE! YES, I'M RUNNING AN EXPERIMENT.
SHE'S A BABY OWL.
SHE'S A BABY OWL WITH SUPERSTRENGTH! AM I THE ONLY ONE HERE WHO WANTS TO FIND OUT WHY?
AND ISN'T ANYONE CURIOUS WHY CAPTAIN HAIRBALL HAS BEEN SO BUSY LATELY?
IT'S A NEW VILLAIN EVERY DAY!
SOMEONE'S BEHIND IT ALL, AND WHILE I APPRECIATE THE EFFORT--BELIEVE ME, I DO--I CAN'T HELP BUT CONNECT THE DOTS...
...THAT THIS ALL STARTED THE DAY HOOT SHOWED UP.

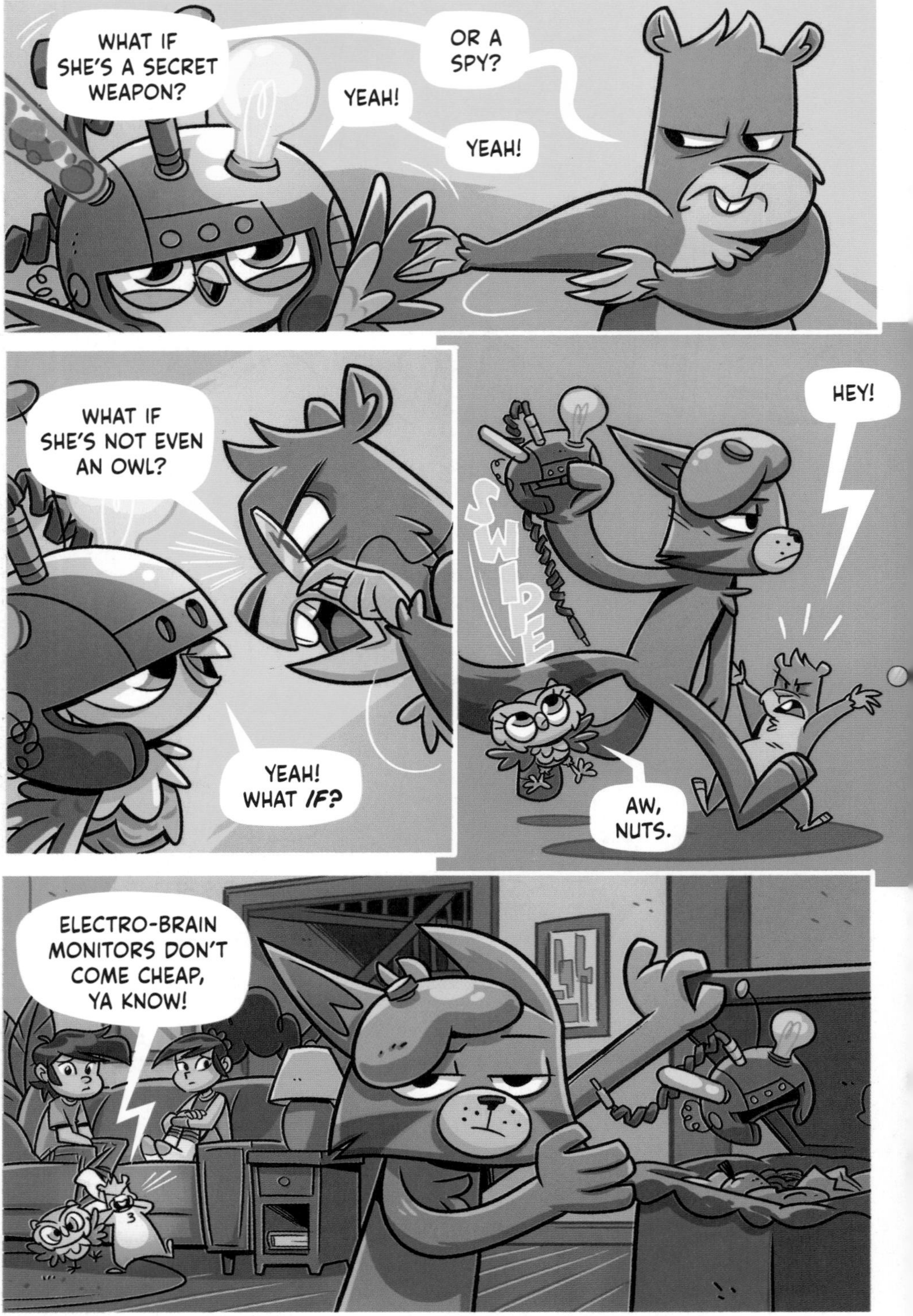
WHAT IF SHE'S A SECRET WEAPON?
YEAH!
OR A SPY?
YEAH!
WHAT IF SHE'S NOT EVEN AN OWL?
YEAH! WHAT IF?
SWIPE
HEY!
AW, NUTS.
ELECTRO-BRAIN MONITORS DON'T COME CHEAP, YA KNOW!

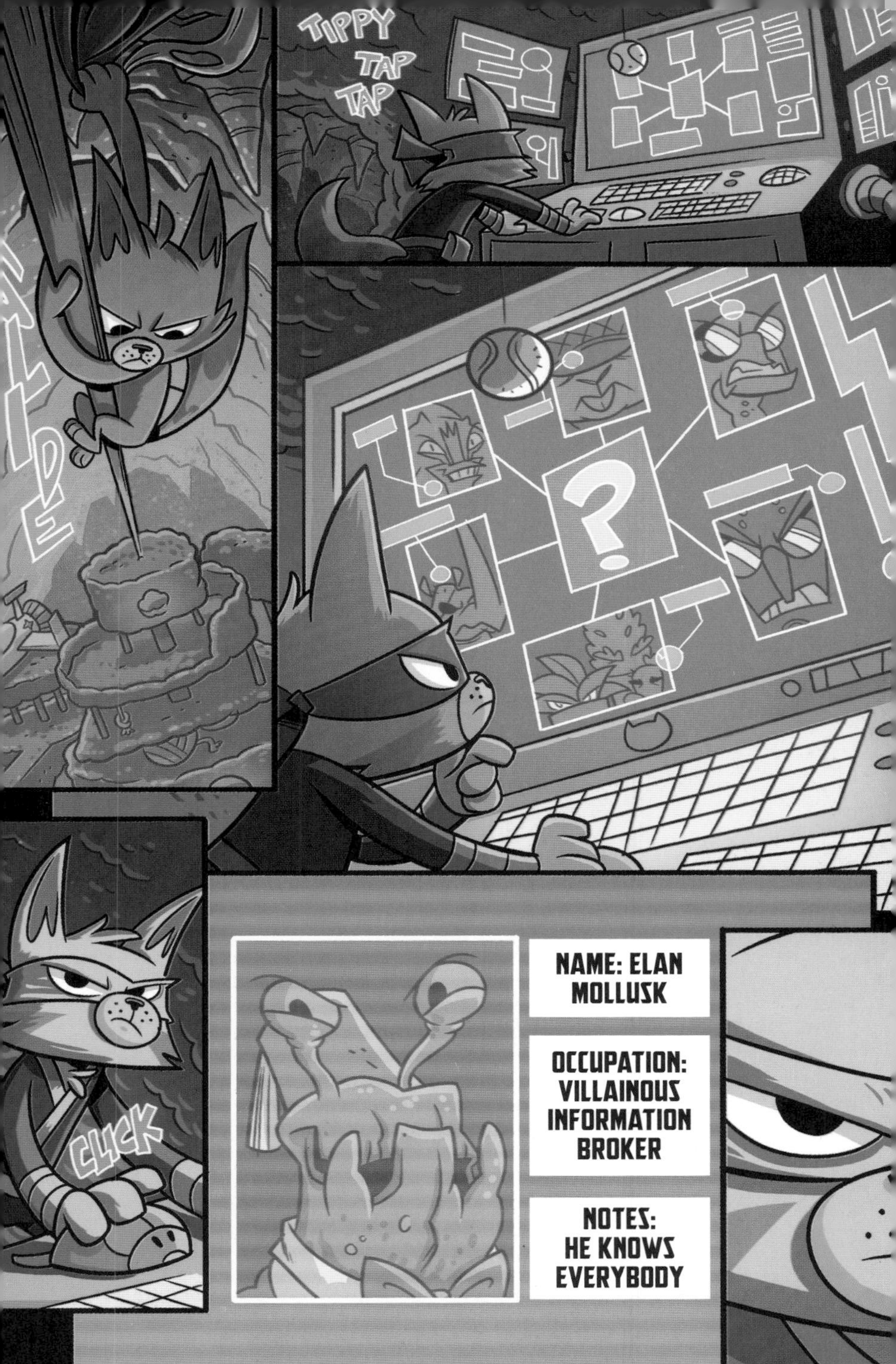
TIPPY
TAP
TAP
CLICK
NAME: ELAN MOLLUSK
OCCUPATION: VILLAINOUS INFORMATION BROKER
NOTES: HE KNOWS EVERYBODY

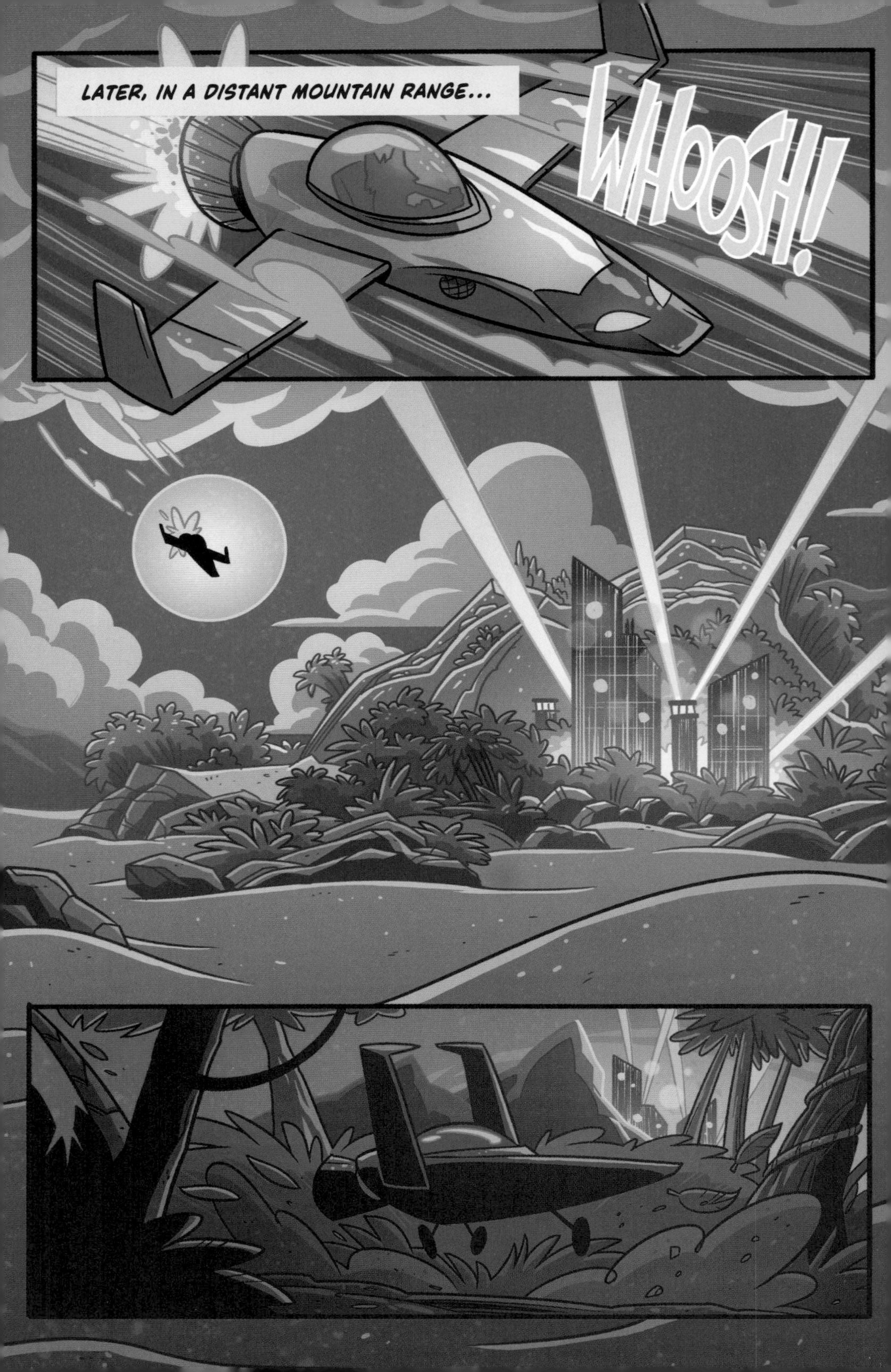
LATER, IN A DISTANT MOUNTAIN RANGE...
WHOOSH!

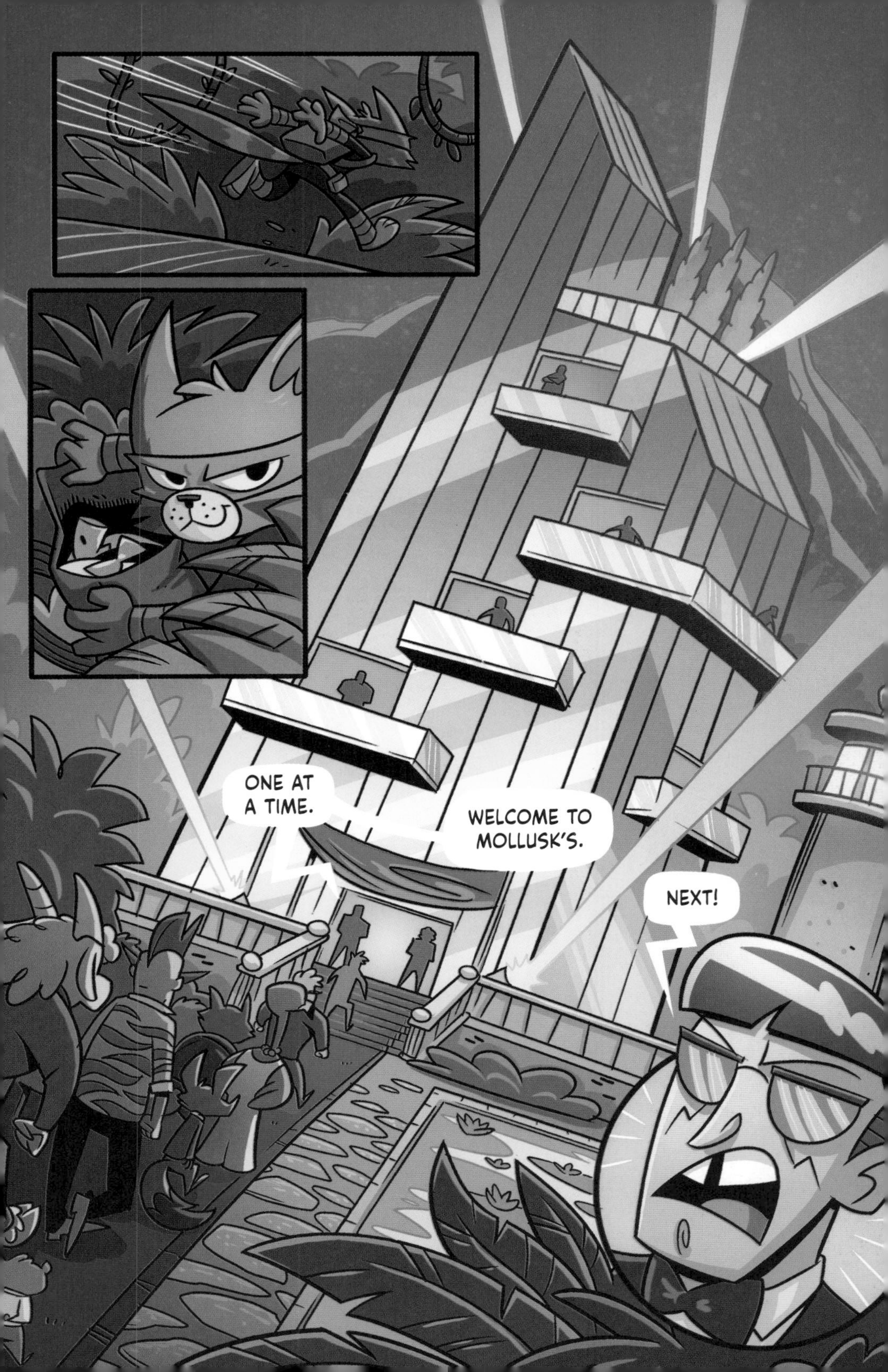
ONE AT A TIME.
WELCOME TO MOLLUSK'S.
NEXT!

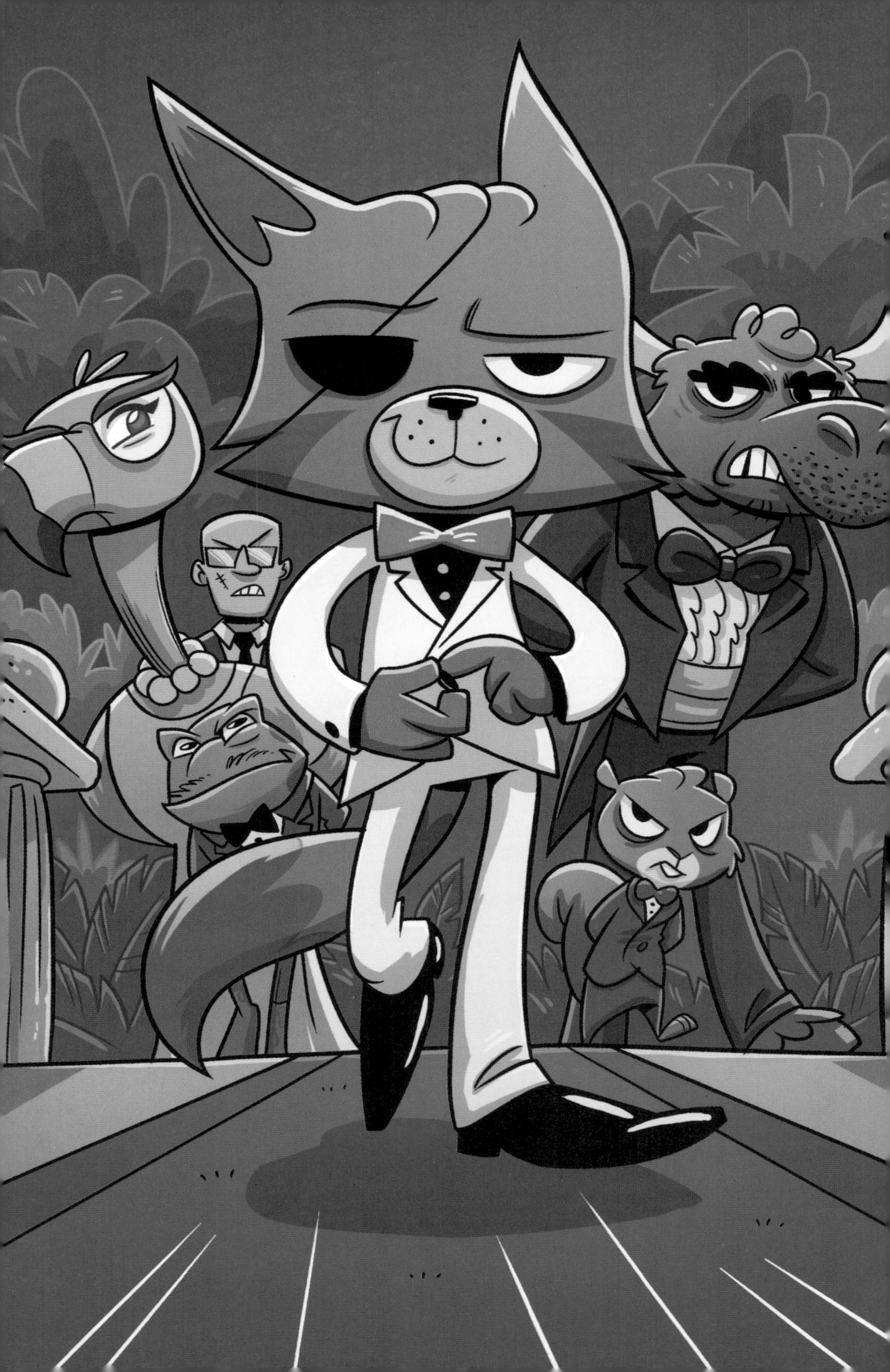

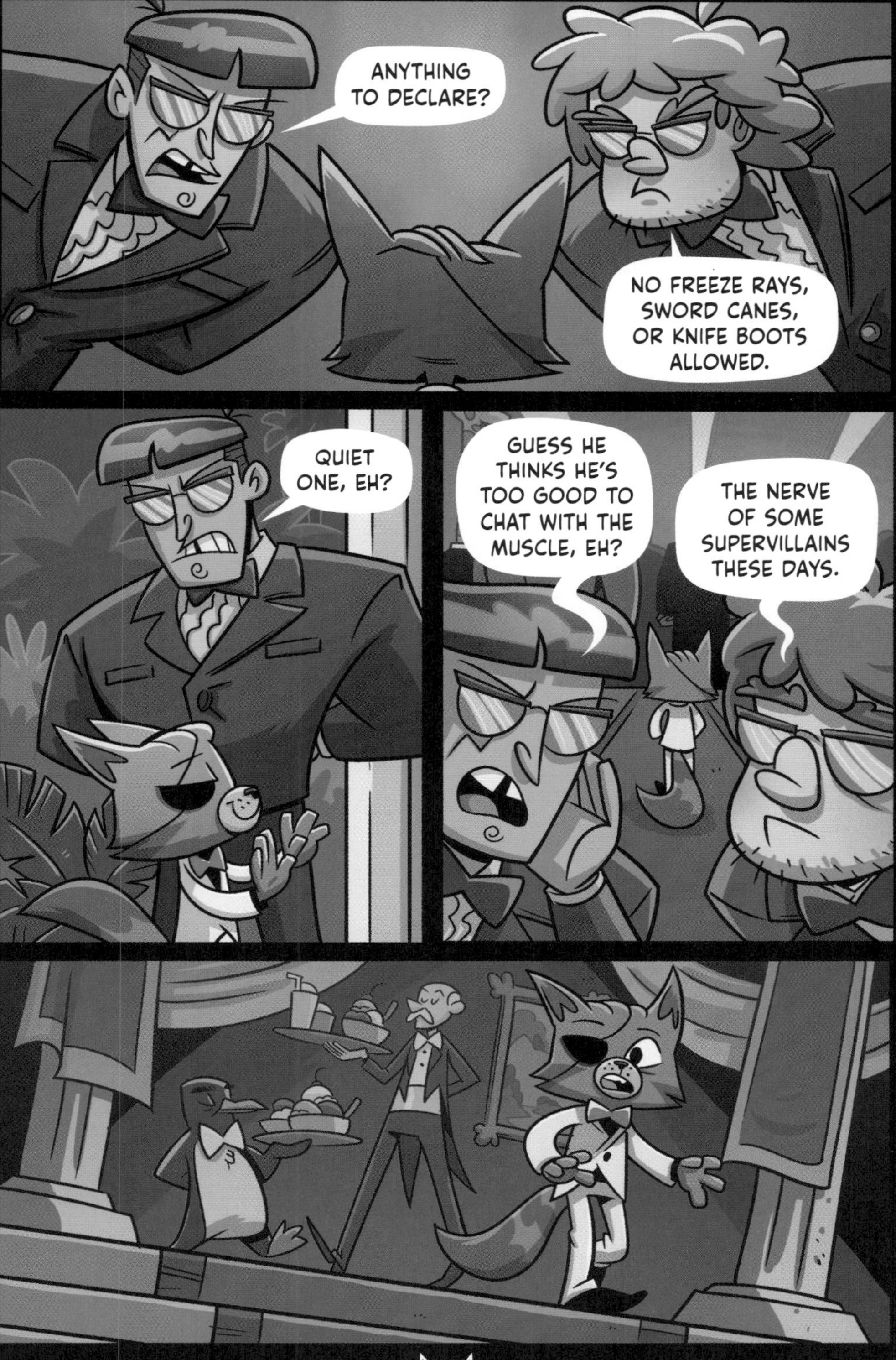
ANYTHING TO DECLARE?
NO FREEZE RAYS, SWORD CANES, OR KNIFE BOOTS ALLOWED.
QUIET ONE, EH?
GUESS HE THINKS HE'S TOO GOOD TO CHAT WITH THE MUSCLE, EH?
THE NERVE OF SOME SUPERVILLAINS THESE DAYS.

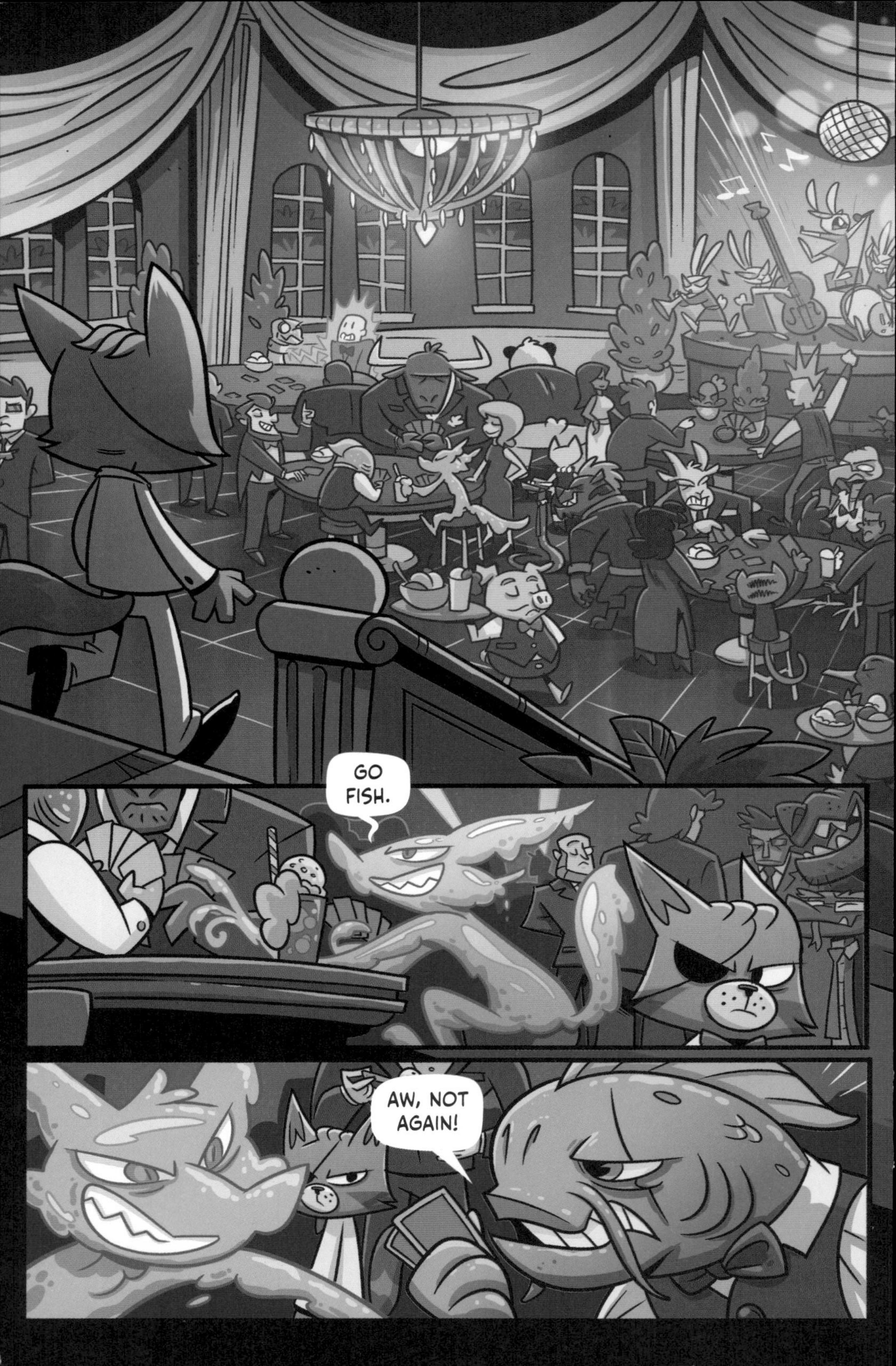
GO FISH.
AW, NOT AGAIN!

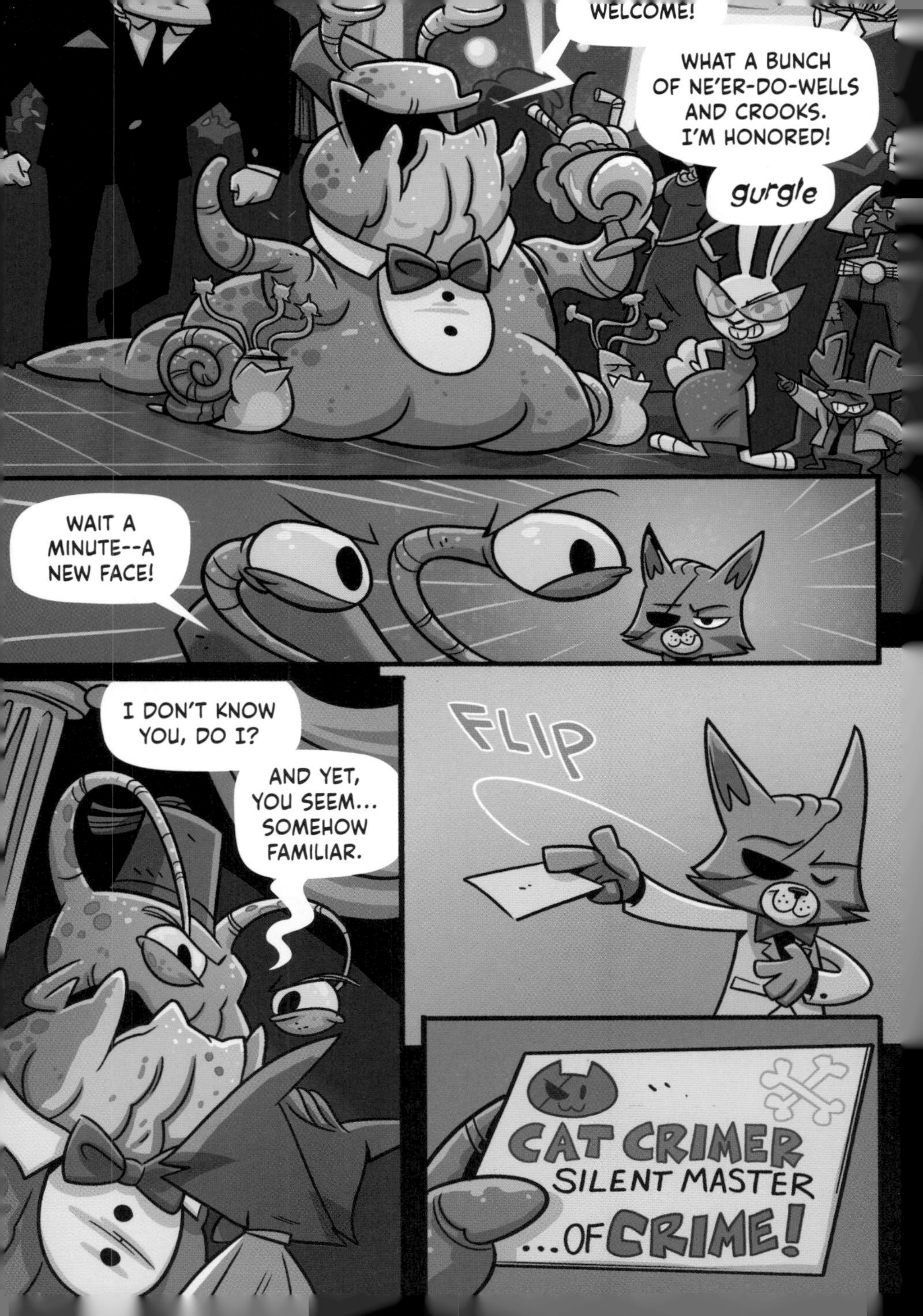
WELCOME!
WHAT A BUNCH OF NE'ER-DO-WELLS AND CROOKS. I'M HONORED!
gurgle
WAIT A MINUTE--A NEW FACE!
I DON'T KNOW YOU, DO I?
AND YET, YOU SEEM... SOMEHOW FAMILIAR.
FLIP
CAT CRIMER
SILENT MASTER
...OF CRIME!

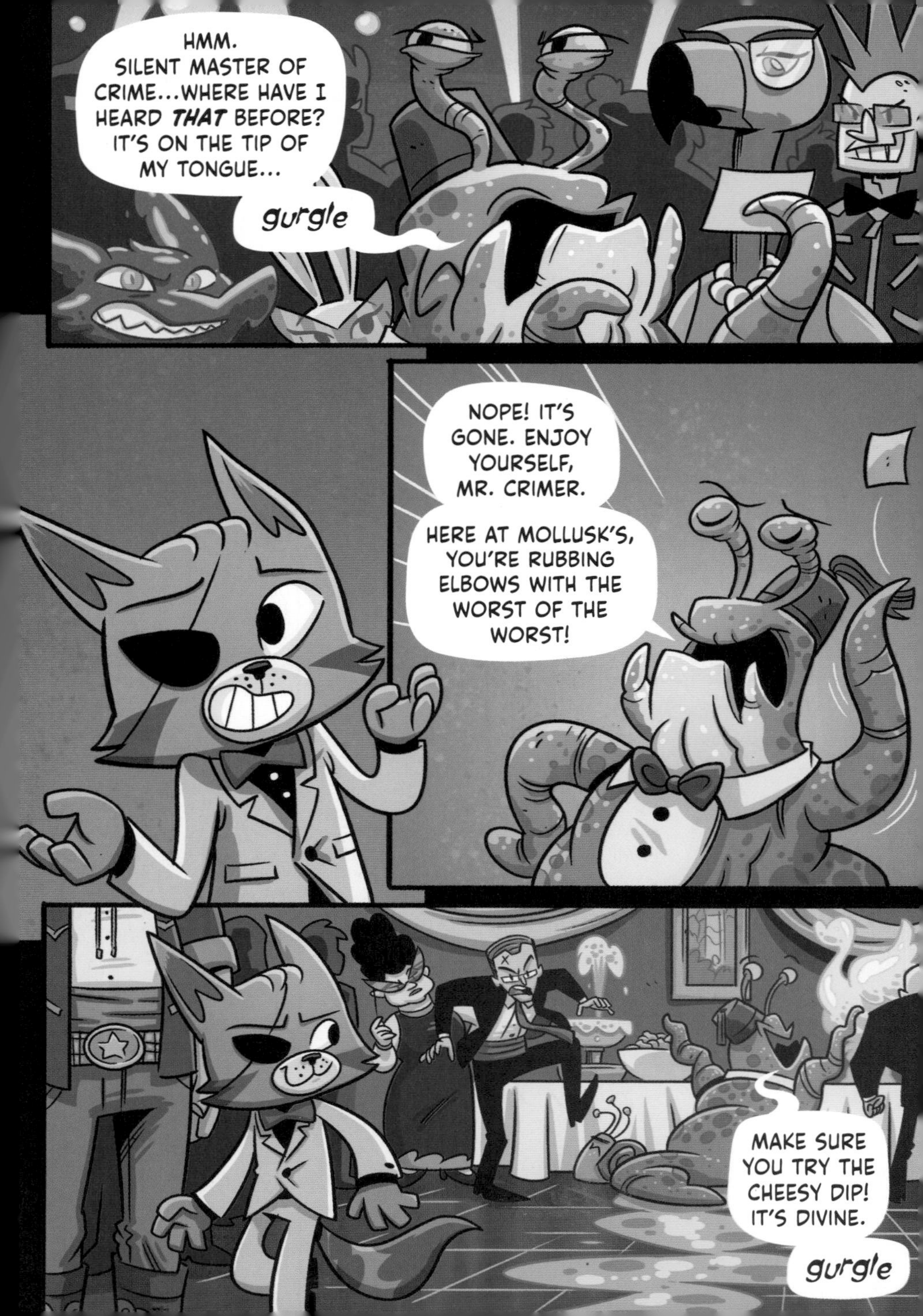
HMM. SILENT MASTER OF CRIME...WHERE HAVE I HEARD *THAT* BEFORE? IT'S ON THE TIP OF MY TONGUE...
gurgle
NOPE! IT'S GONE. ENJOY YOURSELF, MR. CRIMER.
HERE AT MOLLUSK'S, YOU'RE RUBBING ELBOWS WITH THE WORST OF THE WORST!
MAKE SURE YOU TRY THE CHEESY DIP! IT'S DIVINE.
gurgle

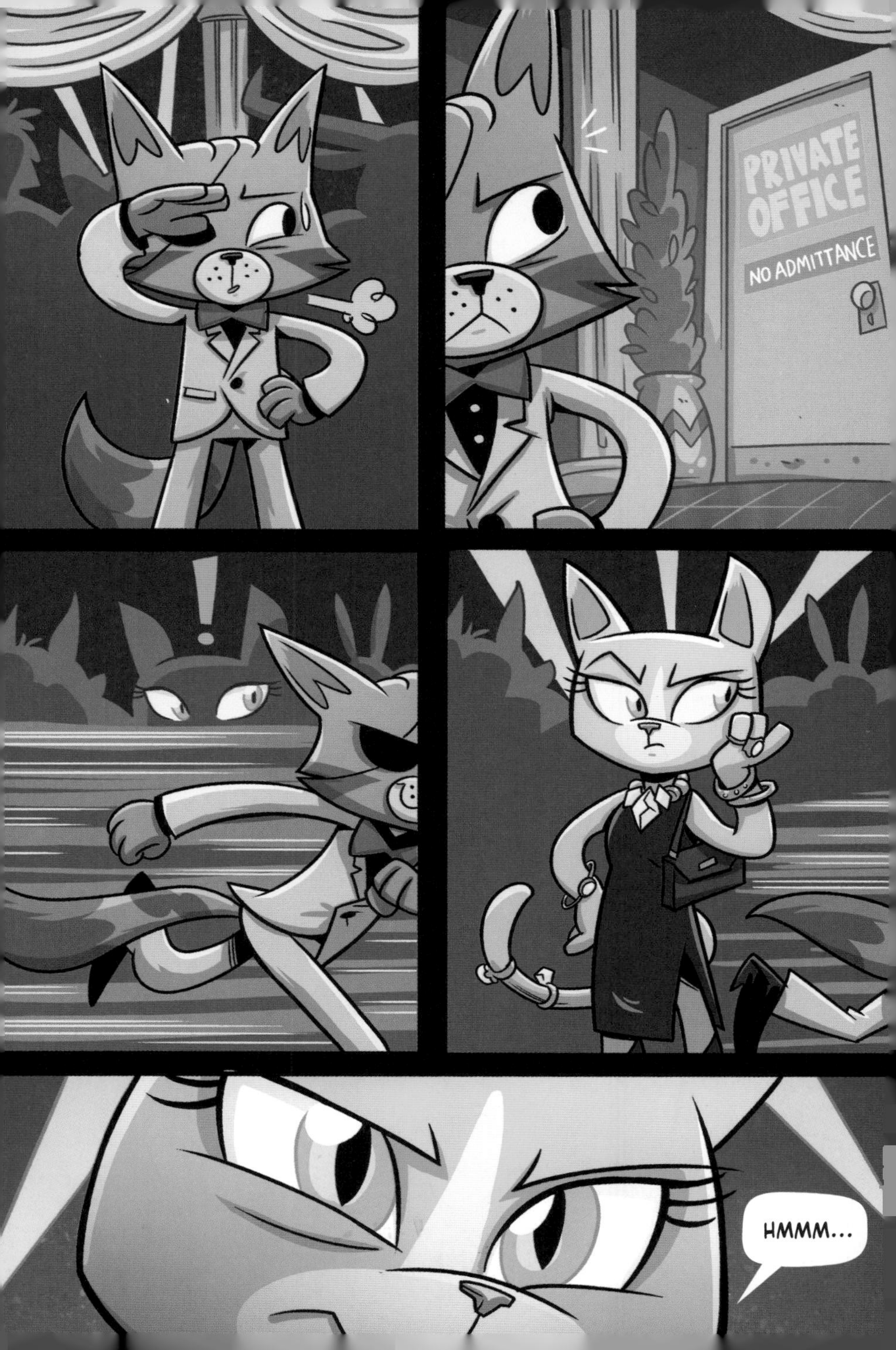
PRIVATE OFFICE
NO ADMITTANCE
!
HMMM...

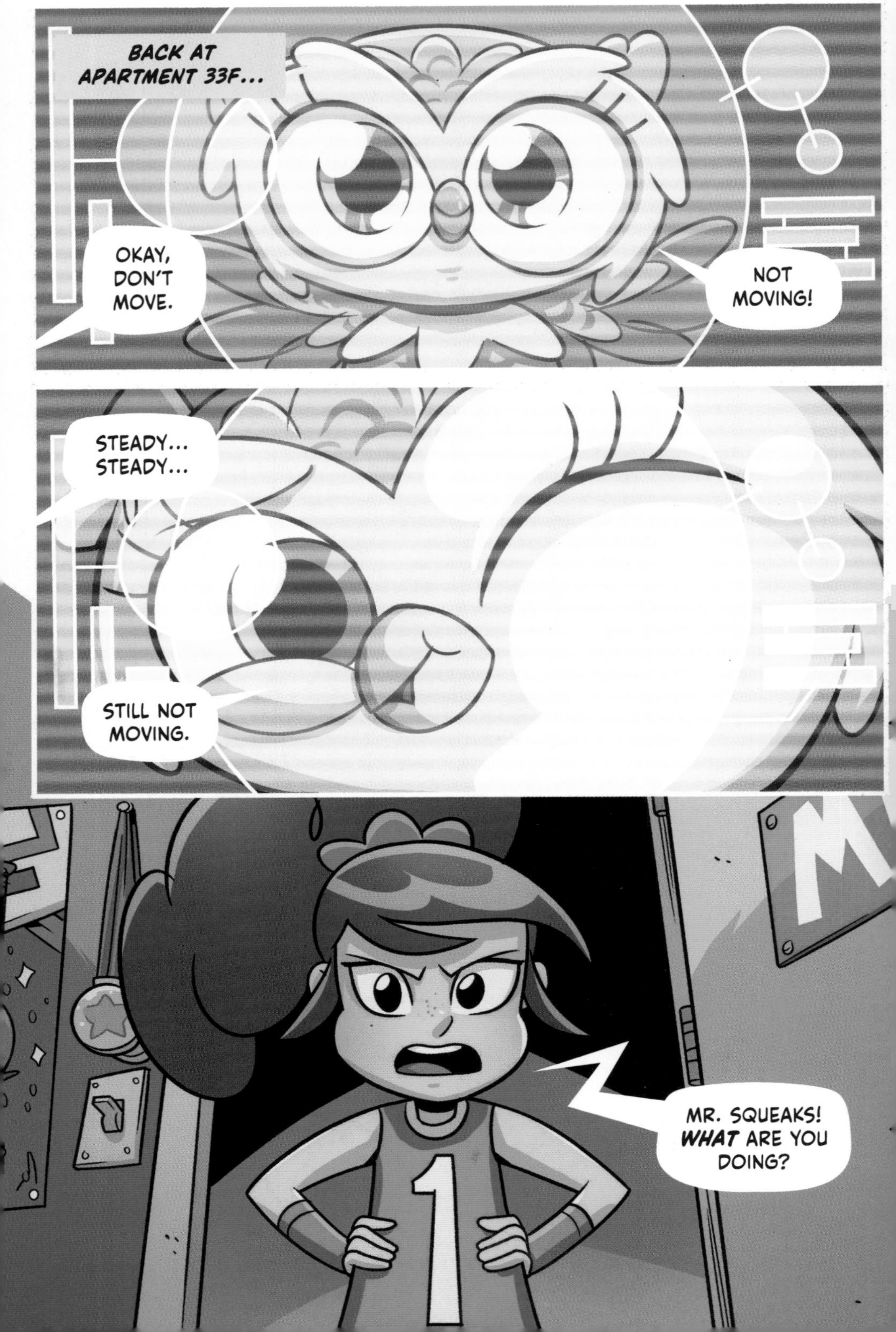
BACK AT APARTMENT 33F...
OKAY, DON'T MOVE.
NOT MOVING!
STEADY... STEADY...
STILL NOT MOVING.
MR. SQUEAKS! *WHAT* ARE YOU DOING?

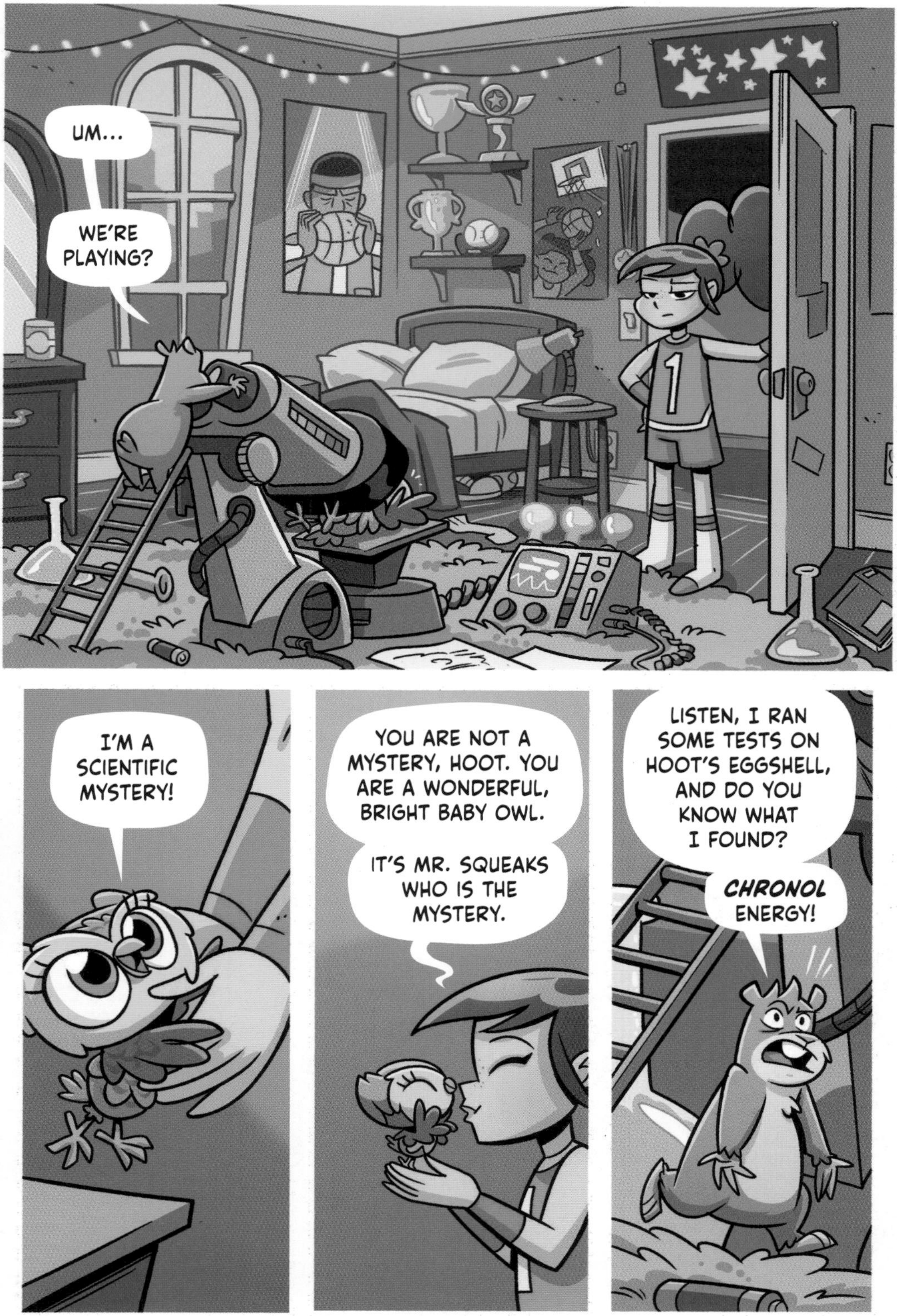
UM...
WE'RE PLAYING?
I'M A SCIENTIFIC MYSTERY!
YOU ARE NOT A MYSTERY, HOOT. YOU ARE A WONDERFUL, BRIGHT BABY OWL.
IT'S MR. SQUEAKS WHO IS THE MYSTERY.
LISTEN, I RAN SOME TESTS ON HOOT'S EGGSHELL, AND DO YOU KNOW WHAT I FOUND?
CHRONOL ENERGY!
1

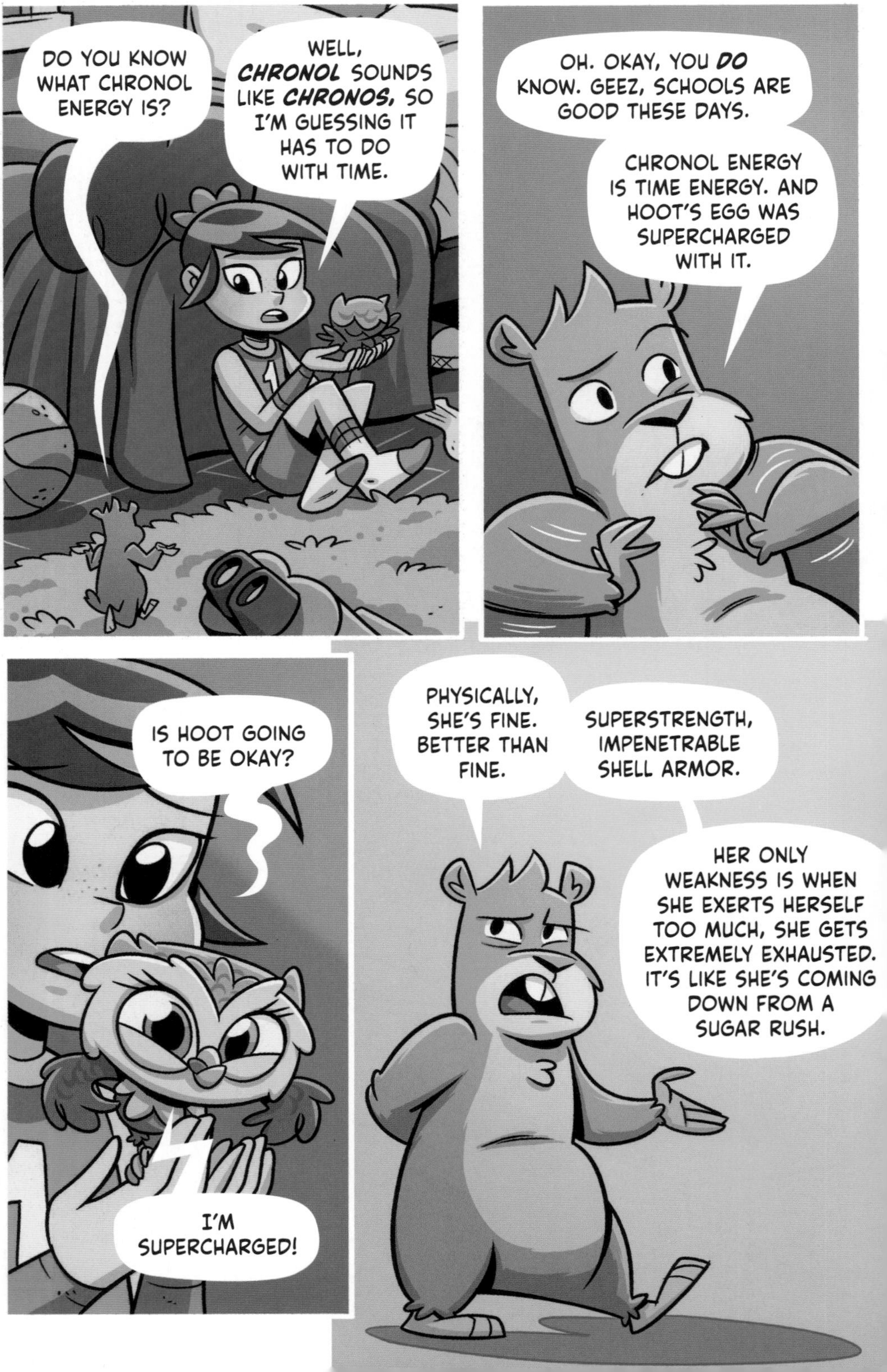
DO YOU KNOW WHAT CHRONOL ENERGY IS?
WELL, *CHRONOL* SOUNDS LIKE *CHRONOS,* SO I'M GUESSING IT HAS TO DO WITH TIME.
OH. OKAY, YOU *DO* KNOW. GEEZ, SCHOOLS ARE GOOD THESE DAYS.
CHRONOL ENERGY IS TIME ENERGY. AND HOOT'S EGG WAS SUPERCHARGED WITH IT.
IS HOOT GOING TO BE OKAY?
I'M SUPERCHARGED!
PHYSICALLY, SHE'S FINE. BETTER THAN FINE.
SUPERSTRENGTH, IMPENETRABLE SHELL ARMOR.
HER ONLY WEAKNESS IS WHEN SHE EXERTS HERSELF TOO MUCH, SHE GETS EXTREMELY EXHAUSTED. IT'S LIKE SHE'S COMING DOWN FROM A SUGAR RUSH.

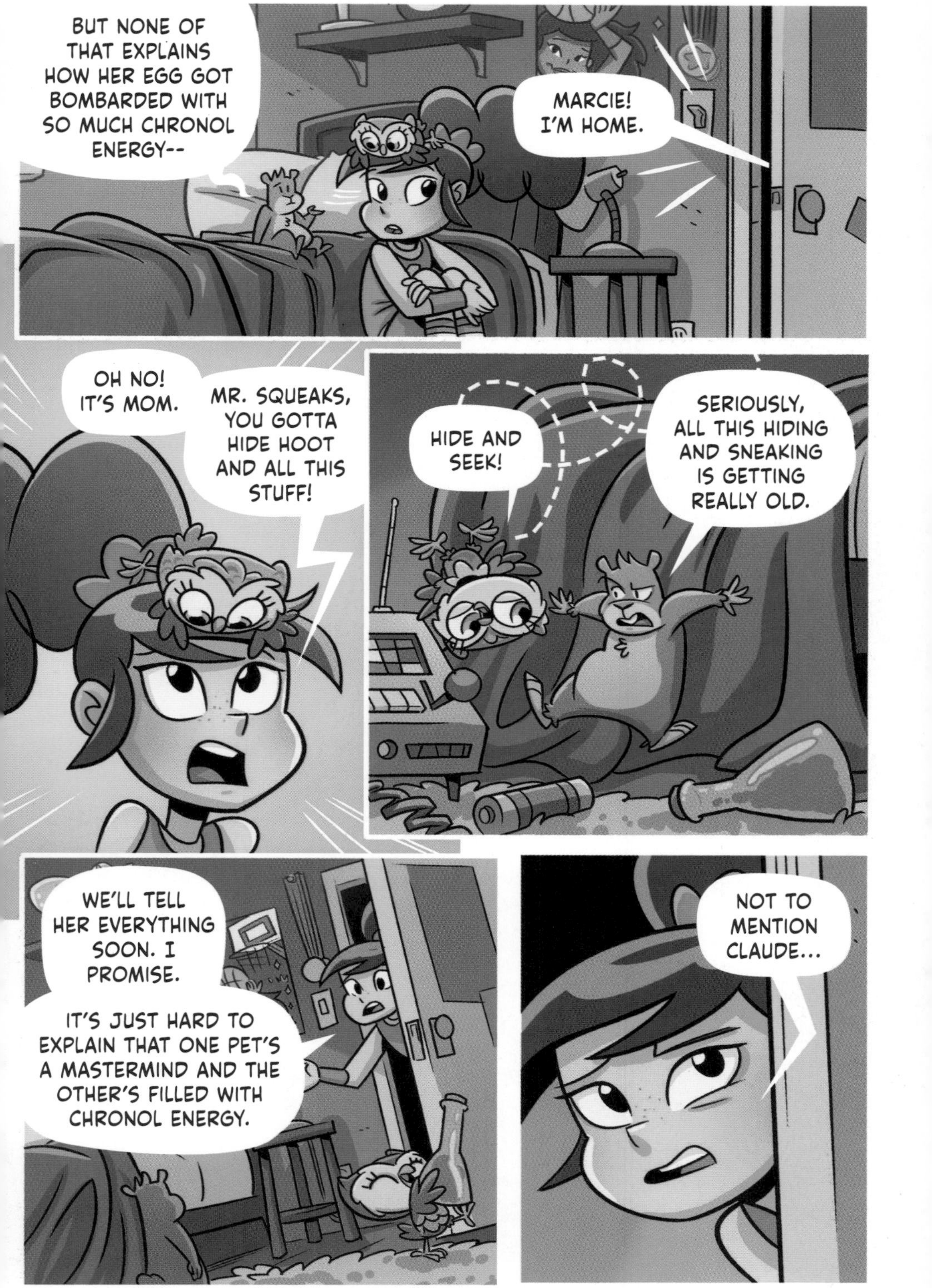
BUT NONE OF THAT EXPLAINS HOW HER EGG GOT BOMBARDED WITH SO MUCH CHRONOL ENERGY--
MARCIE! I'M HOME.
OH NO! IT'S MOM.
MR. SQUEAKS, YOU GOTTA HIDE HOOT AND ALL THIS STUFF!
HIDE AND SEEK!
SERIOUSLY, ALL THIS HIDING AND SNEAKING IS GETTING REALLY OLD.
WE'LL TELL HER EVERYTHING SOON. I PROMISE.
IT'S JUST HARD TO EXPLAIN THAT ONE PET'S A MASTERMIND AND THE OTHER'S FILLED WITH CHRONOL ENERGY.
NOT TO MENTION CLAUDE...

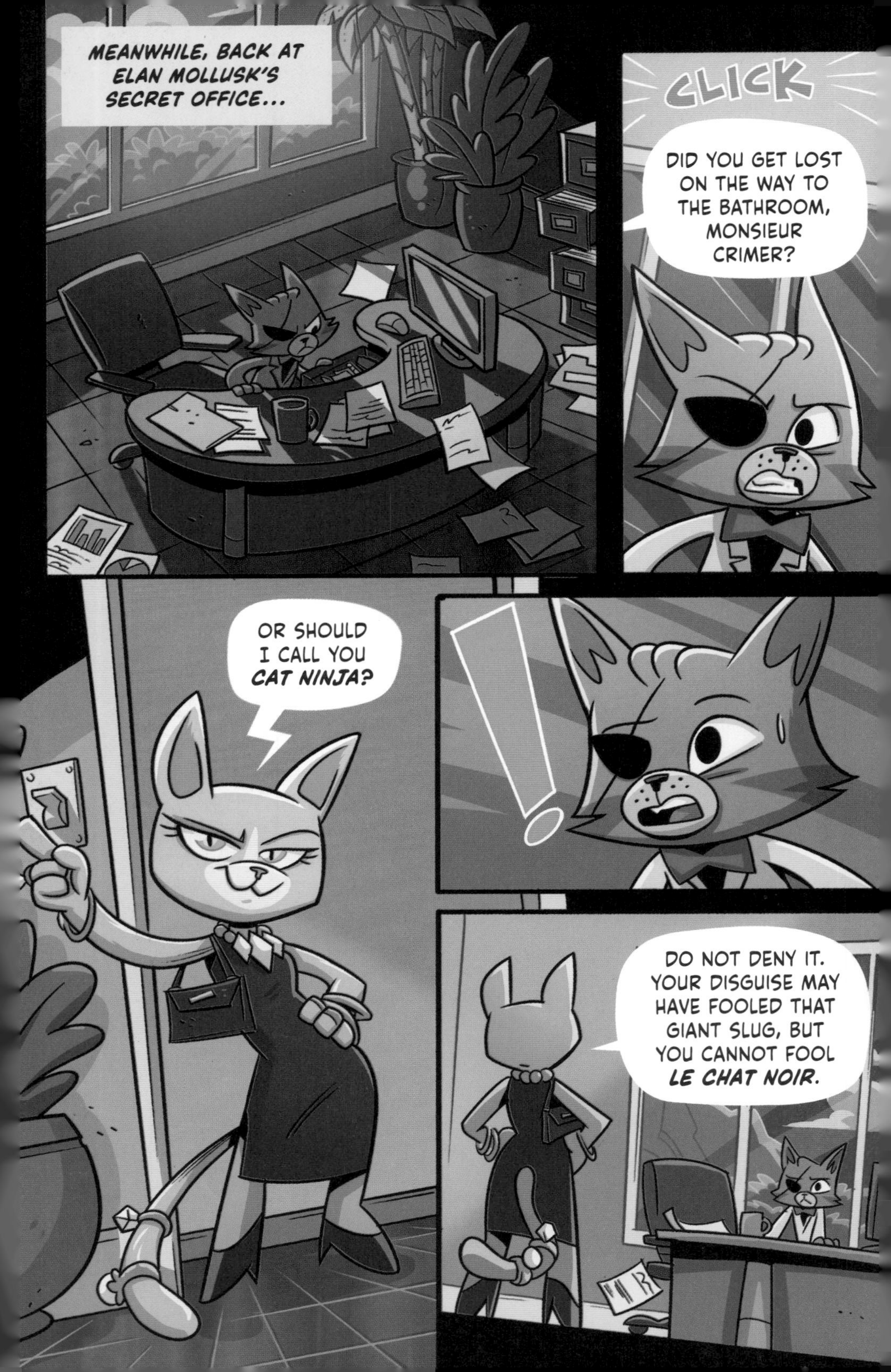
MEANWHILE, BACK AT ELAN MOLLUSK'S SECRET OFFICE...
CLICK
DID YOU GET LOST ON THE WAY TO THE BATHROOM, MONSIEUR CRIMER?
OR SHOULD I CALL YOU *CAT NINJA?*
DO NOT DENY IT. YOUR DISGUISE MAY HAVE FOOLED THAT GIANT SLUG, BUT YOU CANNOT FOOL *LE CHAT NOIR.*

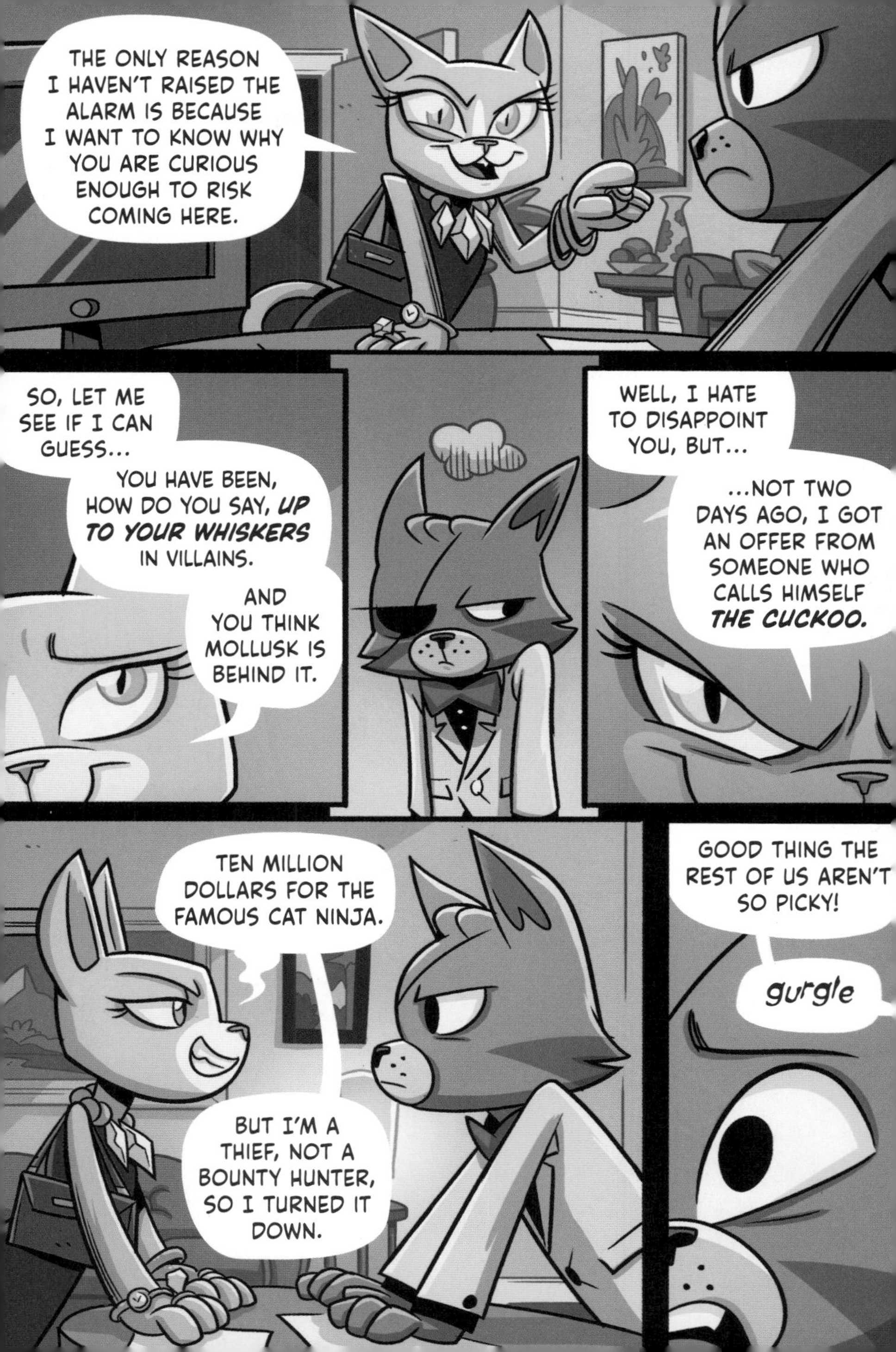
THE ONLY REASON I HAVEN'T RAISED THE ALARM IS BECAUSE I WANT TO KNOW WHY YOU ARE CURIOUS ENOUGH TO RISK COMING HERE.
SO, LET ME SEE IF I CAN GUESS...
YOU HAVE BEEN, HOW DO YOU SAY, *UP TO YOUR WHISKERS* IN VILLAINS.
AND YOU THINK MOLLUSK IS BEHIND IT.
WELL, I HATE TO DISAPPOINT YOU, BUT...
...NOT TWO DAYS AGO, I GOT AN OFFER FROM SOMEONE WHO CALLS HIMSELF *THE CUCKOO.*
TEN MILLION DOLLARS FOR THE FAMOUS CAT NINJA.
BUT I'M A THIEF, NOT A BOUNTY HUNTER, SO I TURNED IT DOWN.
GOOD THING THE REST OF US AREN'T SO PICKY!
gurgle

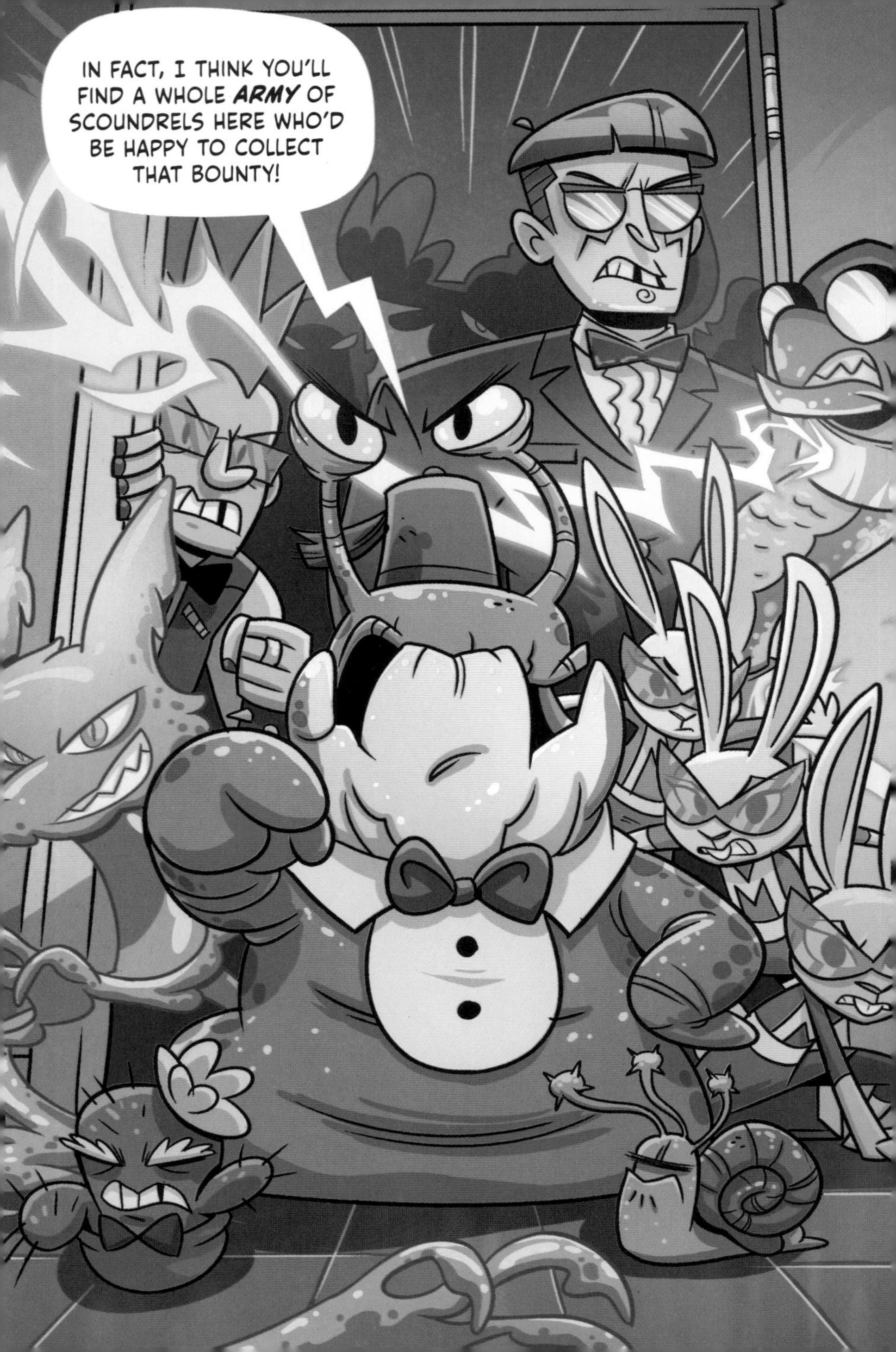
IN FACT, I THINK YOU'LL FIND A WHOLE ARMY OF SCOUNDRELS HERE WHO'D BE HAPPY TO COLLECT THAT BOUNTY!

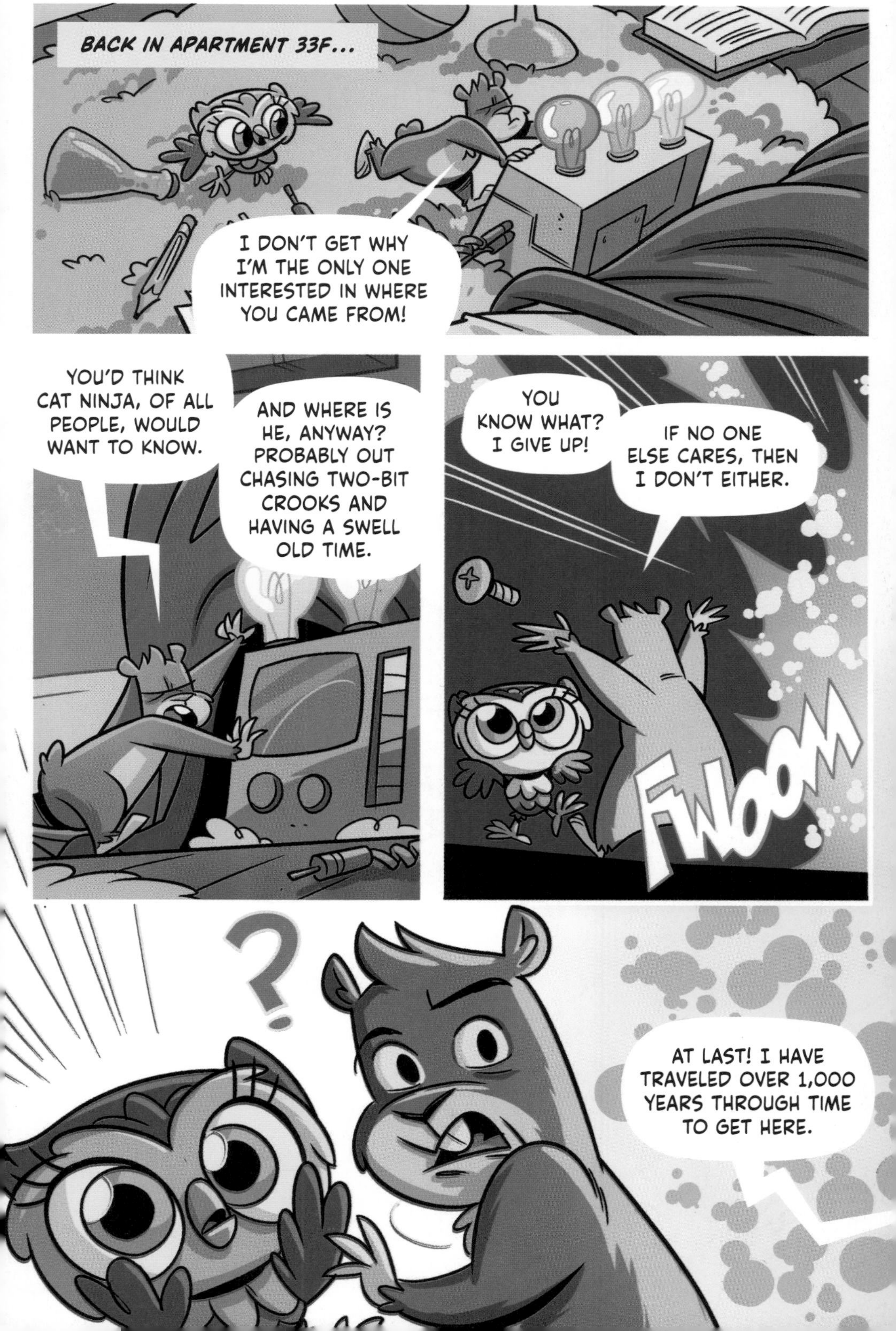
BACK IN APARTMENT 33F...
I DON'T GET WHY I'M THE ONLY ONE INTERESTED IN WHERE YOU CAME FROM!
YOU'D THINK CAT NINJA, OF ALL PEOPLE, WOULD WANT TO KNOW.
AND WHERE IS HE, ANYWAY? PROBABLY OUT CHASING TWO-BIT CROOKS AND HAVING A SWELL OLD TIME.
YOU KNOW WHAT? I GIVE UP!
IF NO ONE ELSE CARES, THEN I DON'T EITHER.
FWOOM
?
AT LAST! I HAVE TRAVELED OVER 1,000 YEARS THROUGH TIME TO GET HERE.

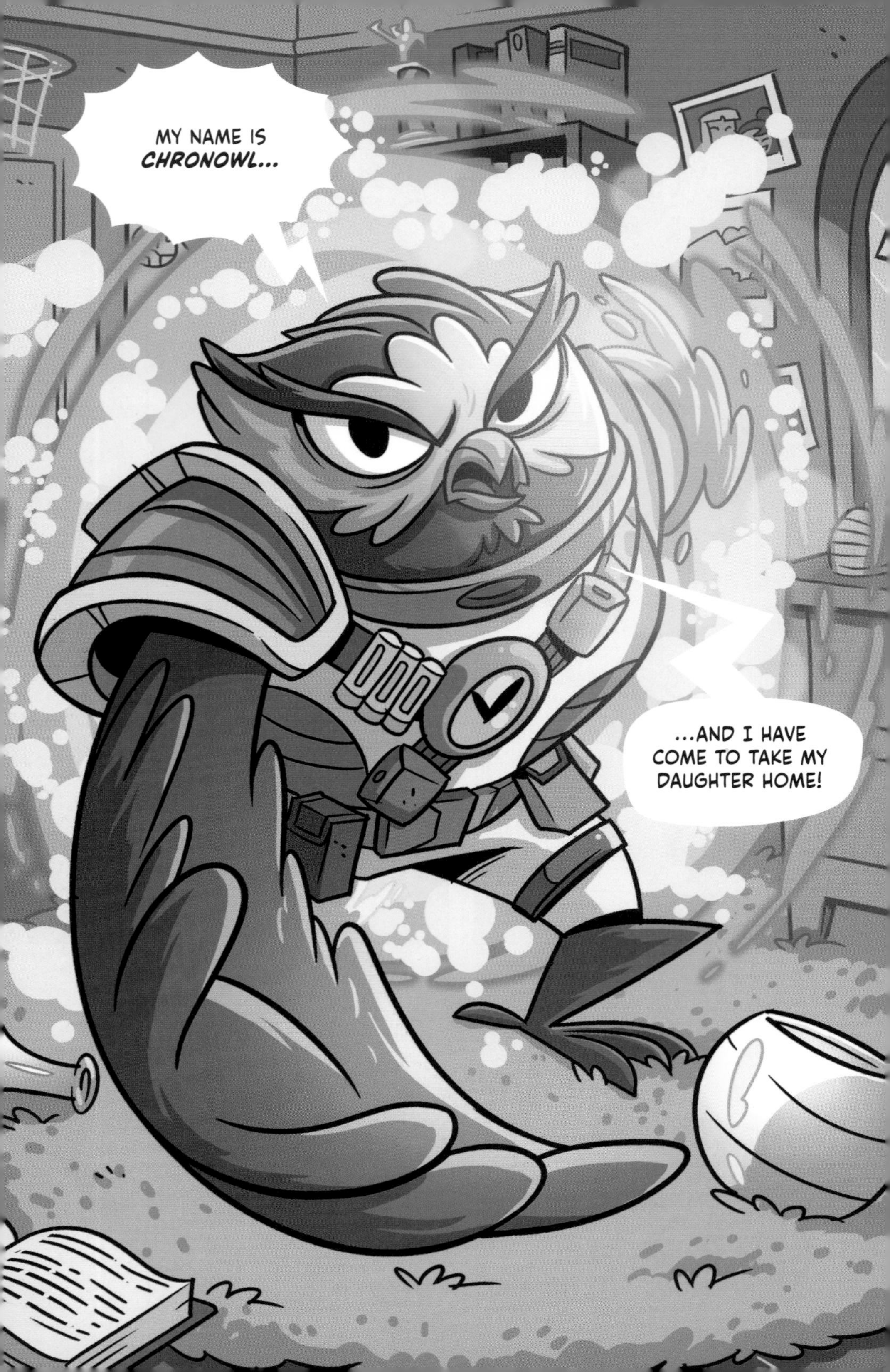
MY NAME IS *CHRONOWL...*
...AND I HAVE COME TO TAKE MY DAUGHTER HOME!

Chapter 4: Night of the Cuckoo

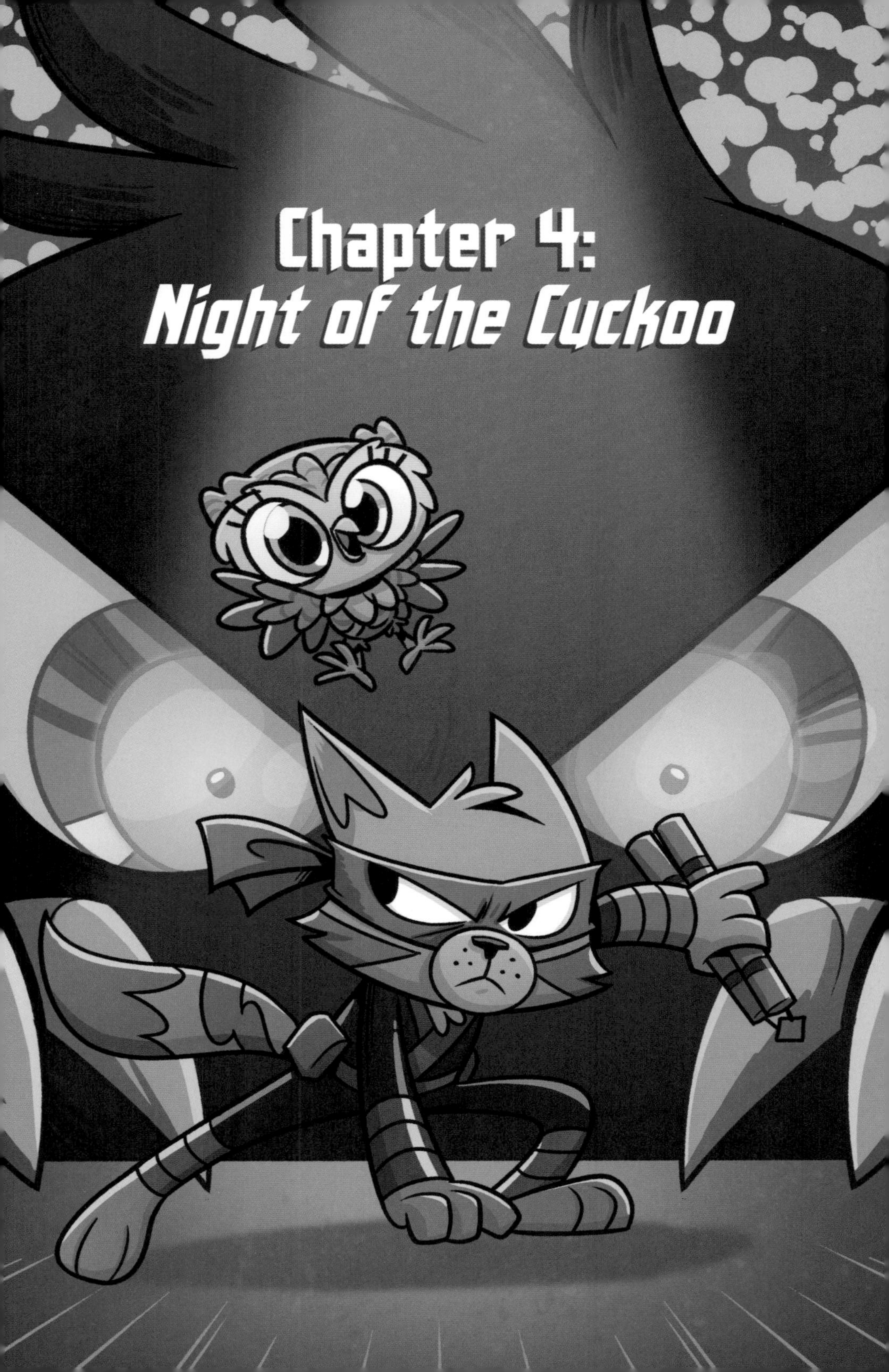

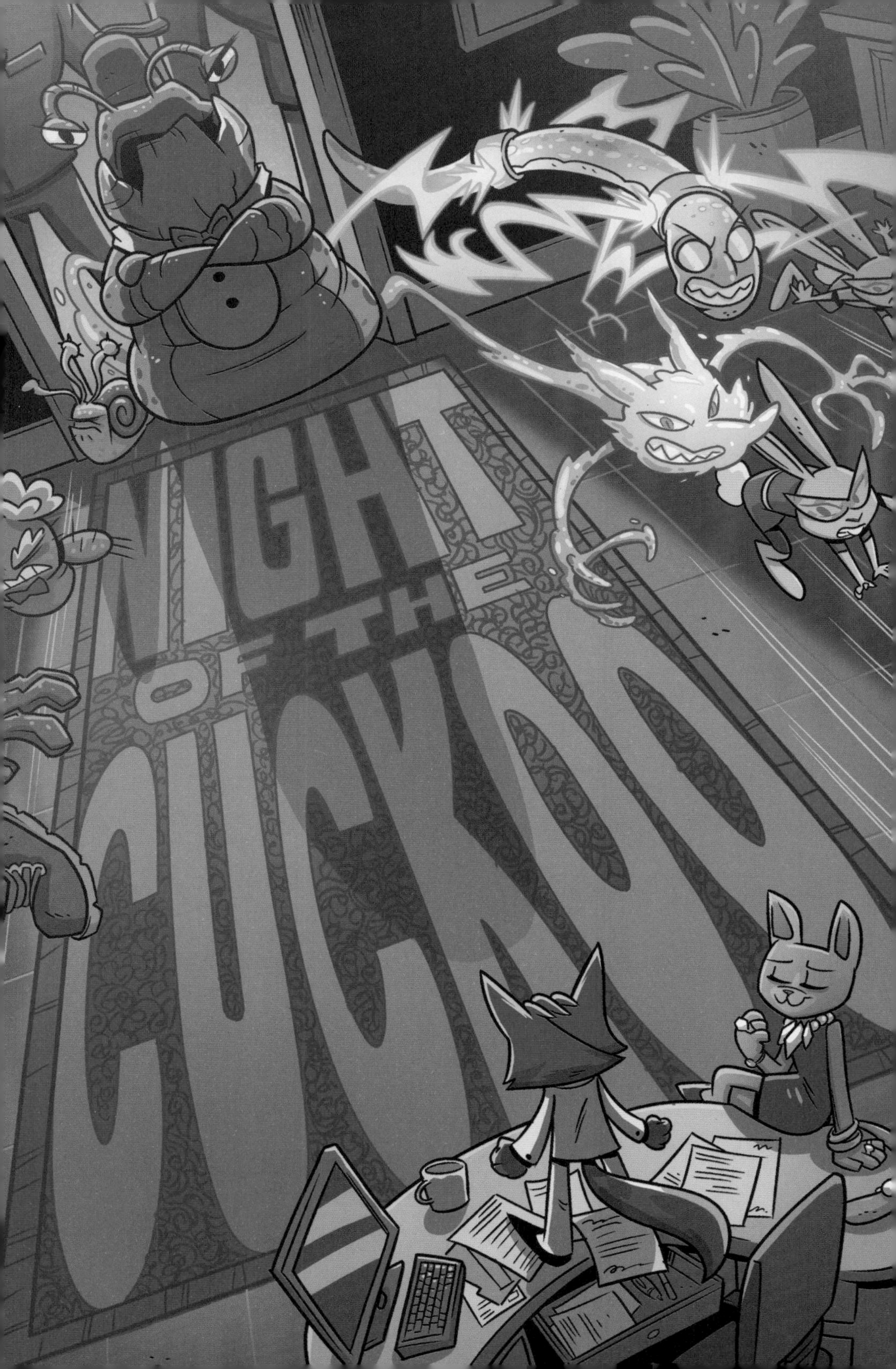
NIGHT
OF THE
CUCKOO

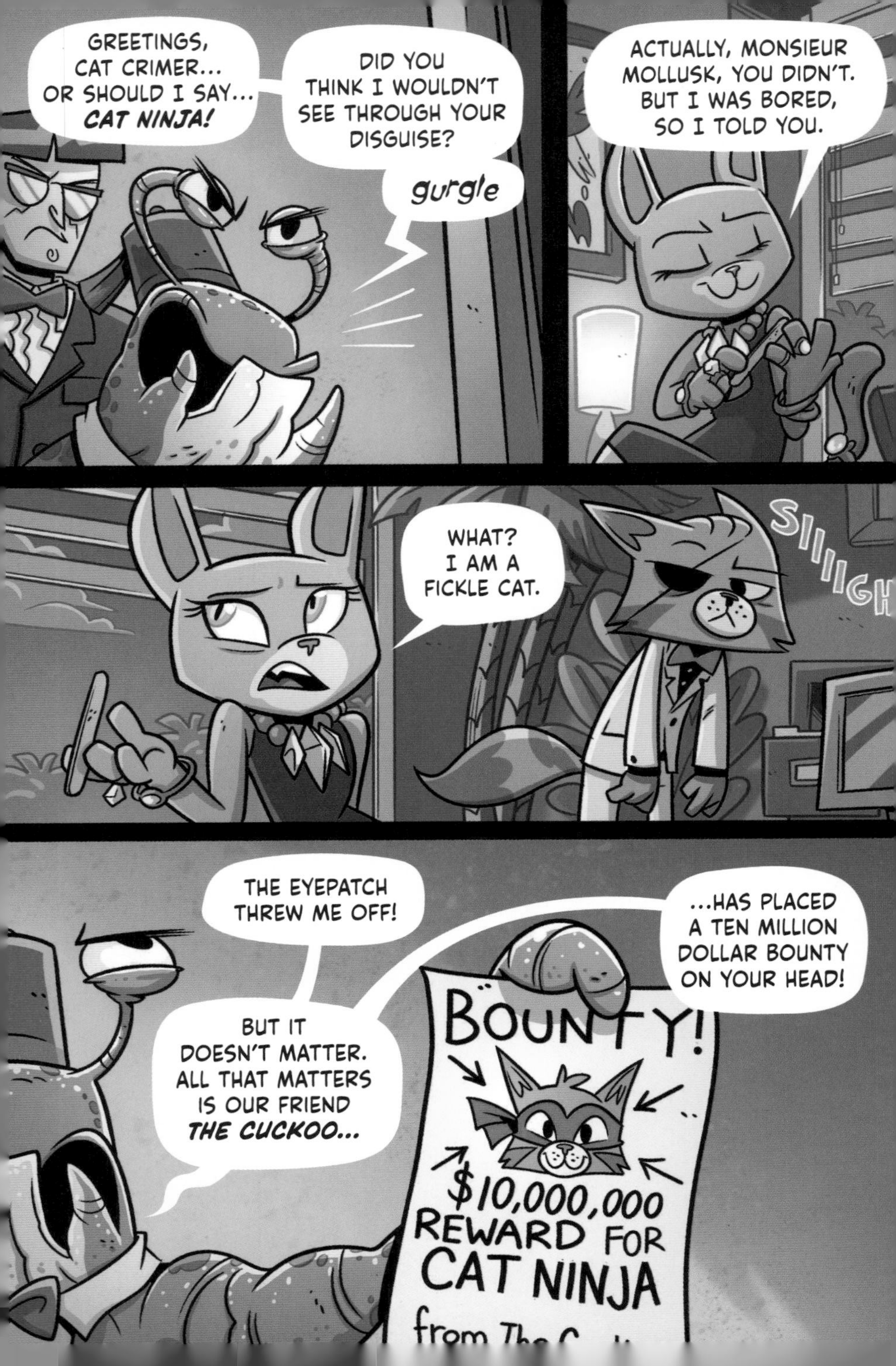
GREETINGS, CAT CRIMER... OR SHOULD I SAY... *CAT NINJA!*
DID YOU THINK I WOULDN'T SEE THROUGH YOUR DISGUISE?
gurgle
ACTUALLY, MONSIEUR MOLLUSK, YOU DIDN'T. BUT I WAS BORED, SO I TOLD YOU.
WHAT? I AM A FICKLE CAT.
SIIIIGH
THE EYEPATCH THREW ME OFF!
BUT IT DOESN'T MATTER. ALL THAT MATTERS IS OUR FRIEND *THE CUCKOO...*
...HAS PLACED A TEN MILLION DOLLAR BOUNTY ON YOUR HEAD!
BOUNTY!
$10,000,000 REWARD FOR CAT NINJA

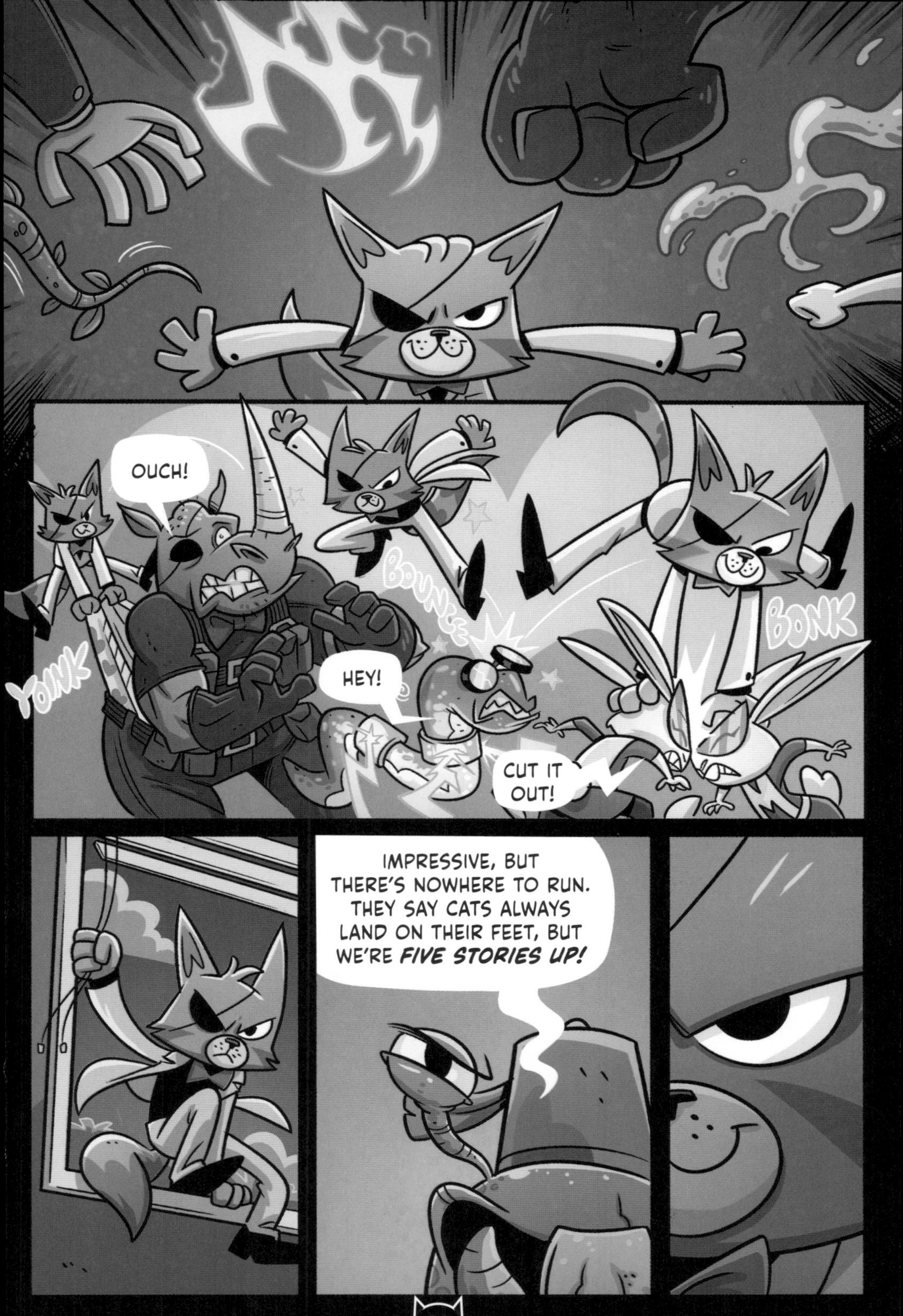
OUCH!
YOINK
BOUNCE
BONK
HEY!
CUT IT OUT!
IMPRESSIVE, BUT THERE'S NOWHERE TO RUN. THEY SAY CATS ALWAYS LAND ON THEIR FEET, BUT WE'RE *FIVE STORIES UP!*

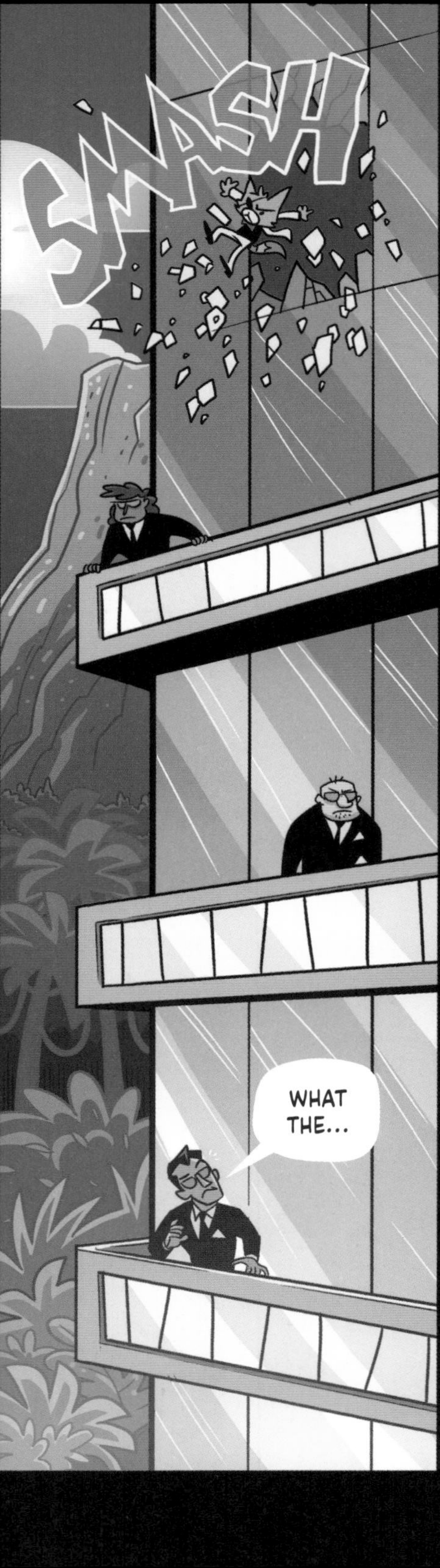
SMASH
WHAT THE...

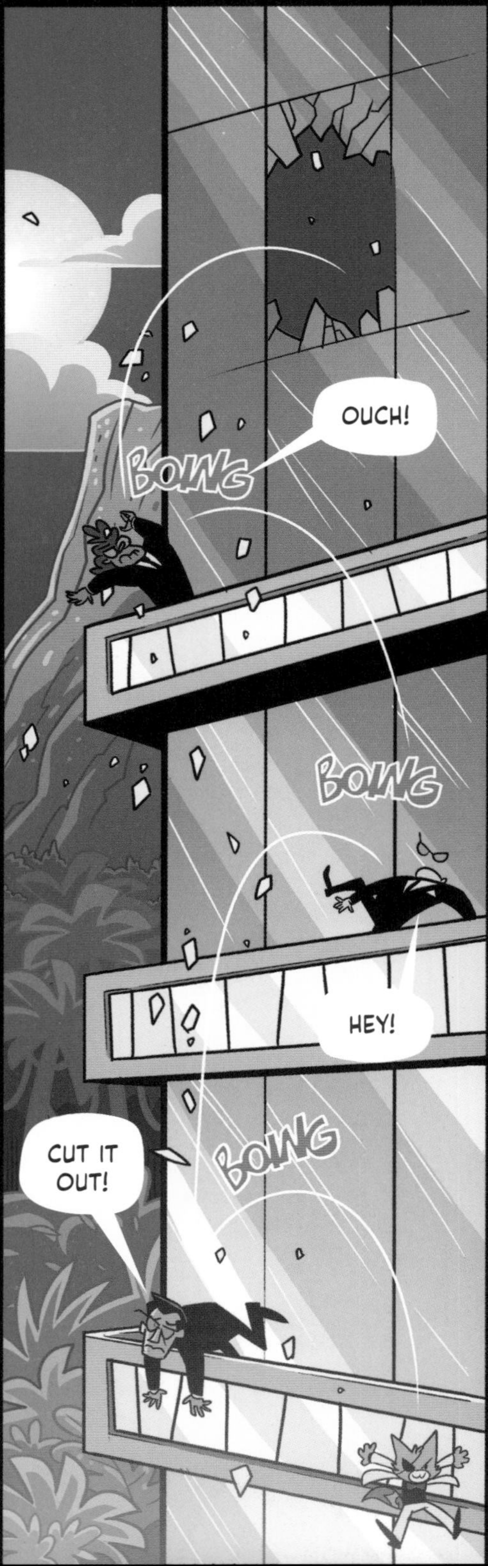
BOING
OUCH!
BOING
HEY!
BOING
CUT IT OUT!

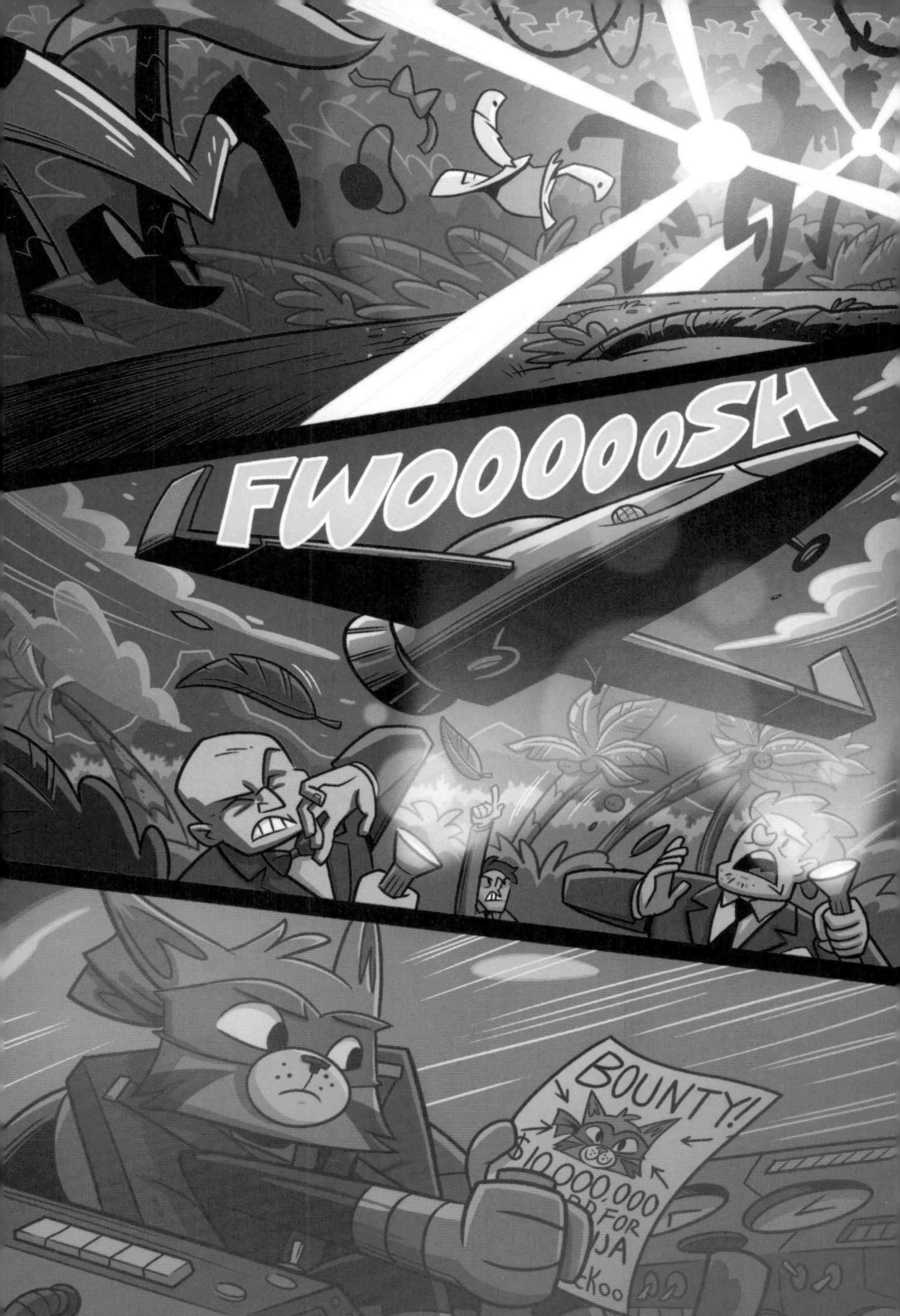
FWOOOOOOSH
BOUNTY!
$10,000,000
FOR

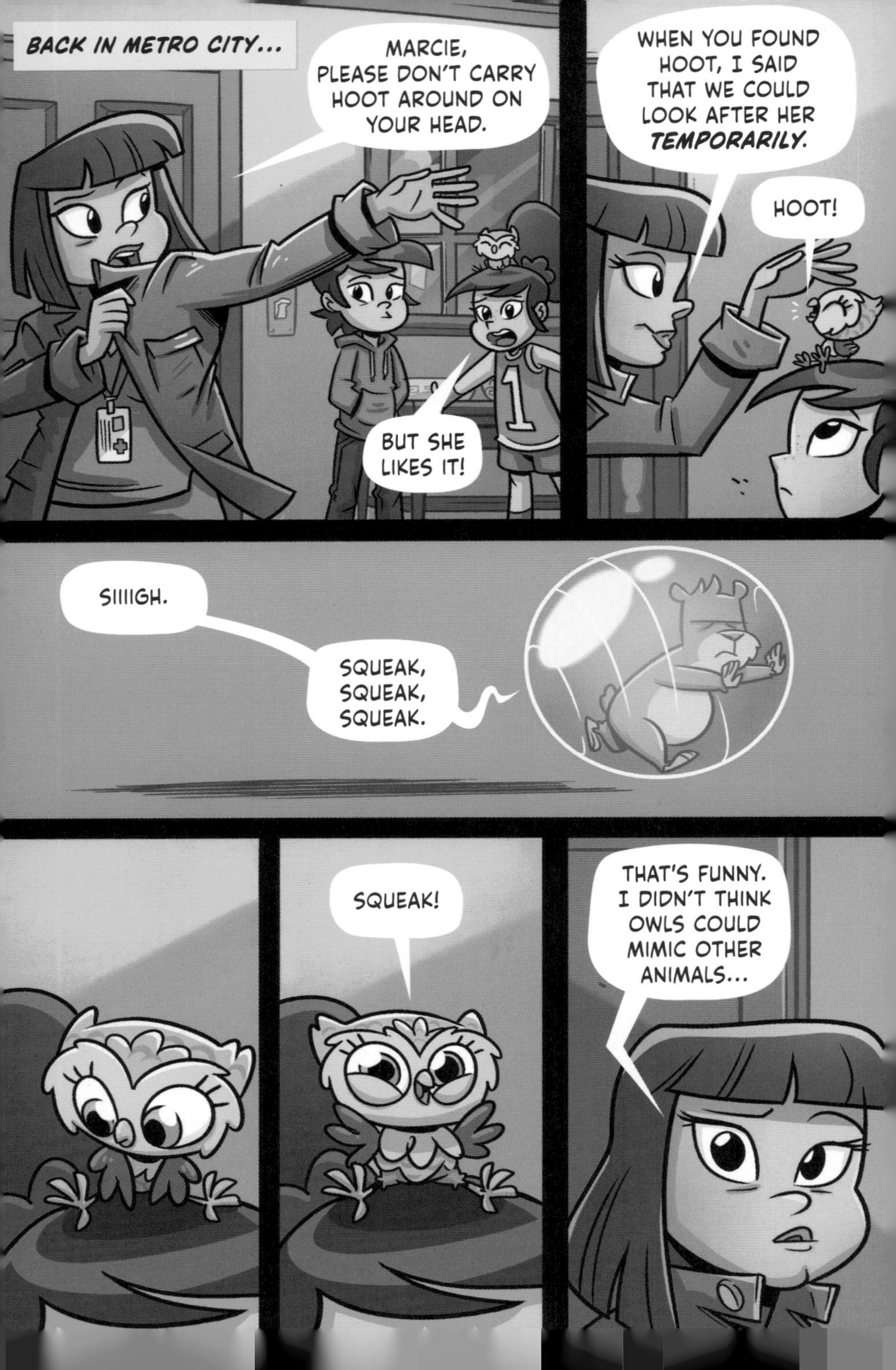
BACK IN METRO CITY...
MARCIE, PLEASE DON'T CARRY HOOT AROUND ON YOUR HEAD.
BUT SHE LIKES IT!
WHEN YOU FOUND HOOT, I SAID THAT WE COULD LOOK AFTER HER *TEMPORARILY.*
HOOT!
SIIIIGH.
SQUEAK, SQUEAK, SQUEAK.
SQUEAK!
THAT'S FUNNY. I DIDN'T THINK OWLS COULD MIMIC OTHER ANIMALS...

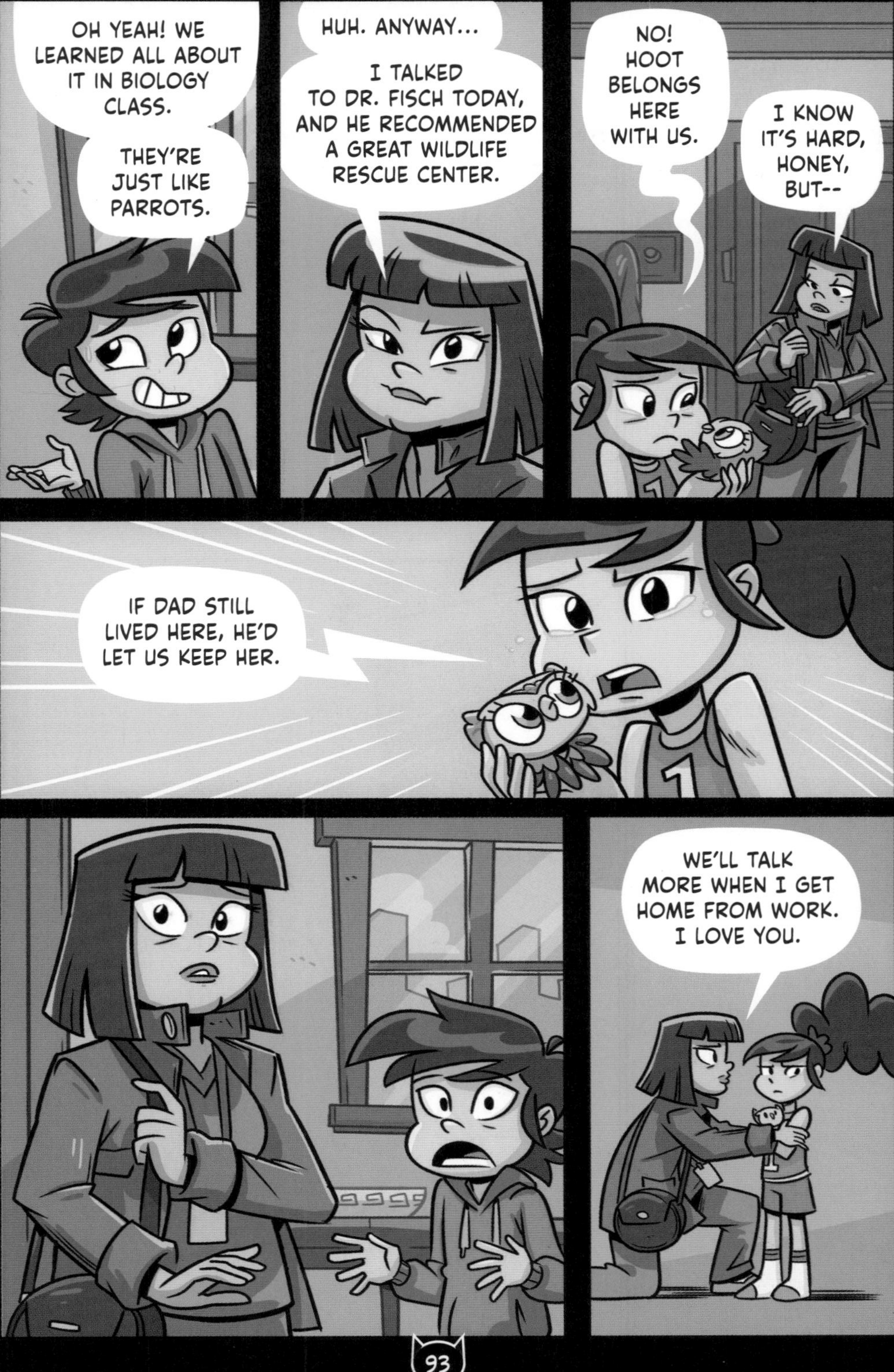
OH YEAH! WE LEARNED ALL ABOUT IT IN BIOLOGY CLASS.
THEY'RE JUST LIKE PARROTS.
HUH. ANYWAY...
I TALKED TO DR. FISCH TODAY, AND HE RECOMMENDED A GREAT WILDLIFE RESCUE CENTER.
NO! HOOT BELONGS HERE WITH US.
I KNOW IT'S HARD, HONEY, BUT--
IF DAD STILL LIVED HERE, HE'D LET US KEEP HER.
WE'LL TALK MORE WHEN I GET HOME FROM WORK. I LOVE YOU.

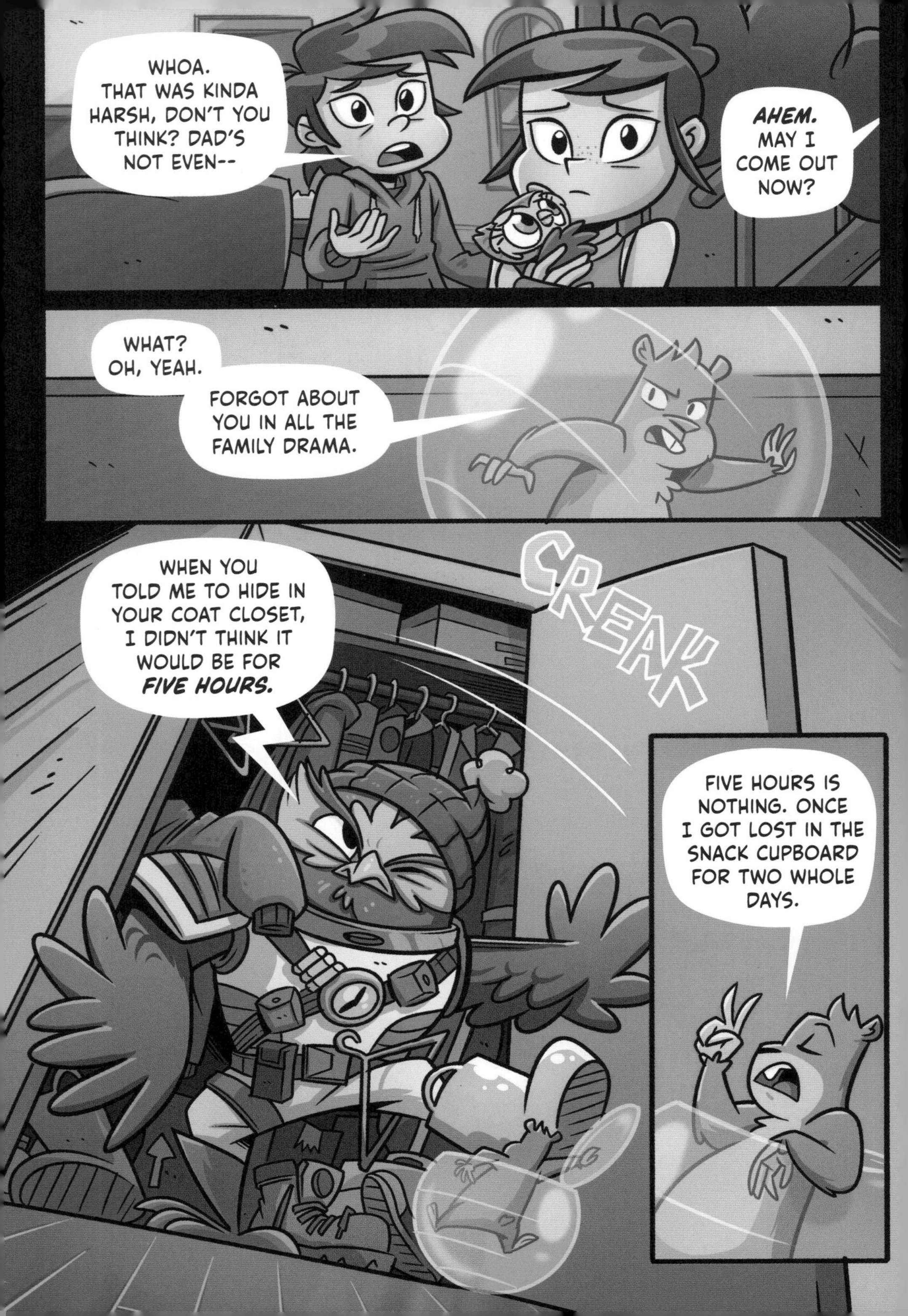
WHOA. THAT WAS KINDA HARSH, DON'T YOU THINK? DAD'S NOT EVEN--
AHEM. MAY I COME OUT NOW?
WHAT? OH, YEAH.
FORGOT ABOUT YOU IN ALL THE FAMILY DRAMA.
CREAK
WHEN YOU TOLD ME TO HIDE IN YOUR COAT CLOSET, I DIDN'T THINK IT WOULD BE FOR ***FIVE HOURS.***
FIVE HOURS IS NOTHING. ONCE I GOT LOST IN THE SNACK CUPBOARD FOR TWO WHOLE DAYS.

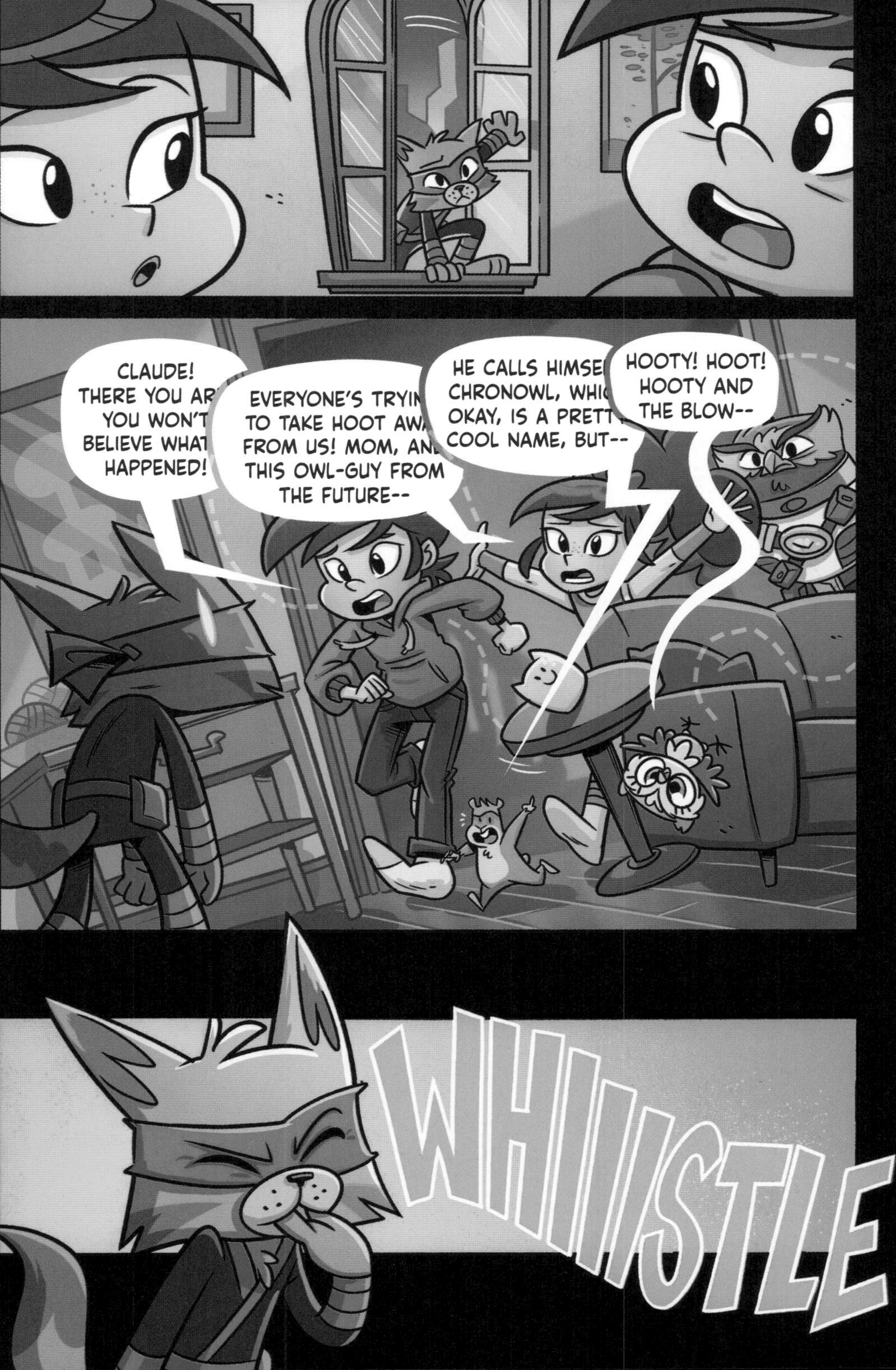

CLAUDE! THERE YOU AR YOU WON'T BELIEVE WHAT HAPPENED!
EVERYONE'S TRYIN TO TAKE HOOT AWA FROM US! MOM, AN THIS OWL-GUY FROM THE FUTURE--
HE CALLS HIMSE CHRONOWL, WHI OKAY, IS A PRETT COOL NAME, BUT--
HOOTY! HOOT! HOOTY AND THE BLOW--
WHIIISTLE

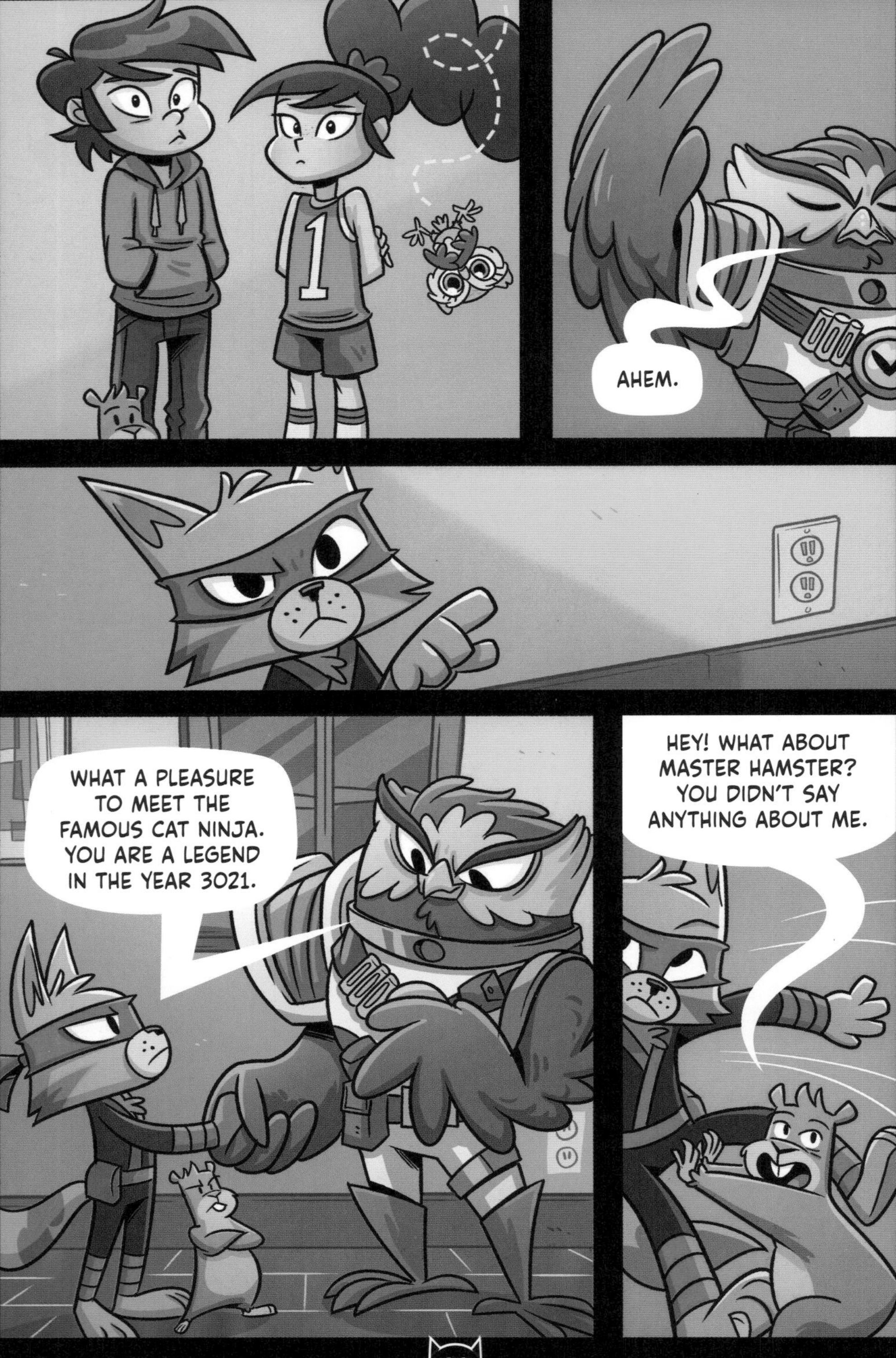
AHEM.
WHAT A PLEASURE TO MEET THE FAMOUS CAT NINJA. YOU ARE A LEGEND IN THE YEAR 3021.
HEY! WHAT ABOUT MASTER HAMSTER? YOU DIDN'T SAY ANYTHING ABOUT ME.

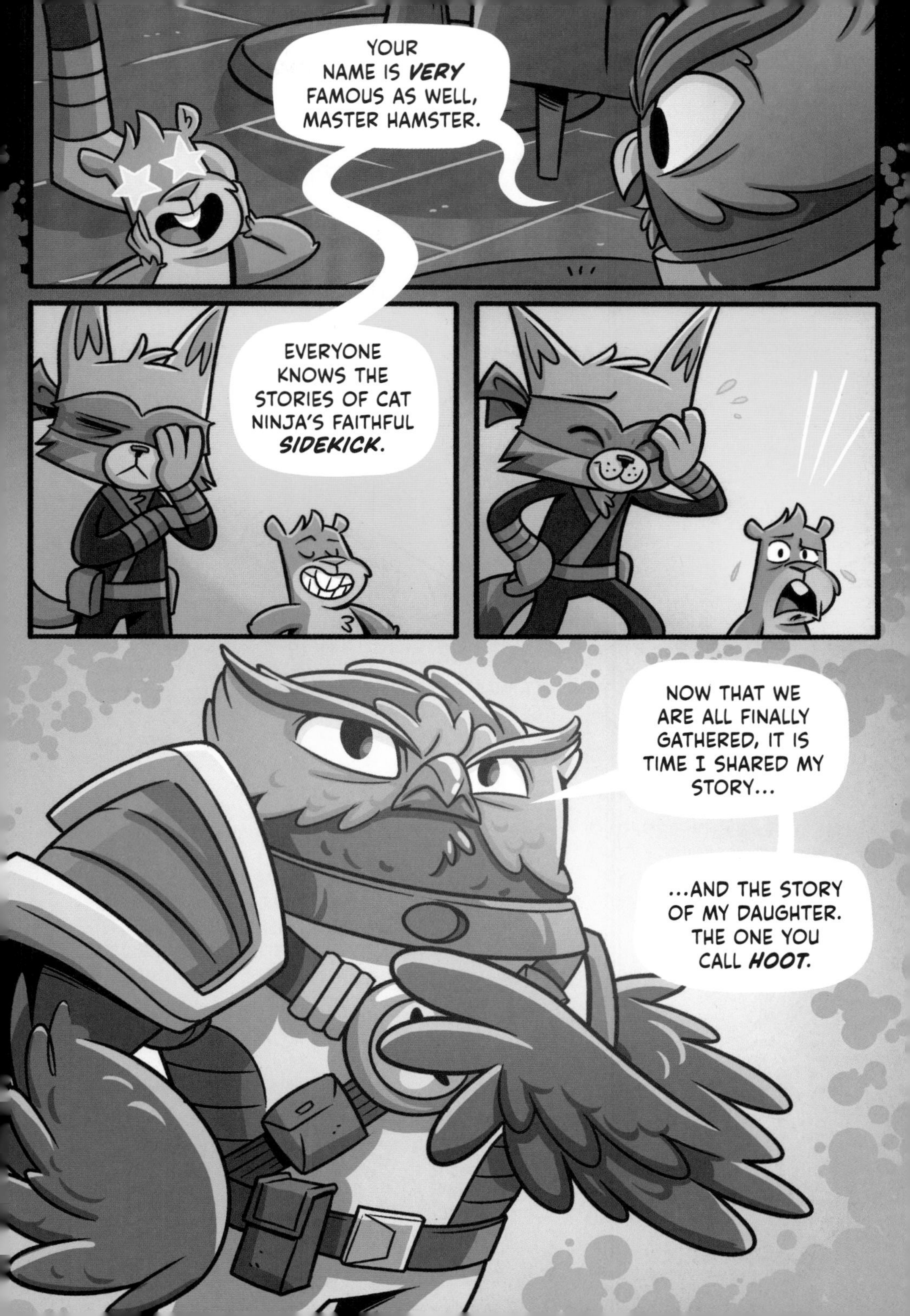
YOUR NAME IS *VERY* FAMOUS AS WELL, MASTER HAMSTER.
EVERYONE KNOWS THE STORIES OF CAT NINJA'S FAITHFUL ***SIDEKICK***.
NOW THAT WE ARE ALL FINALLY GATHERED, IT IS TIME I SHARED MY STORY...
...AND THE STORY OF MY DAUGHTER. THE ONE YOU CALL ***HOOT***.

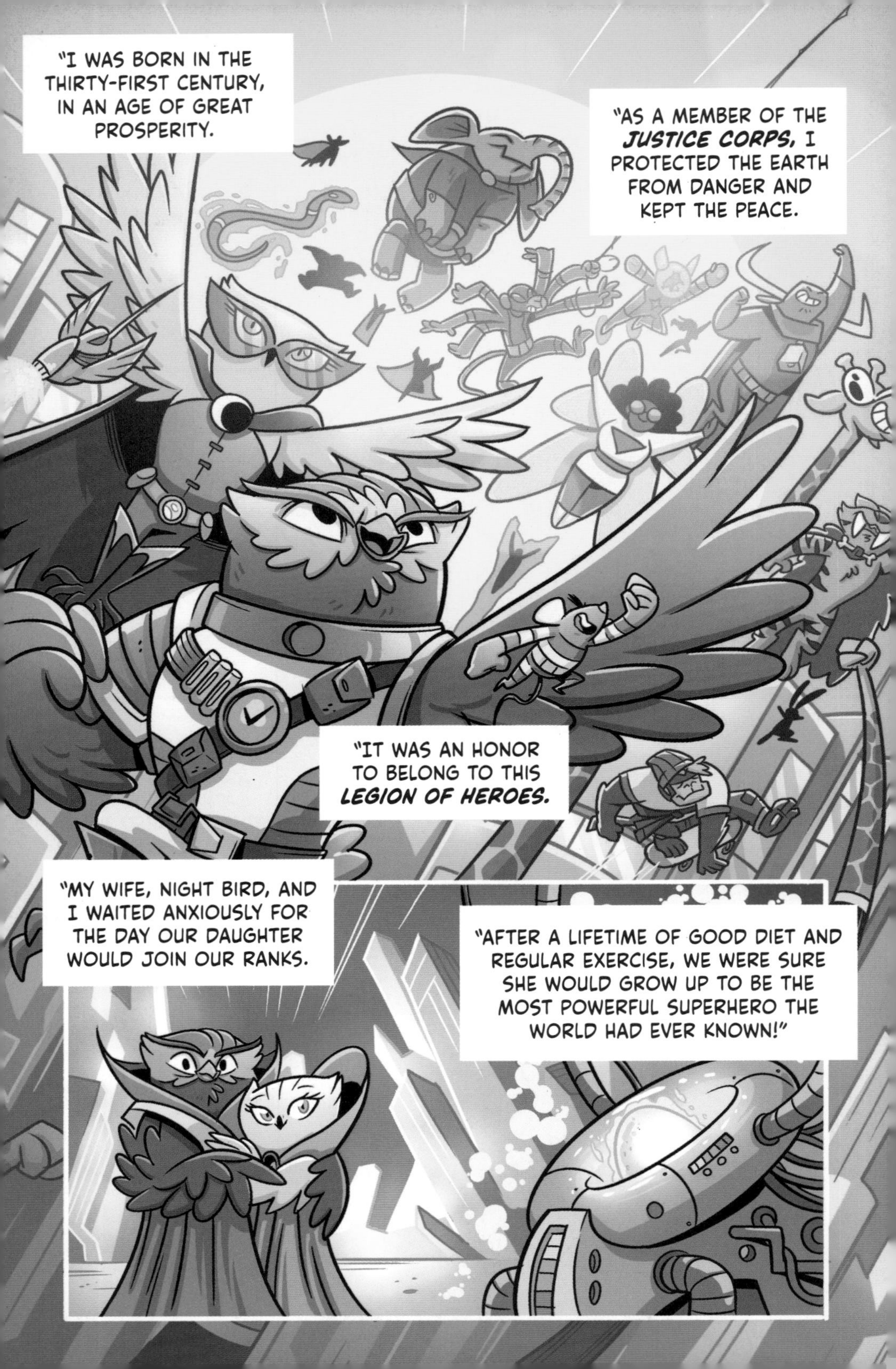
"I WAS BORN IN THE THIRTY-FIRST CENTURY, IN AN AGE OF GREAT PROSPERITY.
"AS A MEMBER OF THE ***JUSTICE CORPS,*** I PROTECTED THE EARTH FROM DANGER AND KEPT THE PEACE.
"IT WAS AN HONOR TO BELONG TO THIS ***LEGION OF HEROES.***
"MY WIFE, NIGHT BIRD, AND I WAITED ANXIOUSLY FOR THE DAY OUR DAUGHTER WOULD JOIN OUR RANKS.
"AFTER A LIFETIME OF GOOD DIET AND REGULAR EXERCISE, WE WERE SURE SHE WOULD GROW UP TO BE THE MOST POWERFUL SUPERHERO THE WORLD HAD EVER KNOWN!"

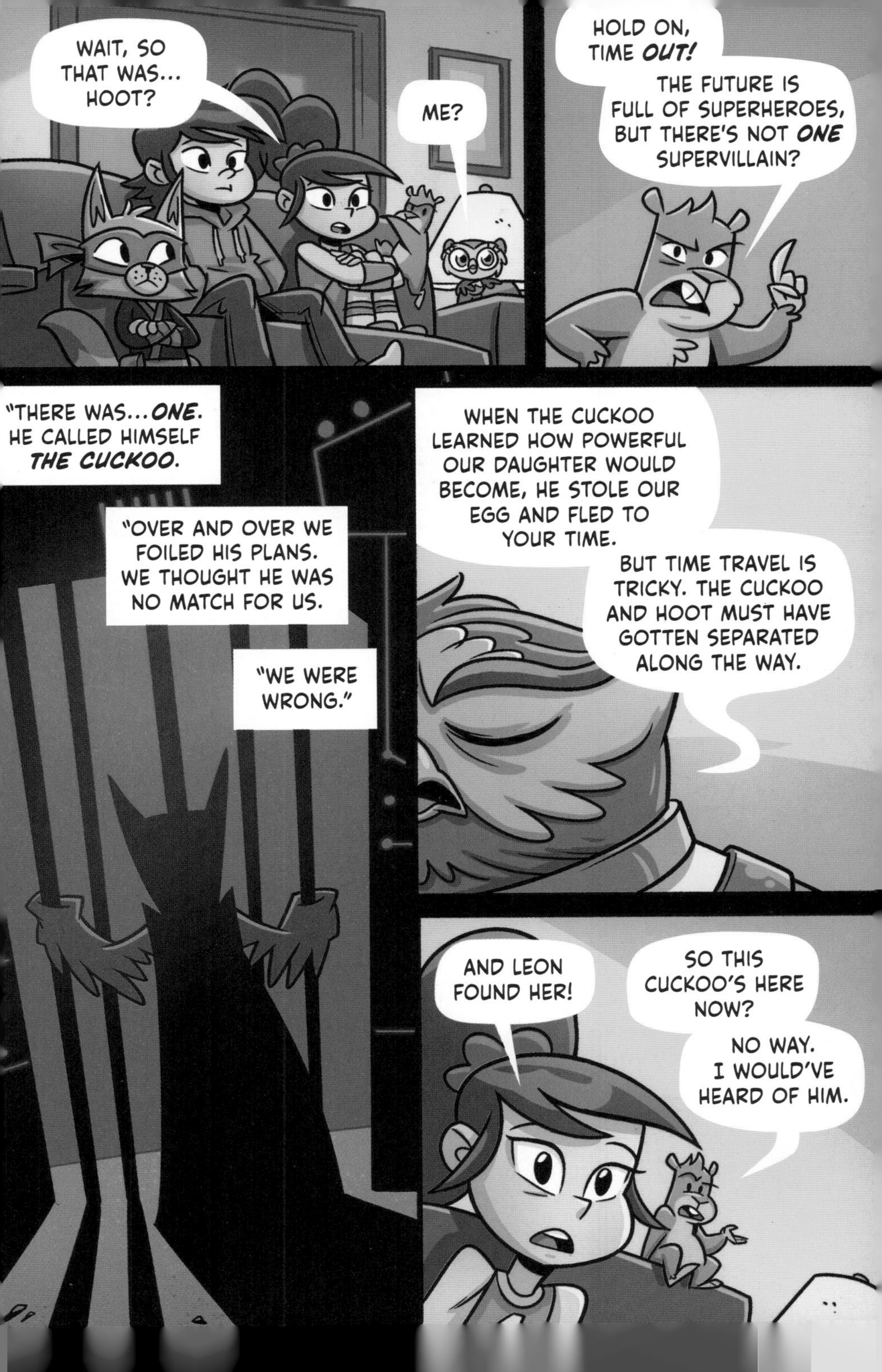
WAIT, SO THAT WAS... HOOT?
ME?
HOLD ON, TIME *OUT!*
THE FUTURE IS FULL OF SUPERHEROES, BUT THERE'S NOT *ONE* SUPERVILLAIN?
"THERE WAS...*ONE*. HE CALLED HIMSELF ***THE CUCKOO***.
"OVER AND OVER WE FOILED HIS PLANS. WE THOUGHT HE WAS NO MATCH FOR US.
"WE WERE WRONG."
WHEN THE CUCKOO LEARNED HOW POWERFUL OUR DAUGHTER WOULD BECOME, HE STOLE OUR EGG AND FLED TO YOUR TIME.
BUT TIME TRAVEL IS TRICKY. THE CUCKOO AND HOOT MUST HAVE GOTTEN SEPARATED ALONG THE WAY.
AND LEON FOUND HER!
SO THIS CUCKOO'S HERE NOW?
NO WAY. I WOULD'VE HEARD OF HIM.

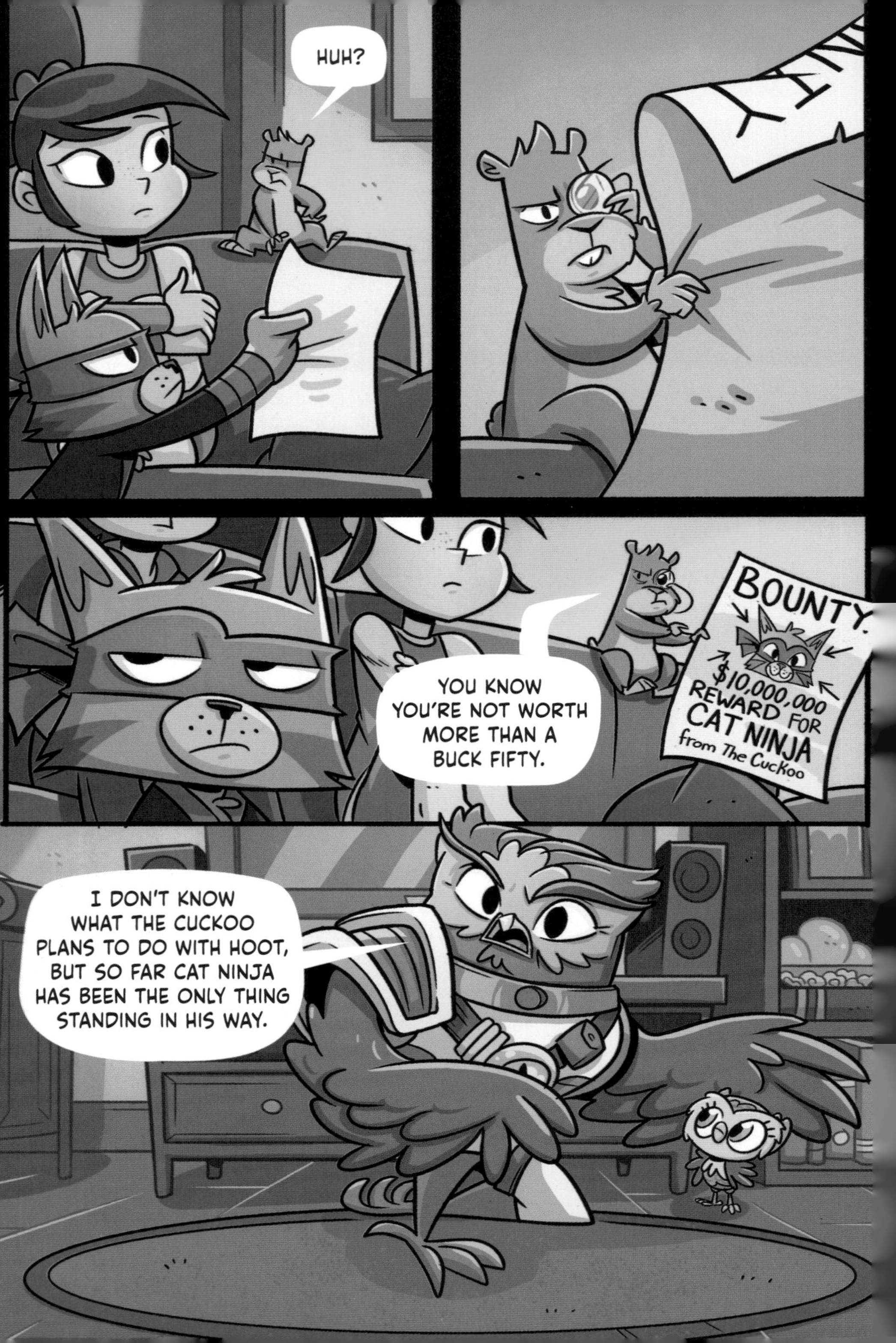
HUH?
YOU KNOW YOU'RE NOT WORTH MORE THAN A BUCK FIFTY.
BOUNTY
$10,000,000 REWARD FOR CAT NINJA
from The Cuckoo
I DON'T KNOW WHAT THE CUCKOO PLANS TO DO WITH HOOT, BUT SO FAR CAT NINJA HAS BEEN THE ONLY THING STANDING IN HIS WAY.

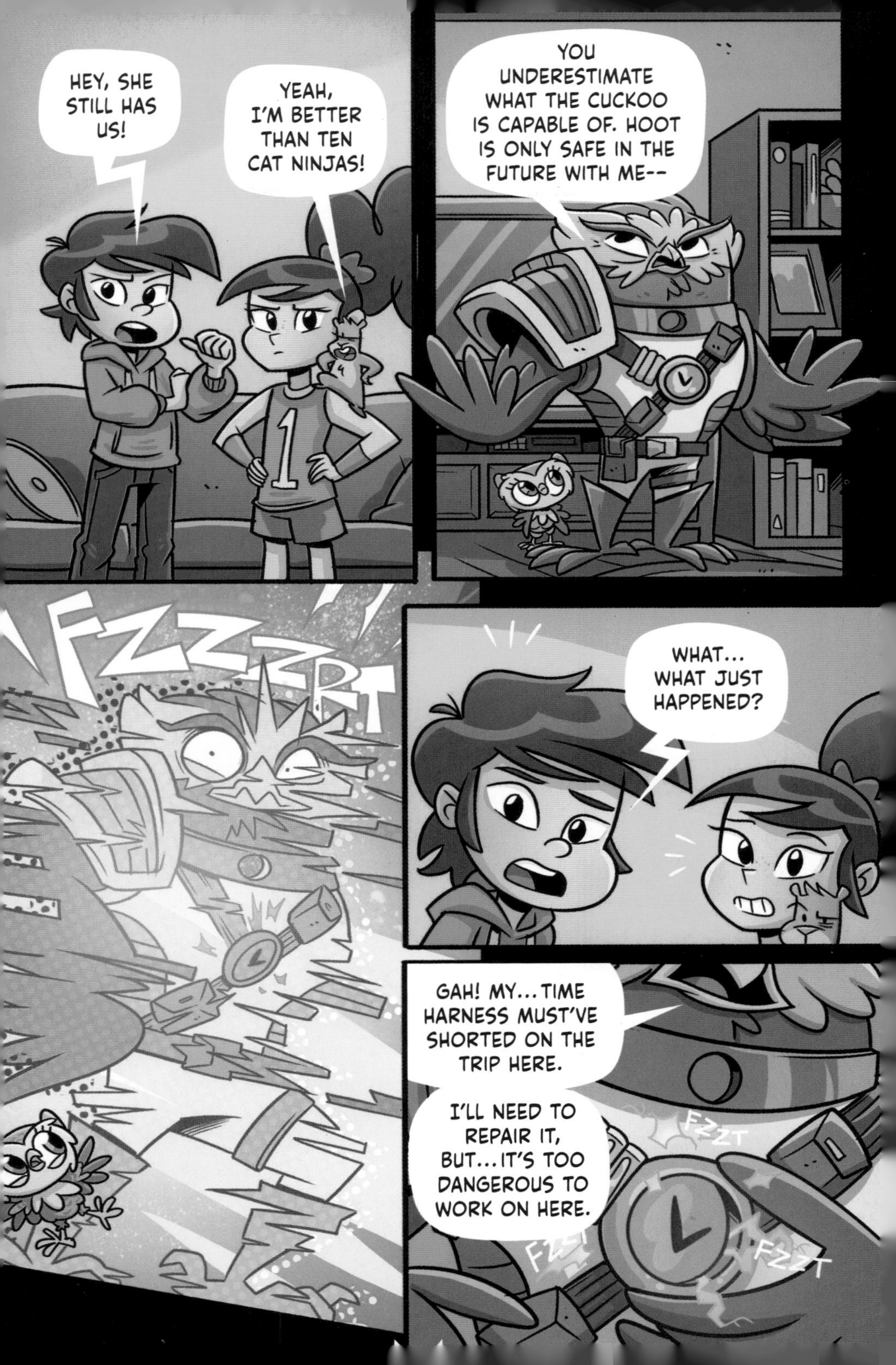
HEY, SHE STILL HAS US!
YEAH, I'M BETTER THAN TEN CAT NINJAS!
YOU UNDERESTIMATE WHAT THE CUCKOO IS CAPABLE OF. HOOT IS ONLY SAFE IN THE FUTURE WITH ME--
FZZZZRT
WHAT... WHAT JUST HAPPENED?
GAH! MY...TIME HARNESS MUST'VE SHORTED ON THE TRIP HERE.
I'LL NEED TO REPAIR IT, BUT...IT'S TOO DANGEROUS TO WORK ON HERE.
FZZT
FZZT
FZZT

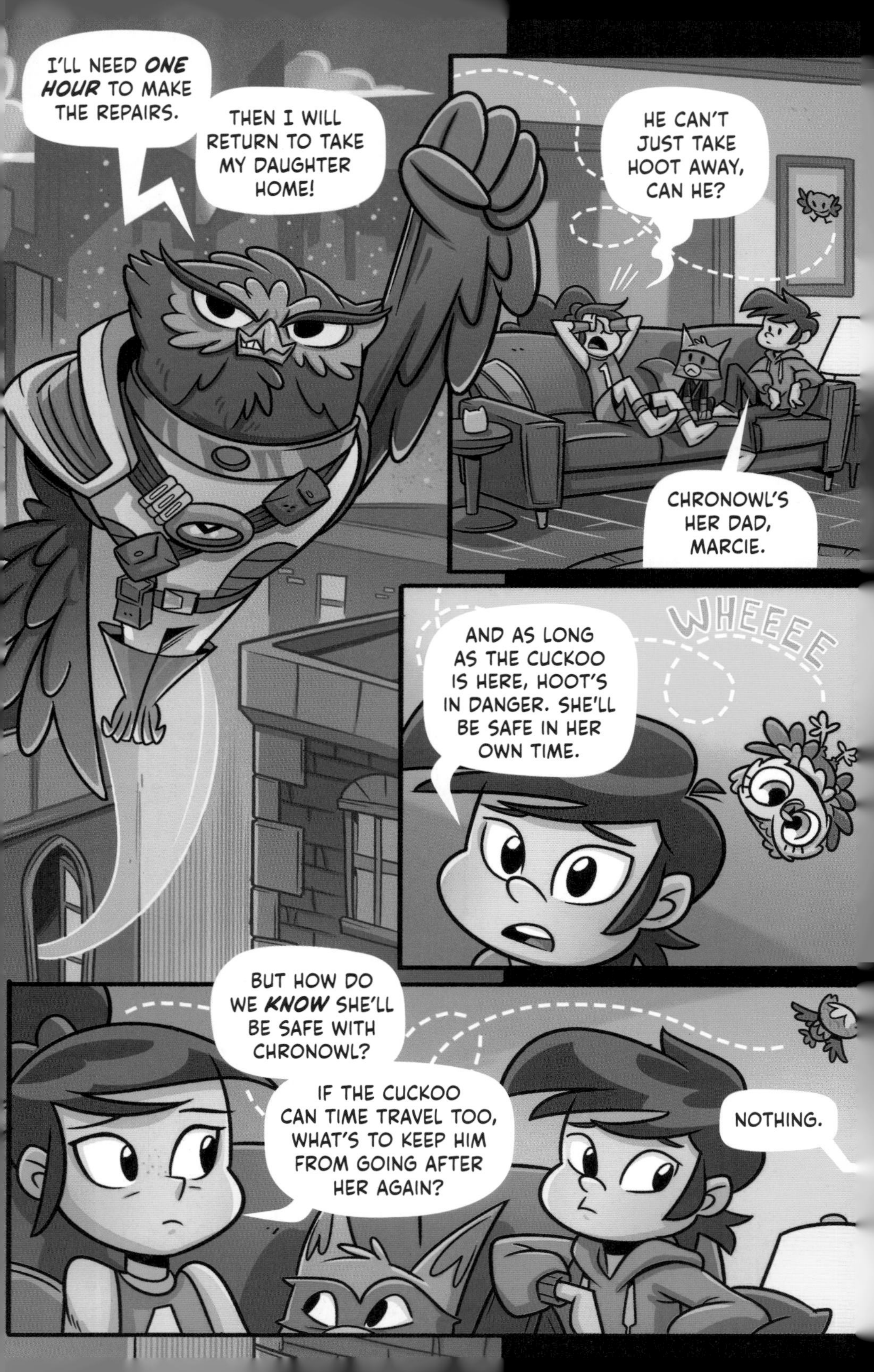
I'LL NEED ONE HOUR TO MAKE THE REPAIRS.
THEN I WILL RETURN TO TAKE MY DAUGHTER HOME!
HE CAN'T JUST TAKE HOOT AWAY, CAN HE?
CHRONOWL'S HER DAD, MARCIE.
WHEEEE
AND AS LONG AS THE CUCKOO IS HERE, HOOT'S IN DANGER. SHE'LL BE SAFE IN HER OWN TIME.
BUT HOW DO WE KNOW SHE'LL BE SAFE WITH CHRONOWL?
IF THE CUCKOO CAN TIME TRAVEL TOO, WHAT'S TO KEEP HIM FROM GOING AFTER HER AGAIN?
NOTHING.

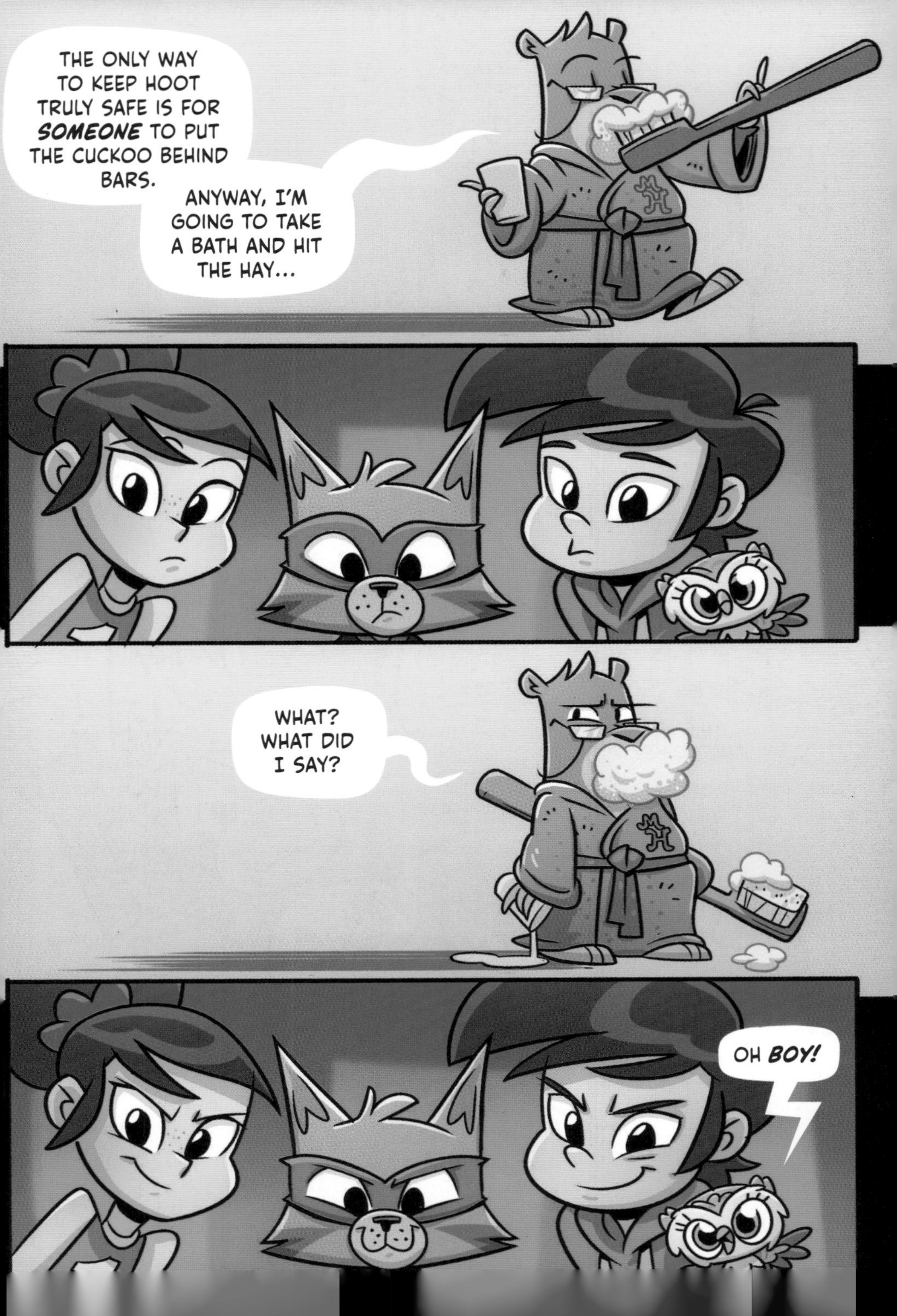

THE ONLY WAY TO KEEP HOOT TRULY SAFE IS FOR ***SOMEONE*** TO PUT THE CUCKOO BEHIND BARS.
ANYWAY, I'M GOING TO TAKE A BATH AND HIT THE HAY...
WHAT? WHAT DID I SAY?
OH ***BOY!***

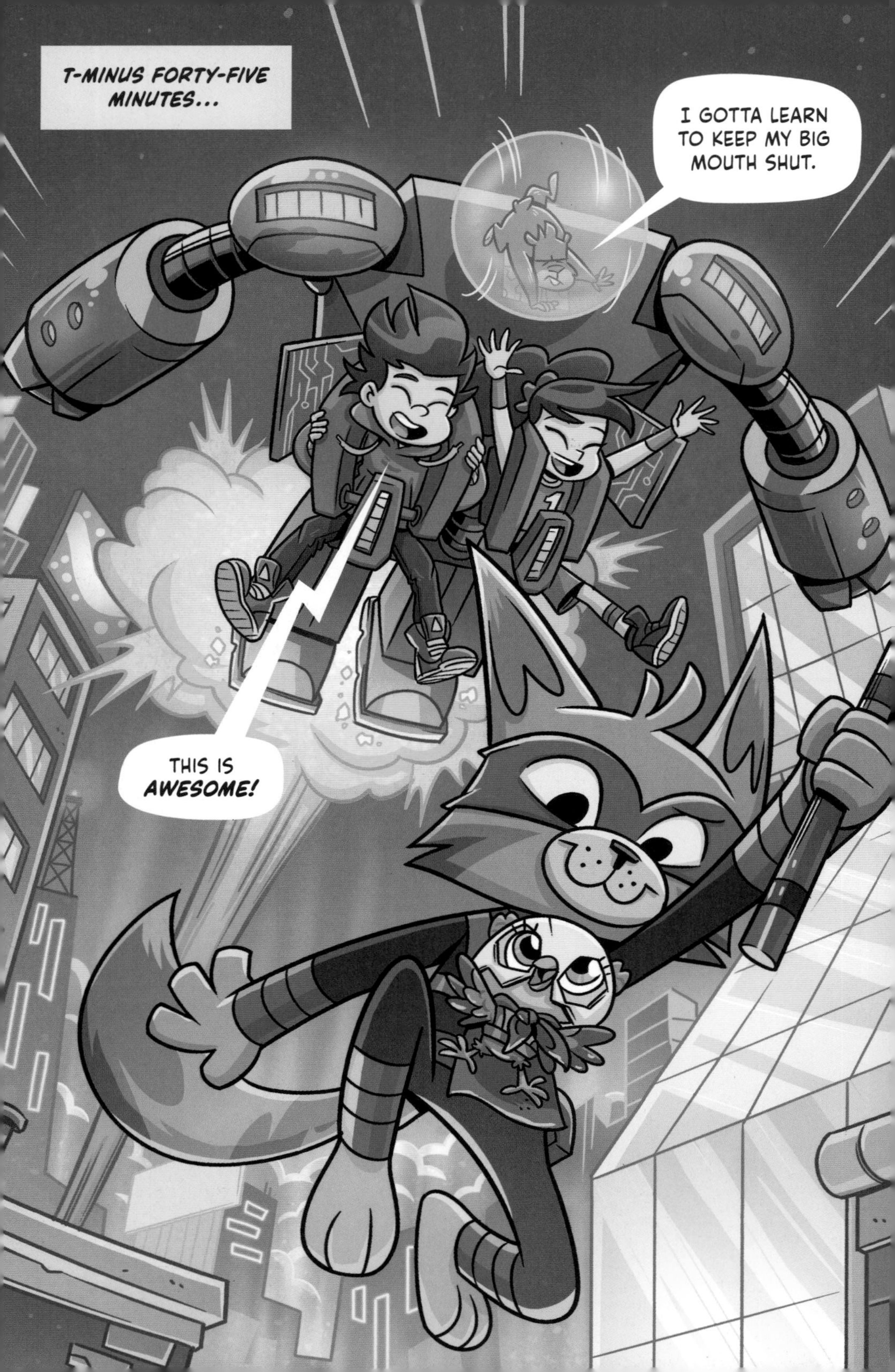
T-MINUS FORTY-FIVE MINUTES...
I GOTTA LEARN TO KEEP MY BIG MOUTH SHUT.
THIS IS AWESOME!

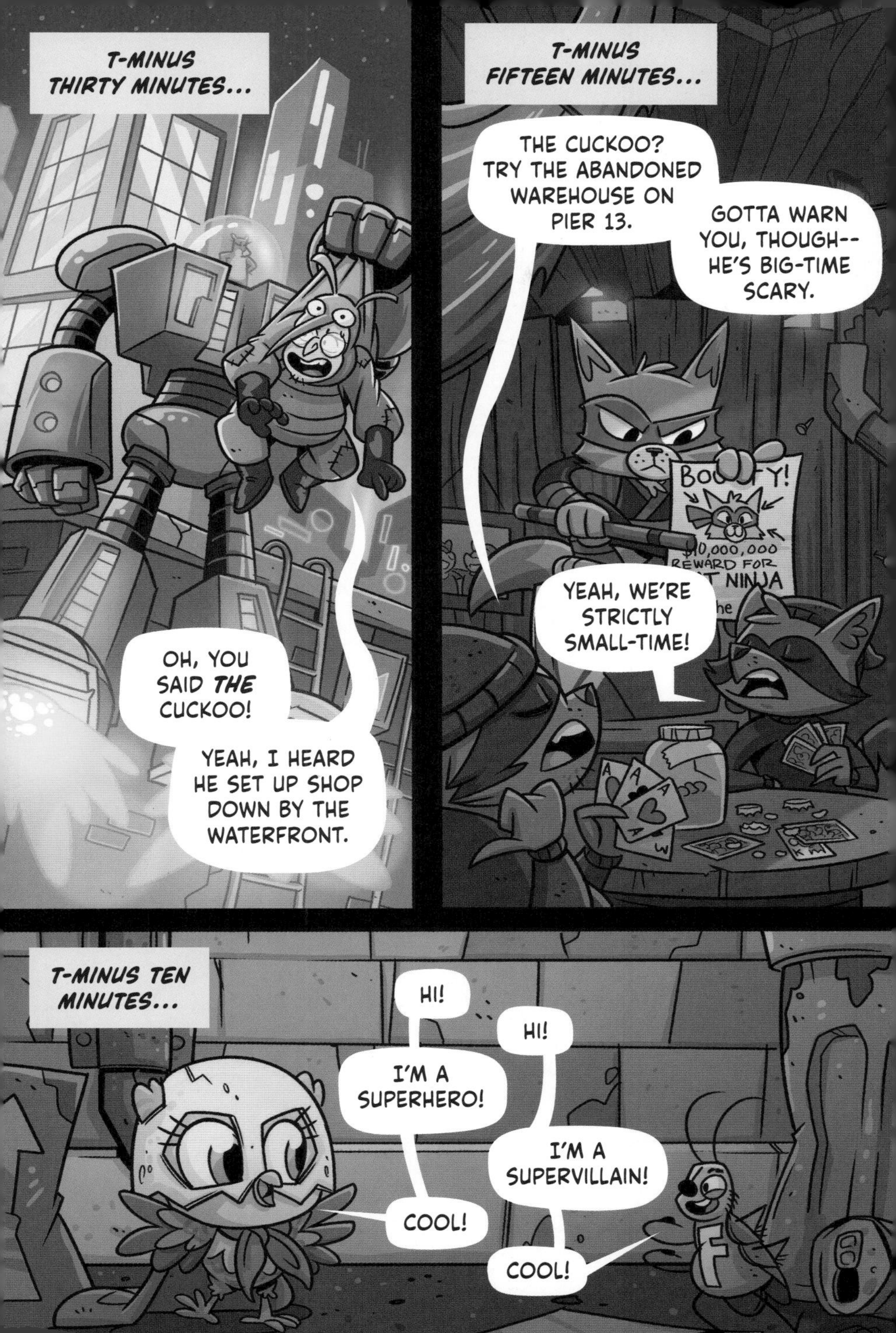
T-MINUS THIRTY MINUTES...
OH, YOU SAID *THE* CUCKOO!
YEAH, I HEARD HE SET UP SHOP DOWN BY THE WATERFRONT.
T-MINUS FIFTEEN MINUTES...
THE CUCKOO? TRY THE ABANDONED WAREHOUSE ON PIER 13.
GOTTA WARN YOU, THOUGH-- HE'S BIG-TIME SCARY.
$10,000,000
REWARD FOR
YEAH, WE'RE STRICTLY SMALL-TIME!
T-MINUS TEN MINUTES...
HI!
I'M A SUPERHERO!
COOL!
HI!
I'M A SUPERVILLAIN!
COOL!

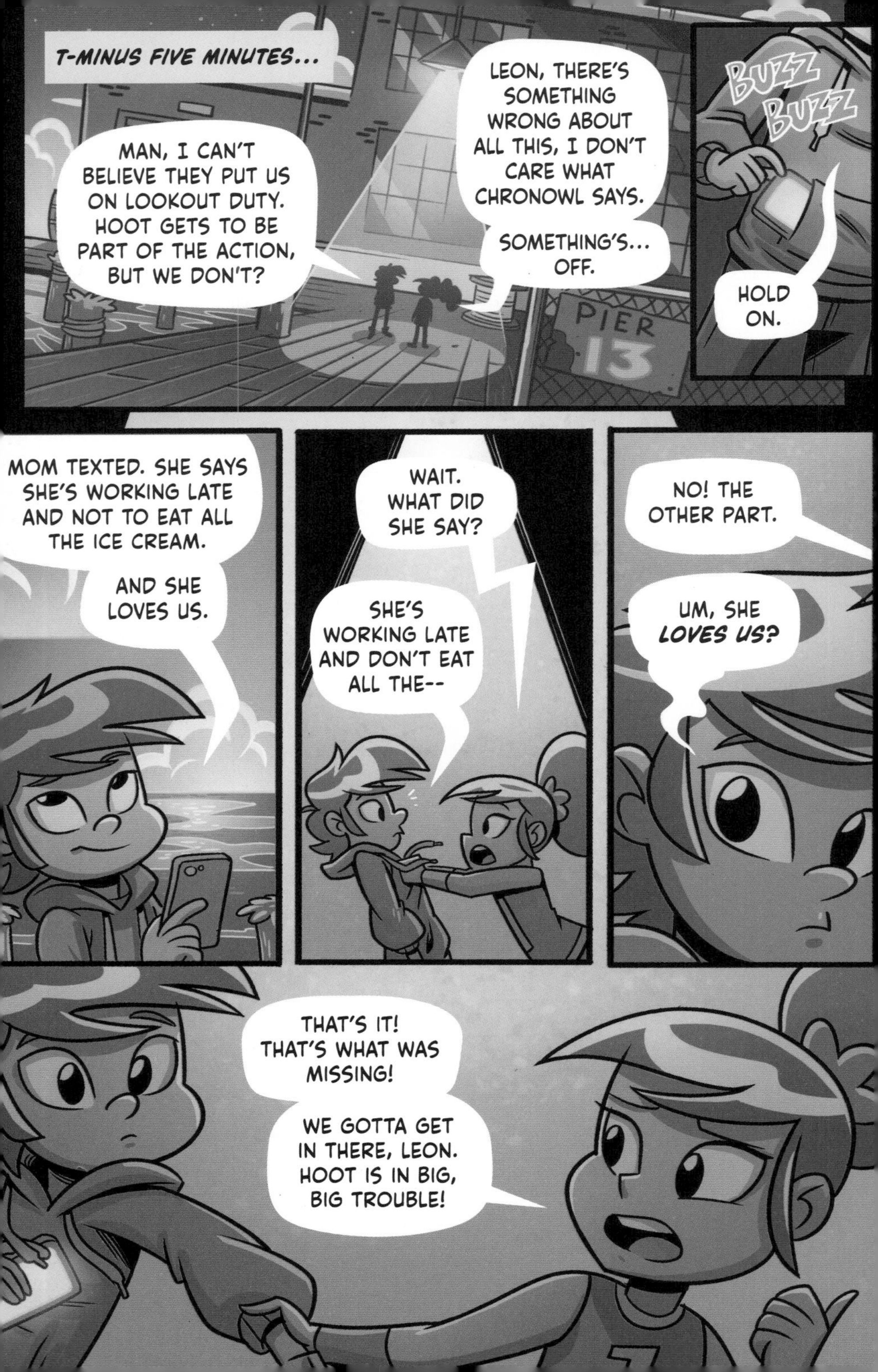
T-MINUS FIVE MINUTES...
MAN, I CAN'T BELIEVE THEY PUT US ON LOOKOUT DUTY. HOOT GETS TO BE PART OF THE ACTION, BUT WE DON'T?
LEON, THERE'S SOMETHING WRONG ABOUT ALL THIS, I DON'T CARE WHAT CHRONOWL SAYS.
SOMETHING'S... OFF.
PIER 13
BUZZ BUZZ
HOLD ON.
MOM TEXTED. SHE SAYS SHE'S WORKING LATE AND NOT TO EAT ALL THE ICE CREAM.
AND SHE LOVES US.
WAIT. WHAT DID SHE SAY?
SHE'S WORKING LATE AND DON'T EAT ALL THE--
NO! THE OTHER PART.
UM, SHE *LOVES US?*
THAT'S IT! THAT'S WHAT WAS MISSING!
WE GOTTA GET IN THERE, LEON. HOOT IS IN BIG, BIG TROUBLE!

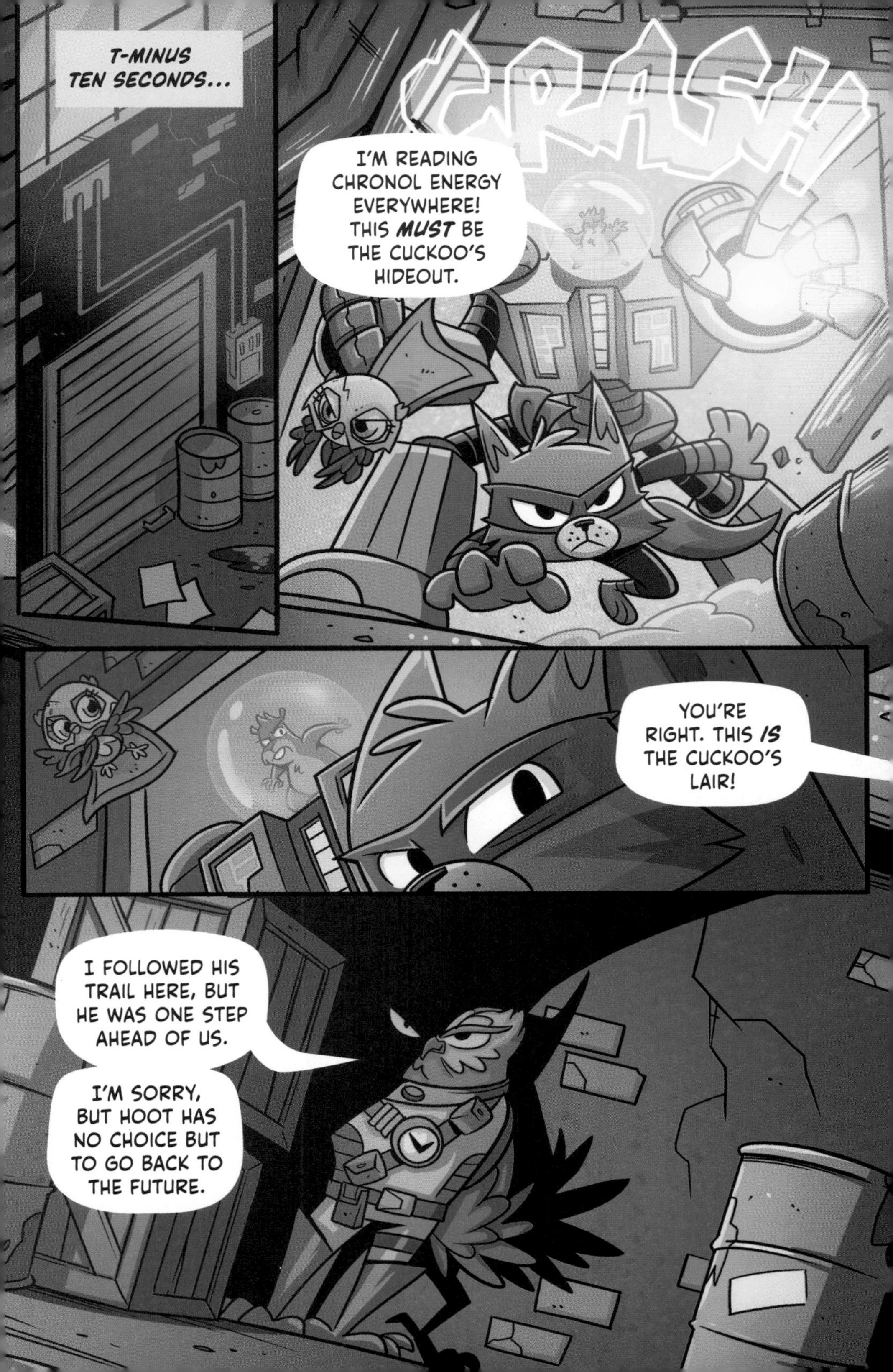
T-MINUS TEN SECONDS...
CRASH!
I'M READING CHRONOL ENERGY EVERYWHERE! THIS MUST BE THE CUCKOO'S HIDEOUT.
YOU'RE RIGHT. THIS IS THE CUCKOO'S LAIR!
I FOLLOWED HIS TRAIL HERE, BUT HE WAS ONE STEP AHEAD OF US.
I'M SORRY, BUT HOOT HAS NO CHOICE BUT TO GO BACK TO THE FUTURE.

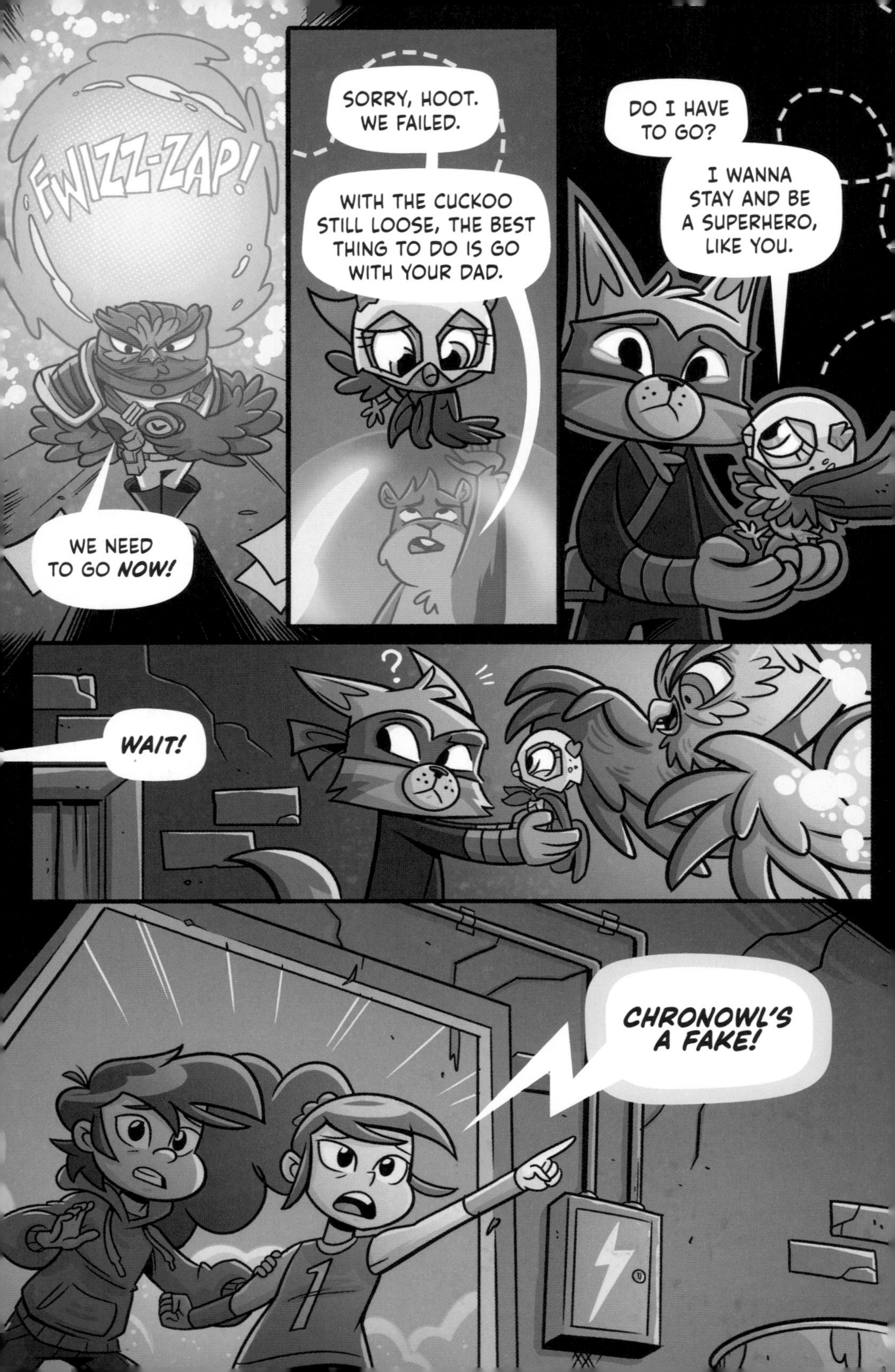
FWIZZ-ZAP!
WE NEED TO GO *NOW!*
SORRY, HOOT. WE FAILED.
WITH THE CUCKOO STILL LOOSE, THE BEST THING TO DO IS GO WITH YOUR DAD.
DO I HAVE TO GO?
I WANNA STAY AND BE A SUPERHERO, LIKE YOU.
?
WAIT!
CHRONOWL'S A FAKE!

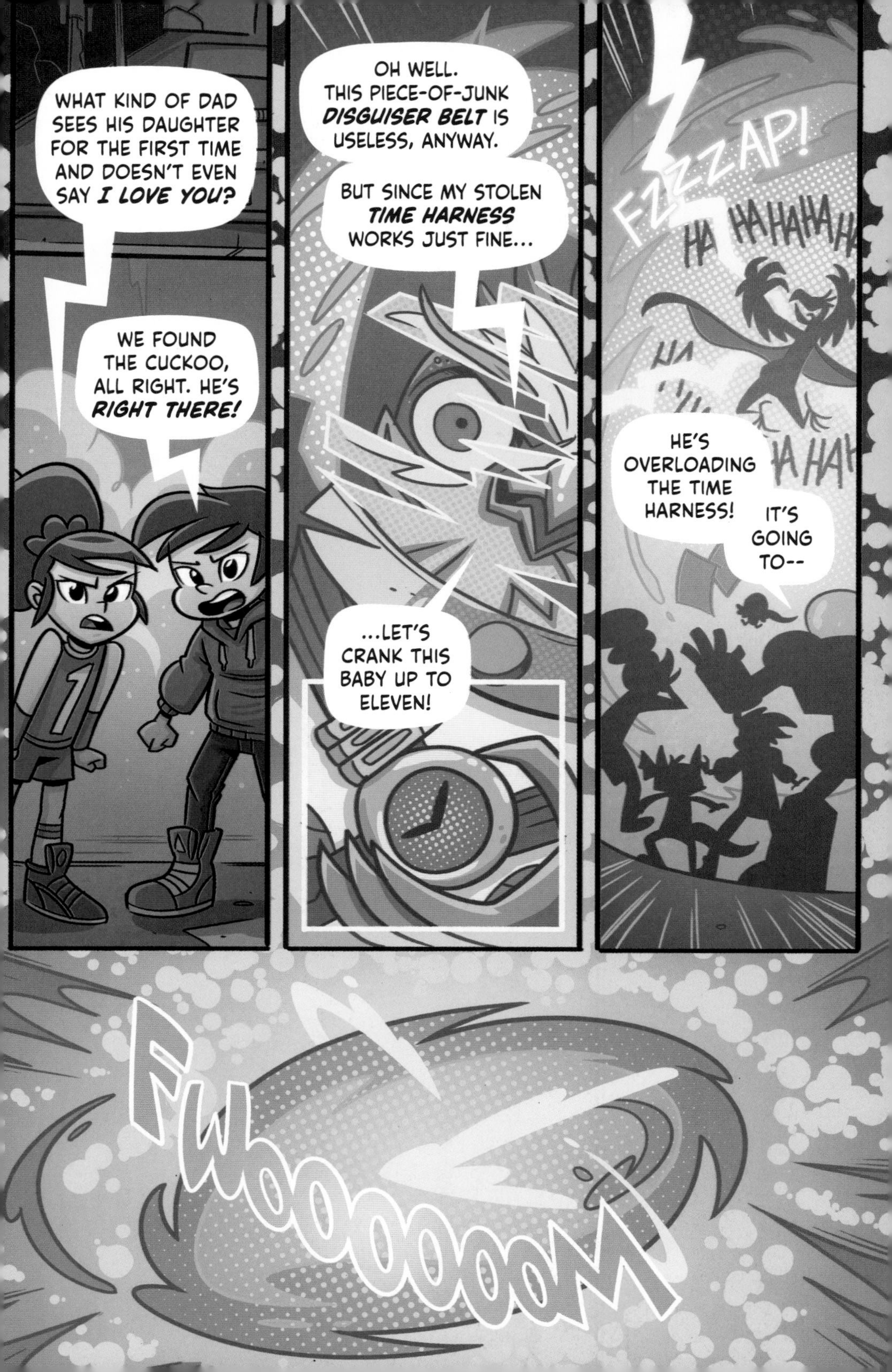
WHAT KIND OF DAD SEES HIS DAUGHTER FOR THE FIRST TIME AND DOESN'T EVEN SAY *I LOVE YOU?*
WE FOUND THE CUCKOO, ALL RIGHT. HE'S *RIGHT THERE!*
OH WELL. THIS PIECE-OF-JUNK *DISGUISER BELT* IS USELESS, ANYWAY.
BUT SINCE MY STOLEN *TIME HARNESS* WORKS JUST FINE...
...LET'S CRANK THIS BABY UP TO ELEVEN!
FZZZZAP!
HA HAHAHAH
HE'S OVERLOADING THE TIME HARNESS!
IT'S GOING TO--
FWOOOOOOM

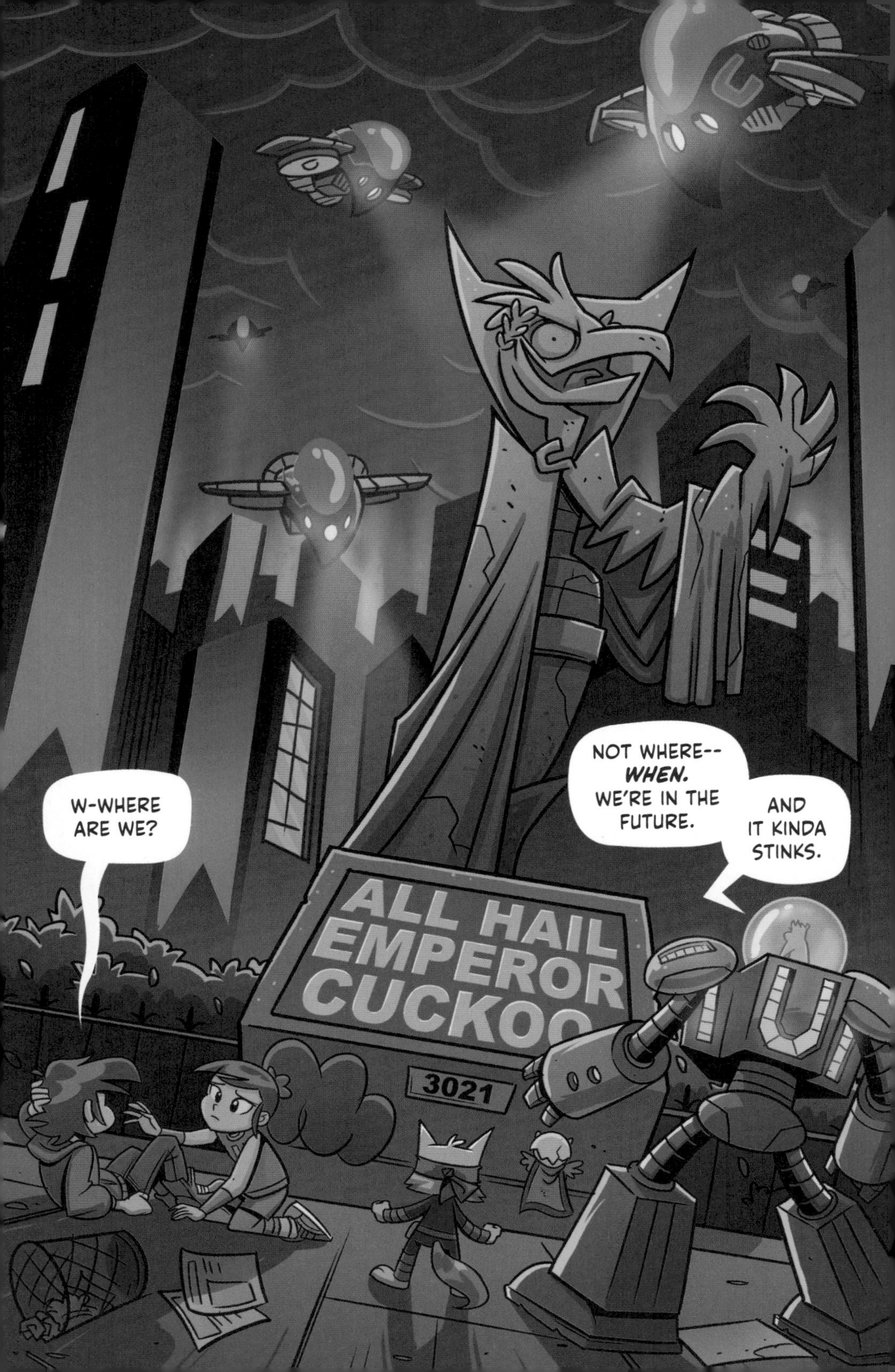
W-WHERE ARE WE?
NOT WHERE-- *WHEN.* WE'RE IN THE FUTURE.
AND IT KINDA STINKS.
ALL HAIL EMPEROR CUCKOO
3021

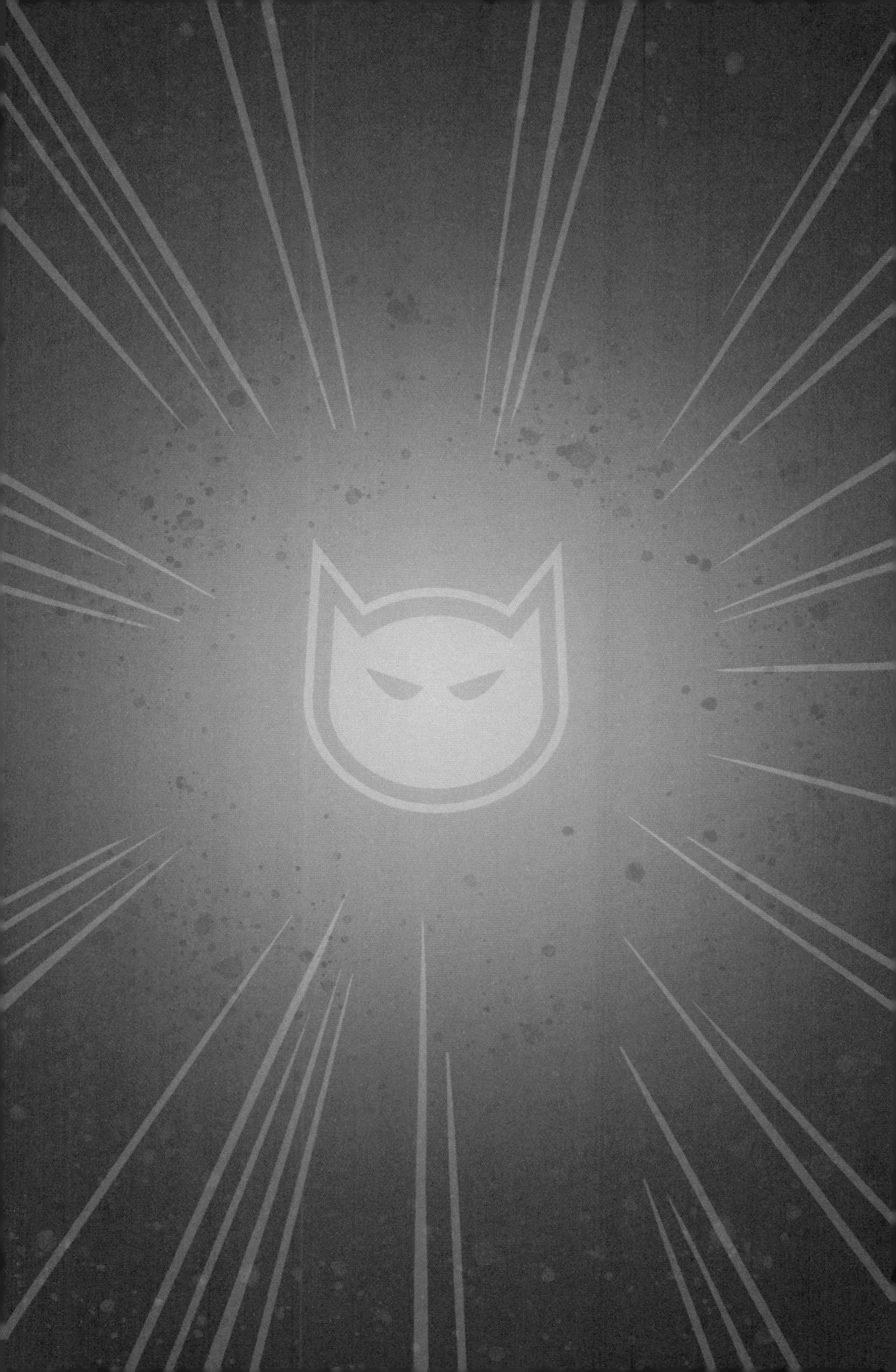

Chapter 5:
Escape from...the Future!

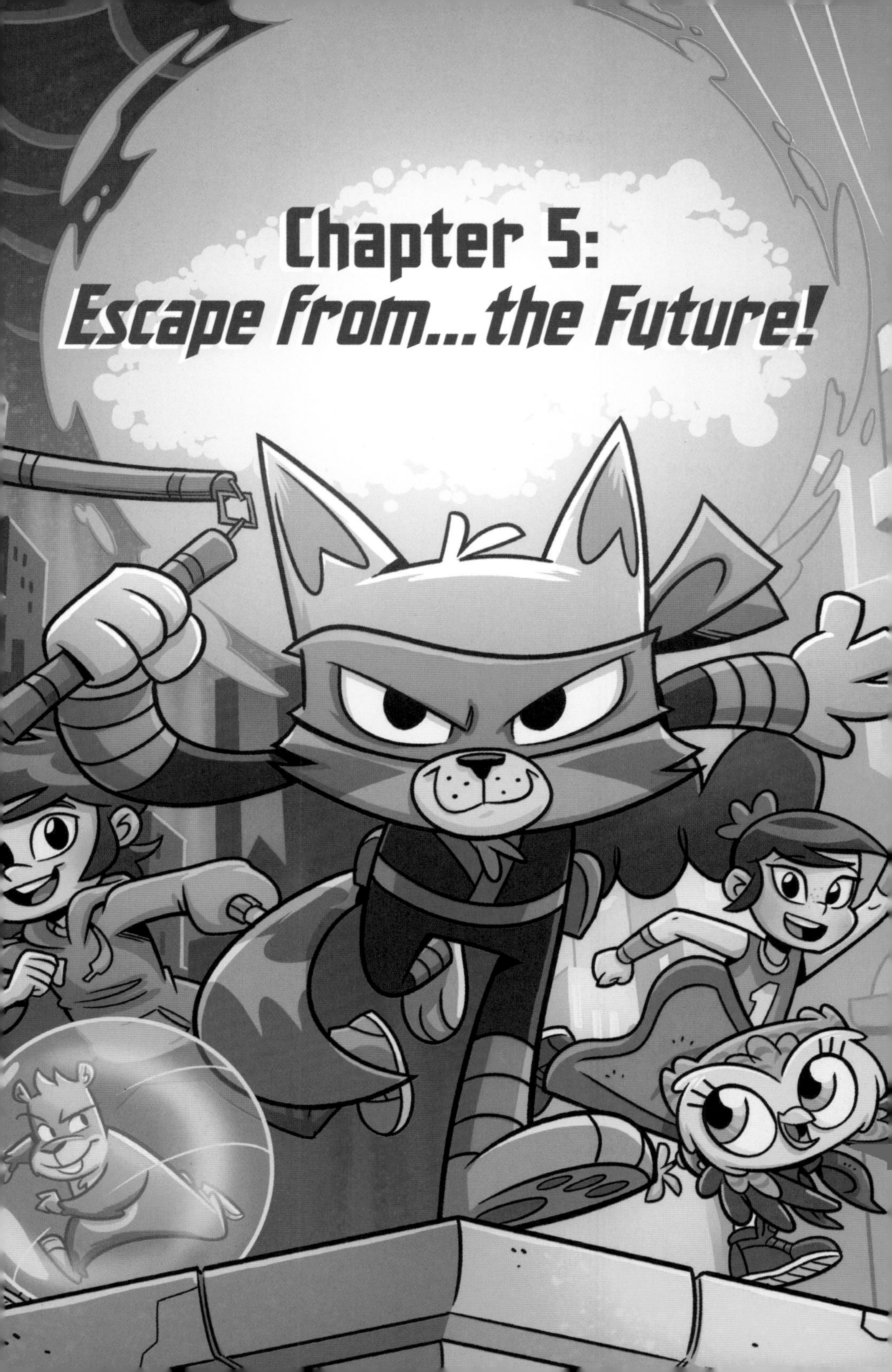

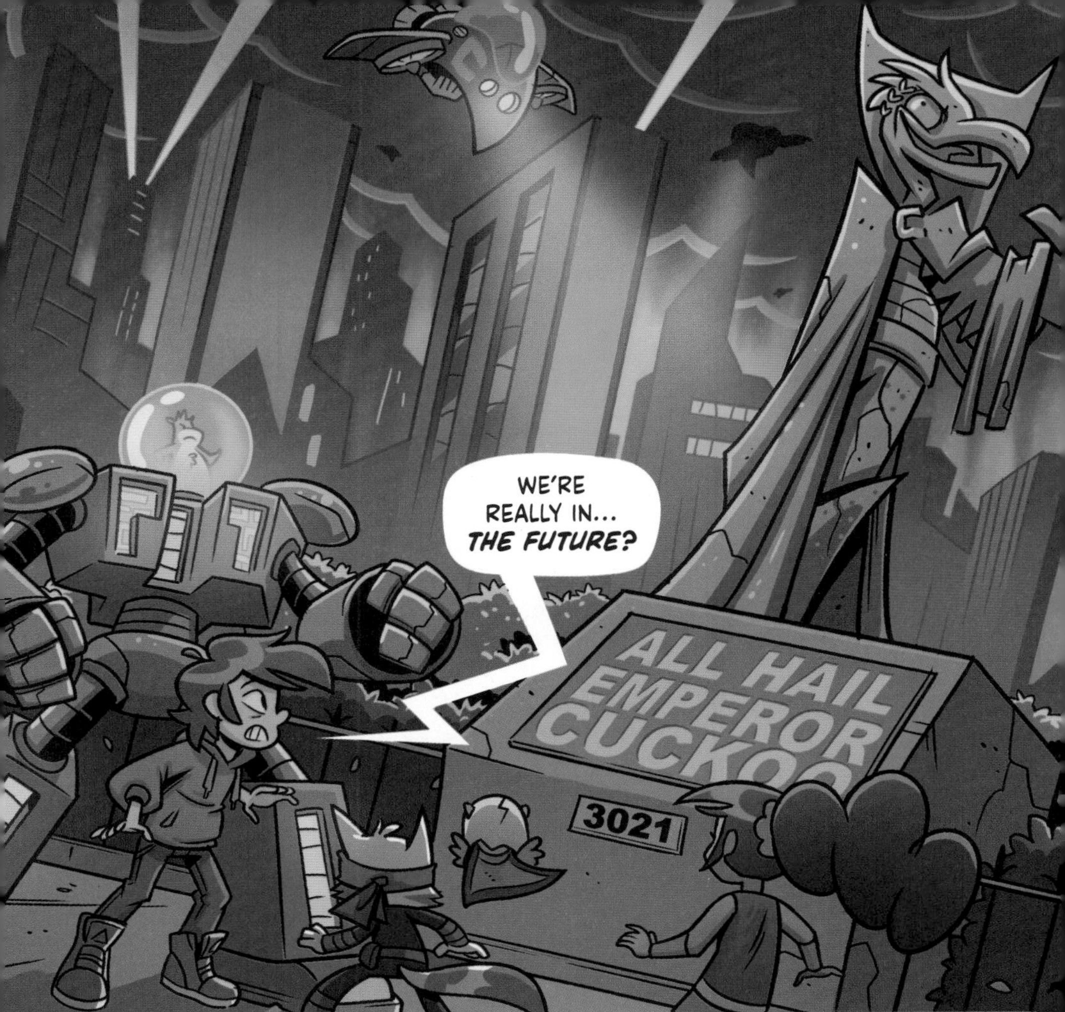
WE'RE REALLY IN... *THE FUTURE?*
ALL HAIL EMPEROR CUCKOO
3021

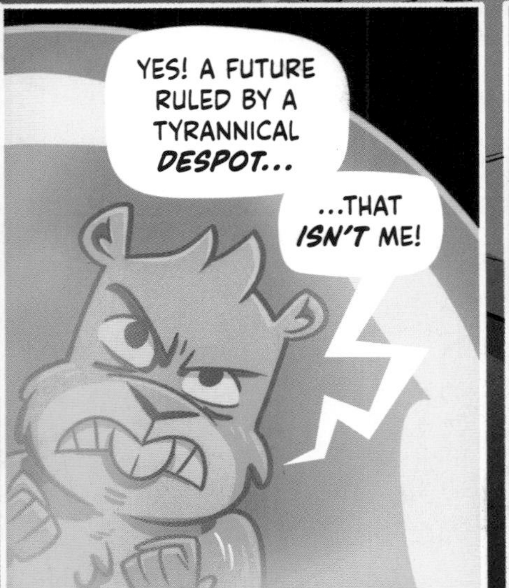
YES! A FUTURE RULED BY A TYRANNICAL *DESPOT...*
...THAT *ISN'T* ME!

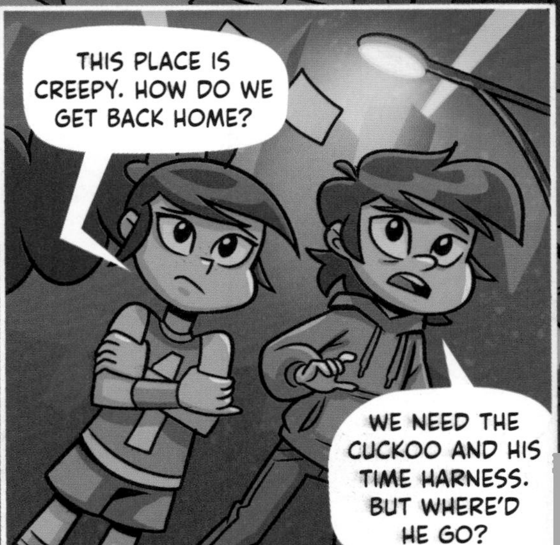
THIS PLACE IS CREEPY. HOW DO WE GET BACK HOME?
WE NEED THE CUCKOO AND HIS TIME HARNESS. BUT WHERE'D HE GO?

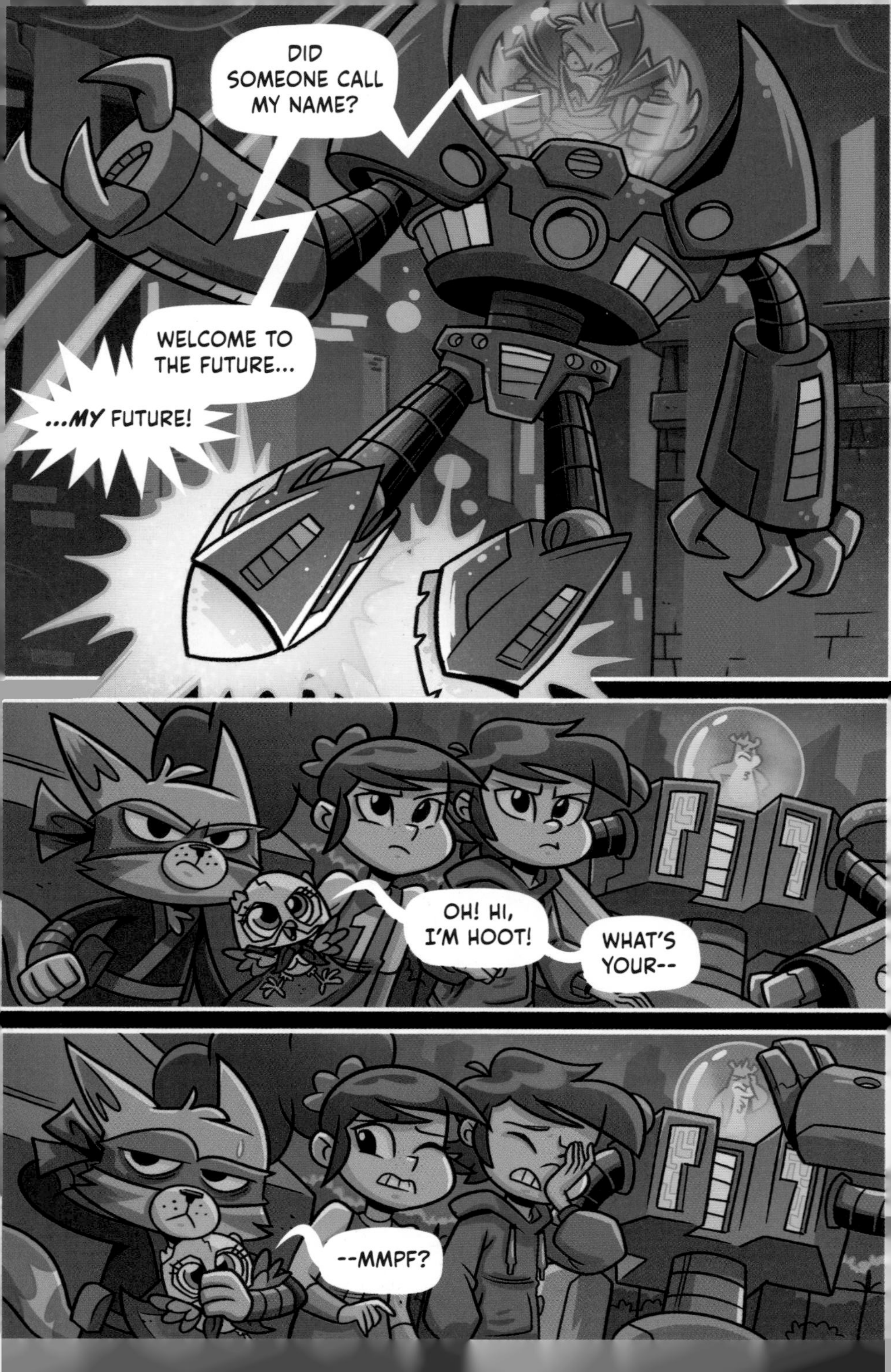
DID SOMEONE CALL MY NAME?
WELCOME TO THE FUTURE...
...MY FUTURE!
OH! HI, I'M HOOT!
WHAT'S YOUR--
--MMPF?

WAIT. A. MINUTE.
HE STOLE *MY* GIANT ROBOT DESIGN!
I HOPE THERE ARE GOOD LAWYERS IN THE YEAR 3021, BECAUSE...
CLICK

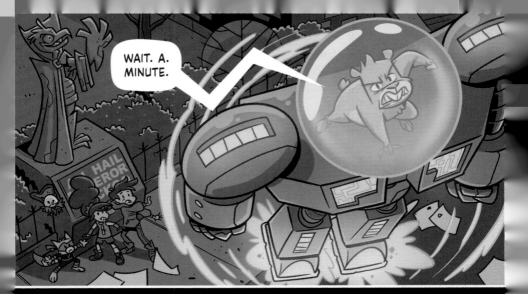

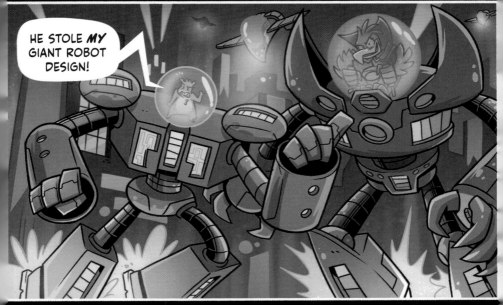

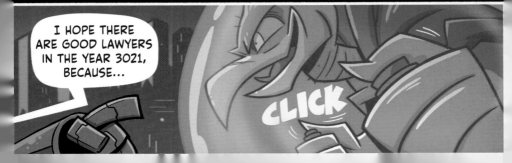

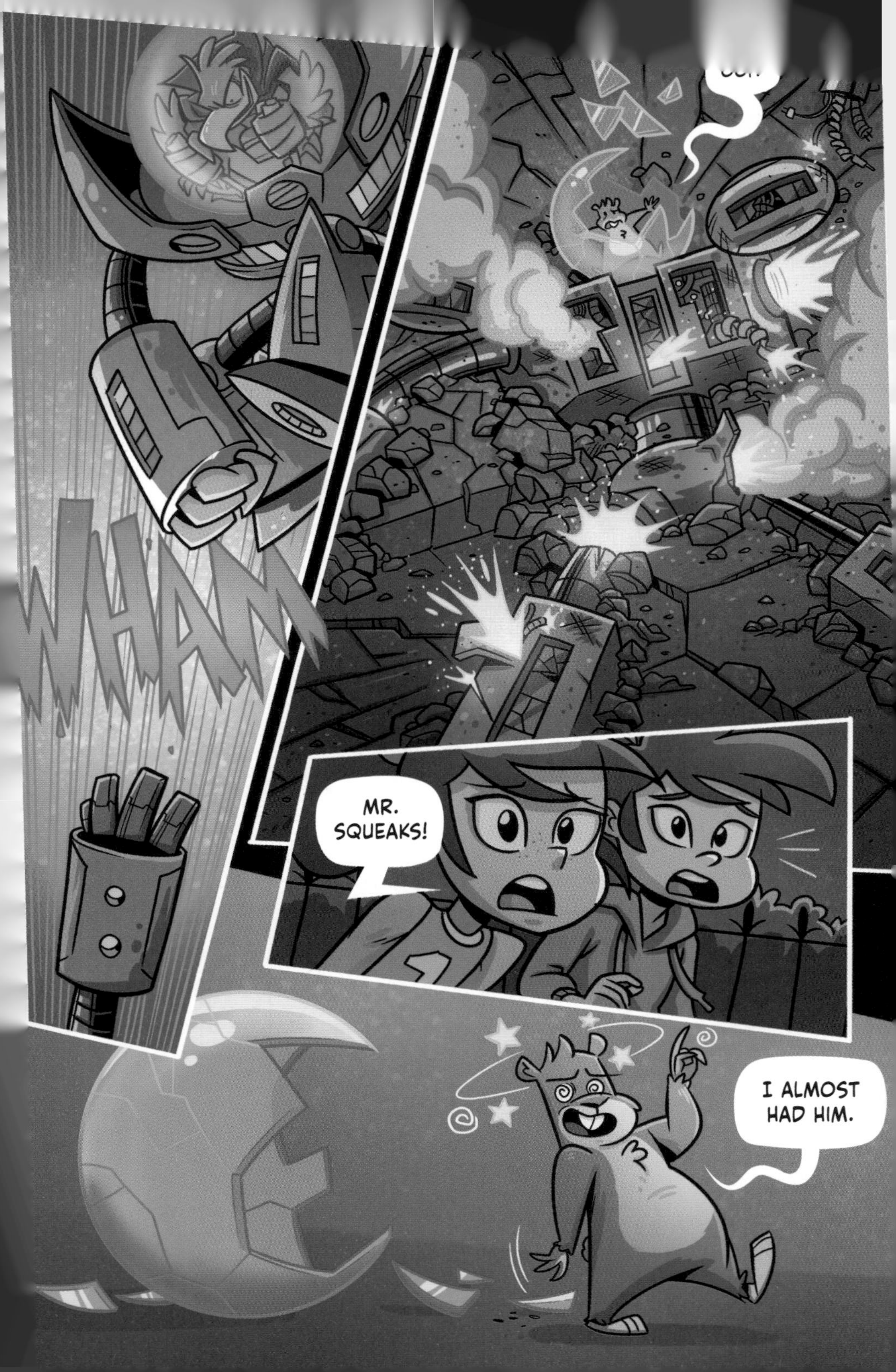
WHAM
MR. SQUEAKS!
I ALMOST HAD HIM.

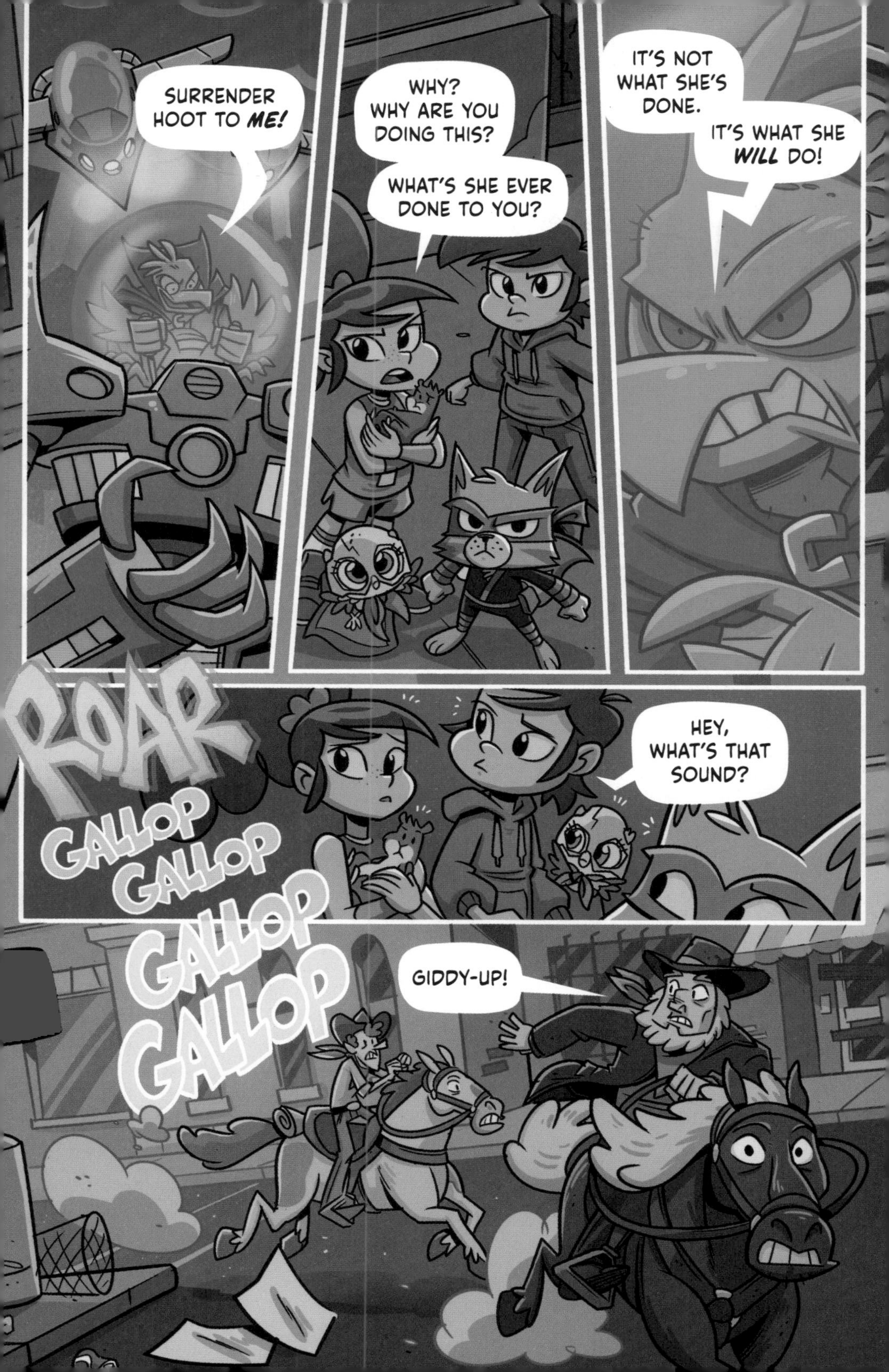
SURRENDER HOOT TO *ME!*
WHY? WHY ARE YOU DOING THIS?
WHAT'S SHE EVER DONE TO YOU?
IT'S NOT WHAT SHE'S DONE.
IT'S WHAT SHE *WILL* DO!
ROAR
GALLOP GALLOP
HEY, WHAT'S THAT SOUND?
GALLOP GALLOP
GIDDY-UP!

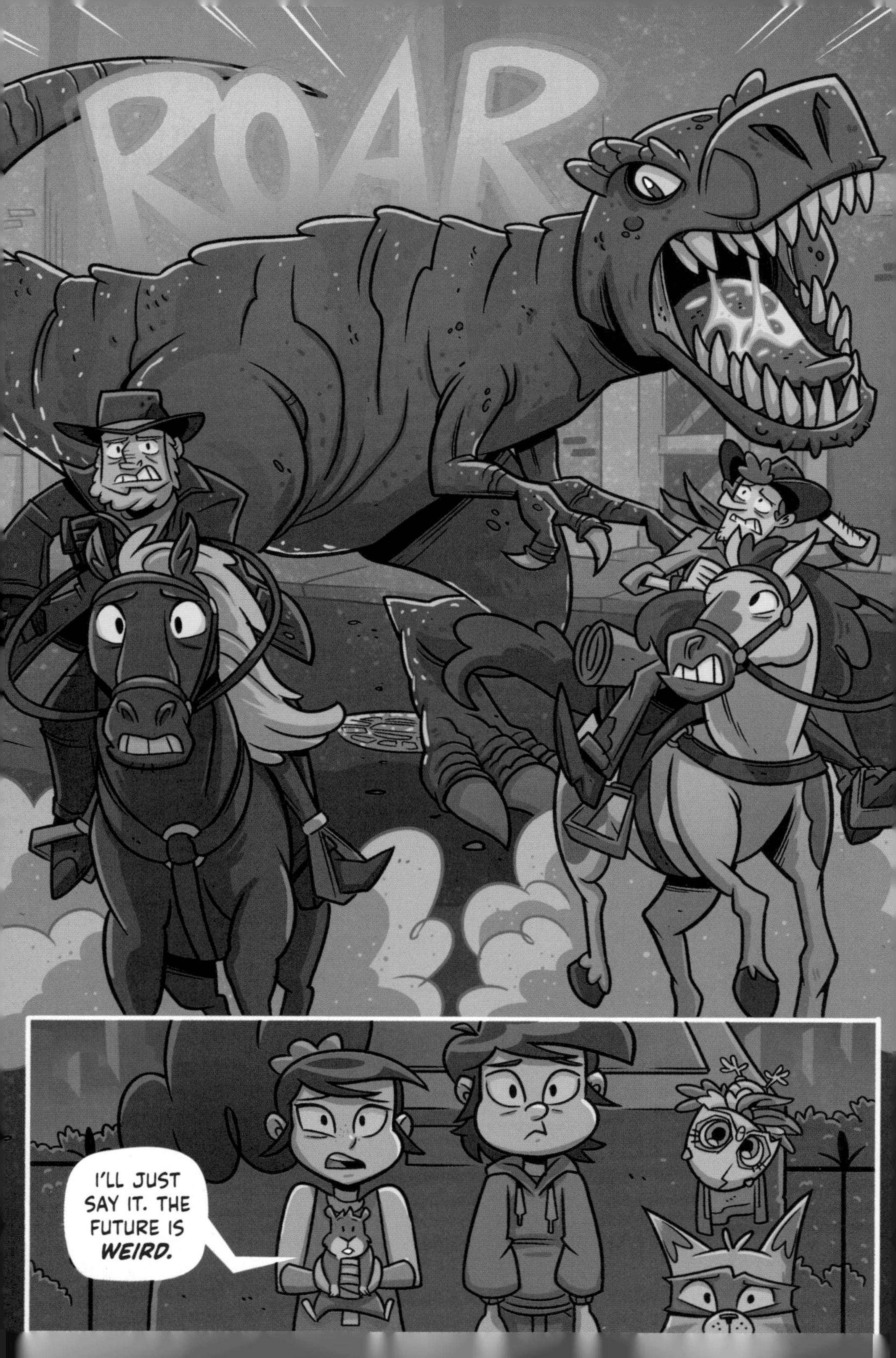
ROAR
I'LL JUST SAY IT. THE FUTURE IS ***WEIRD.***

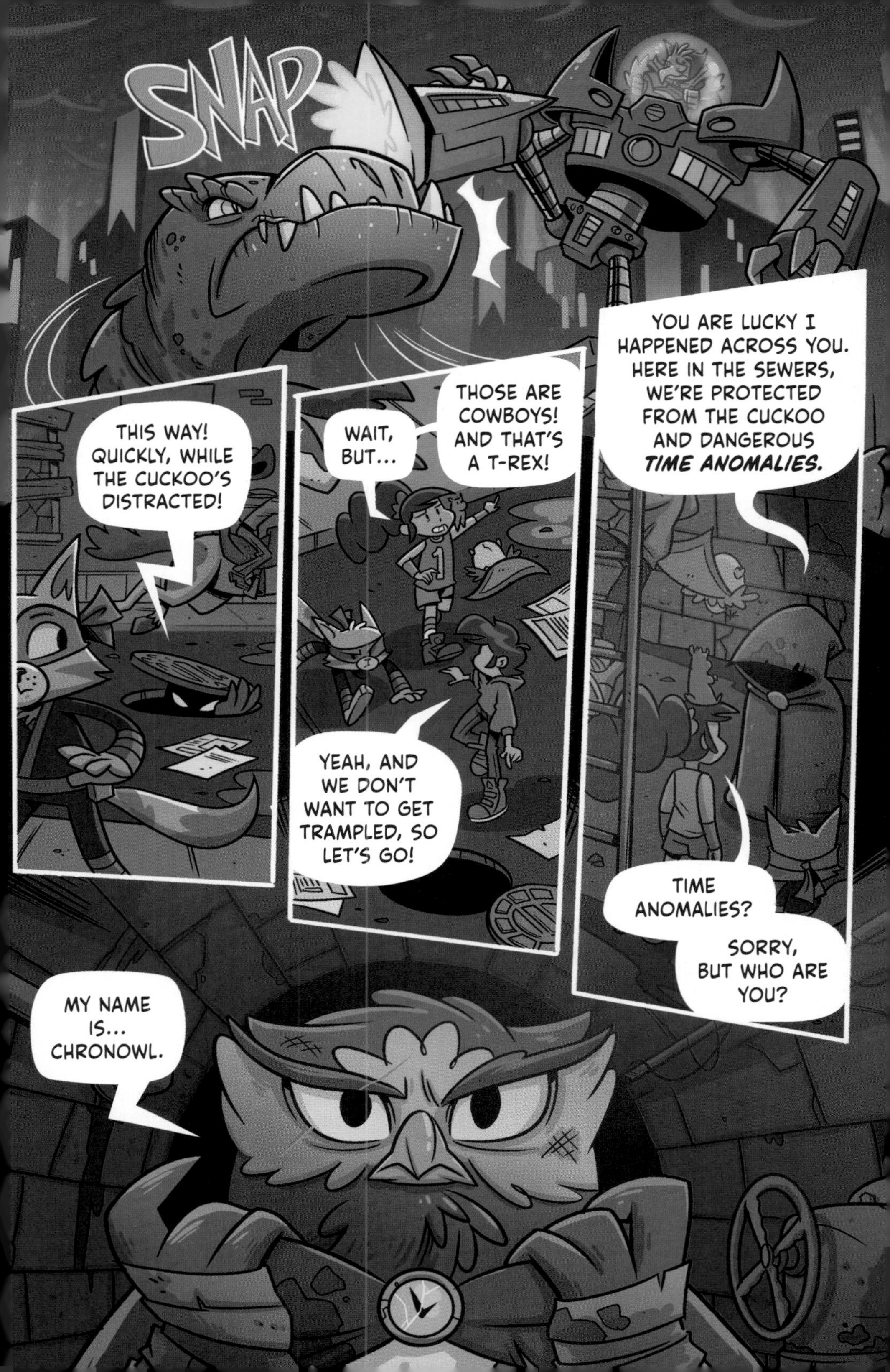
SNAP
THIS WAY! QUICKLY, WHILE THE CUCKOO'S DISTRACTED!
WAIT, BUT...
THOSE ARE COWBOYS! AND THAT'S A T-REX!
YEAH, AND WE DON'T WANT TO GET TRAMPLED, SO LET'S GO!
YOU ARE LUCKY I HAPPENED ACROSS YOU. HERE IN THE SEWERS, WE'RE PROTECTED FROM THE CUCKOO AND DANGEROUS *TIME ANOMALIES.*
TIME ANOMALIES?
SORRY, BUT WHO ARE YOU?
MY NAME IS... CHRONOWL.

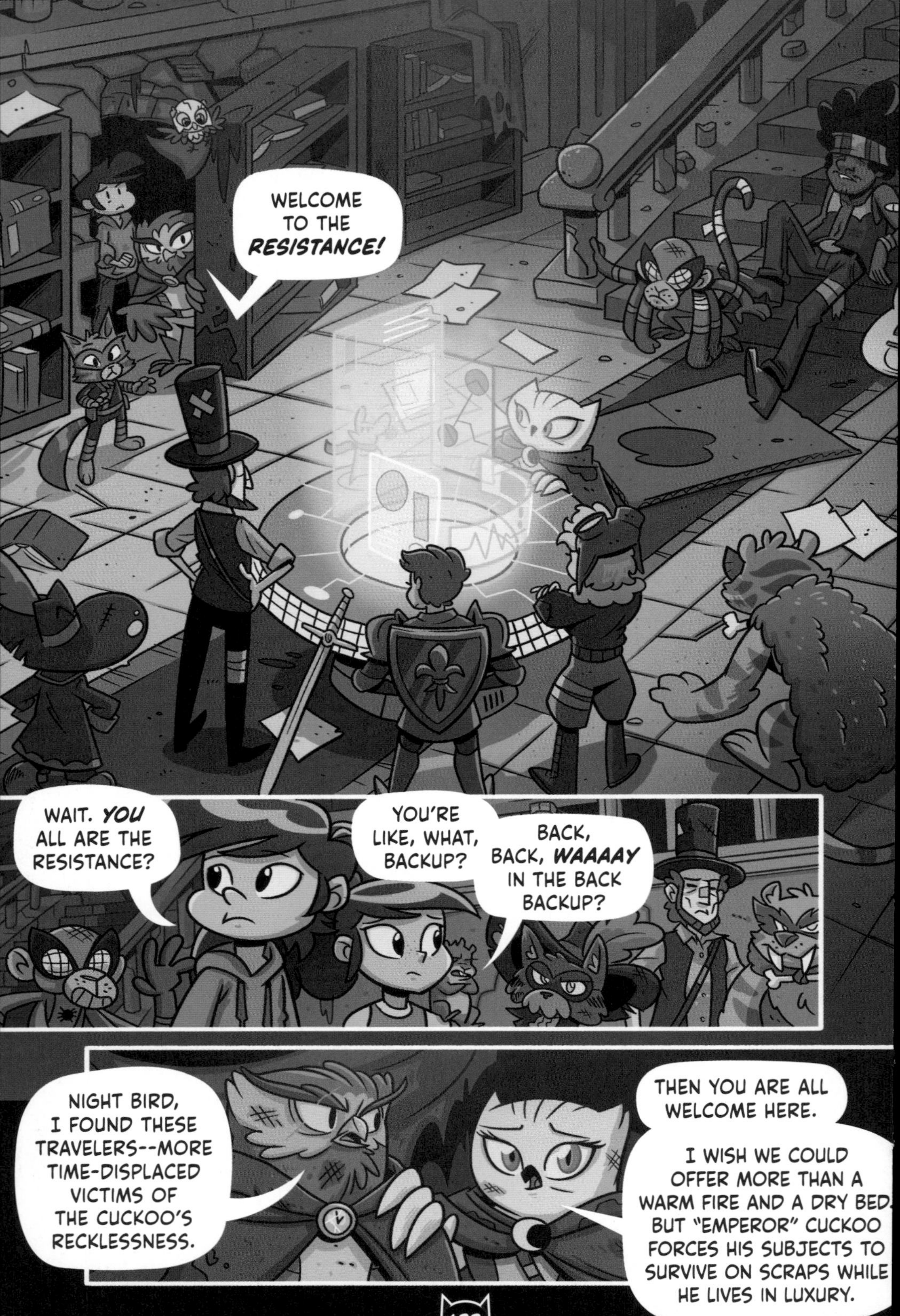
WELCOME TO THE RESISTANCE!
WAIT. YOU ALL ARE THE RESISTANCE?
YOU'RE LIKE, WHAT, BACKUP?
BACK, BACK, WAAAAY IN THE BACK BACKUP?
NIGHT BIRD, I FOUND THESE TRAVELERS--MORE TIME-DISPLACED VICTIMS OF THE CUCKOO'S RECKLESSNESS.
THEN YOU ARE ALL WELCOME HERE.
I WISH WE COULD OFFER MORE THAN A WARM FIRE AND A DRY BED. BUT "EMPEROR" CUCKOO FORCES HIS SUBJECTS TO SURVIVE ON SCRAPS WHILE HE LIVES IN LUXURY.

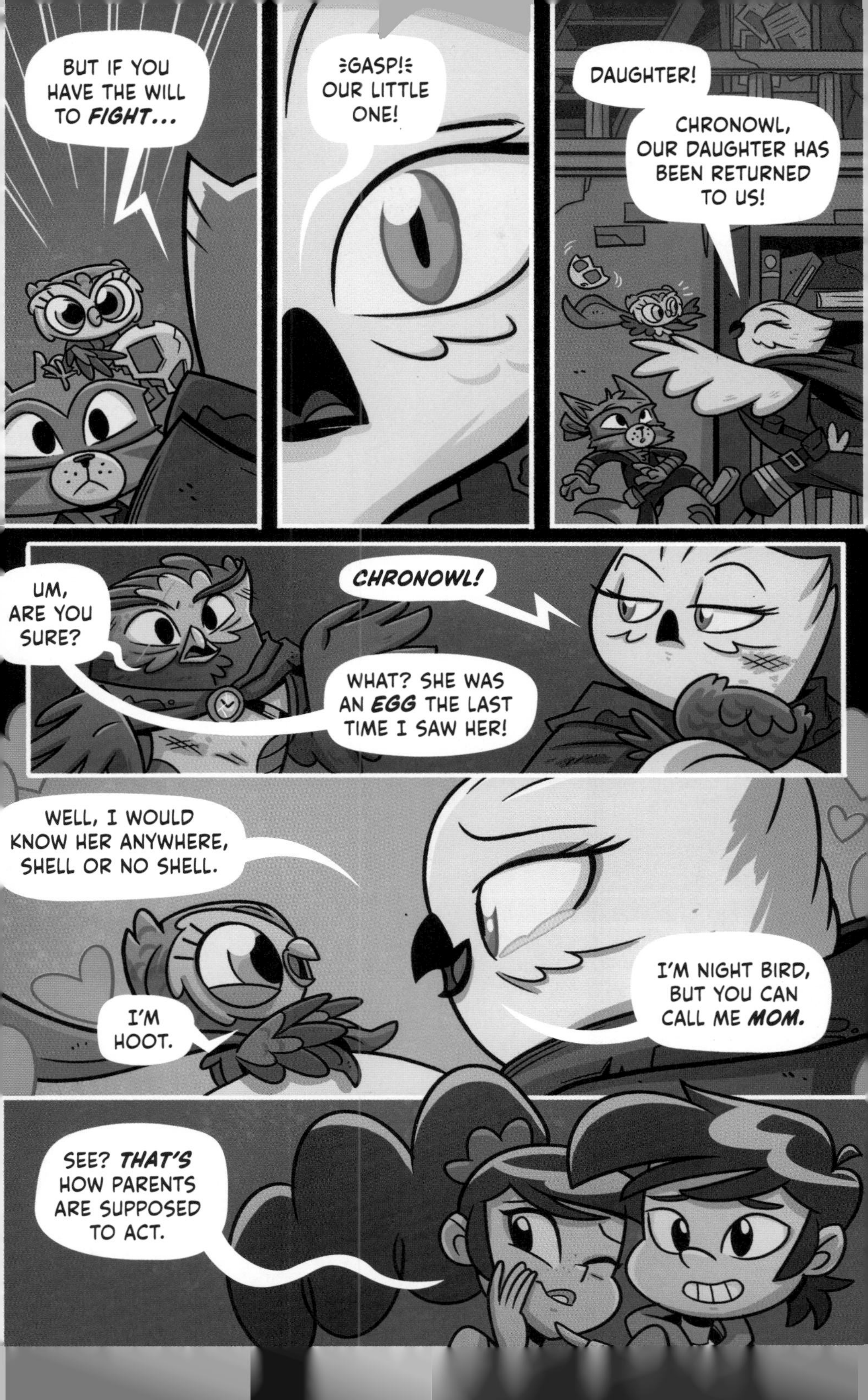
BUT IF YOU HAVE THE WILL TO *FIGHT*...
⁝GASP!⁝ OUR LITTLE ONE!
DAUGHTER!
CHRONOWL, OUR DAUGHTER HAS BEEN RETURNED TO US!
UM, ARE YOU SURE?
CHRONOWL!
WHAT? SHE WAS AN *EGG* THE LAST TIME I SAW HER!
WELL, I WOULD KNOW HER ANYWHERE, SHELL OR NO SHELL.
I'M HOOT.
I'M NIGHT BIRD, BUT YOU CAN CALL ME *MOM.*
SEE? *THAT'S* HOW PARENTS ARE SUPPOSED TO ACT.

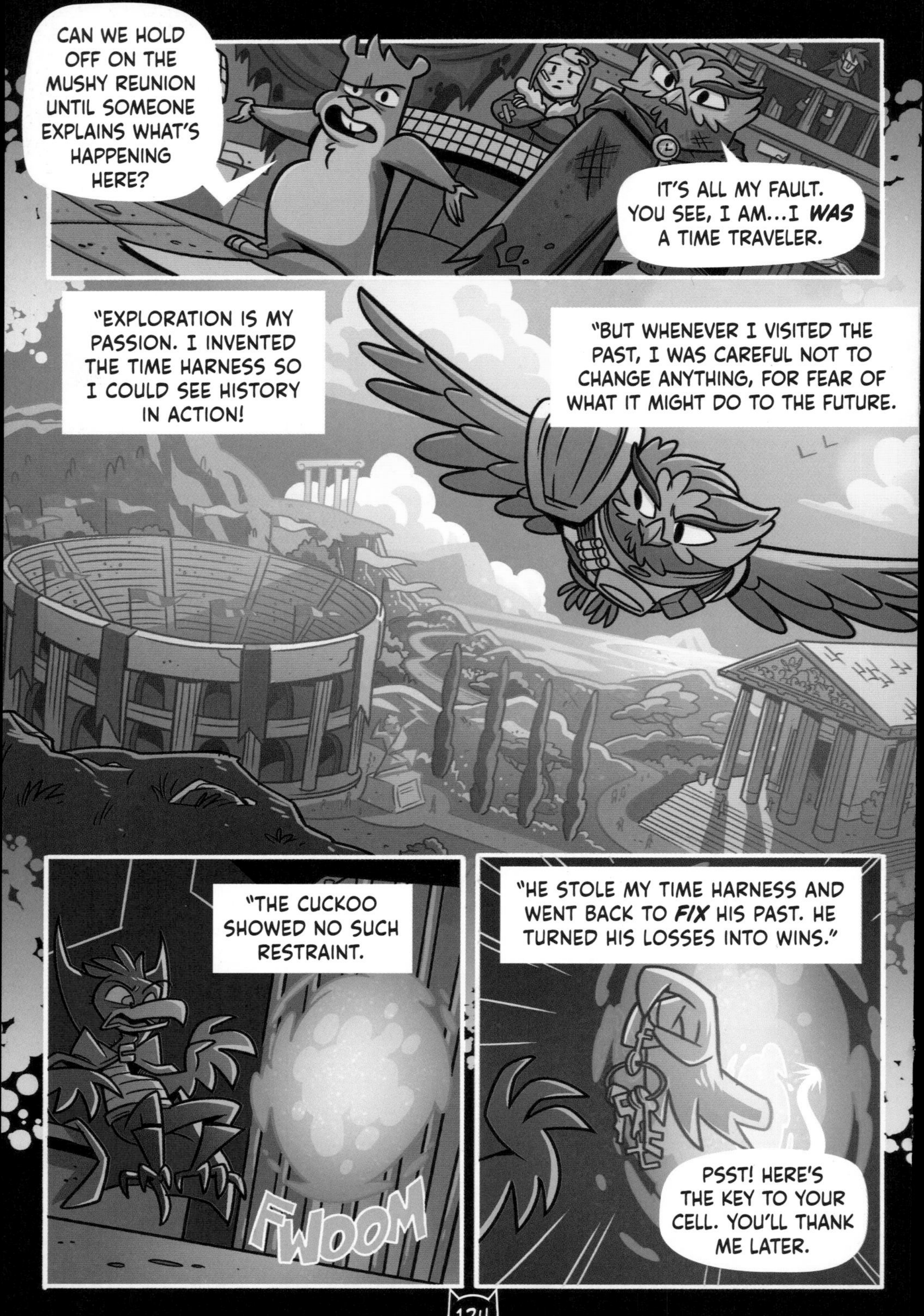
CAN WE HOLD OFF ON THE MUSHY REUNION UNTIL SOMEONE EXPLAINS WHAT'S HAPPENING HERE?
IT'S ALL MY FAULT. YOU SEE, I AM...I *WAS* A TIME TRAVELER.
"EXPLORATION IS MY PASSION. I INVENTED THE TIME HARNESS SO I COULD SEE HISTORY IN ACTION!
"BUT WHENEVER I VISITED THE PAST, I WAS CAREFUL NOT TO CHANGE ANYTHING, FOR FEAR OF WHAT IT MIGHT DO TO THE FUTURE.
"THE CUCKOO SHOWED NO SUCH RESTRAINT.
FWOOM
"HE STOLE MY TIME HARNESS AND WENT BACK TO *FIX* HIS PAST. HE TURNED HIS LOSSES INTO WINS."
PSST! HERE'S THE KEY TO YOUR CELL. YOU'LL THANK ME LATER.

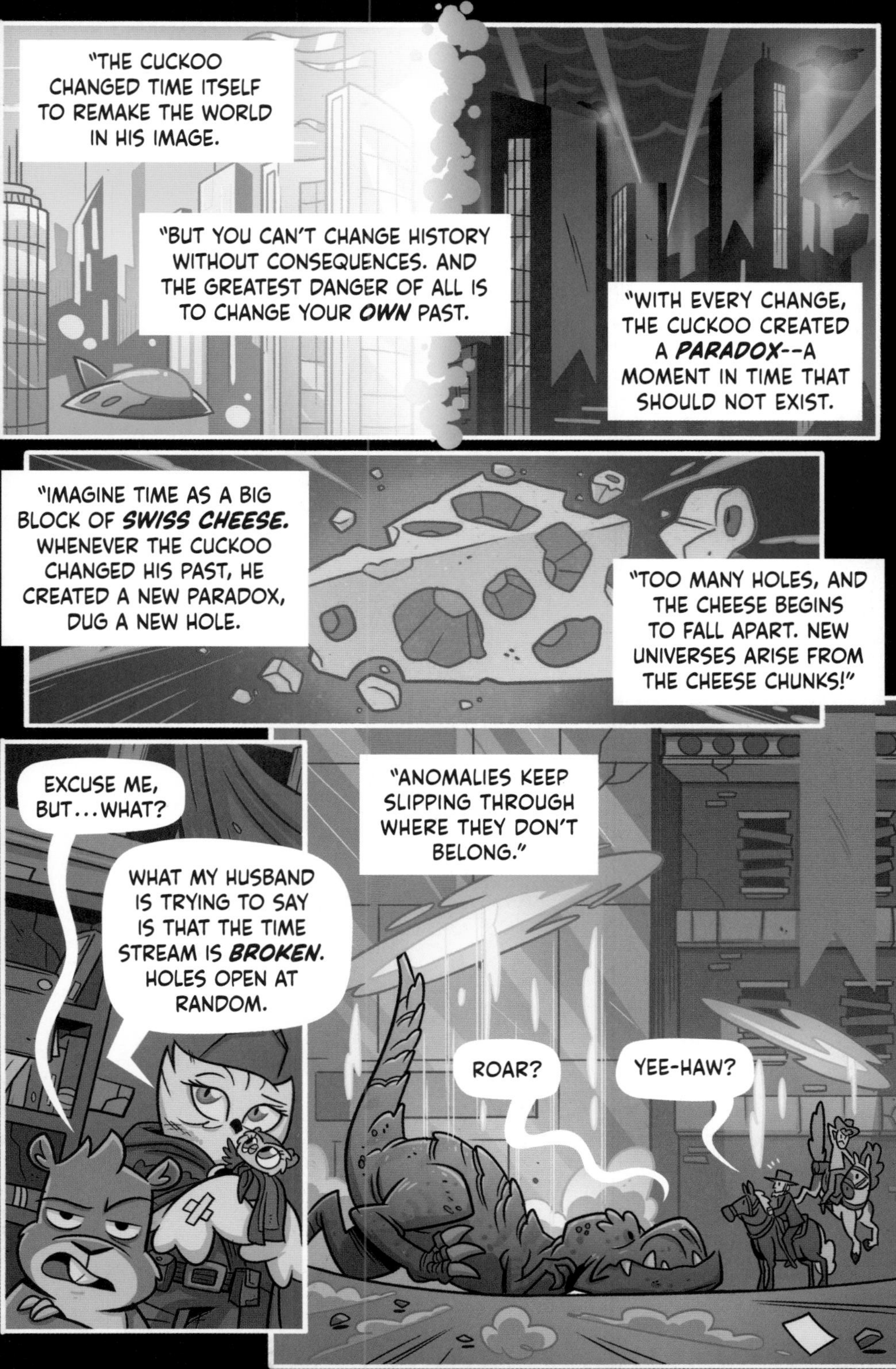
"THE CUCKOO CHANGED TIME ITSELF TO REMAKE THE WORLD IN HIS IMAGE.
"BUT YOU CAN'T CHANGE HISTORY WITHOUT CONSEQUENCES. AND THE GREATEST DANGER OF ALL IS TO CHANGE YOUR *OWN* PAST.
"WITH EVERY CHANGE, THE CUCKOO CREATED A *PARADOX*--A MOMENT IN TIME THAT SHOULD NOT EXIST.
"IMAGINE TIME AS A BIG BLOCK OF *SWISS CHEESE.* WHENEVER THE CUCKOO CHANGED HIS PAST, HE CREATED A NEW PARADOX, DUG A NEW HOLE.
"TOO MANY HOLES, AND THE CHEESE BEGINS TO FALL APART. NEW UNIVERSES ARISE FROM THE CHEESE CHUNKS!"
EXCUSE ME, BUT...WHAT?
WHAT MY HUSBAND IS TRYING TO SAY IS THAT THE TIME STREAM IS *BROKEN.* HOLES OPEN AT RANDOM.
"ANOMALIES KEEP SLIPPING THROUGH WHERE THEY DON'T BELONG."
ROAR?
YEE-HAW?

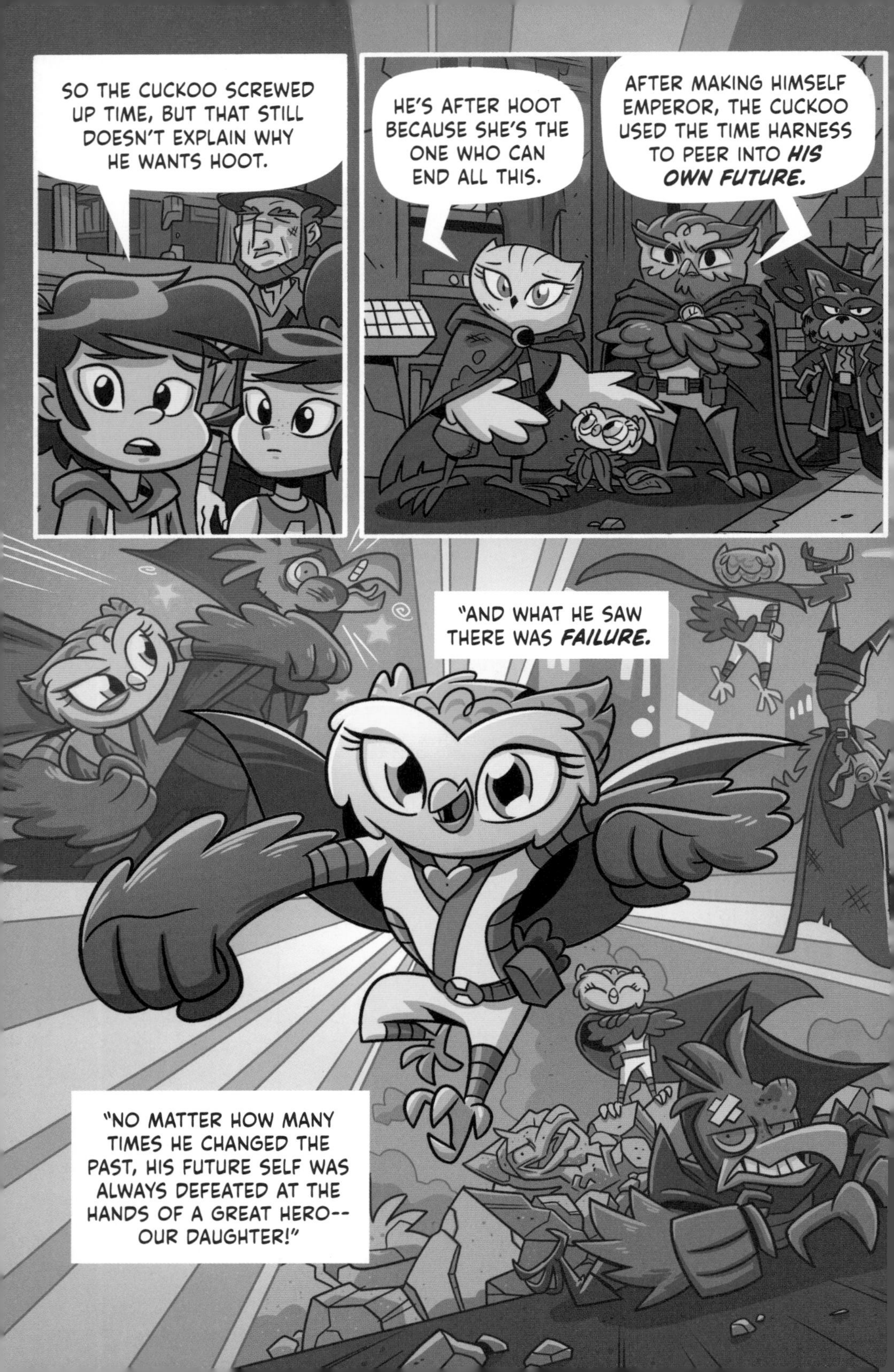
SO THE CUCKOO SCREWED UP TIME, BUT THAT STILL DOESN'T EXPLAIN WHY HE WANTS HOOT.
HE'S AFTER HOOT BECAUSE SHE'S THE ONE WHO CAN END ALL THIS.
AFTER MAKING HIMSELF EMPEROR, THE CUCKOO USED THE TIME HARNESS TO PEER INTO ***HIS OWN FUTURE.***
"AND WHAT HE SAW THERE WAS ***FAILURE.***
"NO MATTER HOW MANY TIMES HE CHANGED THE PAST, HIS FUTURE SELF WAS ALWAYS DEFEATED AT THE HANDS OF A GREAT HERO-- OUR DAUGHTER!"

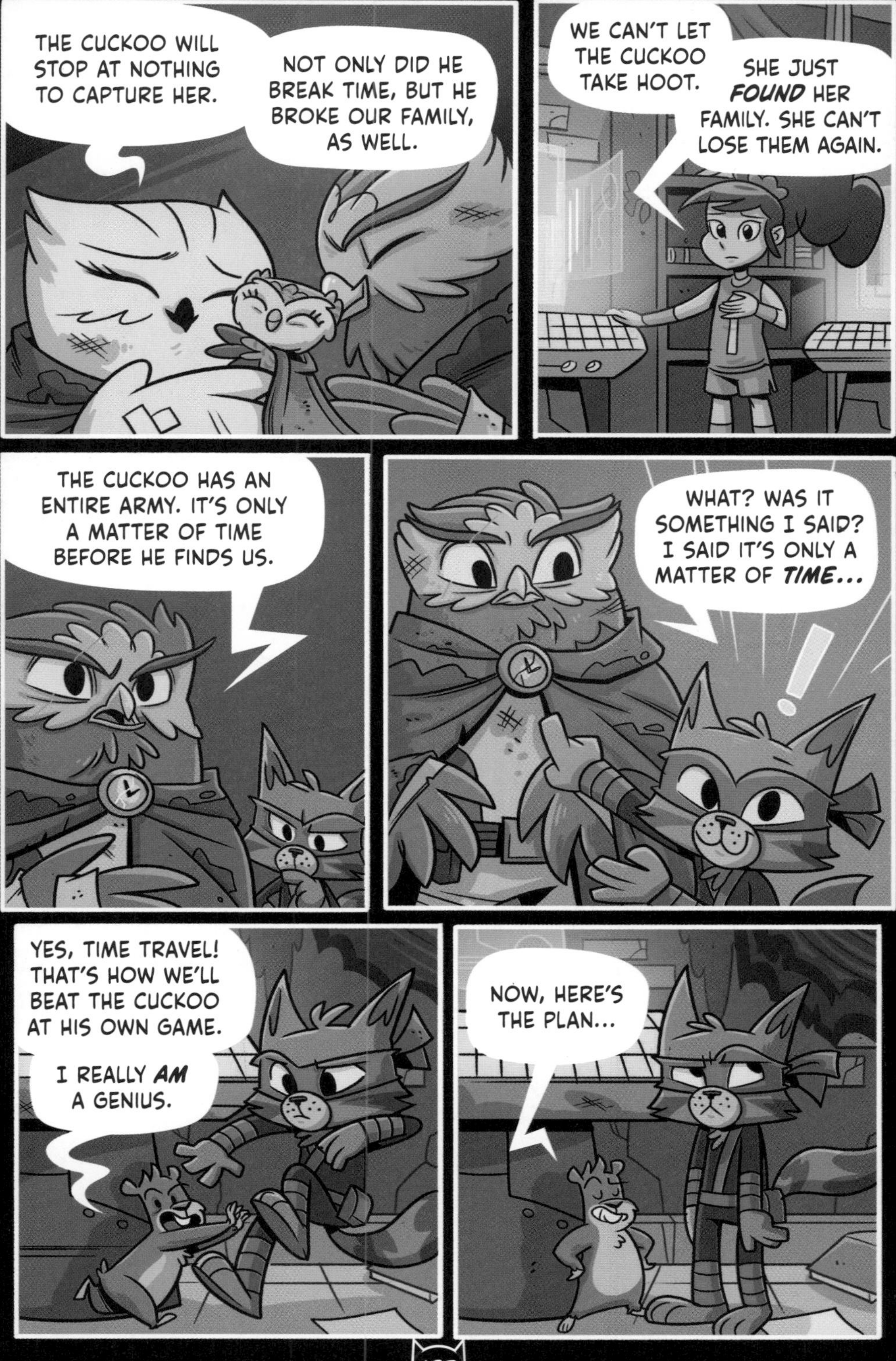
THE CUCKOO WILL STOP AT NOTHING TO CAPTURE HER.
NOT ONLY DID HE BREAK TIME, BUT HE BROKE OUR FAMILY, AS WELL.
WE CAN'T LET THE CUCKOO TAKE HOOT.
SHE JUST FOUND HER FAMILY. SHE CAN'T LOSE THEM AGAIN.
THE CUCKOO HAS AN ENTIRE ARMY. IT'S ONLY A MATTER OF TIME BEFORE HE FINDS US.
WHAT? WAS IT SOMETHING I SAID? I SAID IT'S ONLY A MATTER OF TIME...
!
YES, TIME TRAVEL! THAT'S HOW WE'LL BEAT THE CUCKOO AT HIS OWN GAME.
I REALLY AM A GENIUS.
NOW, HERE'S THE PLAN...

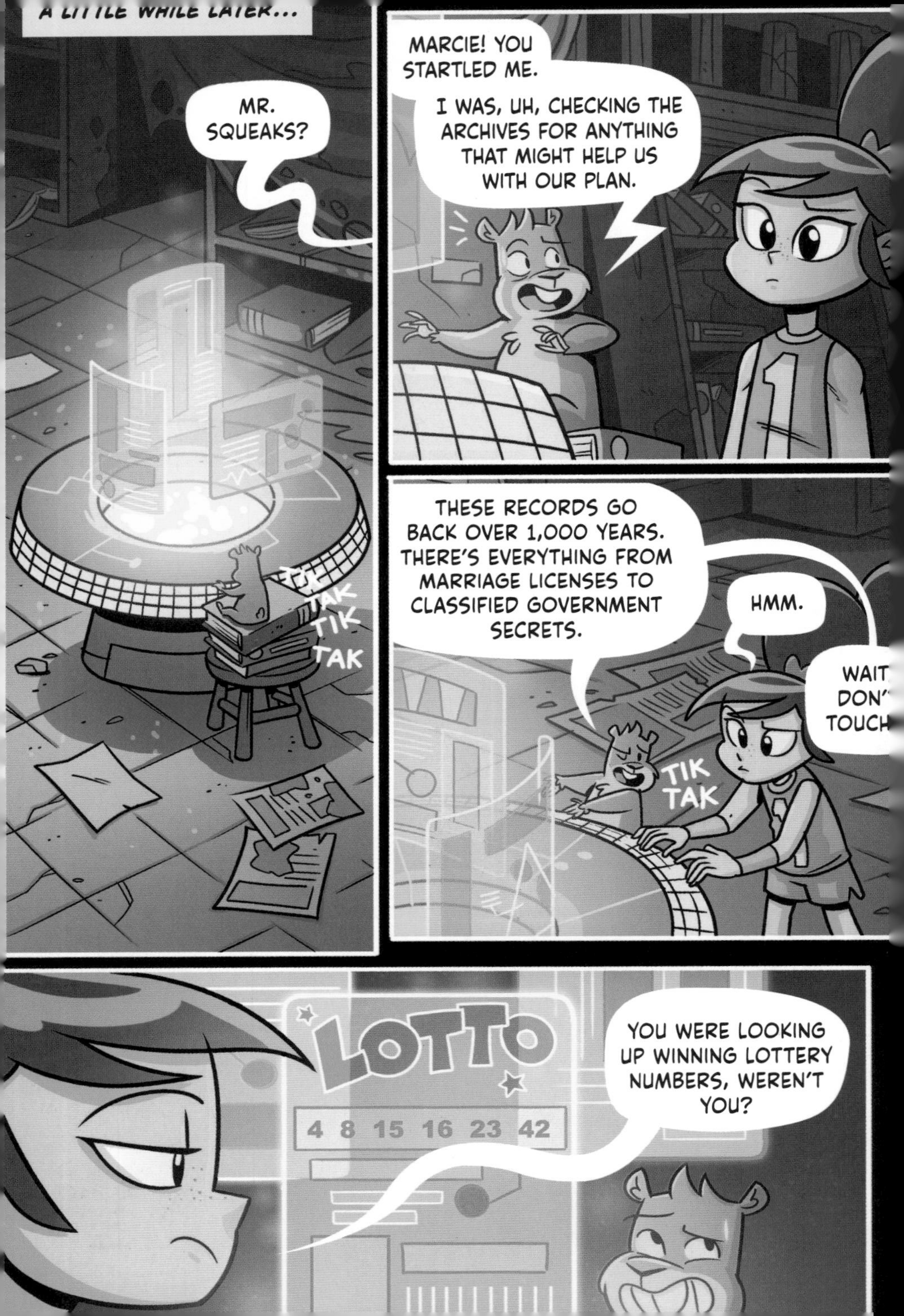
A LITTLE WHILE LATER...
MR. SQUEAKS?
TIK TAK TIK TAK
MARCIE! YOU STARTLED ME.
I WAS, UH, CHECKING THE ARCHIVES FOR ANYTHING THAT MIGHT HELP US WITH OUR PLAN.
THESE RECORDS GO BACK OVER 1,000 YEARS. THERE'S EVERYTHING FROM MARRIAGE LICENSES TO CLASSIFIED GOVERNMENT SECRETS.
HMM.
TIK TAK
LOTTO
4 8 15 16 23 42
YOU WERE LOOKING UP WINNING LOTTERY NUMBERS, WEREN'T YOU?

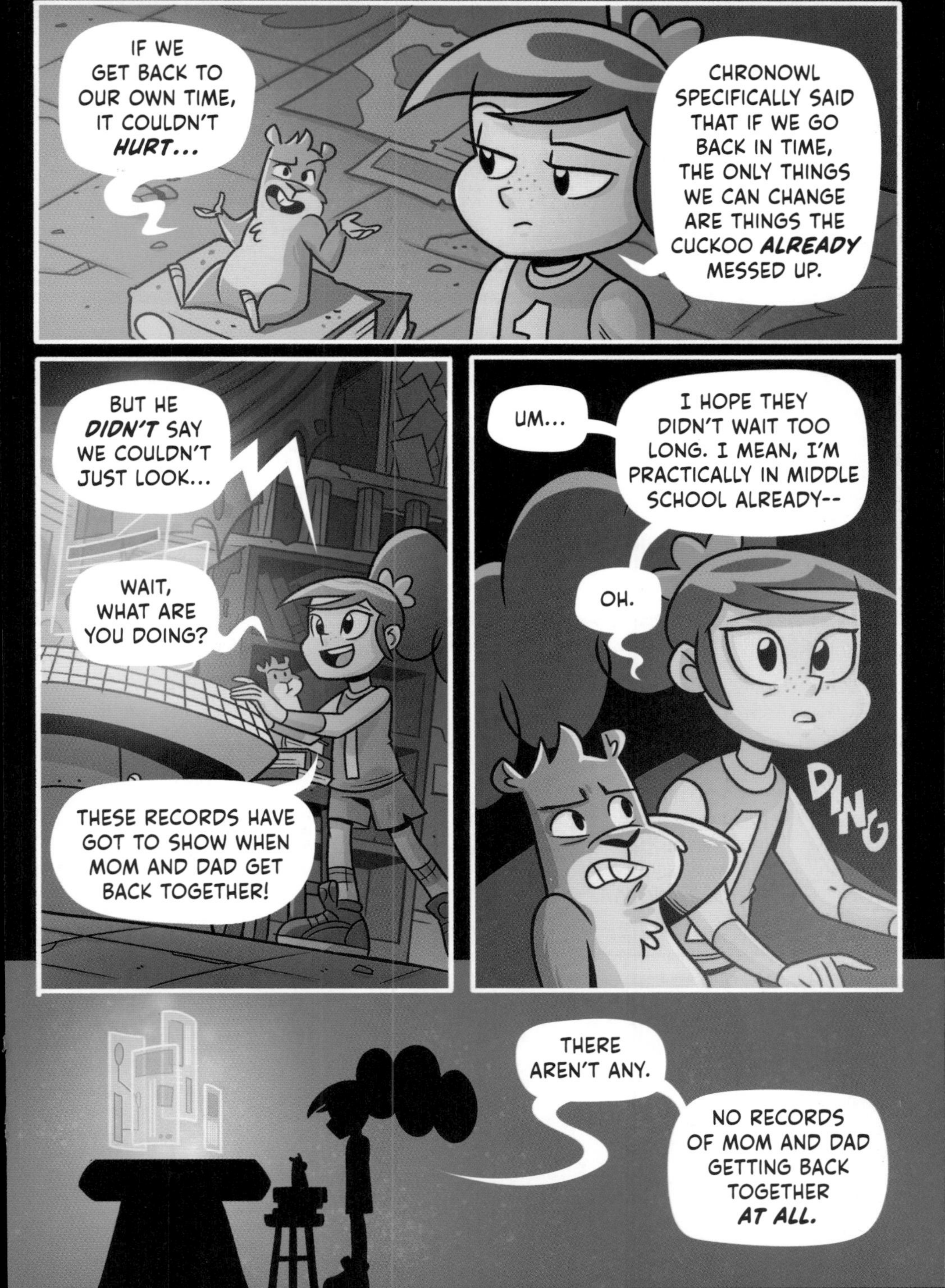
IF WE GET BACK TO OUR OWN TIME, IT COULDN'T *HURT...*
CHRONOWL SPECIFICALLY SAID THAT IF WE GO BACK IN TIME, THE ONLY THINGS WE CAN CHANGE ARE THINGS THE CUCKOO *ALREADY* MESSED UP.
BUT HE *DIDN'T* SAY WE COULDN'T JUST LOOK...
WAIT, WHAT ARE YOU DOING?
THESE RECORDS HAVE GOT TO SHOW WHEN MOM AND DAD GET BACK TOGETHER!
UM...
I HOPE THEY DIDN'T WAIT TOO LONG. I MEAN, I'M PRACTICALLY IN MIDDLE SCHOOL ALREADY--
OH.
DING
THERE AREN'T ANY.
NO RECORDS OF MOM AND DAD GETTING BACK TOGETHER *AT ALL.*

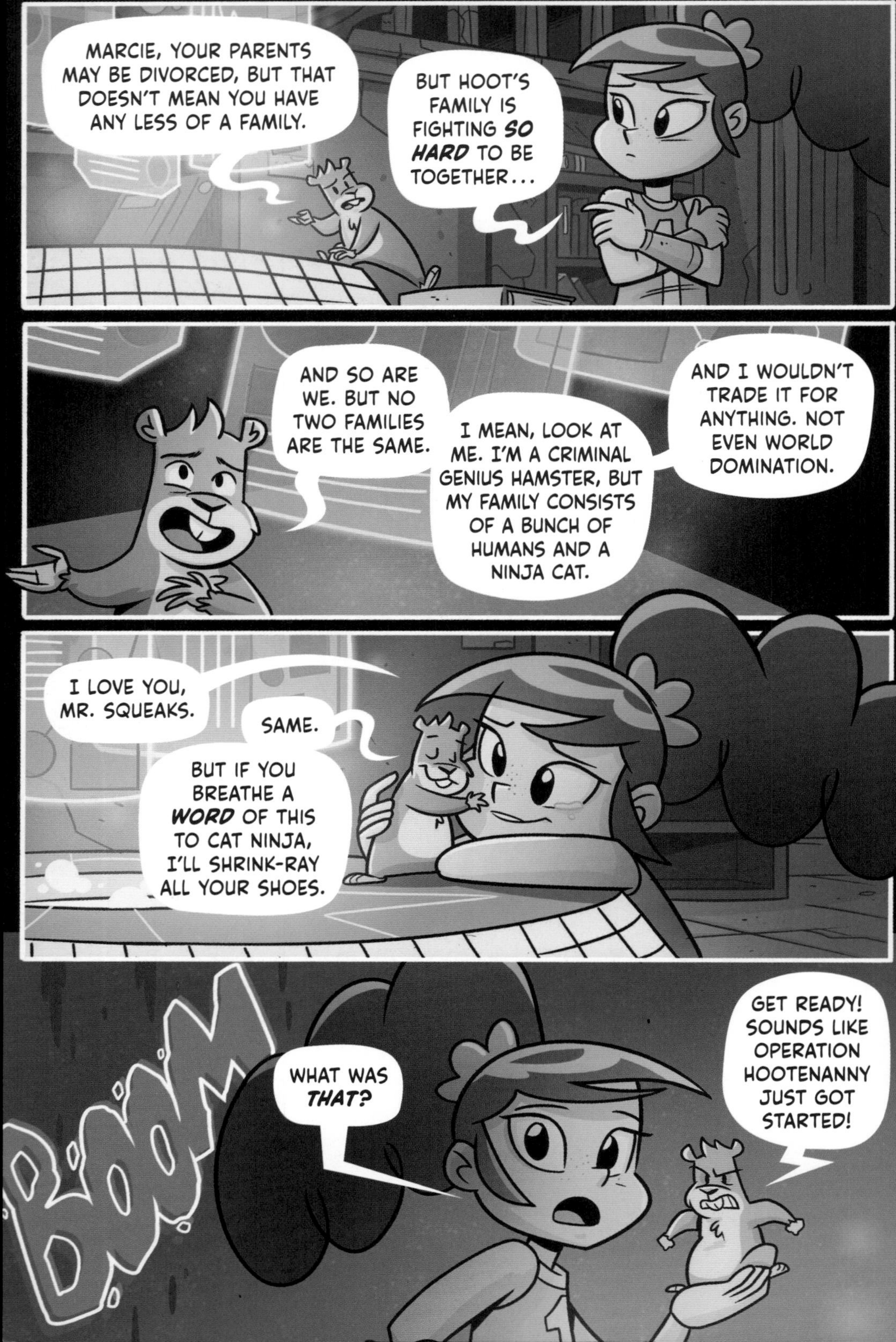
MARCIE, YOUR PARENTS MAY BE DIVORCED, BUT THAT DOESN'T MEAN YOU HAVE ANY LESS OF A FAMILY.
BUT HOOT'S FAMILY IS FIGHTING ***SO HARD*** TO BE TOGETHER...
AND SO ARE WE. BUT NO TWO FAMILIES ARE THE SAME.
I MEAN, LOOK AT ME. I'M A CRIMINAL GENIUS HAMSTER, BUT MY FAMILY CONSISTS OF A BUNCH OF HUMANS AND A NINJA CAT.
AND I WOULDN'T TRADE IT FOR ANYTHING. NOT EVEN WORLD DOMINATION.
I LOVE YOU, MR. SQUEAKS.
SAME.
BUT IF YOU BREATHE A ***WORD*** OF THIS TO CAT NINJA, I'LL SHRINK-RAY ALL YOUR SHOES.
BOOOM
WHAT WAS ***THAT?***
GET READY! SOUNDS LIKE OPERATION HOOTENANNY JUST GOT STARTED!

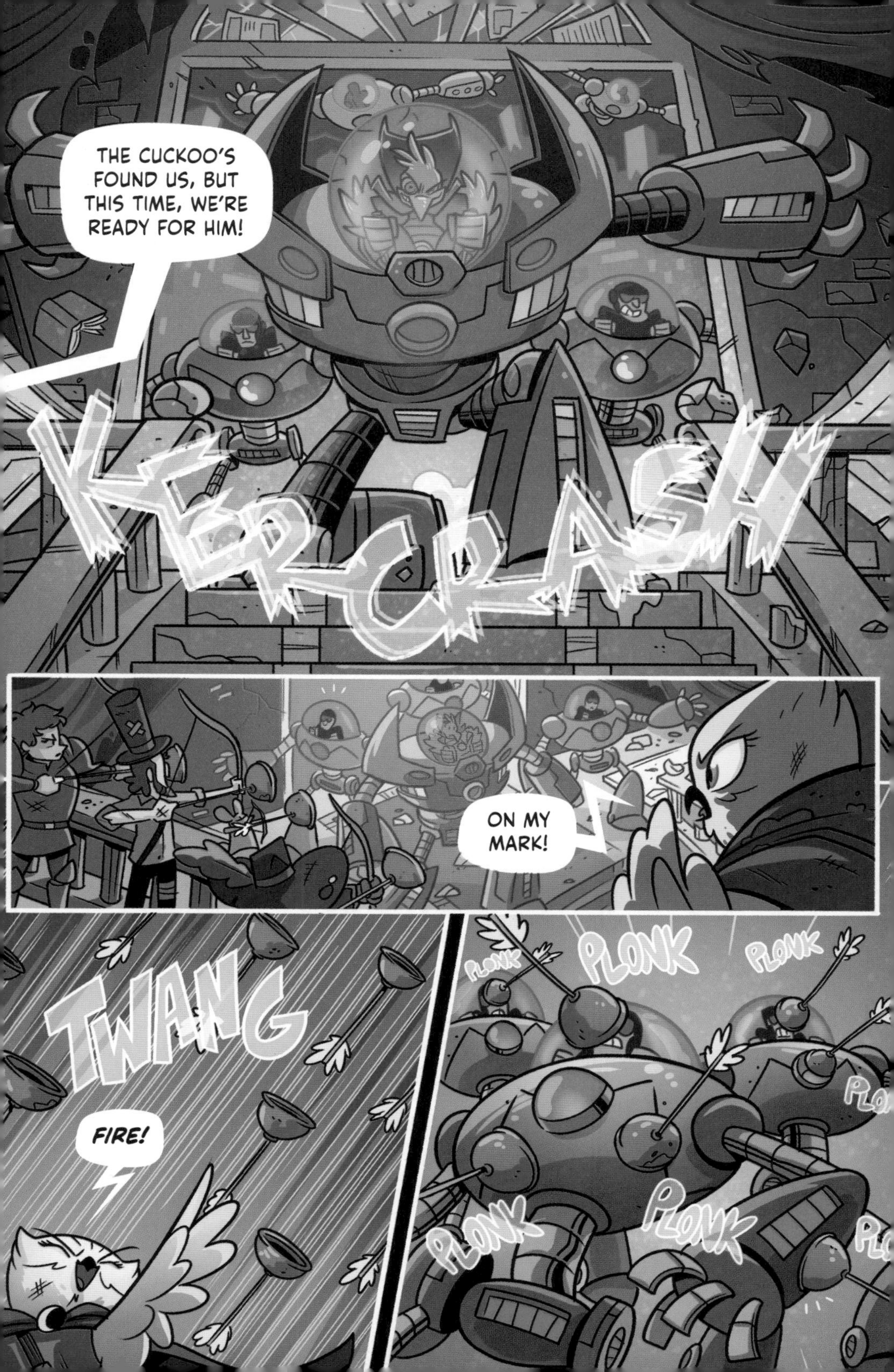

THE CUCKOO'S FOUND US, BUT THIS TIME, WE'RE READY FOR HIM!
KERCRASH
ON MY MARK!
TWANG
FIRE!
PLONK
PLONK
PLONK
PLONK
PLONK

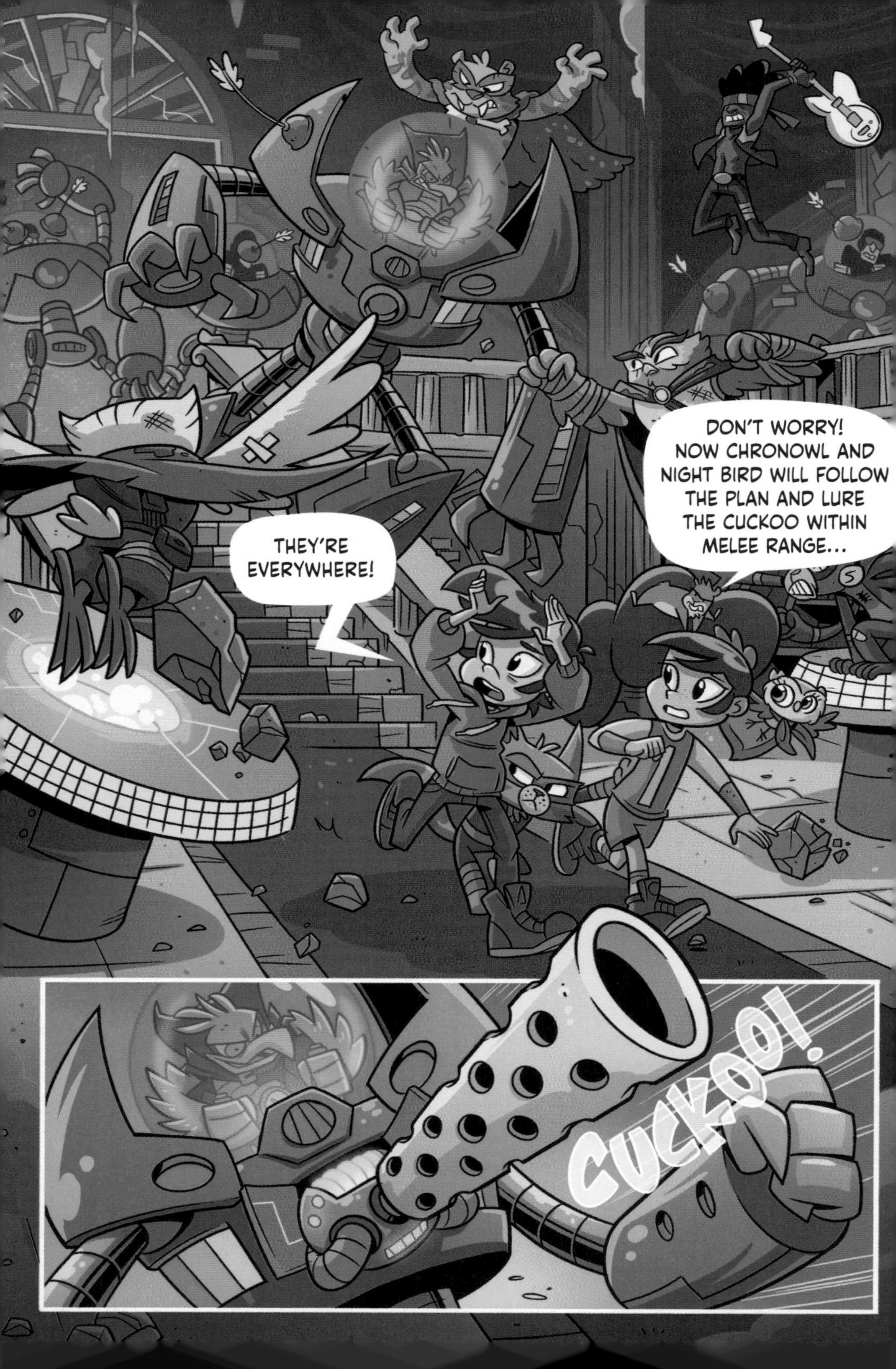
THEY'RE EVERYWHERE!
DON'T WORRY! NOW CHRONOWL AND NIGHT BIRD WILL FOLLOW THE PLAN AND LURE THE CUCKOO WITHIN MELEE RANGE...
CUCKOO!

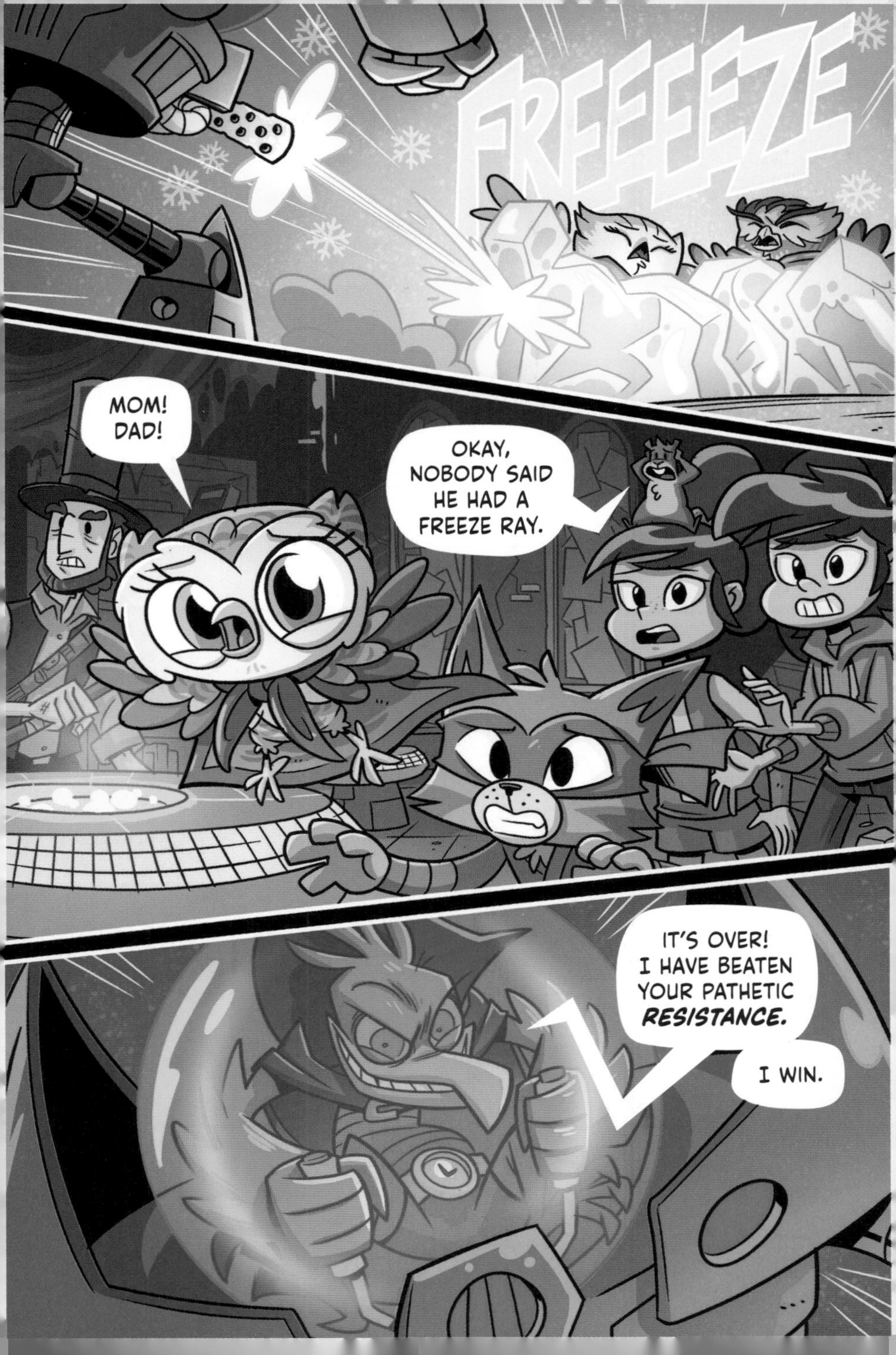
FREEEEZE
MOM! DAD!
OKAY, NOBODY SAID HE HAD A FREEZE RAY.
IT'S OVER! I HAVE BEATEN YOUR PATHETIC *RESISTANCE.*
I WIN.

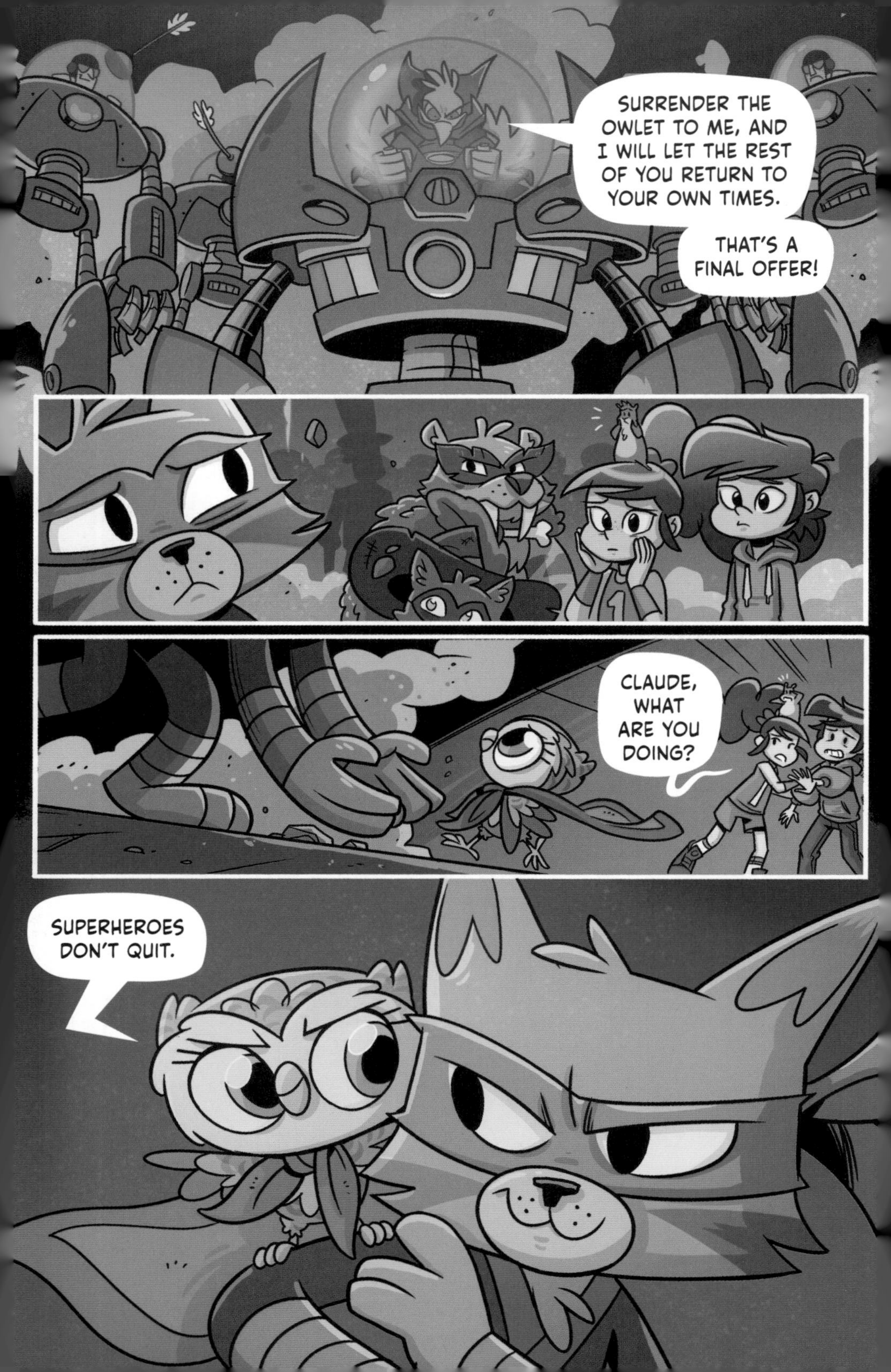
SURRENDER THE OWLET TO ME, AND I WILL LET THE REST OF YOU RETURN TO YOUR OWN TIMES.
THAT'S A FINAL OFFER!
CLAUDE, WHAT ARE YOU DOING?
SUPERHEROES DON'T QUIT.

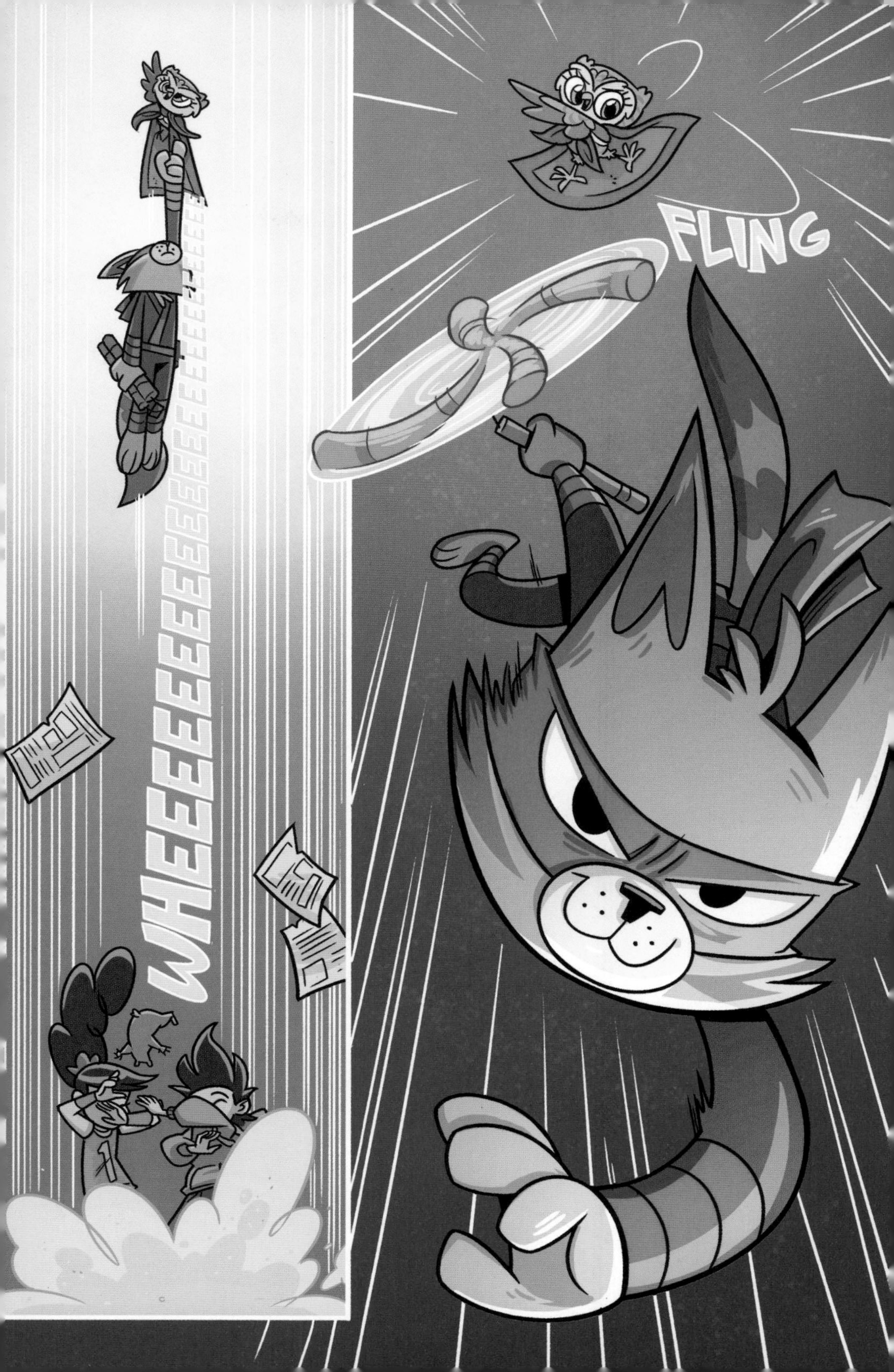
WHEEEEEEEEEEEEEEEEEEEEEEEEEEEEEE
FLING

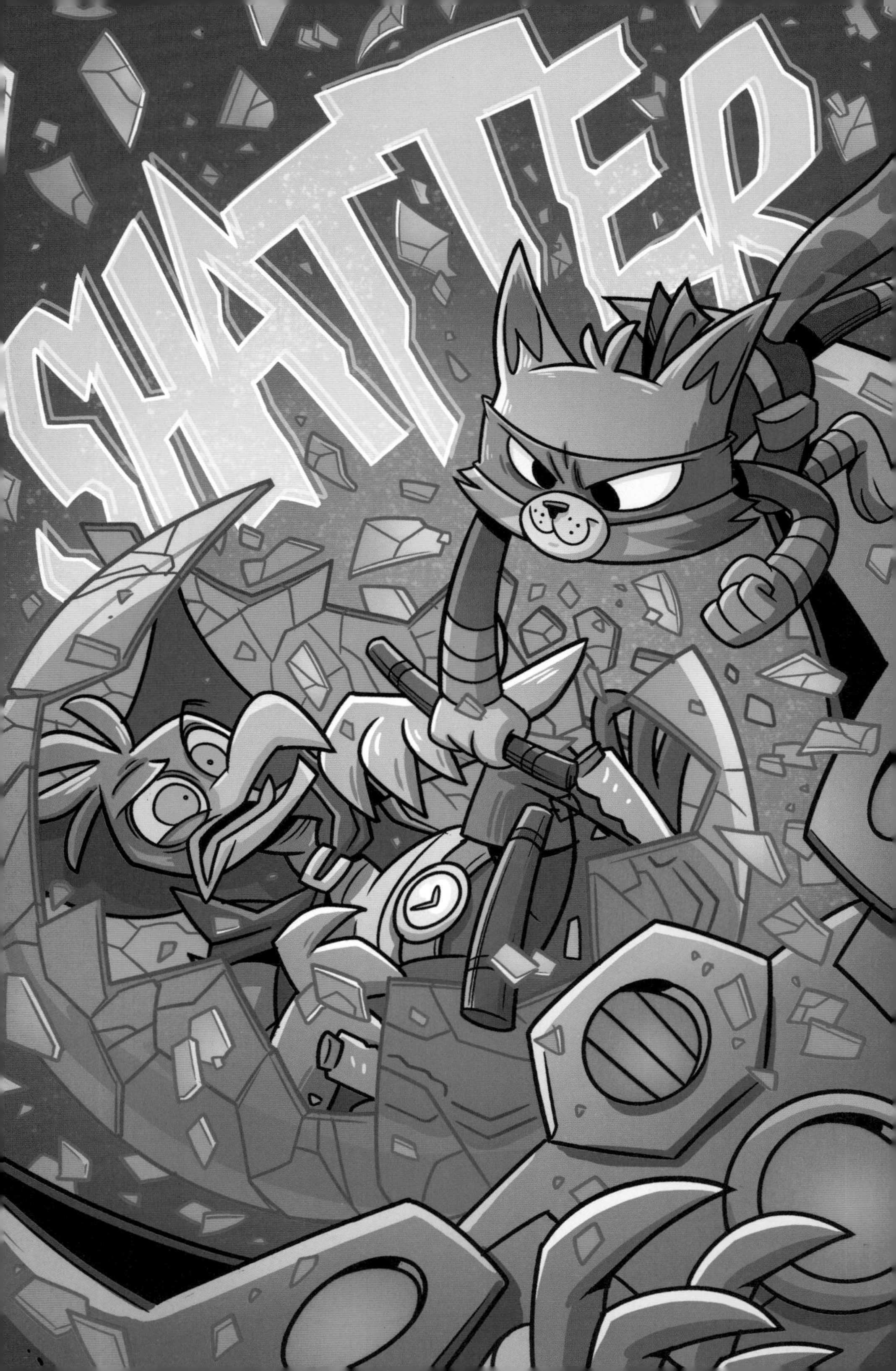
SHATTER

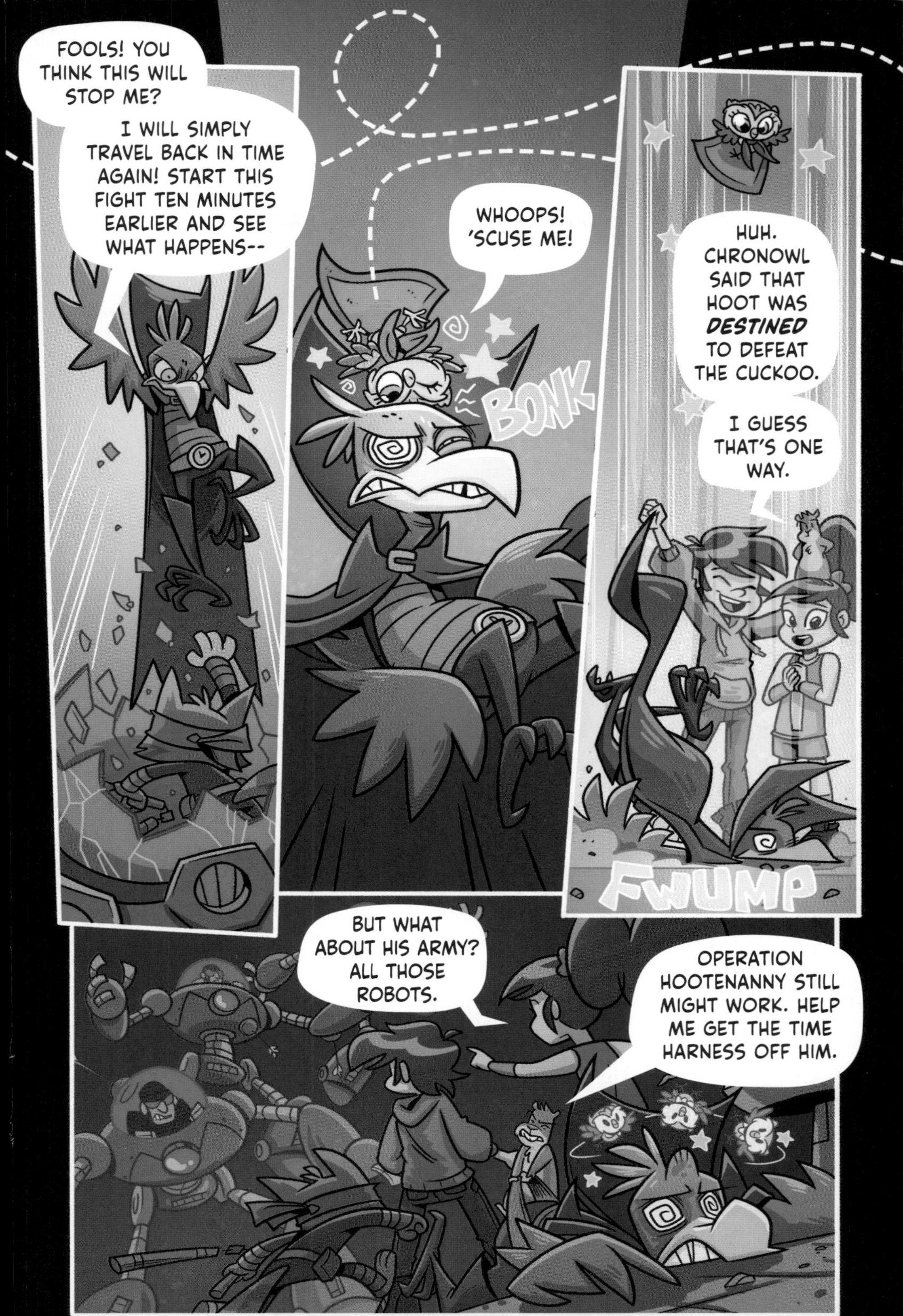
FOOLS! YOU THINK THIS WILL STOP ME?
I WILL SIMPLY TRAVEL BACK IN TIME AGAIN! START THIS FIGHT TEN MINUTES EARLIER AND SEE WHAT HAPPENS--
WHOOPS! 'SCUSE ME!
BONK
HUH. CHRONOWL SAID THAT HOOT WAS ***DESTINED*** TO DEFEAT THE CUCKOO.
I GUESS THAT'S ONE WAY.
FWUMP
BUT WHAT ABOUT HIS ARMY? ALL THOSE ROBOTS.
OPERATION HOOTENANNY STILL MIGHT WORK. HELP ME GET THE TIME HARNESS OFF HIM.

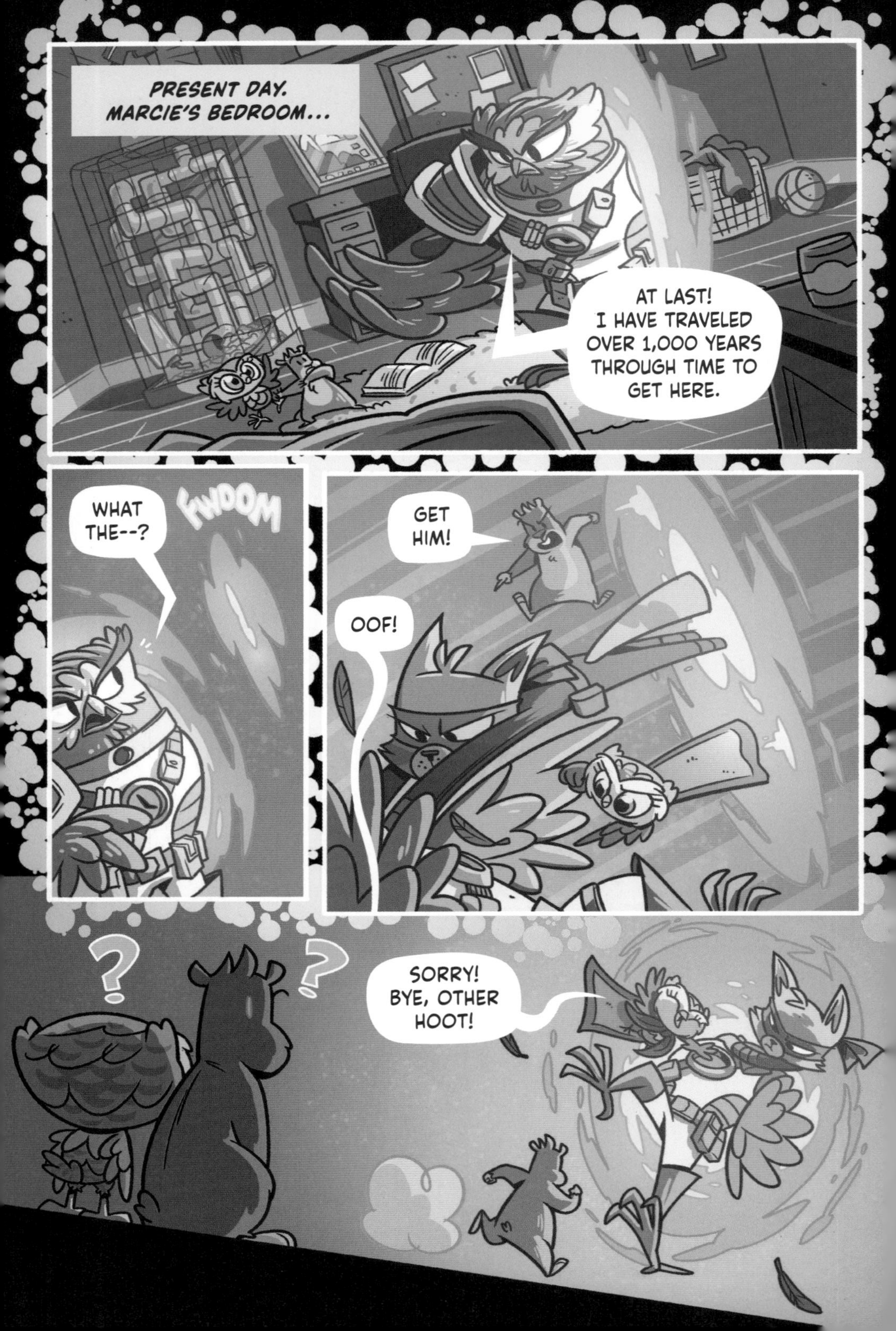
PRESENT DAY.
MARCIE'S BEDROOM...
AT LAST! I HAVE TRAVELED OVER 1,000 YEARS THROUGH TIME TO GET HERE.
WHAT THE--?
FWOOM
GET HIM!
OOF!
?
?
SORRY! BYE, OTHER HOOT!

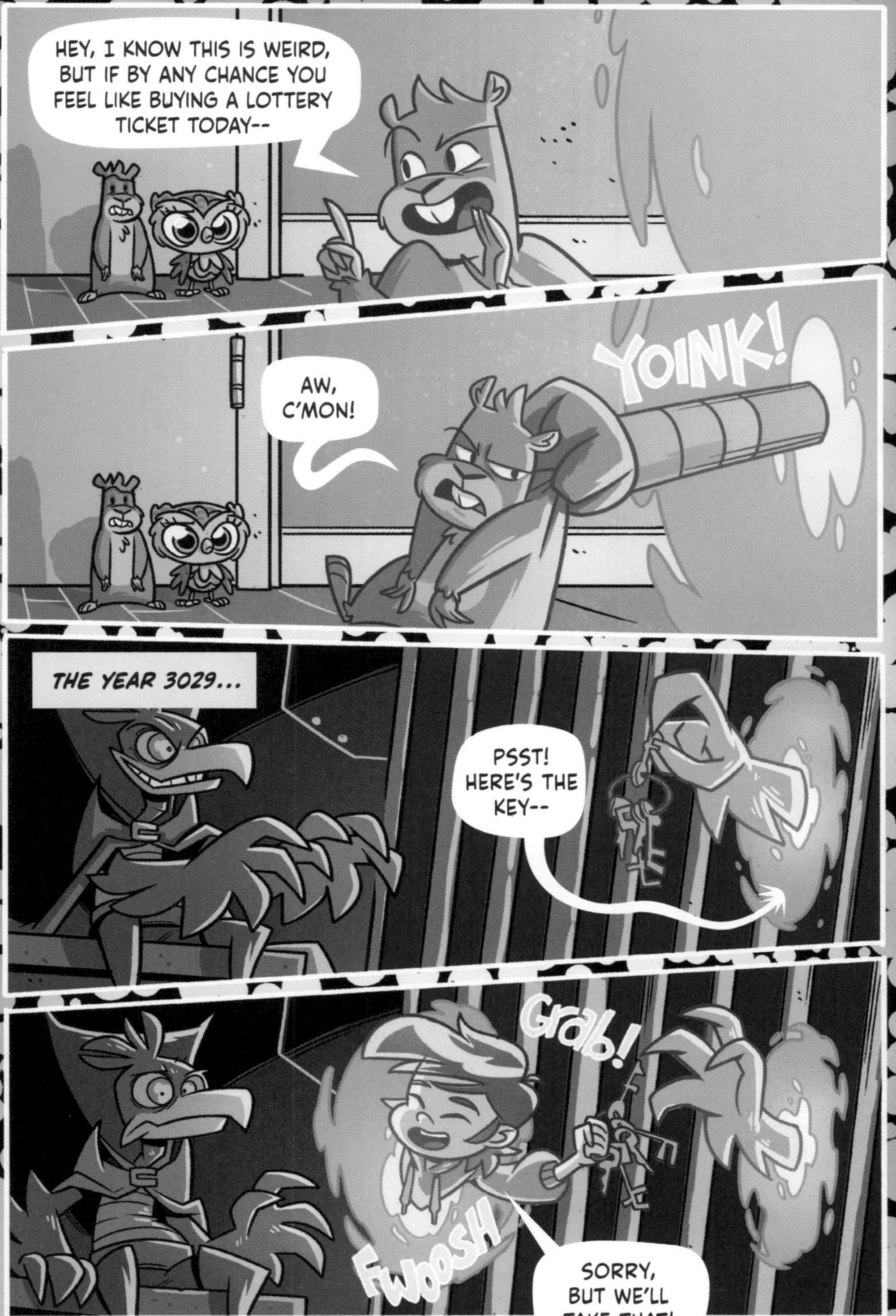
HEY, I KNOW THIS IS WEIRD, BUT IF BY ANY CHANCE YOU FEEL LIKE BUYING A LOTTERY TICKET TODAY--
YOINK!
AW, C'MON!
THE YEAR 3029...
PSST! HERE'S THE KEY--
GRAB!
FWOOSH
SORRY, BUT WE'LL TAKE THAT!

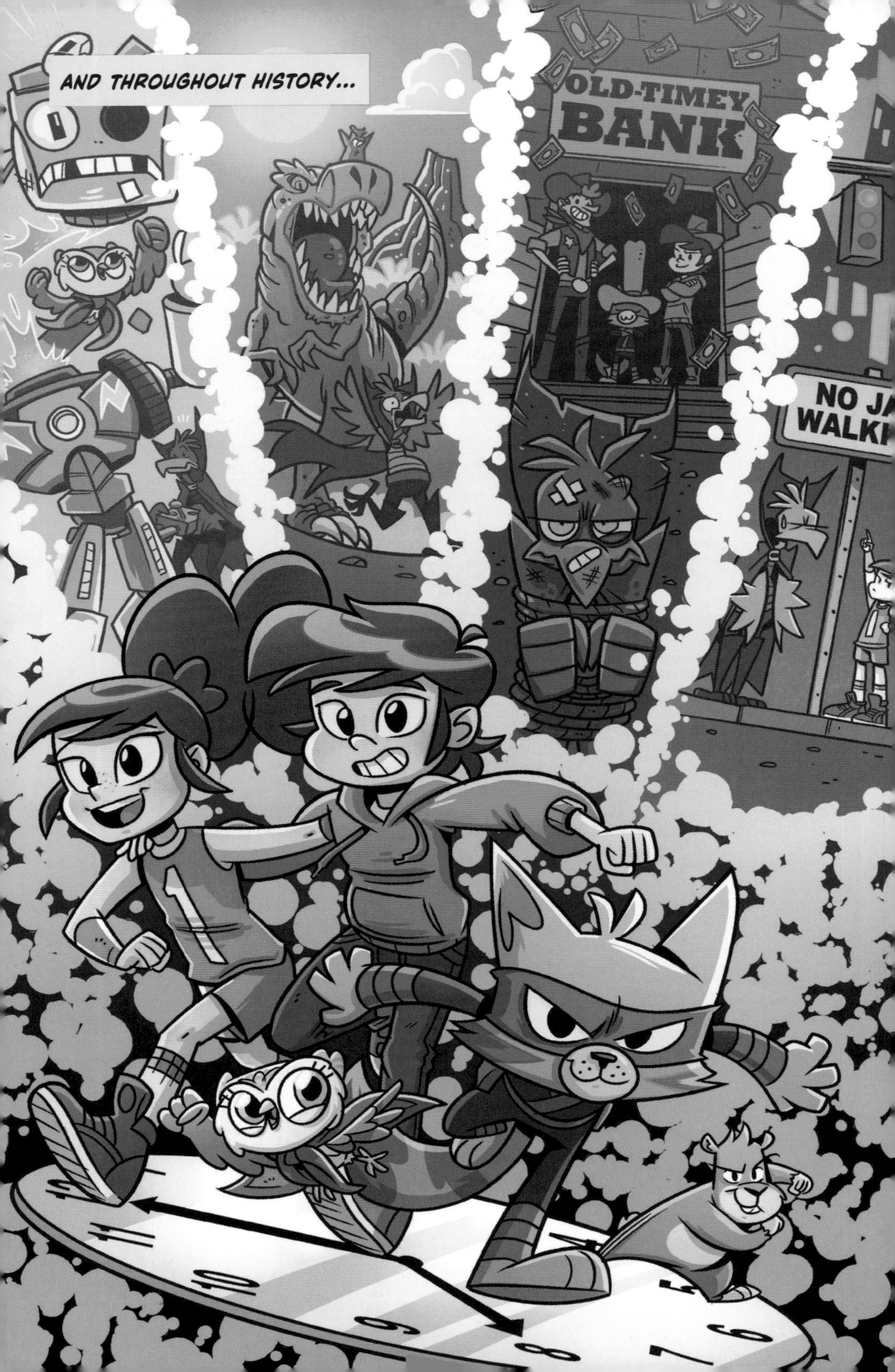
AND THROUGHOUT HISTORY...
OLD-TIMEY
BANK

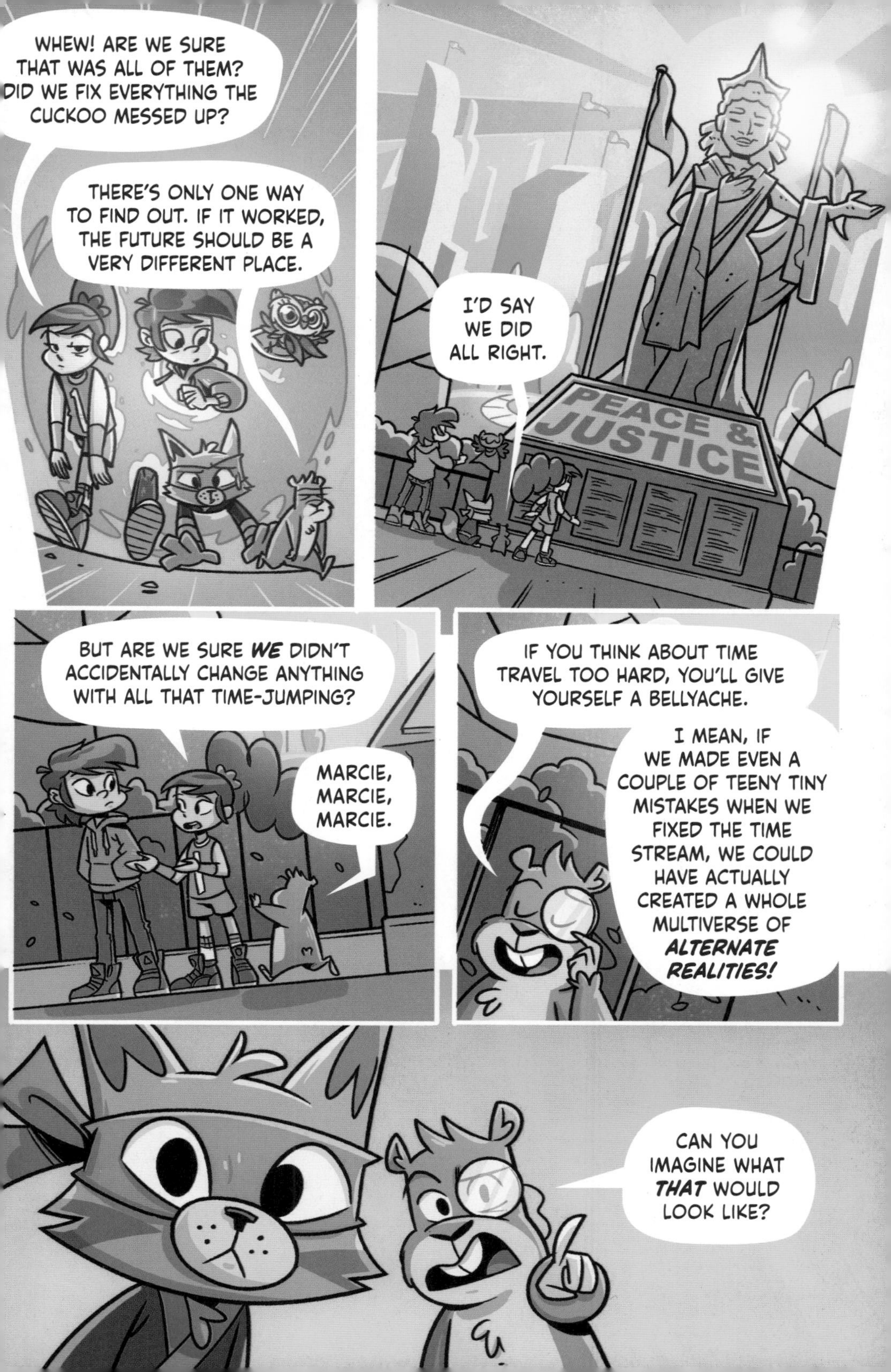
WHEW! ARE WE SURE THAT WAS ALL OF THEM? DID WE FIX EVERYTHING THE CUCKOO MESSED UP?
THERE'S ONLY ONE WAY TO FIND OUT. IF IT WORKED, THE FUTURE SHOULD BE A VERY DIFFERENT PLACE.
I'D SAY WE DID ALL RIGHT.
PEACE & JUSTICE
BUT ARE WE SURE *WE* DIDN'T ACCIDENTALLY CHANGE ANYTHING WITH ALL THAT TIME-JUMPING?
MARCIE, MARCIE, MARCIE.
IF YOU THINK ABOUT TIME TRAVEL TOO HARD, YOU'LL GIVE YOURSELF A BELLYACHE.
I MEAN, IF WE MADE EVEN A COUPLE OF TEENY TINY MISTAKES WHEN WE FIXED THE TIME STREAM, WE COULD HAVE ACTUALLY CREATED A WHOLE MULTIVERSE OF ***ALTERNATE REALITIES!***
CAN YOU IMAGINE WHAT *THAT* WOULD LOOK LIKE?

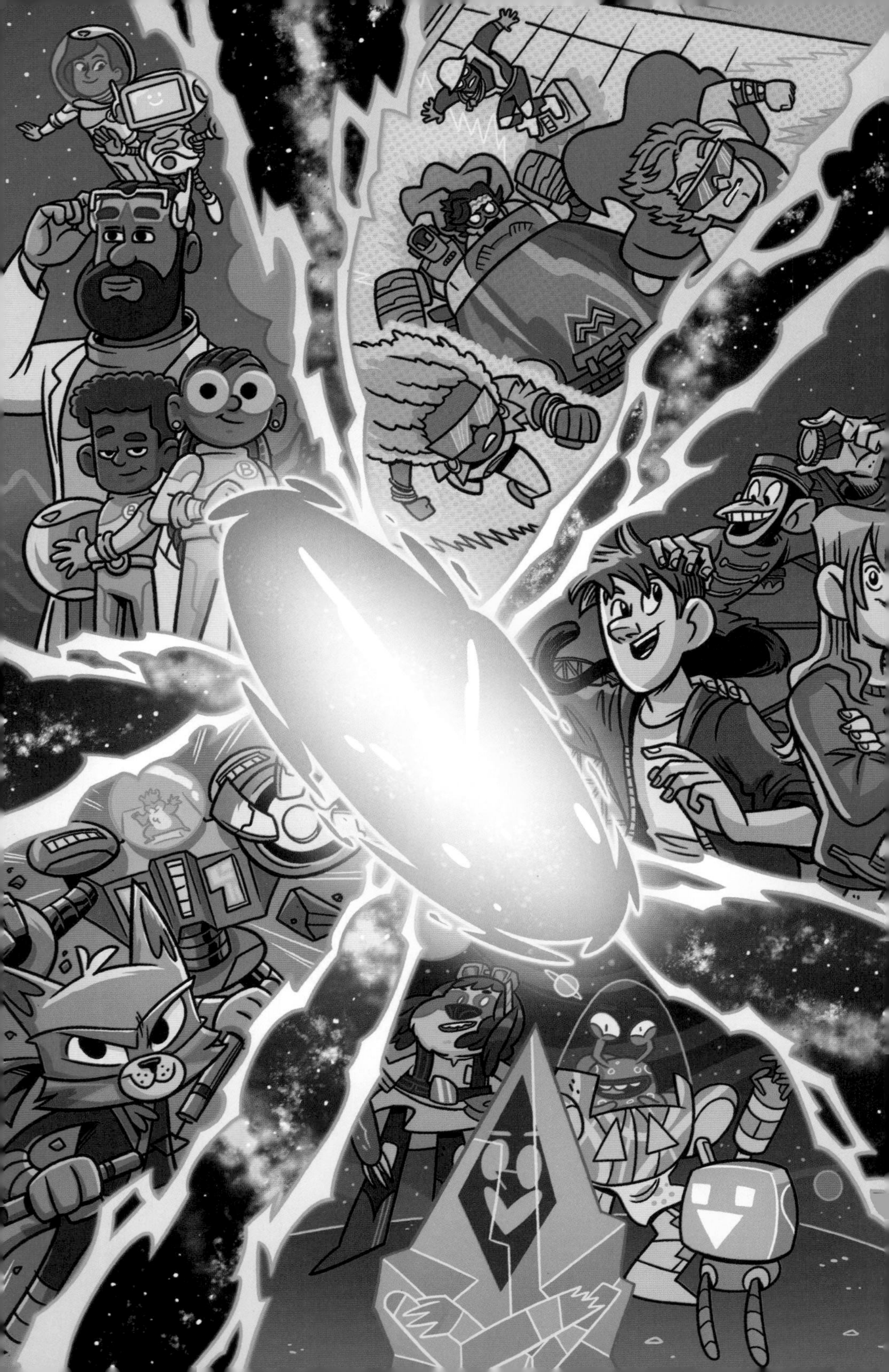

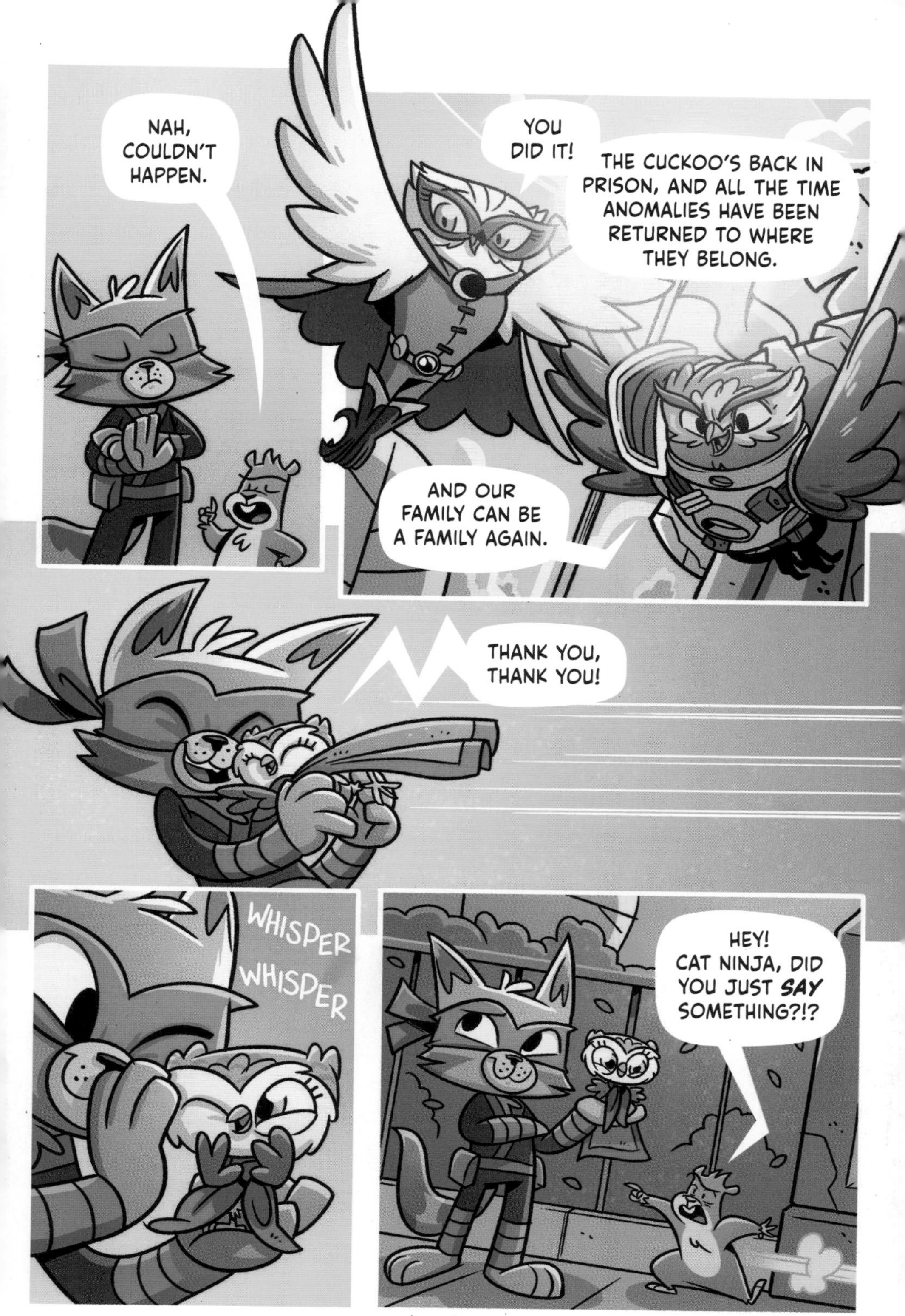
NAH, COULDN'T HAPPEN.
YOU DID IT!
THE CUCKOO'S BACK IN PRISON, AND ALL THE TIME ANOMALIES HAVE BEEN RETURNED TO WHERE THEY BELONG.
AND OUR FAMILY CAN BE A FAMILY AGAIN.
THANK YOU, THANK YOU!
WHISPER
WHISPER
HEY! CAT NINJA, DID YOU JUST *SAY* SOMETHING?!?

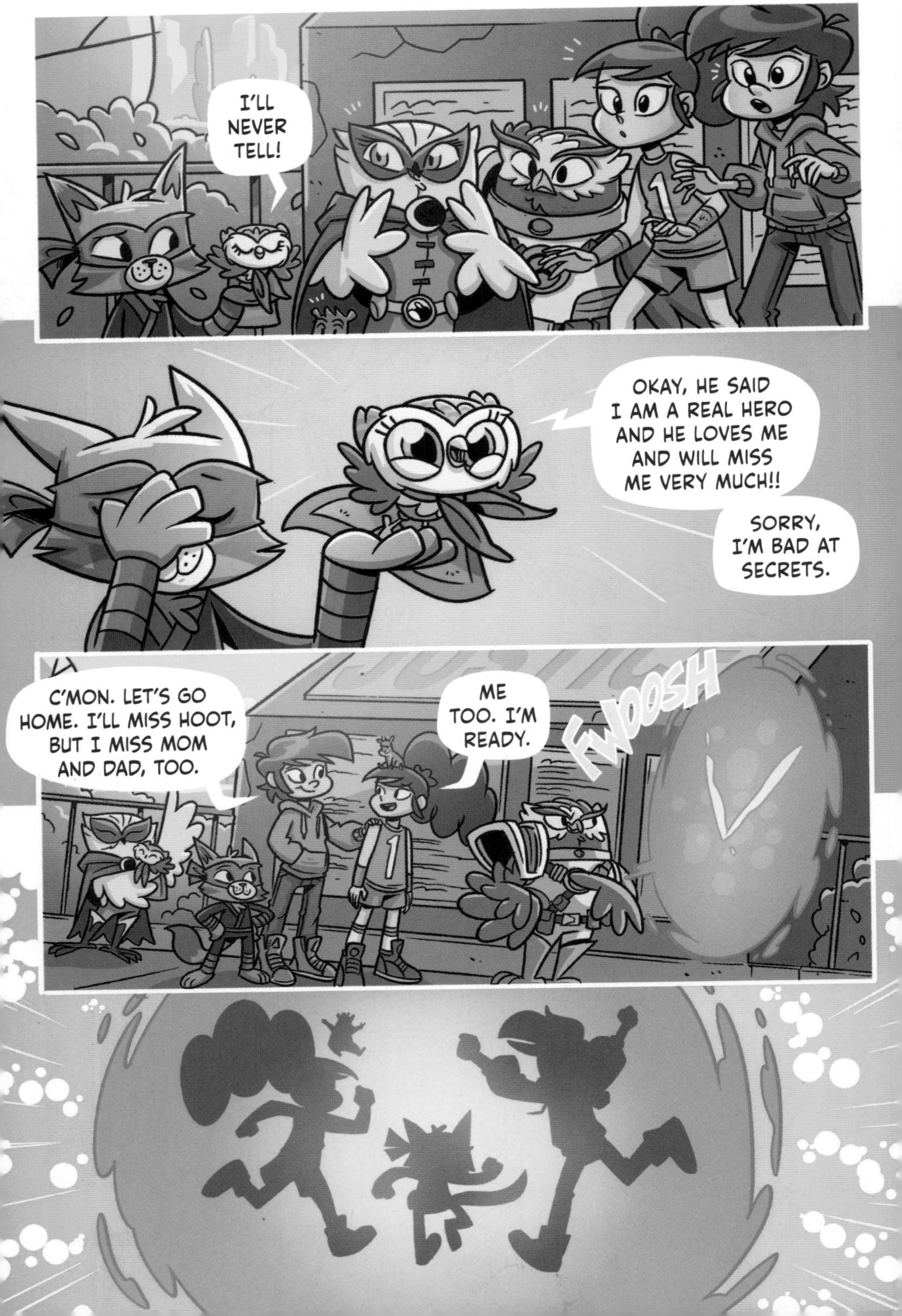
I'LL NEVER TELL!
OKAY, HE SAID I AM A REAL HERO AND HE LOVES ME AND WILL MISS ME VERY MUCH!!
SORRY, I'M BAD AT SECRETS.
C'MON. LET'S GO HOME. I'LL MISS HOOT, BUT I MISS MOM AND DAD, TOO.
ME TOO. I'M READY.
FWOOSH

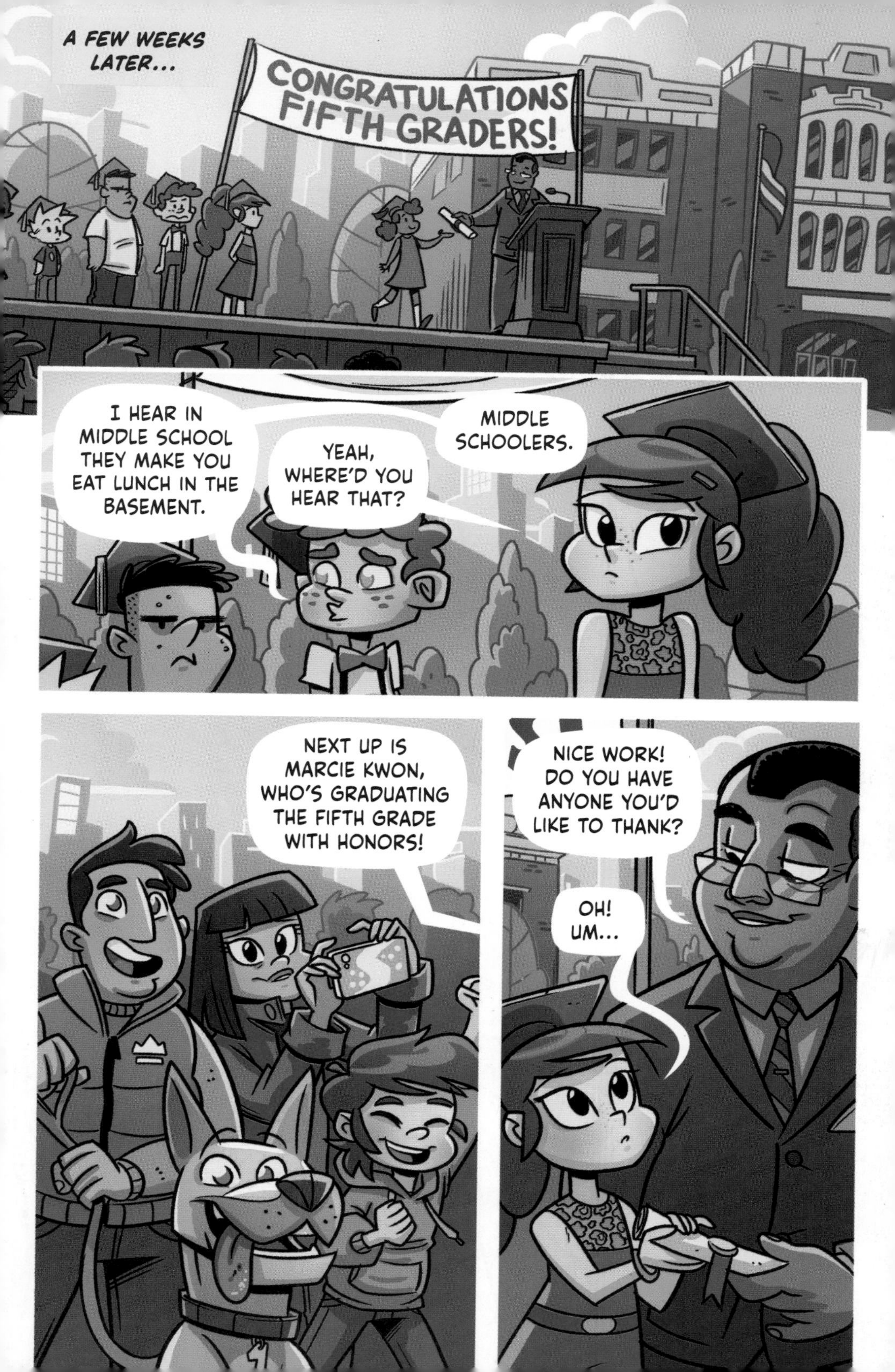
A FEW WEEKS LATER...
CONGRATULATIONS FIFTH GRADERS!
I HEAR IN MIDDLE SCHOOL THEY MAKE YOU EAT LUNCH IN THE BASEMENT.
YEAH, WHERE'D YOU HEAR THAT?
MIDDLE SCHOOLERS.
NEXT UP IS MARCIE KWON, WHO'S GRADUATING THE FIFTH GRADE WITH HONORS!
NICE WORK! DO YOU HAVE ANYONE YOU'D LIKE TO THANK?
OH! UM...

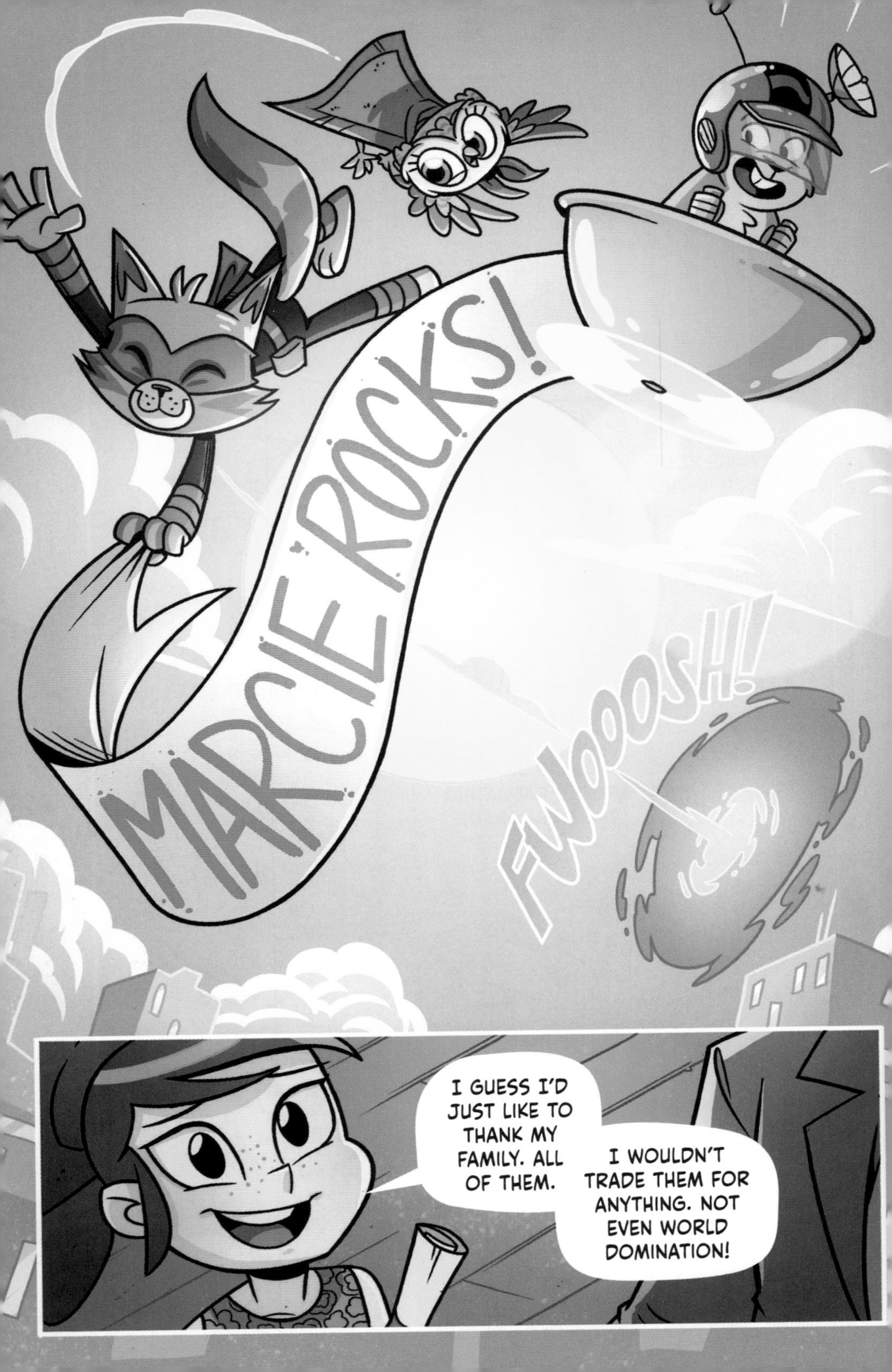
MARCIE ROCKS!
FWOOOSH!
I GUESS I'D JUST LIKE TO THANK MY FAMILY. ALL OF THEM.
I WOULDN'T TRADE THEM FOR ANYTHING. NOT EVEN WORLD DOMINATION!

About the Author

MATTHEW CODY is the author of several popular books, including the award-winning Supers of Noble's Green trilogy: *Powerless*, *Super*, and *Villainous*. He is also the author of *Will in Scarlet* and *The Dead Gentleman*, as well as the graphic novels *Zatanna and the House of Secrets* from DC comics and *Bright Family* from Epic/Andrews McMeel. He lives in Manhattan, New York, with his wife and son.

About the Illustrator

CHAD THOMAS is an illustrator and cartoonist living with his family in McKinney, Texas. He's worked on books such as *TMNT*, *Star Wars Adventures*, and *Mega Man* and also illustrates activity and educational books. He loves his family, comic books, and Star Wars and will let his children beat him in checkers, but never in *Mario Kart.*

About the Colorist

WARREN WUCINICH is a comic book creator and part-time carny who has been lucky enough to work on such cool projects as *Invader ZIM*, *Courtney Crumrin*, and *Cat Ninja*. He is also the cocreator of the YA graphic novel *Kriss: The Gift of Wrath*. He currently resides in Dallas, Texas, where he spends his time making comics, rewatching '80s television shows, and eating all the tacos.

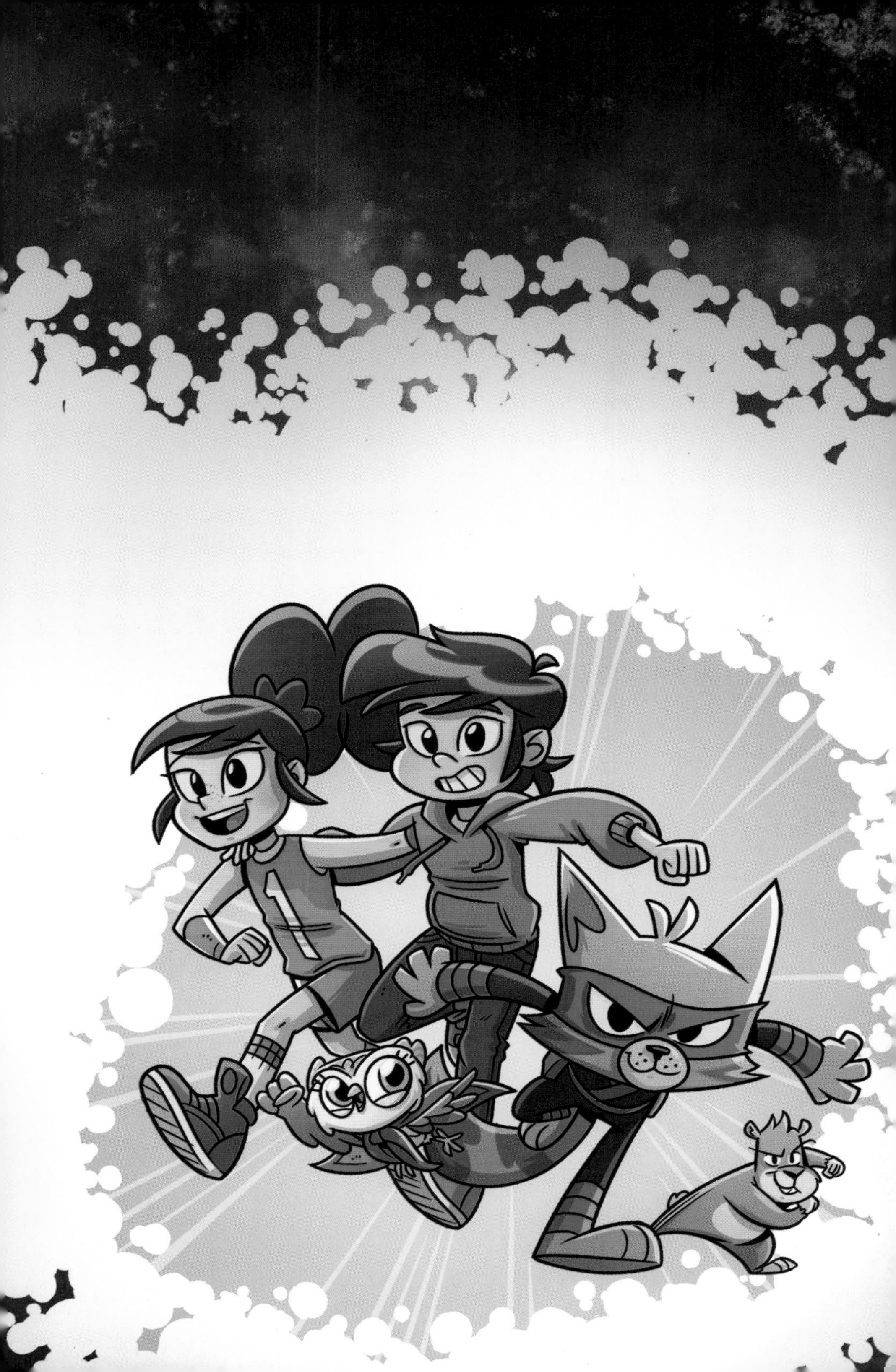

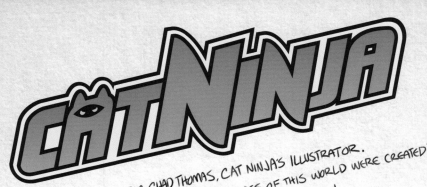

CAT NINJA

HEY THERE! I'M CHAD THOMAS, CAT NINJA'S ILLUSTRATOR.
EVER WONDER HOW THE VILLAINS AND HEROES OF THIS WORLD WERE CREATED?
PEEK INTO MY SKETCHBOOK TO FIND OUT!

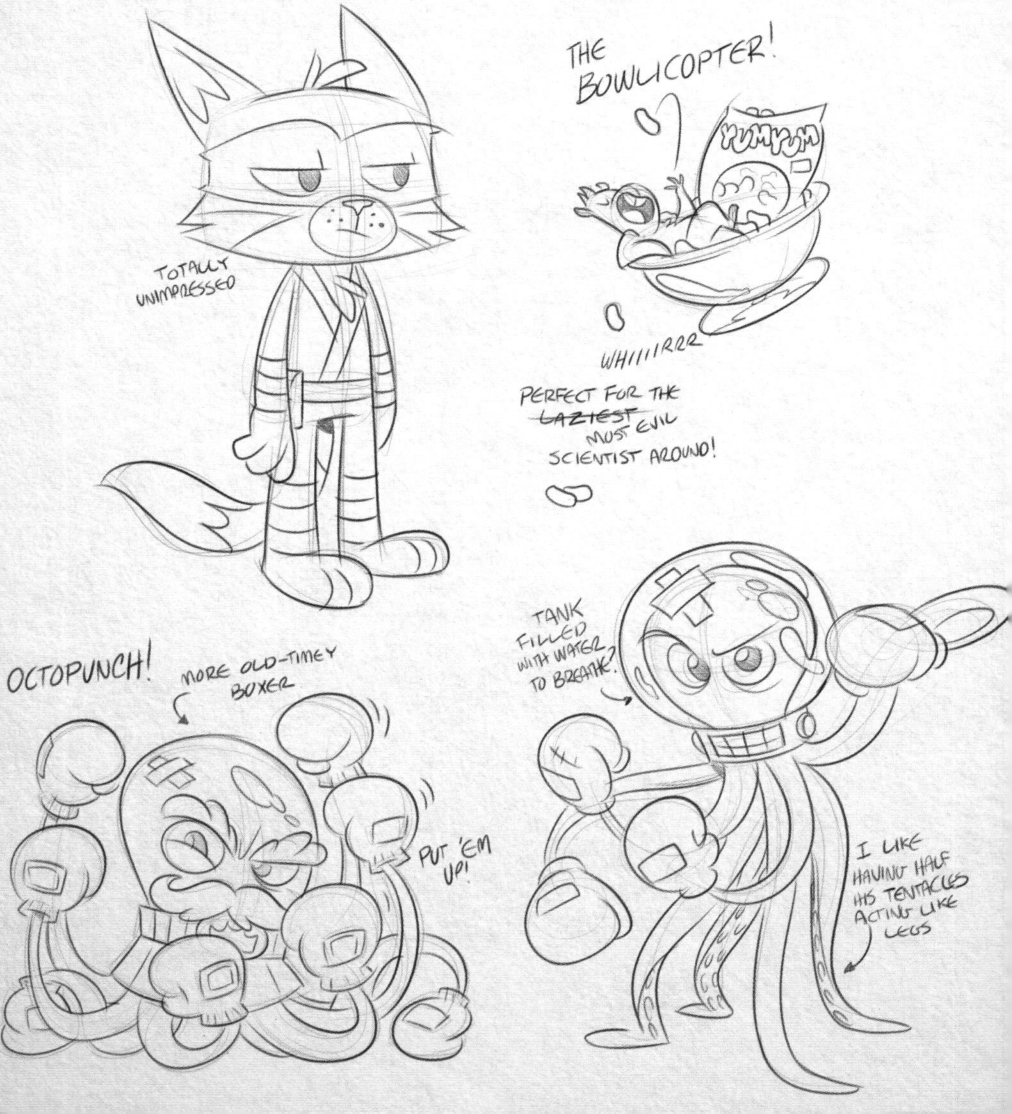
TOTALLY UNIMPRESSED
THE BOWLICOPTER!
YUMYUM
WHIIIIRRR
PERFECT FOR THE ~~LAZIEST~~ MOST EVIL SCIENTIST AROUND!
OCTOPUNCH!
MORE OLD-TIMEY BOXER
PUT 'EM UP!
TANK FILLED WITH WATER TO BREATHE?
I LIKE HAVING HALF HIS TENTACLES ACTING LIKE LEGS

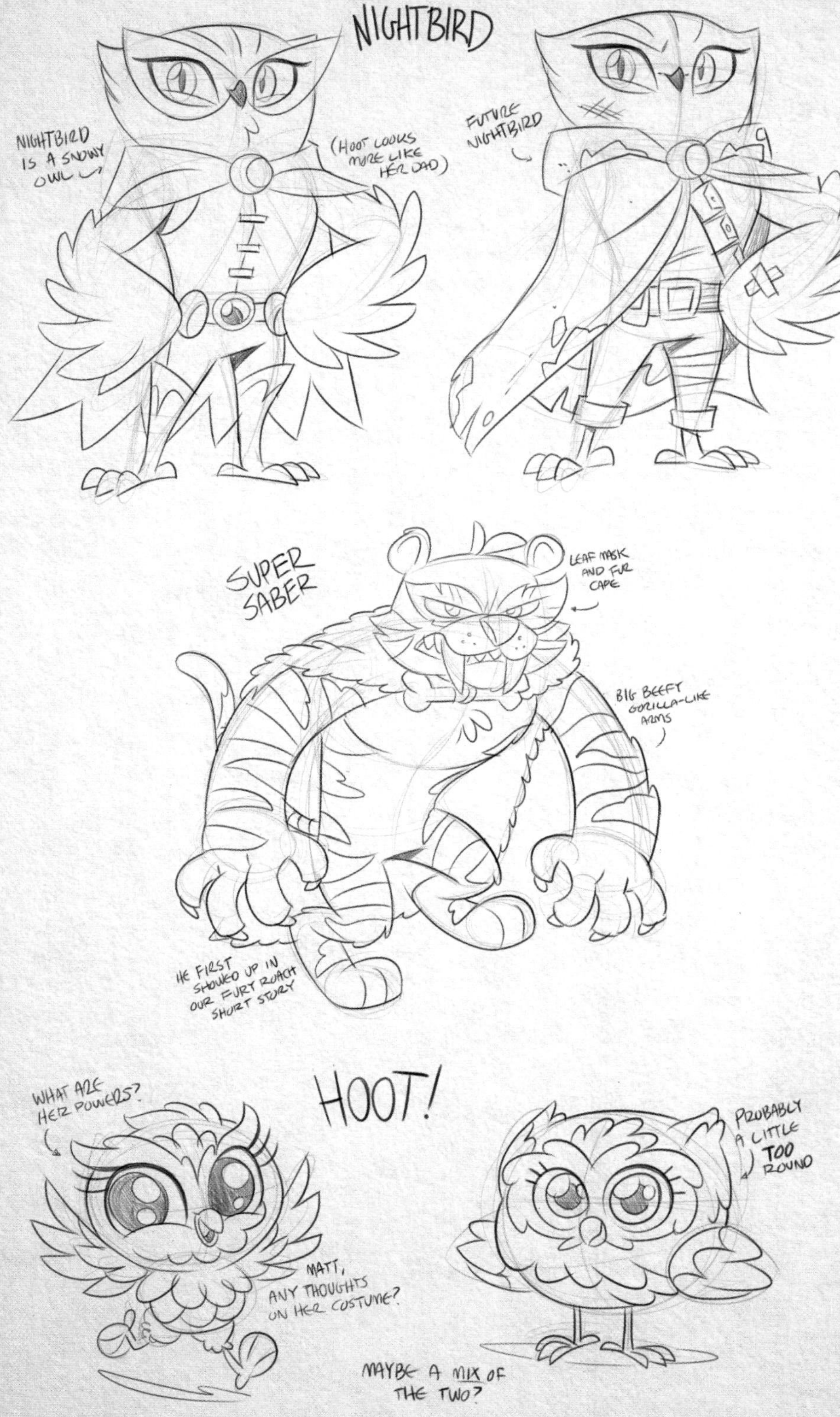
NIGHTBIRD
NIGHTBIRD IS A SNOWY OWL
(HOOT LOOKS MORE LIKE HER DAD)
FUTURE NIGHTBIRD
SUPER SABER
LEAF MASK AND FUR CAPE
BIG BEEFY GORILLA-LIKE ARMS
HE FIRST SHOWED UP IN OUR FURY ROACH SHORT STORY
HOOT!
WHAT ARE HER POWERS?
PROBABLY A LITTLE TOO ROUND
MATT, ANY THOUGHTS ON HER COSTUME?
MAYBE A MIX OF THE TWO?

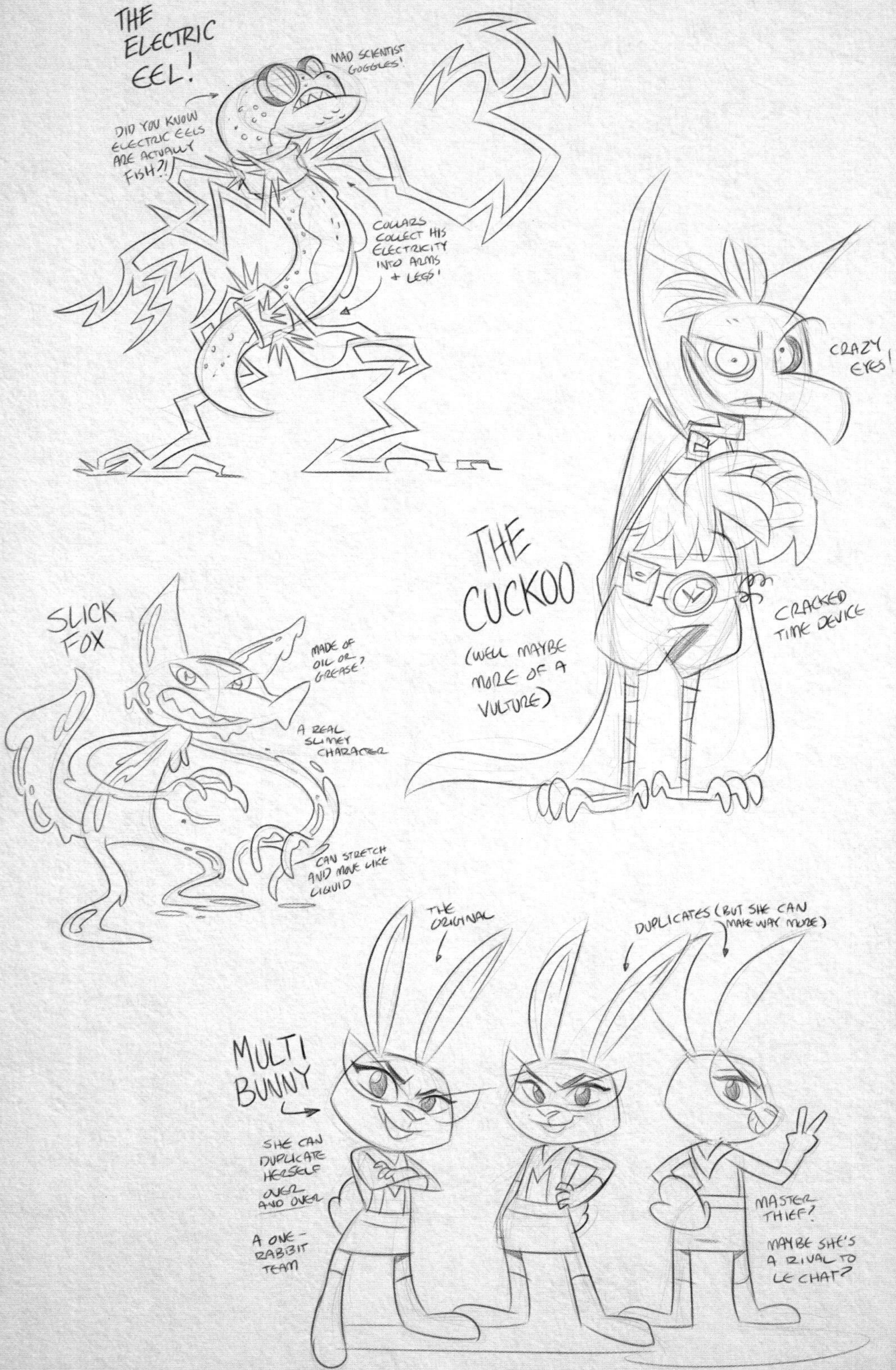

THE ELECTRIC EEL!
MAD SCIENTIST GOGGLES!
DID YOU KNOW ELECTRIC EELS ARE ACTUALLY FISH?!
COLLARS COLLECT HIS ELECTRICITY INTO ARMS + LEGS!
CRAZY EYES!
THE CUCKOO
(WELL MAYBE MORE OF A VULTURE)
CRACKED TIME DEVICE
SLICK FOX
MADE OF OIL OR GREASE?
A REAL SLIMEY CHARACTER
CAN STRETCH AND MOVE LIKE LIQUID
THE ORIGINAL
DUPLICATES (BUT SHE CAN MAKE WAY MORE)
MULTI BUNNY
SHE CAN DUPLICATE HERSELF OVER AND OVER
A ONE-RABBIT TEAM
MASTER THIEF?
MAYBE SHE'S A RIVAL TO LE CHAT?

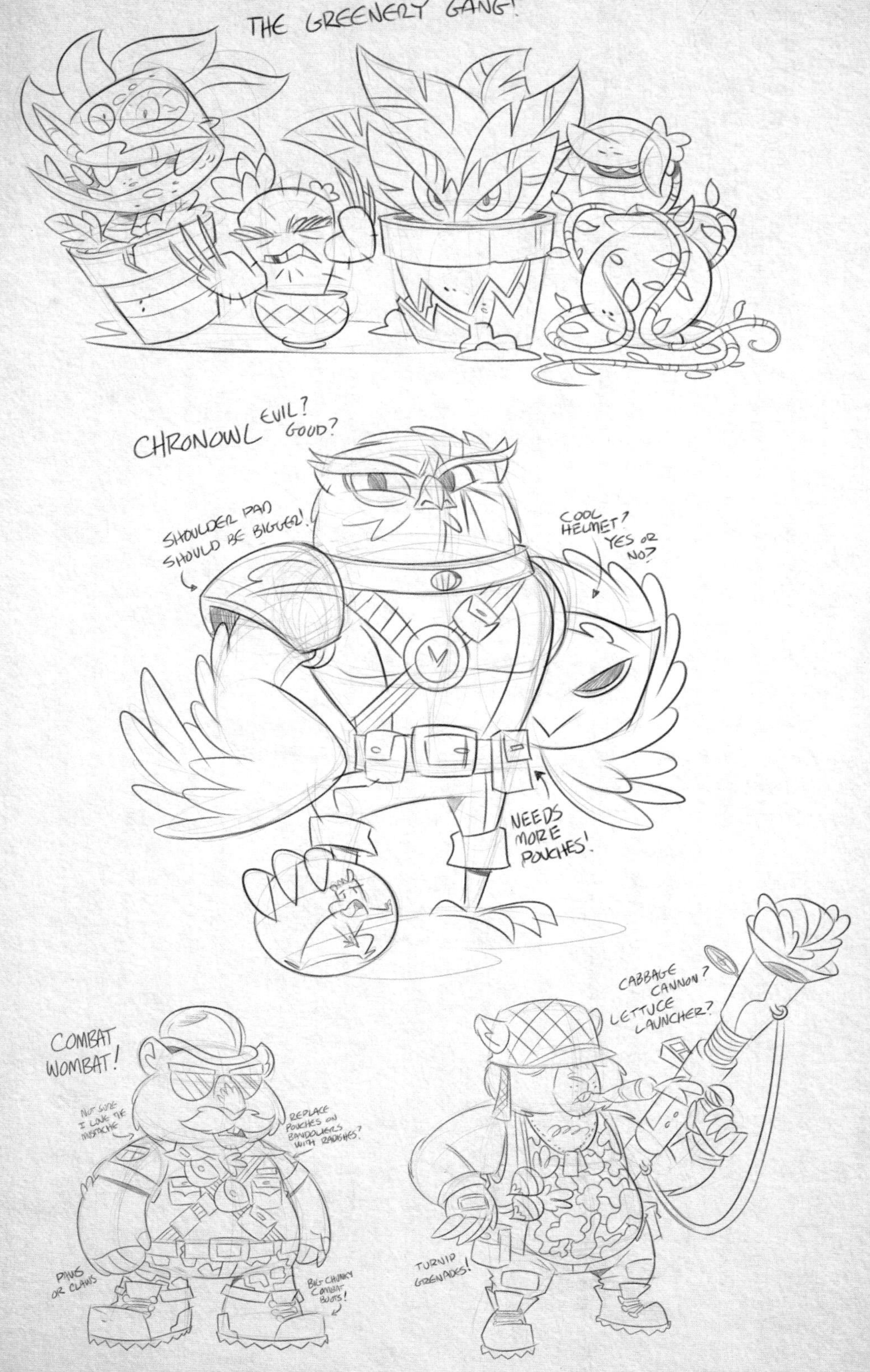
THE GREENERY GANG!
CHRONOWL
EVIL? GOOD?
SHOULDER PAD SHOULD BE BIGGER!
COOL HELMET? YES OR NO?
NEEDS MORE POUCHES!
CABBAGE CANNON?
LETTUCE LAUNCHER?
COMBAT WOMBAT!
NOT SURE I LOVE THE MUSTACHE
REPLACE POUCHES ON BANDOLIERS WITH RADISHES?
PAWS OR CLAWS
BIG CHUNKY COMBAT BOOTS!
TURNIP GRENADES!

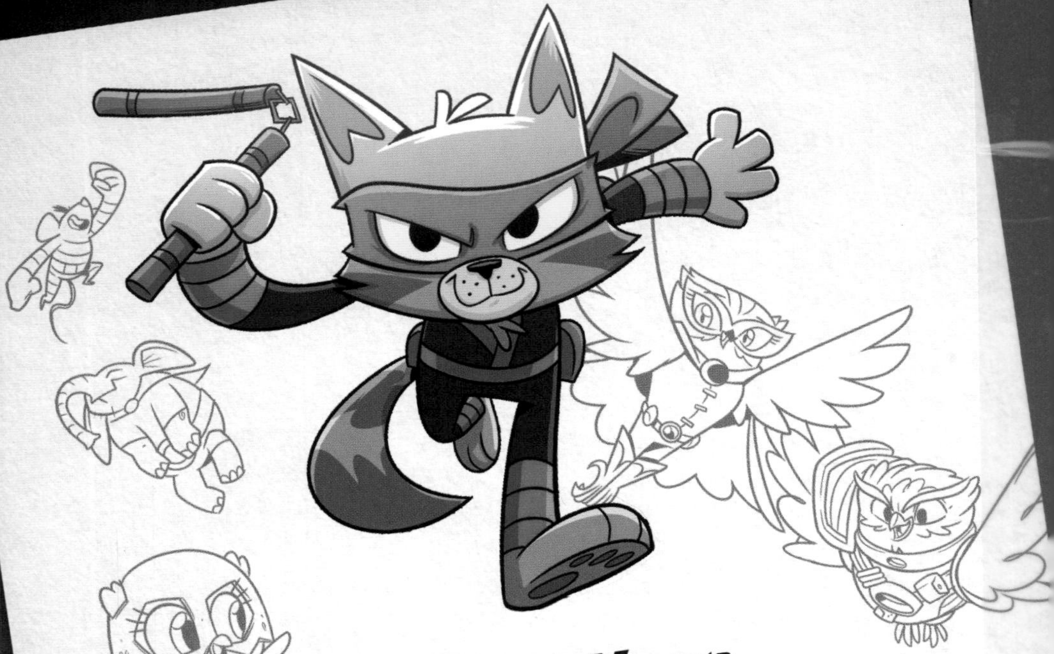

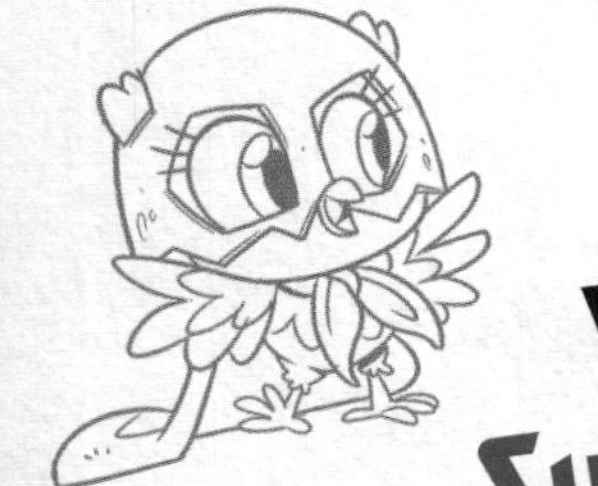

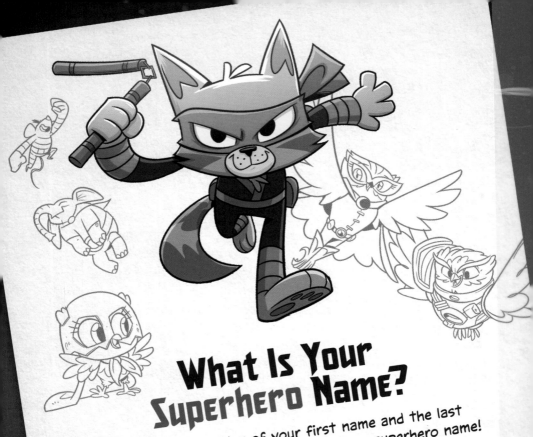

What Is Your Superhero Name?

Use the first letter of your first name and the last number of your birth year to learn your superhero name!

A - Marvelous
B - Captivating
C - Spectacular
D - Amazing
E - Brilliant
F - Extraordinary
G - Mind-Blowing
H - Incredible
I - Golden
J - Stupendous
K - Astonishing
L - Powerful
M - Glorious
N - Fabulous
O - Superb
P - Scarlet
Q - Sensational
R - Crafty
S - Royal
T - Astounding
U - Clever
V - Super
W - The Great
X - Giant
Y - Ultimate
Z - Nifty

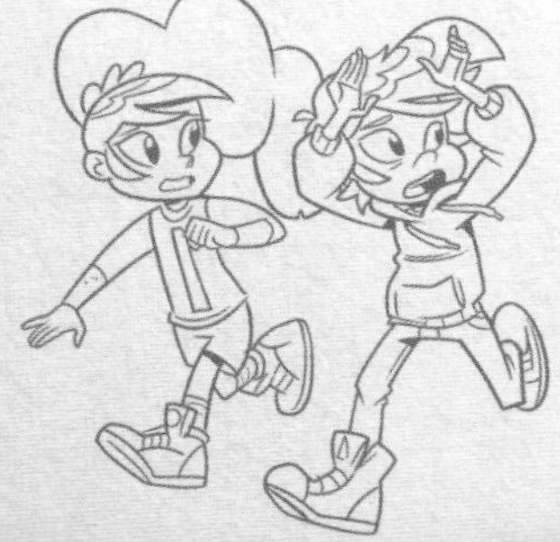

1 - Genius
2 - Justice
3 - Blaster
4 - Prodigy
5 - Ninja
6 - Brain
7 - Might
8 - Protector
9 - Guardian
0 - Defender

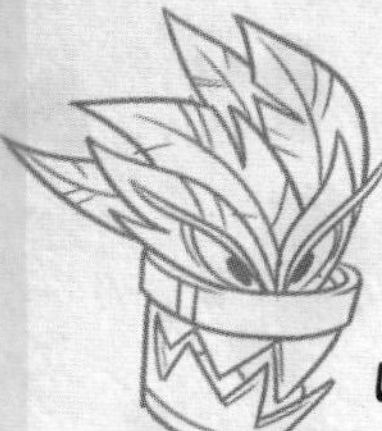

What Is Your Supervillain Name?

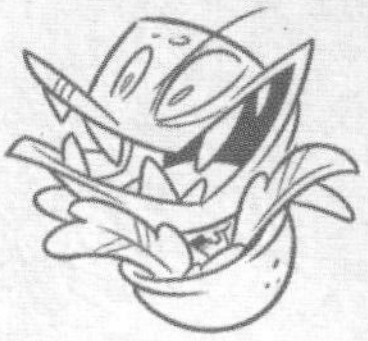

Use the month you were born and the day you were born to learn your supervillain name!

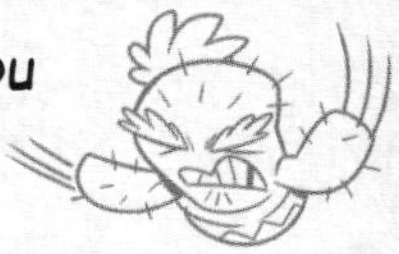

January – Rotten
February – Evil
March – Crusty
April – Diabolical
May – Hairy
June – Dastardly
July – Doomed
August – Vile
September – Cursed
October – Sinister
November – Foul
December – Malicious

1 – Sewer Rat
2 – Snot Spewer
3 – Denture Mouth
4 – Joker
5 – Twinkle Tamer
6 – Bubble Bottom
7 – Stinkbug
8 – Dumpster Diver
9 – Furball
10 – Garlic Nose
11 – Banana Peel
12 – Mastermind
13 – Garbage Gopher
14 – Jelly Belly
15 – Toothbrush
16 – Lobster Breath
17 – Doodler
18 – Tuna Tub
19 – Vermin
20 – Maniac
21 – Gunk Grabber
22 – Skunkmaster
23 – Mold Eater
24 – Opossum Poker
25 – Crustacean
26 – Milk Mustache
27 – Wubby Bubby
28 – Slimer
29 – Spinach Sniffer
30 – Fish
31 – Burp Thief

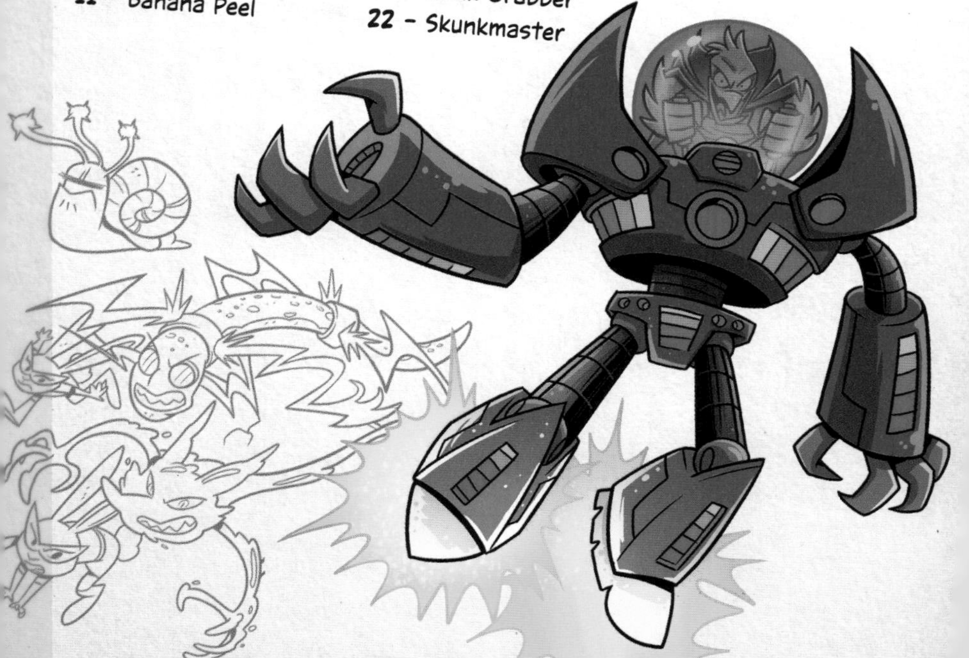